Finding Santa

Mikael Carlson

WARRINGTON
PUBLISHING

Danbury, Connecticut

Finding Santa
Copyright © 2025 Warrington Publishing

All rights reserved. No part of this publication may be reproduced, stored in a retrieval system, or transmitted by any means – electronic, mechanical, photographic (photocopying), recording, or otherwise – without prior permission in writing from the author. For such requests, contact the author at www.mikaelcarlson.com/contact.

Printed in the United States of America
First Edition
ISBN: 978-1-944972-80-6 (paperback)
978-1-944972-79-0 (ebook)
978-1-944972-82-0 (hardcover)

Book cover designed by JD&J
Edited by Mike Waitz at Stick & Stones

This book is a work of fiction. Names, characters, places, and incidents are either products of the author's imagination or are used fictitiously. Any resemblance to actual persons, living or dead, events, or locales is entirely coincidental.

Chapter One

SAINT NICHOLAS

10 Days Until Christmas

Santa stands at his office door and looks out at the white line that marks the Arctic Circle. Even at this late hour, the sight of tourists straddling it as they mug for a camera is commonplace. Not in this weather. He glances up at the sky as an avalanche of flakes settles on his hair and beard.

Rovaniemi, Finland, is a magical destination and a true winter wonderland in December, but lousy weather like this often sends the throngs of tourists back to their lodgings for hot cocoa around a warm fireplace. Almost nobody is here, and a cursory glance at the quiet post office where he receives hundreds of thousands of letters confirms that the village is nearly devoid of people. It's a shame. With only a couple of weeks left in the year, this should be his busiest time. It's the calm before the metaphorical storm, so to speak. He looks up again. The literal storm is already here.

Christmas feels magical because it resonates emotionally and culturally. The holiday is often associated with cherished childhood memories – everything from decorating a tree and baking sugary treats to watching festive movies and waiting for Santa. Twinkling lights, the smell of freshly baked cookies, and festive music delight the senses, creating an enchanting environment that evokes a mental slideshow filled with happy memories.

What makes this village so special is how it relates to the whimsical stories of Santa Claus, with his flying reindeer and his North Pole workshop filled with elves. Tales that have fueled imagination and wonder since childhood come to life in this place. The children who meet him are filled with awe, but the experience resonates with adults as well. Unfortunately, the winter storms in Lapland sometimes put a damper on the festivities.

"Why don't you knock off for the day, Aurielle?"

The chief elf blinks a few times before staring apprehensively at the door. "Are you sure, Santa?"

"Yes, this storm isn't going to let up anytime soon. We won't have many more visitors today, if any. I can handle any stragglers."

"Okay. Do you need anything before I leave?" the blonde-haired, rainbow-eyed elf asks.

"No, I'm fine. Thank you."

"I'll see you in the morning, then. Good night."

Santa wishes her a pleasant evening as she leaves. He never tires of being in his "office." It's more like an old woodshop than a typical workspace with a desk and chair. The smells of candy canes and a hint of sawdust waft into his nostrils. The honey-stained wood, pine boughs, ornaments, and twinkle lights add to the warmth of the room. There is no place on Earth where he would rather spend his day.

He hears the string of sleigh bells on the door announce his next visitor. Maybe this village isn't as empty as he thought it was. Santa takes a seat on the wooden bench, listening to a pair of boots shuffle on the hardwood floors. Only one set...that's odd. He can always make out the pitter-patter of small shoes to determine how many children have come to see him.

"Hello?" a man's voice calls out from the entry.

"Come in. Come in."

A man slowly comes around the corner and nods at Santa before admiring the room. He checks every inch of it, including the ceiling. He knows how to appreciate being in the moment. So few people do.

"Merry Christmas, Santa."

"And a very Merry Christmas to you. Come, have a seat," the jolly old elf says, patting the bench beside him.

The man looks around again. He wrings his hands in front of him. "I'll stand if that's okay."

Santa chuckles. "Suit yourself."

He doesn't look like any of the thousands of people who visit this cozy village on the Arctic Circle. He's dressed in a black overcoat and a holiday-colored plaid wool scarf, not the ski jacket and warm boots that most people wear. He also has no wife or kids with him...at least, not yet.

"Did you come here with your family?"

"No, I'm afraid that things aren't going well in that department these days," the man says, frowning. "I do have a couple of friends with me. They wanted to see you, too."

"I'm glad to hear that. Everyone is welcome here," Santa says, outstretching his hands.

"I have to be honest," the man says, cocking his head to the side and furrowing his brow. You're not at all what I expected."

"I hear that a lot," Santa says, smiling. "The myth of me is, unfortunately, more impressive than reality."

The man nods. "Yeah, and that's the problem."

St. Nick is about to ask what he means when the bells affixed to the door announce more guests, and two severe-looking men appear in the opening to the foyer. Outside of the dopey dollar store Santa hats they are wearing, they look more like beefy bodyguards than friends. Each one of them looks like he could play on the offensive line for an American professional football team. Maybe they do.

"I hope they don't expect to sit on my lap," Santa says with another merry laugh.

"No, I don't think they have an interest in that. They're here because I was hoping you could grant me a Christmas wish."

"Oh? I can do my best, but I make no promises. Some wishes are beyond my capacity to grant."

The man pulls out a gun and points it at Santa's chest. Surprise morphs into confusion, but a plea for an explanation refuses to slip from his lips. He can only stare wide-eyed at the sleek black firearm that is now trained directly on him. Finally, he pries his eyes off the weapon to stare at the man.

"My wish is for you to come with us quietly, Santa. If you don't grant that simple request…well, I'm afraid that I will have to kill you."

Chapter Two

WYATT HUFFMAN

Wyatt swings the ax hard over his head and slams it down, cleaving the hunk of wood in half with ease. He's been splitting firewood since he was old enough to lift an ax. It's practically a rite of passage in his part of Montana. The bittersweet irony is that his father owned and frequently used a gas-powered log splitter. Not that he let either him or his brother lay a hand on it.

The premise behind that prohibition is simple: manual labor builds character, and that's the Bill Huffman way. He's old-school, and doing even menial tasks the hard way before learning the shortcuts was the way the Huffman children were raised. His brother Colt towed the line to their father's satisfaction and is the heir apparent to take the reins of the sprawling ranch someday. Wyatt got payback for that slight by going into politics.

The nice thing about such physical tasks that don't require much mental energy is that they give Wyatt time to think. About the past. About the present. About the future. Of those three things, the future is what occupies most of his thoughts. He's happy with the present, and there isn't much use in doting on the past. What's done is done. It's the next move that he's obsessing over.

He moved in with Stowe and her grandparents over the summer. It was a decision that even his father accepted with little resistance. In the mind of the old rancher, any place is better than Washington. That's a city that most Montanans think is a rotting cesspool of human debris. They aren't completely wrong about that conclusion.

Everything has been great since his arrival. Stowe is in school, and he is working at a nearby farm, tending to horses and offering trail rides to tourists and locals who want an outdoor experience. It's relaxing...and peaceful.

What it isn't is a future. Wyatt wants a family someday. He is going to need a far better job than that to provide for them. His current job is a welcome break from the machinations of political bickering inside the Beltway, but it's not a career. It's nothing that will put kids through school or fund family vacations. In other words, it's a short detour in his life's journey. Or, so he hopes.

A family. This is the first time in his life he's even considered that. Of course, the traditional way to start one is to propose to the woman you love. That's the challenge he's spent sleepless nights contemplating. The decision is easy. The circumstances are making the execution a touch more challenging.

"Whatever's bothering you must be a doozie," PopPop says from his seat on the wooden stairs leading up to the kitchen door.

"Why would you say that?"

"Well, we have enough firewood to last through February of next year, which means you came out here to think. Since I've been sitting out here freezing my ass off for five minutes without your noticing, whatever is on your mind must be serious. You're locked in. Did you and Stowe get into a fight?"

Wyatt shakes his head. "Would you want to hear about it if we did?"

PopPop chuckles. "Not really. I've been married for over fifty years. I have my own problems with the women who live in this house."

Walter and Dorothy have the ultimate love story. They were high school sweethearts and have lived quiet lives on this mountain in Central Vermont. The death of their only son and daughter-in-law in a tragic car accident meant they had to raise Stowe from the time she was just a child. Dorothy is sweet but tough, and Stowe is one of the most spirited women Wyatt has ever met. He understands what PopPop is saying.

"That just happens to be my problem."

"A woman or marriage?"

"Since we're talking about the same person, both," Wyatt says, slamming the ax into the large piece of wood he was using as a chopping block.

PopPop rises from his seat on the stairs and brushes off his pants before walking over to Wyatt. "Ah. Are you finally going to make an honest woman out of her?"

"Would I have your blessing if I did?"

"Hell, son, I'd engrave it on stone tablets if you asked me to. After what happened with Bobby, her grandmother and I didn't think she would ever date again, let alone consider marriage. Then, she met you."

The tale of Bobby and Stowe is your typical enemies-to-lovers romance trope. A stolen kiss under the mistletoe led to months of annoyance and then a hero moment at a Vermont lake that summer. The subsequent romance blossomed into an engagement, and their future was bright until Stowe took the job with Congresswoman Angela Pratt in her Washington office. Bobby didn't handle the separation well and sought other companionship, or so Stowe learned when she returned home one weekend as a surprise and found him in bed with another woman.

One of the biggest obstacles between Wyatt and Stowe early on was how much he reminded her of her ex. Wyatt has long hated the comparison, and that was cemented when he finally met the man in town one day. To say he wasn't impressed by Bobby Sinclair is an exercise in understatement.

"Don't tell me that you're worried that Stowe will say 'no.'"

Wyatt smirks at PopPop. "No, I'm worried about what happens when she says 'yes.' We've been through a lot in the last two years. Factor in the career changes, and…. I think she wants me to pop the question, but I can't be sure."

"And you never will be. It'd require you to understand women. If you ever manage to crack that code, they'll build statues of you in town squares across America."

That's probably true. Women are mysteries shrouded in enigmas on their best days. By comparison, men are much easier to understand. The stereotypes of loving beer, women, and sports while wanting to be left alone and not nagged hold true for the vast majority of males in this country. At least, the straight ones.

"You're no help."

"Which is why you came out here to chop dead trees apart instead of asking me in the first place. Look, Wyatt, I know that Stowe loves you. I know that you love her. The rest is noise. You'll know when the time is right to ask her."

"And then what?"

PopPop shrugs. "You figure it out, just like the rest of us. Look, son, life wouldn't be worth living if we were handed a map at birth and just told to follow it."

Wyatt bites his lower lip. That isn't the sage advice he was looking for. "Fifty percent of marriages end in divorce."

"Yeah, and the other half ends in death. What's your point? Marriage is a lose-lose proposition, Wyatt, but love can conquer mountains and oceans. That's what really matters."

"Oh, God," Nana says from the doorway to the kitchen. "Is he sharing his mountain man wisdom with you again, Wyatt?"

"I asked for it this time, ma'am."

She scoffs. "Stop with the ma'am stuff. You make me feel old. For the millionth time, the name is Dorothy. You two really should come in."

PopPop rolls his eyes. "We're fine. Stop nagging, will ya?"

Nana folds her arms and frowns. "Fine. Then I'll tell our guest you won't be greeting her anytime soon."

"Guest?"

"Who's here?" Wyatt follows PopPop's question. He didn't hear a car pull up, and he couldn't see the driveway from this spot in the back of the cabin.

Nana smiles as she waves them in before disappearing into the kitchen.

"You go first and watch the damn mistletoe. I love you like a son, Wyatt, but not enough to lock lips with you."

Dorothy Bessette's mistletoe antics are a thing of legend in central Vermont. She hangs the sprigs everywhere in the house during the holiday season, and the kissing rule is enforced without mercy. Wyatt should know. The first kiss he shared with Stowe was in the kitchen under one of those weeds. They don't count it as the first, as it was coerced. But it technically was. He doesn't know if Nana's mistletoe edict applies to two men, but it's best not to tempt fate.

The thought brings a smile to his face as he enters the kitchen and heads for the living room. The grin he's wearing vanishes when he sees his sister sitting on the sofa, her eyes red and puffy and her cheeks wet from tears.

"Ellie? What's wrong?"

"My husband's an asshole."

"Oh, Lord. That's my cue to make coffee," PopPop says, spinning on his heels and retreating into the kitchen.

Wyatt pulls an ottoman from next to the easy chair over and sits across from his sister on the couch. It dawns on him that this is the moment. He's been waiting his whole life to toss the line she uses with him back at her.

"All right, tell me what's wrong. The doctor is in."

Chapter Three

STOWE BESSETTE

The Central Vermont Medical Center is a non-profit hospital located in the small city of Berlin, serving as the primary healthcare provider for approximately 66,000 area residents. It's also become a second home for Stowe since her abrupt career change. That's the way life works sometimes.

She stops at the door to Room 204 and pokes her head in to see one of her favorite patients. The CVMC provides comprehensive family-centered care services to children through its Pediatric Primary Care clinic. The focus is on preventive health and early development, and Stowe likes working with the children and their families who are here for the treatment of acute and chronic conditions.

That's what brings her to Ava – a pale six-year-old with big eyes and a skinny body who is slowly recovering from pneumonia. Naturally shy and almost painfully aloof, she barely spoke at all the first day Stowe met her. Ava's breaths were shallow, her body curled under an oversized hospital gown, and her only movement was to weakly regrip an old orange blanket that she refused to release.

Stowe gently took her temperature with a temporal thermometer and spoke softly about snow angels and sledding. She tried to cheer up Ava by telling her that the cafeteria was serving strawberry Jell-O, to no avail. All the child did was cling to the blanket and stare at her with fearful eyes.

The next day, Stowe brought in a picture book of animals dressed as doctors and nurses, already having donned some themed attire because the children seemed to like it. She sat by Ava's bed and read aloud while adjusting the IV drip and oxygen tubing. On the third day, her young patient finally whispered to her parents, "Where's the nurse with the funny lion socks?"

It was the breakthrough that Stowe was hoping for when she was told what happened. While on rounds, she visited her young patient, smiled, and tugged up the hem of her scrub pants. "I'm right here, Ava. Do you want to help me pick which pair I will wear tomorrow?"

Ava nodded slowly, a flicker of life returning to her eyes. That afternoon, they made a game out of the sock-picking as Ava ate her strawberry Jell-O. By the end of the week, Ava was recovering faster, and her smile was much brighter. She still held the orange blanket, but her grip was looser now, even though the strength in her hands had returned. Her eyes weren't as afraid. She was overcoming her fear.

Now, she is being discharged. Her overjoyed and grateful family greets Stowe as she enters the room. Ava shyly hands Stowe a crayon drawing of a nurse with lion socks holding hands with a small girl in a big bed.

"You made me feel better," she says in a near-whisper. "Thank you."

Stowe crouches to meet the young girl's eyes. "That's what nurses do. I should thank you. You did most of the work."

The two share a hug before Ava takes her father's hand and leaves the room with her orange blanket draped over one of her shoulders. Stowe follows the family to the elevator and waves as the doors close. She smiles as she admires the crayon picture in her hands. It's the first gift a patient has ever given her. If all goes according to plan, it will be far from the last.

"You're much better at this than I ever thought you'd be."

Stowe's head shoots up, and she turns to see the head nurse behind her. Stowe knows that's the closest thing to a compliment that she'll ever get from the resident thirty-year veteran. Nurse Barker is tough as nails. She is cranky, demanding, and almost always here. This is her domain, and she wants things done her way. Countless numbers of Stowe's peers have been driven to tears by the woman's brutal verbal assaults.

"Thank you."

"I'm not gonna lie," Nurse Barker says, coming up alongside her. "I cringed when I heard you were training here. Then I wanted to scream when I found out it was in pediatrics."

That explains the less-than-warm reception she got from the hard-boiled nurse when she started work in this ward. "Why?"

"You were in Washington. It's a city full of uncaring liars."

Stowe presses her lips together before speaking. "That's true, but I only worked there. I wasn't elected to serve there."

"That's not as good a justification as you think it is. In fact, it may be worse," Nurse Barker concludes. "Either way, my expectations for you were low. I thought your wanting to work with kids was a joke. Then you came here and listened to me. You listened to others. You learned."

Stowe shrugs. "All I could do was listen when you were screaming at me."

Army drill sergeants have nothing on Nurse Barker. She can make the smallest detail feel like it's an earth-shattering breach of trust. She amped up the pressure to the point where this ward was almost a hostile work environment. Stowe has seen nurses quit because of it, fleeing the floor in tears. For that reason, many of the nurses here call her "Gunny Hartman," after the infamous Marine drill instructor in *Full Metal Jacket*. Wyatt was more than happy to oblige Stowe with a private screening, watching the movie with her so that she could understand the reference. Now, she gets it.

"Yeah. Do you know why I do that? Nursing isn't for the faint of heart, Miss Bessette. You have to deal with cranky patients, worried parents, arrogant doctors, and stubborn bureaucrats. You'll learn firsthand what *real* stress is."

"I understand," Stowe says with a nod.

She actually does. The best way to learn to deal with pressure and stress is to subject yourself to it.

"You're nearing the end of your training program, right?" Nurse Barker asks.

Nursing certifications validate a nurse's expertise and are credentials awarded to nurses only when specific qualifications are met. In Vermont, instead of earning a Certified Nursing Assistant certification, participants in this program are employed as LNAs-in-training, allowing them to earn a wage while completing the course. The program is about eight weeks and combines classroom instruction with lab work and clinical practice. Once Stowe successfully finishes, there is only one more hurdle to becoming a licensed nursing assistant.

"I sit for the Vermont State Board of Nursing licensure exam immediately after the new year," Stowe informs her.

"And then onto becoming a licensed practical nurse?"

"An LPN is the ultimate goal, yes."

Nurse Barker nods. "I know that graduates are expected to work full-time in the system once they get their certification. Are you staying in the pediatric care clinic?"

"I'd like to. I was inspired when I went to the children's hospital in St. Louis last year. I don't think I can imagine doing anything else now."

Of all the amazing things that happened during her journey across the globe with Santa last year, her meeting with Cynthia may have had the greatest impact. Sure, reconnecting with Wyatt has been…magical. But the young cancer patient there touched her heart in a way that she never thought imaginable. That is why she left Washington and came home to enroll in the nursing program. She wants to feel that again and again. It's something that working for Angela Pratt could never replicate.

"Good. It would be nice to have someone competent on this floor. I need to take a little time off."

"To do what?"

Nurse Barker grins. "You are rare, Nurse Bessette. You're a hard worker, a good listener, have a great work ethic, and are great with our patients and their families. Most of all, you handled everything I threw at you with grace and poise, even though I'm certain you were wondering what it would feel like to wrap your hands around my neck and choke me until I stopped twitching."

Stowe smiles. The woman even talks like Gunny Hartman.

"I need to find a dozen more nurses just like you before I retire."

"Thank you," Stowe says, her heart warming at the high praise. "That means a lot to me."

"No. Thank you. Now, get out of here and enjoy your Christmas, Stowe. Hopefully, it will be less eventful than the last two."

Chapter Four

KEITH MEADOWS

Working as a reporter covering the White House is one of the most high-pressure, high-prestige beats in journalism. Most days, it's a mix of excitement, exhaustion, access, and frustration. Keith knows that covering the most powerful office in the world is a privilege. Every word the president utters or purposely omits can affect financial markets, international diplomacy, or national sentiment. It can even start or stop wars.

That makes the White House both a workplace and a stage. During his years here, Keith has observed how narratives are shaped, how messaging is tested, and how power is exercised. That makes him part of the accountability mechanism, meaning his reporting is often read globally within minutes.

Despite what television shows as *The West Wing* suggest, it's not all glamour. Even as a veteran journalist, he's often stuck waiting in briefing rooms for hours, freezing outside during press gaggles, or chasing sources who are intent on artfully dodging calls. The presidency isn't a nine-to-five job, and neither is reporting on it. There are plenty of early mornings, late nights, weekend call-ins, and the occasional trip around the world with Santa Claus on Air Force One…or "Santa Sleigh One," as they called it.

His years of covering the White House have been thrilling but exhausting. Sleep has long become a luxury for Keith. He's growing increasingly weary, even doing something that he feels matters. The press is the public's eyes and ears in the halls of power. That's why Keith digs so hard for the truth and rarely takes a spokesperson's words at face value. He understands policy, politics, law, and history, and has learned to ask the right questions that end up making national headlines.

Snowflakes are lazily drifting outside the West Wing's windows. It won't accumulate this early in the year, but it's a signal to everyone in this city that it's time to start winding down for the holidays. The growing public infatuation with the Finnish Santa over the past two years has brought new meaning to the season, even in a place as jaded as the nation's capital. People are spending far more time with their families, have rosier dispositions, and are feeling less stress. That has everything to do with his Congressional testimony two years ago, and his world travels to save a sick child last year.

That doesn't mean work has stopped, and it's why Keith has been pressing to get an audience with the president's sharp and unflappable communications director. MacKenzie Walsh is known for her grace under pressure. She also hates Keith with a burning passion.

"I have a press secretary who can answer your questions, Keith. Why are you standing in my office?"

"We haven't spoken much since our time traveling to St. Louis last Christmas," the senior reporter concludes. "I thought we developed a nice rapport while you were eating lasagna and drinking wine in Florence."

"You were wrong. Any hint of one evaporated when you tried to hijack a beautiful moment at a children's hospital for your own gain."

He heard about that from the masses. The scoop of knowing that Heilung, the vilified pharmaceutical company, was Malcolm Chapman's employer quickly turned into an albatross around his neck. He received hate mail throughout most of the winter and into the spring after the incident. If there were a Hall of Fame for epic backfires, that disaster may have earned Keith an induction on the first ballot. It's made most of this year absolutely miserable.

"I didn't do it for that. I was only—"

"I don't care," MacKenzie says, scrawling a note on a pad before looking up at him. "Get to the point, Keith. What do you want?"

The reporter inhales sharply. "I've heard rumors that the president is planning on appointing three agency heads and a federal judge on Christmas Eve while Congress is in pro forma session."

MacKenzie offers a tight smile. "The Constitution grants the president authority to make recess appointments when the Senate isn't in session, Keith."

"I'm aware of that. Isn't that a deliberate end-run around a legitimate confirmation, especially when considering that the Senate is holding these pro forma sessions every three days to block recess appointments?"

"The Senate has had over six months to hold hearings," MacKenzie says after scoffing. The president made a judgment call – one rooted in the need to keep the government functioning."

Keith inhales sharply through his nose. Ah, the sweet stank of political B.S. He knows it as soon as he smells it, and that happens a lot in this building and in this city.

"MacKenzie, the government has managed to function this long without them. Why not wait for the normal process instead of using a legal gray area on Christmas Eve?"

"I see you're busy plotting another Christmas ambush."

"I'm reporting a story," Keith says with a shake of his head. "Can you honestly say the timing isn't political? The president knows most Americans won't be watching, and Congress can't immediately respond. Doesn't that erode public trust?"

"What erodes public trust is a system where qualified nominees are held hostage by partisan gridlock," MacKenzie says, her composed and firm voice dropping a note.

Keith scribbles something in his notebook before looking up quickly. "So, what's next? Fight off the lawsuits? Prepare for a Supreme Court challenge?"

The comms director nods. "If challenges come, we'll meet them, as we always do. But in the meantime, if the president makes these appointments, the appointees will be doing the work they were selected to do – work that Congress has failed to support through its inaction."

It's the typical spin that Keith expects to come from the West Wing. It doesn't matter if it's constitutionally ambiguous or borderline illegal. So long as they can make a case, they are going to "do" now and apologize later. If it comes to that…or anyone even cares. That's what a nation built on laws has come to.

"You make it sound like democracy in action."

MacKenzie grins. "It's the snow shovel version of it."

"You've all but confirmed the president's intentions. I have to run with this."

She shrugs. "Run with whatever you like. It's Christmas. Now, if you don't mind…."

Keith leaves the office and finds his way back to the press area. That was too easy. MacKenzie didn't offer any denials. She all but confirmed the rumor and dared him to write an article about it. Only a fool goes where his enemy leads him, and this has all the hallmarks of a setup. After what happened last year at the children's hospital, he wouldn't put it past the White House communications director to arrange to drive the final nail into his journalistic coffin. That leaves Keith with only one option. It's time to run it past his workaholic news director and get his take on it.

Chapter Five

SPECIAL AGENT GAVIN KINNAIRD

9 DAYS UNTIL CHRISTMAS

The Washington Field Office of the Federal Bureau of Investigation is one of the largest and most prominent bastions of law enforcement in the country. Located in downtown D.C., it's close to the National Mall, federal courthouses, other law enforcement agencies, and the legacy J. Edgar Hoover Building on Pennsylvania Avenue. The field office operates out of a large, secure, and modern facility purpose-built for high-level federal law enforcement and investigative work.

After passing through multiple layers of security, agents have access to command centers, briefing rooms, interview and interrogation rooms, evidence labs, forensics areas, a communications hub, and office space. Thousands of special agents, analysts, staff, and task force members from local and state agencies are posted here under the command of an assistant director in charge.

Conference Room 3B is quiet, save for the low hum of the overhead fluorescent lights. That quiet is unnerving to Gavin Kinnaird. It would almost be easier if his boss were shouting at him like a Marine Corps drill instructor. She isn't, even though a dressing down is deserved. Instead, Supervisory Special Agent Jenna Roth sits at the head of the long table, her arms crossed and a scowl on her face that could make paint melt off the walls.

"You broke procedure, Special Agent Kinnaird," she says in a calm, but razor-edged voice. "You made a call you weren't cleared to make."

Gavin and Jenna have always maintained a friendly relationship despite his being her subordinate. Her using his last name and title instead of calling him Gavin is a clear indication of the seriousness of this discussion. It isn't a friendly one, and she is leaving no room for confusion over their friendship interfering with what she needs to do.

"I had to make a judgment call, ma'am," he says, adding the "ma'am" in for good measure. "The CI was spooked. If I didn't move, we would've lost him—"

"You did lose him!" Roth cuts in, raising her voice for the first time. "You went into that café without surveillance in place and without backup. You didn't even alert Ops. What was the result? A missing informant, a compromised safehouse, and a surveillance unit playing catch-up across three D.C. blocks."

Operations sometimes go to hell. That's what his instructors told Kinnaird and his Quantico classmates right before graduation. Boy, were they right about that. Despite all the classroom and practical exercises in Hogan's Alley, agents make mistakes. He did what he thought he needed to, but it only made things worse.

Gavin clenches his jaw. "I made a judgment call I thought was right in the heat of the moment."

"That's the problem," Roth says. "Protocol exists so you don't have to improvise and make a call when the stakes are that high. You weren't even out of Quantico when I lost two agents because one of them decided to 'make a judgment call' that got them both killed."

Gavin doesn't flinch, but his shoulders stiffen. He heard about the case that she's referring to. Everyone in the FBI was talking about it after the fact because the consequences were so severe.

"I've read the manual. I know the rules," he quietly murmurs.

"I'm sure you do, but knowing them isn't the same as respecting them." Roth uncrosses her arms and places her forearms on the table. "You've got instincts, Gavin. That much is clear. But instincts serve procedure, not override it. It's crucial to ensure your safety. And if you don't care about that, it's also about ensuring the safety of everyone involved – including that CI, who may be dead because of your actions."

That's probably not true, but Gavin doesn't have any evidence to back up a denial. She may be wrong in making the accusation, but refuting it will only make matters worse. The truth is, he did jeopardize the CI's life, even if that wasn't the intent. Everyone who lives and works in Washington's seedy underground will be looking to catch up with him to exact some retribution.

"Am I off the case?"

"Off the case? Are you kidding? You're benched pending the internal review that's already underway. The only reason you still have your badge is that the ADIC wants to wait for the outcome of the investigation before initiating any personnel action. Don't hold your breath for a positive outcome. Until then, you'll be on desk duty coordinating field logistics. Understood?"

Gavin swallows hard. "Understood."

Agent Roth stands to leave but looks down at her charge before taking a step toward the door. "You're good, Gavin, but being good isn't enough in this business. You have to follow the rules. If this were a one-off, I could pass it off as a rookie mistake. But you've flouted procedures since the day you stepped foot in this office. I thought you would change, but you haven't. It's who you are, and I have to be honest –I don't think the FBI is the right place for you."

"Is that what you are going to tell the investigators?"

She frowns. "You need to think about making a career change. It might be better if you leave the Bureau on your terms instead of letting them drum you out. There isn't a person in this building who thinks they won't, me included. I can't save you. Not this time."

She walks out of the conference room, sharp and silent. Gavin follows suit, trying to hold his head high as he navigates between the cubicles to his workspace. It's not exactly a walk of shame, but it might as well be.

Gavin collapses into his chair and pinches the bridge of his nose. He knows that his career in federal law enforcement is all but over. That was evident the moment his CI vanished like a fart in hurricane-force winds, and the entire team went ballistic on him. At this point, he'll be lucky if he can get a job as a deputy sheriff in some backwater Mississippi county. He needs to start thinking about what comes next. The problem is that he has no idea where to start. Merry friggin' Christmas.

Chapter Six

WYATT HUFFMAN

Nana and PopPop made an excuse to avoid being here. They rarely go into town for lunch, but they wanted to give Wyatt and his sister some privacy. The mountaintop cabin isn't small, but it isn't big either. So, they each gave an exhausted Ellie a hug and climbed into the SUV for the trek into Montpelier.

Ellie sits on the sofa and holds her tea with both hands, looking as fragile and insecure as Wyatt has ever seen her. She's given him only the highlights of what happened so far. Now, the time has come to get the details about what could only be considered a shocking infidelity.

"When did you start to suspect something?"

"Umm…two weeks ago? Around that time. I was digging through Bill's coat for his truck keys and found a scarf wadded up in the pocket. Not a wool one…a silky, red thing. I don't even own one of those."

"That doesn't mean anything."

"No, I suppose it doesn't, at least on its own. Then, last week, I caught a glimpse of a text Bill received on his phone. It read, 'Thanks for yesterday – you looked great in the saddle' and had one of those winky face emojis."

"Who was it from?"

"There was no name. Just a Montana number that I didn't recognize."

In most places in the country, that wouldn't be considered odd. It is in Montana, or at least in their part of it. Everybody knows everybody within thirty miles of the Huffman family ranch. If someone outside of a telemarketer texts you, their name is definitely in your contacts.

"Billy was cagey after that – like he knew I saw it."

Wyatt nods. "Did you confront him?"

"No."

"Why not?"

"I didn't really have any evidence…"

Wyatt rewards her with a disapproving look. He knows she's lying. Ellie is a closet therapist who can read people like nobody better than most shrinks. It drives their father crazy, and Wyatt has gotten more than a few helpings of her psychobabble throughout his life. The most recent time was last year, and it saved his relationship with Stowe.

Now, he gets to do it to her, if only a little. Ellie is one of the most self-aware women he has ever met. She knows why she didn't confront her philandering husband.

"Fine. I was afraid of the truth."

Wyatt nods. That's more like it.

"Billy didn't get back to the ranch until after eight last night. I met him outside when he climbed out of his truck, brushing hay from his jeans and carrying a feed sack like nothing was wrong. He apologized for being late, claiming he ran into Nate at the store."

"That sounds normal."

"It does, only every fiber of my being screamed that he was lying. His boots were dirty, but his hair was damp from a shower. So, I challenged him. I told him that he smelled like lavender."

"Did he?"

"Not really. But I guessed right. Billy's expression shifted. His jaw twitched. The two of you play Texas Hold 'Em. You know his tells better than anyone."

That much is true. There isn't much to do in Big Sky Country once the sun goes down. Sure, everyone could gather around the television, but there really hasn't been much of interest aired in the past decade. So, poker games spring up, and the ranch has hosted its fair share of them. It's only nickel blinds and a small ten-dollar buy-in, but Ellie's husband has turned losing into an art form. His mannerisms betrayed him every time he was holding a straight draw or got a full house on the river. If he won hands, they were always small. When he was bluffing, everyone at the table knew it.

"I told him that I'm not stupid and can feel when someone's lying. I didn't want to hear a sob story. I didn't want lame excuses. I wanted the truth. I told him that he had ten seconds to tell me who owned the red scarf, who had texted him the other day, and where he had been. So, he did. I just wasn't ready for the answer."

"Where was he?" Wyatt asks, almost bracing himself.

Ellie has to fight back a wave of tears. "At Missy Petersen's."

That throws Wyatt for a loop. After he broke up with Stowe and moved back to Montana, he went on exactly one date with the perpetually single and always looking Missy Petersen. She was infatuated with Wyatt and was heartbroken when she learned that he had returned to his ex after their Christmas adventure last year. Is this revenge, or just her moving on? It's not a question Wyatt wants to ask his sister.

"I had the same reaction. Billy tried to explain why he was with her, but I was already walking back into the house. His words sounded like white noise. I didn't cry. Didn't scream. I just needed to get away from him…and Mom and Dad…and the ranch. So, I threw some clothes into a small suitcase and stayed at a hotel near the airport after booking a flight here."

"I'm glad you did. And I'm so sorry you have to go through this."

"We've been tested before, Billy and I. You know the story," Ellie says, staring down at her now tepid tea. "Our relationship has bent and even buckled a couple of times. But even during the worst of them, he never lied to me…never betrayed me. I never would have thought he would so willingly destroy our marriage."

"Assuming that's what he did," Wyatt says, immediately earning a look of scorn.

"What? Tell me you aren't taking his side. You don't even really like him, Wyatt!"

"I'm not taking his side at all. You are my little sister…and my rock. I will always have your back. But—"

"No buts."

"But," Wyatt continues, "you also didn't let him explain."

"I don't need an explanation!"

"Yes, you do. Ellie, how many times have you threatened to kill, maim, poison, or disappear me?"

"I've lost track."

"Exactly. Hell, if I recall, you even threatened to break Stowe's legs and make it look like a skiing accident if she hurt me. If you were convinced that Billy was *actually* cheating on you, he'd be dead by now. That plane ticket you bought would have been to a non-extradition country instead of Vermont, and you would have flown there. Go ahead…tell me I'm wrong."

"You're not wrong."

"Good. You spent months last year explaining how I needed closure with Stowe. And you were right, as it turned out. I'm just saying that you deserve the same thing. I don't know if Billy did or didn't cheat. But I know that you won't be able to live with yourself until you find out that answer for sure."

Chapter Seven

SAINT NICHOLAS

You don't need to travel the world in a reindeer-powered sleigh to know this sprawling metropolis at first glance. London is one of the most recognizable cities in the world, even from a few thousand feet. Gatwick and Heathrow are the two most notorious airports, but this jet is heading for London Farnborough. That makes sense. It's exclusive to business aviation.

The jet glides into a landing without incident and taxis to hangars on the far end of the field. It parks alongside one of them, and the engines spool down. Santa would like nothing more than to signal one of the ground crew, but they pay no attention to anything outside of their assigned tasks. He isn't even certain the men can see him through the window.

Inside the aircraft, the man who took him puts on a suit jacket and grabs his briefcase. He signals his two beefy henchmen, who stand. As spacious and comfortable as this jet is, the two men look like they would need a 747 or A380 to not appear like they are taking too much space.

"Stay with St. Nick. I will only be a couple of hours. If he tries to escape or signal anyone, you know what to do." The two guards nod. "Now, Santa, you need to be on your best behavior. If you do anything reckless, there will be consequences. I don't want to have to hurt you."

"That's refreshing. Why are we in London?"

The man offers Santa a brief look of puzzlement. "We have some stops to make before reaching our final destination. You know, to keep up appearances. You'll remain on the plane under Skut's and Kram's watchful eyes."

Santa looks at the two men, neither of whom looks inclined to smile. Are those nicknames or their real names? It doesn't matter much. They have no negative reaction to the monikers and are clearly comfortable with their use.

"Feel free to help yourself to anything in the galley or bar," the man continues. I would recommend the whisky, but I know you prefer milk and cookies, so we have plenty of both."

It's a cliché, but one that also happens to be true. Actually, Aurielle's cocoa is his drink of choice. It's food for the soul. It also wreaks havoc on his waistline, but that is a secondary consideration after even a single sip.

"What is this all about?"

The man stops and cocks his head near the aircraft's door. "You're Santa Claus. You don't know?"

Santa smiles at him with a twinkle in his eye. "I know for sure that you're on the naughty list. As for why you have taken me, unfortunately, I'm not clairvoyant. I have no idea."

"What name did you write on that list?" the man asks, resting his arms against the headrest of the closest seat. "Hmm? What's my name, Santa?"

He doesn't get a response.

"That's what I thought. The naughty list is as much a myth as you are. Since there isn't anything magical about you, I'm sure this is all a big mystery."

"It is," Santa confirms.

"Then, for now, let's just say that it's necessary to prove a point."

Santa strokes his beard. "You think kidnapping an old man from his workplace is making a point?"

He smirks. "Yes."

There was strength and commitment in that answer. Whatever this man has planned, he believes in it. What that could be is anyone's guess. Santa certainly doesn't know what this could be about.

"People will be looking for me."

"Of course," the man says, a grin marching across his lips. "You're Santa Claus. Or at least that's what you have people believing. They will search the globe for you."

"If you know that, then why do this?"

"Because I also know they won't find you before Christmas. Whether they ever do will be determined by your behavior. So, be good for goodness' sake!"

Santa isn't amused at the nefarious use of one of his favorite Christmas carols. His kidnapper nods at the two guards and leaves the business jet. He watches out the window as the man strides across the hangar without looking back.

At least he was kidnapped in style. This is a nice way to travel. Santa looks around the high-performance, long-range Gulfstream IV. Most have been refurbished with new avionics, noise-reduction insulation, and enhanced interiors. He prefers his sleigh…or Air Force One. Cruising around last year in the president of the United States's plane was a treat.

"He's a pleasant one, isn't he?" Santa asks the two severe-looking guards sitting at the front of the aircraft.

The men don't respond.

"Are Skut and Kram your real names?"

Again, nothing. Santa presses his lips together and stares out the small window at the empty hangar. This is going to be a long trip, and he could really use a cup of hot cocoa right now.

Chapter Eight

STOWE BESSETTE

Stowe pauses on the stairs. Wyatt is on the couch, staring at the fire in the fireplace. He doesn't look relaxed…more like…pensive. She almost doesn't want to disturb his thoughts, but also doesn't want him to think she's indifferent, especially when family is involved. He is close to his sister, and she's hurting. No man wants to see his mother upset, and she imagines that extends to a sister.

"She put her head down and went straight to sleep," Stowe says, curling up next to Wyatt on the couch. "You okay?"

"I've never seen Ellie like this before."

"And that bothers you."

"Outside of you and my mother, she's the strongest woman I've ever known. To see her like this…it's unnerving."

Stowe understands why. He's right about Ellie's strength. She has only met his sister a handful of times, but has always regarded her as decisive and headstrong. It is no easy feat to shake that confidence.

"Do you think her husband is cheating on her?"

Wyatt exhales hard. "A big part of me doesn't think he would be that stupid."

"But?"

"It wouldn't be the first time. There is a long history between them. They were high school sweethearts."

"Really?"

"It's not that uncommon in Montana. Billy was sixteen and still acted like a toddler. She was fifteen, going on thirty. They met one night at a bonfire at a nearby ranch. For some reason, she took to him. My brother and I didn't think it would amount to much. But the late-night truck rides, trail rides on the horses, and lying under the stars became their thing. The perfect Montana couple. They shared their first kiss on a tractor during a thunderstorm."

"How Montanan," Stowe observes, a wry smile creasing her lips.

"Yeah. Billy and Ellie didn't say they were in love back then, thank God. My father was protective of her. He despised Billy, and hearing the word 'love' out of either of their mouths would have sent the old man off the edge. But we all saw it for what it was. Colt and I eventually accepted it. Mom was tolerant and supported Ellie's decision, even if she didn't like it. My father made it well known that Billy Olson wasn't his first choice of suitors for his only daughter."

Stowe understands that sentiment. The family patriarch didn't like her very much the first time they met at the ranch. She was surprised to hear that it was Wyatt's father who convinced him to help deliver Santa to the children's hospital in St. Louis after she went there and awkwardly asked for his help. The reception she has received since has been much warmer.

"What happened next?"

"The usual. Billy went to work on a ranch in a different part of the state after graduation. Things between them got tense. Phone calls grew shorter. Trips home became less frequent. Then, the calls ended. A week passed. Then two.

"Things reached a boiling point when Billy came back to tend his family's ranch for his ill father. It turns out that he had been unfaithful. Ellie was livid, but he worked hard to regain her trust. They didn't fix everything overnight. They fought. They learned. When he came home permanently, they built a stronger relationship.

"Three years later, on the same tractor that they first kissed on, Billy held up a tiny silver ring in shaking fingers and asked her to marry him. She said yes, of course, and my father wore black for a week. We were all surprised when he agreed to host the wedding at our ranch. When they exchanged vows, it was against a painted backdrop of orange, pink, and purple streaks in an endless sky. It was the most amazing Montana sunset I've ever seen. I thought they were blessed."

"You didn't answer my question. I asked if you think Billy cheated. Yes or no?"

Wyatt shrugs. "I don't have an answer. Ellie isn't the easiest woman to deal with. It takes a strong man, and her husband…well, he doesn't quite fit that mold. And that's the problem. If he gets caught stepping out on her again now that they're married, he's going to learn the hard way how Wild Bill Huffman got that nickname. When my father finishes with him, my brother Colt gets whatever is left of his carcass. It's a hell of a risk for Billy to take, especially in small-town Central Montana."

"But?" Stowe presses, sensing that there is another side to this explanation.

"My sister has a keen intuition about people. It's downright uncanny. She must have sensed that something was wrong even before the clues presented themselves. If she came here to talk to me, it's because something is *very* wrong. I think there is more to the story than we know."

"This is shaping up to be an interesting Christmas," Stowe says, watching the fire.

"Yeah, we have a history of those, don't we? It makes me wonder what happens next."

Almost on cue, there's a knock at the front door. Stowe's grandparents live in a beautiful mountain cabin. The driveway is long and steep, so they don't get much foot traffic here, and he didn't hear a car pull up. If a neighbor is knocking, it's because they desperately need something.

Neither of them wants to move, but Wyatt manages to struggle off the sofa first. He walks over and opens the front door to see Santa's head elf staring at him through watery eyes.

"Aurielle? What are you doing here?"

"I'm sorry to bother you," she says, her normally sweet, chipper voice laced with hints of despair and panic. "I didn't know who else I could turn to."

"What's wrong?" Stowe asks, coming up alongside Wyatt when she hears the same tone and feels the rush of adrenaline.

"Santa is missing."

Chapter Nine

KEITH MEADOWS

Keith is old, but not that old. He wasn't around for the day when newsrooms relied on typewriters, landline phones, fax machines, and printed wire reports. However, he is old enough not to fully understand modern tools of the trade, such as digital publishing systems, cloud collaboration tools, content management systems, and AI for content generation.

Gone are the days of operating on fixed publishing cycles like the morning newspaper or evening news broadcast. Information flows in real time now and is instantly distributed through blogs and social media posts. The internet has surpassed physical media and even television as the primary means of news consumption. YouTube and TikTok posts get far more viewership than most cable news broadcasts.

The one-way relationship with the audience has changed now that readers or viewers have direct feedback opportunities via social media and live chats. That has forced a change in how the news is delivered. Reporters, editors, photographers, and designers used to have distinct, narrow duties. Today's journalists must be multi-skilled Swiss Army knives who can write, shoot video, edit, and publish across platforms. They are mobile newsrooms and, as a result, are rarely in the office. Thank God, Keith works at the White House and doesn't typically have to deal with much of that.

The newsroom smells like burnt coffee and flop sweat. Cheap twinkle lights and plastic garlands are spread haphazardly around the office. A fake pine wreath is hung off-center on Ben Haverson's door, probably due to his slamming it throughout the day. It's a surprise it has stayed put at all.

"Did you get my email?" Keith asks after a quick knock on the door jamb. Without waiting for an acknowledgment, he sits in the chair opposite his editor's desk and checks the length of his fingernails. He'll get an answer to his question eventually.

"The one about the president making recess appointments?" Ben mumbles after a few moments, not looking up from his laptop. "Yeah, I got it. And?"

Keith doesn't understand his boss's flippant attitude. This is a big story. The president of the United States is openly flouting the Constitution, and people should care about that. He knows it doesn't have the spice of oral sex in the Oval Office or the presidency-ending consequences of breaking into the other party's campaign headquarters, but it's still a huge story.

"And? The Senate isn't in recess, Ben. At least, not officially. What the president is doing is likely unconstitutional."

Ben waves a dismissive hand. "Who cares?"

"A lot of people."

"Inside the Beltway, sure. The president's political enemies, absolutely. The rest of America will shrug and let the courts figure it out. It doesn't affect their daily lives."

"It's an important story."

"Does it have a drunk mall Santa? A reindeer on the run? A grieving widow who saved a town with gingerbread? Because it's almost Christmas, and that's about all our subscribers care about right now."

The senior correspondent scoffs. "No. But it has numbers and accountability. You know, the journalism you expect from your senior White House correspondent."

"Keith, in eight days, people around the world will start opening gifts with their families. No one wants civic outrage under the tree, especially after what happened last year. They want another Santa Claus trip around the world-type story, and I want something to boost us like it did last year…despite your best efforts to sabotage it."

He didn't intend to sabotage anything. Keith discovered who Malcolm Chapman was and who he worked for. That Santa would take a high-ranking Heilung Pharma executive with him was a story that nobody else had broken. It was a question of whether MacKenzie or anyone on the plane even knew. That had to be called out. He had no idea that events would unfold as they did, turning a globe-trotting Santa into the year's best feel-good story.

"You want more fluff."

Ben leans forward slightly. "I want more *traffic*. I want something that makes our homepage sparkle like Rockefeller Center at the tree lighting. Find me another Christmas miracle."

"I work at the White House. If you want stories like that, talk to the city desk."

"I have. Now, I'm talking to you."

Keith will never understand the need to cater to the masses. Their job is to deliver the news. His job isn't sexy, but it's important.

"Well, I did hear about this dog who bit a mailman dressed as an elf. Twice."

Ben rubs his chin theatrically. "Good headline, but it has no heart."

"Neither do I."

"I'm well-aware. Your grinchiness was on full display for the entire world at that children's hospital. I'm still reading hate mail over it a year later."

"Crazy people aside, are you ever going to let me live that down?"

"Only when you make me forget by finding me a compelling Christmas story. I don't much care how or why you hate Christmas. You have a therapist for that. Give me the kind of story that makes people smile while their in-laws fight in the background."

Keith shakes his head. "I work at the White House. The government doesn't do that kind of thing."

"Recent stories say otherwise. Santa Claus testified before Congress and traveled around the world on Air Force One. Those stories gave us the best ratings we've seen in years."

"Santa Sleigh One, actually."

Ben scowls. "Get out of my office and find me another one."

It wasn't a rude dismissal. At least, it wasn't intended to be one. It was a command...almost a plea. The pressure from their corporate overlords to produce the clicks and views that generate advertising revenue is immense, and there aren't enough hours in the day for Ben to get through the workload heaped upon him. He issues orders, makes demands, and gets busy clearing the to-do list. That's how things work around here.

Keith stands and turns before stopping. "How do you sleep at night?"

"Easy," Ben says without looking up from his computer. "With a belly full of spiked eggnog, a weighted blanket, and three million unique monthly visitors."

Chapter Ten

SPECIAL AGENT GAVIN KINNARD

It is just past midnight when Gavin manages to unlock the door and step into his apartment. He thinks about what excuse he can make for his lateness this time. It will be work-related, even if that has nothing to do with the truth. He's been at the bar for hours. The smell of beer and the taste of barley and hops on his lips will be tough to hide from her. Of course, there is always the option of telling Julie the truth. She will be elated to hear that he's not going to be in the Bureau for much longer when that bomb gets dropped. Of course, that means he will also be unemployed....

It's late, but his fiancée is usually awake, even at this hour. The alcohol has fogged his senses. He doesn't notice the silence at first or realize that the apartment is bathed in darkness. There is no light in the kitchen or coming from the switched-off television. He flips the switch and listens. There is no stirring or soft laughter coming from the other room. The wine glass that should be next to the sink is conspicuously missing. The only thing on the counter is the likely explanation for the dark, quiet apartment.

A small, pale envelope is propped against a mason jar of pine boughs tied with red ribbons. His name is written in her handwriting — looped and gentle and familiar in the way that a favorite song or worn flannel feels. She often leaves notes, preferring them to bland text messages unless necessity dictates otherwise. Not one of those notes was ever tucked inside an envelope.

Gavin

She sealed it. That's another first. He runs his finger inside the flap to defeat the glue. He can feel something hard in it and turns it upside-down to pour the contents out into his hand. A diamond engagement ring drops into his palm and glints like a shard of ice in the dim kitchen light.

Gavin doesn't sit. He doesn't curse. He simply pulls out the letter from the envelope, braces himself for the words on the page, and reads:

You never come home angry or raise your voice at me.
You support me, treat me well, and always kiss me
goodbye — even when you are already out the door. By

all measures, you're the perfect man when you're here…except you never really are.

Your job is demanding, and I thought I could live with that. I thought love was enough to overcome your constant absence and the fear that, one day, something could happen to make that absence permanent. I was wrong.

I know you love me. Know that I love you, too. But love isn't always enough when our lives are lived in two different worlds. I cannot live in yours, and you aren't willing to live in mine.

So, I'm releasing you from the promise you made to me when you proposed. It's the best thing for both of us. Please don't come looking for me or beg that things will be different. They won't be…they can't be. Just be safe. That's all I ask of you now.

Jules

Gavin stands in the dim light of the kitchen for a long time, the letter in one hand and the ring in the other. He has talked people off ledges. He's stared down the barrels of guns, taken criminals off the streets, worked undercover, and convincingly lied to dangerous men. But he's never felt this helpless.

Outside, the small Virginia city they live in keeps moving. He can hear the wail of distant sirens, the rumble of truck engines, and even the sound of the brisk December wind rattling the windows. But inside the confines of this plain vanilla apartment, he stands alone in absolute stillness, lamenting a history that was meant to serve as a foundation for the future.

He drops into the chair by the table, the letter now creased from how tightly he holds it. The ring – her ring – is set on the counter as a silent verdict in their now failed engagement. Gavin knows he did everything right. He long ago laid bare the trials and tribulations of his life for Jules as she sat across from him at a rickety table outside their favorite coffee shop.

They were sharing funny stories. Jules laughed and tossed a sugar packet at him. The sun had caught in her hair that day, turning it the color of honey. He remembered thinking that she could be the one. It was an odd thought for a second date, but he felt he needed to warn her about his mistress. That's what the FBI is.

Gavin turned more serious, explaining that being a federal agent is complicated. He told Jules to imagine him always being on call, even when off duty. Birthdays, dinners, vacations – anything can be interrupted at a moment's notice. He has learned to keep his phone charged and his emotions in check. He holds things back because the job takes a lot from him – time, trust, and, more often than not, sleep.

That didn't deter her, so he got really honest about the walls he builds to shield himself from the work trauma and how they often unintentionally keep people out, too. He stated point-blank that he needs someone who understands the barriers he needs to erect for his mental survival, and is patient, trusting, and okay with his not talking about what happened that day when he comes home from work. She said that she was good with secrets so long as she was not one of them.

Gavin actually thought she meant that. Maybe she did. That's why he proposed. But, in a line of work that always demands sacrifices, he never thought Jules would be one of them. Words can be empty. Talk can be cheap. It turns out that her assuring words that she was different were both of those things.

The refrigerator clicks on. A dog barks in the distance. The world goes on, oblivious to his pain. At Quantico, Gavin trained to chase fugitives, intercept threats, and uncover lies. All he can do now is sit here and try not to break apart. He has no future in federal law enforcement, no rosy prospects for a bright future, and no future wife to share his troubles and fears with. All he's left with is a diamond ring that once graced her finger and the quiet goodbye she left behind.

Chapter Eleven

WYATT HUFFMAN

Aurielle is a far cry from the chipper woman who faintly smelled of cinnamon and pine the first time they met her inside Santa's cozy wooden office. She is even dressed differently than she was when she accompanied St. Nick on his world tour. The chief elf is dressed in street clothes that look normal in Vermont during winter. The only way he recognizes Santa's closest companion is her trippy rainbow eyes. Although it's easy to believe they are, Wyatt is beginning to think they aren't actually contact lenses.

He takes her coat and gets her settled on the sofa while Stowe makes coffee. Nana's brew is the best in New England, but Aurielle makes the best hot cocoa on the planet. That she opted for the cup of joe instead of a mug of pure happiness is a stark warning about how bad this must be.

Nana and PopPop return from their outing, and introductions are made. Everyone sits, and Aurielle begins her recount of what happened in the village. She doesn't provide a lot of detail. Wyatt worked in Washington long enough to learn how to sift lies from the truth like he was panning for gold in the Yukon. It's not that the chief elf is purposely deceiving them. It's more like she isn't divulging all the details.

"Aurielle, this is going to sound crass, but—"

"No, this isn't one of Santa's reindeer games. This is real. I can't help but think something happened to him."

"Oh, it's probably nothing," Nana tries to assure her in the grandmotherly voice Wyatt finds more soothing than a massage.

"Let me be clear," Aurielle says, shaking her head as she grips the mug with two hands. "Santa Claus does not miss work…ever. The only days he has missed in years were going to Washington to testify in front of that committee and the days it took to make it to St. Louis last year. This isn't some nine-to-five job. There are no weekends off."

"Everybody deserves a break from work, dear," Nana argues.

"It's not work…at least, not for Santa. We are used to big crowds in December, but this whole year has been…incredible. Santa's Village was packed even in spring and summer. We had school trips in April, social media influencers in May and June, and more than quadruple the normal number of Christmas fanatics in July. Santa rests after the holiday right before New Year's Eve. There is no way he would take a break in mid-December during peak holiday merriment. Not ever."

"Aren't there other Santas who can fill in for him?"

Aurielle looks at PopPop in confusion. It was an innocent question asked without any real understanding of the man Wyatt and Stowe met. How could he know? While people may have drawn a conclusion about the man based on what they saw on television, it takes being with him to understand the magic. Their St. Nick isn't a person…he's an experience.

"He's not a mall Santa," Aurielle argues.

"We can vouch for that," Stowe mutters, getting nods from her grandparents. They heard the stories about Tax Evasion, Sauced, Jaded, and Streaker Santa from their search two years ago. They have become nothing short of a legacy in the Bessette household.

"He doesn't do what he does for a paycheck. He's special…as you two have undoubtedly figured out. Even when Santa isn't in his office, he's always working. Yes, occasionally, he takes a quiet sleigh ride through the forest to recharge his batteries, but he has never gone missing like this."

"He didn't leave a note or anything?"

The red envelopes on their journey to St. Louis became a thing. The last one, wishing them to live happily ever after, has a permanent place in a shadowbox hung upstairs on their bedroom wall. It's not inconceivable that he would have left something for his chief elf.

"Nothing. I left for the night. There was nothing out of the ordinary when I arrived the next morning. I waited for him for over an hour…but he never arrived…never showed up. He has always shown up."

"You checked his…house?" Stowe asks.

"He lives in the village. It was the first place I went when people started arriving with their children to meet him. He wasn't there. It doesn't even look like his bed was slept in."

Nana looks at PopPop and then at Stowe and Wyatt with pleading eyes. "Is there anything you can do?"

Stowe answers first. "We're not investigators."

"Maybe the authorities—"

"They won't do anything," Aurielle interrupts Wyatt. "At least, not in time for Christmas. To them, Santa is just a missing person – an old man who probably didn't want to play the part anymore. They don't realize the truth like both of you do. That's why I came here. Santa has a soft spot for you two. His eyes twinkle whenever your names come up. You are my last and only hope."

Wyatt is sold. If that was meant to be a guilt trip, it worked like a charm. But he doesn't think Aurielle is trying to manipulate them. She means every word she says. He glances at Stowe, who nods. She knows it, too.

"We can make some calls."

"Thank you, Stowe. Anything you can do would be greatly appreciated. I have no idea where to start. We have to find him, and quickly."

There is nothing in the world more synonymous with the holiday than Santa Claus. He may only be a symbol, but he's a powerful one. Millions of children believe he will bring them gifts. The stakes for this are very high, especially in light of what has happened over the past two years.

Aurielle exhales slowly. "If word leaks out that he's missing, it'll...."

Nana and PopPop know what the end of that sentence is. They look with concerned eyes at their granddaughter and the man they hope she marries.

"Ruin Christmas," they both say.

Chapter Twelve

STOWE BESSETTE

The West Wing of the White House never stops working, even during Christmas. When Stowe was in Washington, she noticed a distinct seasonal shift in tone that accompanied the holiday decorations. Staffers still manage the day-to-day business of government, national security, communications, and policy, but meetings are shorter, visitors are fewer, and the press briefings are lighter.

The same is true in Congress. They recess soon, so workloads will be very light on Capitol Hill. Nobody wants legislation to ruin people's holidays. That's what made the hearings about banning Santa Claus so jarring two years ago.

She pulls up the contact on her cell and punches the call icon. Until last year, MacKenzie hated Christmas. Stowe wonders if her tune has changed since reconnecting with her old flame in Morocco, courtesy of Santa. She's about to find out as she switches the audio to the speaker so Wyatt can listen in.

"Hello?"

"Merry Christmas, MacKenzie."

"Stowe?"

"Yeah, and Wyatt is here with me."

"Hi, Mac. How's Cliff doing?"

Stowe tries and fails to stifle a frown. She hates it when he calls MacKenzie by her shortened name. It's a leftover trauma from last year's adventure when she thought the man she had fallen in love with had an interest in the very not unattractive communications director. They were chummy on the flight to Finland, and it bothered the hell out of her. Even though she and Wyatt are together now, and she trusts him implicitly, his calling her "Mac" is still like hearing fingernails scraping a chalkboard.

"Very busy. He's keeping Malcolm Chapman hopping. We're all looking for some good downtime for the holidays."

"It's great to hear that," Wyatt says, meaning it.

Cliff left government service to form a non-profit organization that aimed to make a difference in the world by teaching critical work skills to local villages, helping them become self-sufficient in a modern global economy. From what he read, their first year has been a rousing success, thanks in no small part to the corporate charity the former Heilung marketing executive secures.

"It's been a long time since we've talked, although I suppose it wouldn't be Christmas without hearing from you two."

"Well, it wouldn't be Christmas these days without a Santa-related crisis," Stowe admits.

"Uh, oh. Is that why you're calling?"

"Pretty much."

Stowe begins to explain how Aurielle arrived in Vermont and relays the story she told them. MacKenzie listens with few interruptions for questions, and they are the same ones they already thought to ask the chief elf. At the end of the synopsis, they get a heavy sigh from the other end of the line.

"I appreciate the call and the heads up, but I'm the White House communications director, not the head of the FBI. Why are you telling me this?"

"Because you have connections, and we need your help to find someone who *can* help us," Stowe pleads.

"Guys, I get it, but a missing Santa isn't the U.S. government's problem."

"Yes, it is," Wyatt argues, his eyes locked on the phone like it is about to get up and do a dance routine. "You made it that way."

"You brought Santa to testify, if memory serves."

"And you took him on a world tour with Air Force One," Stowe says, taking up the argument. "You came up with the 'Santa Sleigh One' moniker. MacKenzie, do you really want to follow up on last year's amazing Christmas miracle with a series of stories about the administration's indifference to the current crisis?"

"Phew," Wyatt says, grinning. "Those would be stories worth reading about on blogs and watching on every political YouTube channel in the country. Usain Bolt wouldn't catch the new media running with those tales of conspiracy and looming Christmas disaster."

"And then there are the administration's haters. I mean, really, I can only imagine what Keith Meadows will—"

"Okay, okay, I get it! Why did you two ever leave Washington?" MacKenzie asks.

"We value our sanity. Why?"

"You two are very good at this game, Wyatt. Look, I can't make promises, but let me make some calls. A few people inside the Beltway owe me some favors. I can try to cash in one or two of them, but don't expect too much. It's almost Christmas, and getting people to take this seriously will be a struggle."

"Thank you, MacKenzie."

"Oh, you two aren't off the hook that easily. There's a political storm brewing with the president, so I can't take the lead on this."

"Recess appointments?"

"It seems you haven't completely checked out of the Washington mindset, after all, Wyatt."

He frowns. "Old habits die hard."

"What do you need from us?" Stowe presses. She can almost hear MacKenzie smile.

"How fast can you get to Washington?"

Chapter Thirteen

KEITH MEADOWS

There was a point in time when Keith was ready to give up the demanding, high-pressure world of journalism to become a novelist. The idea of sitting in his pajamas on the couch and pecking away at a laptop all day with a warm cup of coffee and some quiet music in the background seemed relaxing. Then, he tried it.

It wasn't so much relaxing as it was boring. Keith stared at the open document as if words would magically appear on the page without any interaction. They didn't. Someday, they will. Computers will replace humans in the arts. By the time people realize that the stories an AI tells are soulless and absent real creativity, it will be too late.

Computers aside, Keith knew he wasn't introverted enough to be an author. He enjoys talking to people in an effort to uncover the truth. He likes cutting through the lame excuses and outright lies. And he's good at it.

So, he stayed in journalism and has had a great career that saw him rise to become the chief White House correspondent for a major news publication. Of course, that decision and the changing media landscape have also landed him here, on a laptop, reminiscing about the path not chosen as he looks for a Christmas story.

No Christmas stories are coming out of the White House, feel-good or otherwise. After two years of government involvement with Santa, it looks like they are taking this one off. Since he refuses to do an article about the First Lady's awful taste in Christmas decorations, he's going to have to get creative. That's easier said than done, so close to the 25th.

Keith is perusing social media when a shared article catches his attention. He clicks on the linked post, which takes him to a local Finnish news site. Of all the places where he expects to see breaking news, Scandinavia isn't near the top of the list. Then again, it is close to Christmas, and Santa's Village is on the Arctic Circle, so he shouldn't be that surprised.

Rovaniemi, Finland — December 17th

Tourists disappointed as Santa Claus missing from his village in Rovaniemi

By Elina Korhonen

A wave of disappointment is sweeping through the Arctic Circle as visitors to Santa Claus Village in Rovaniemi take to social media to express frustration: Santa is nowhere to be seen.

Typically, a cheerful stop for thousands of tourists year-round, Santa Claus Village has recently been at the center of online criticism after multiple visitors complained on social media that they were unable to meet Santa during their visits.

"We came all the way from Tokyo to see Santa, and he's not even here? Heartbroken is an understatement," wrote one user on Instagram, posting a photo in front of a locked door labeled "Santa's Office."

Another visitor posted a TikTok video showing crowds gathering in the square bisected by the Arctic Circle as a harried employee tries to explain the situation. The caption read: "Santa, where are you? #RovaniemiLetDown"

According to the official website, Santa Claus is "available every day of the year," a promise that has attracted international tourists even during off-season months.

A spokesperson for Santa Claus Village released a brief statement: "Due to unforeseen circumstances, Santa has had to step away temporarily. We apologize to all visitors and assure them that Santa will return shortly."

No further explanation was given, leading to more speculation online, including humorous theories ranging from "Santa burnout" to enrollment in a rehabilitation center to overcome a milk and cookie addiction.

Local tourism officials are now under pressure to clarify the situation and restore visitor confidence with less than ten days until Christmas.

Meanwhile, souvenir shops and husky tours remain open, and staff are encouraging visitors to enjoy the "magic of the Arctic" despite Santa's mysterious absence.

"We understand the disappointment," said a tour guide. "But there's always some magic here in Lapland."

Keith leans back in his chair. That's not like the Santa he remembers from last year. That jolly old man may or may not be the real thing, but he wasn't lazy, apathetic, or prone to disappear at this time of year. Even if he wasn't at his office during his world tour, people understood why. They were caught up in the adventure. This is different.

Keith picks up his cell. It's time to get to the bottom of this. He surfs over to the appropriate website and punches in the numbers. It's picked up on the third ring.

"Hello, Santa Claus Village. How can I help you?" a cheerful voice asks in accented English.

"Hi," Keith says, trying to match her enthusiastic tone. "My name is Keith Meadows. I'm a reporter in the United States who accompanied Santa on his journey last year. I read reports that he isn't at the village and was concerned, so I thought I would check in. Is he okay?"

There is a long pause on the other end of the line. "Thank you for calling. Santa is fine. He's currently unavailable due to personal reasons. We expect him back soon. Thank you for calling. We recommend checking our website for updates. Thank you."

A script. That's what the pause was for. Keith is about to press for more details when the line goes dead. He stares at the phone. "Interesting."

This time, he makes a call to someone not involved at all. Mika was one of the tour guides who brought the press pool to see the Northern Lights when they spent an extra day in Rovaniemi last year. He has no horse in this race and will likely be more candid.

"Nobody knows what's going on," Mika says after the two exchange greetings and provide brief updates on how things are going in their lives. "Santa is there 24/7. I've seen the man greet people while recovering from the flu, after breaking his ankle, and even during a power outage following a nasty snowstorm. Other than his two visits to the U.S., he's always there. This is a new development."

"So I gathered. Could this be something health-related?"

Keith can almost hear the man shrug. "Maybe, but I doubt it. They would be more forthcoming about something like that."

That's probably true. Fifteen minutes later, he ends the call with Mika and dials the number for the Rovaniemi Tourism Board to request an official explanation. All he gets is more stonewalling. Nobody knows what's happening, and everyone is on edge about it. This is not a planned absence. It's not an illness or something easily explained. That much is clear. What escaped from the spokesman's mouth were the poetic stanzas of a man well-versed in uttering lots of words that have no meaning.

This is a mystery. If this is a PR stunt, it has gone sideways. But Keith doesn't think this is a fabrication to attract attention because nobody up in Lapland is giving straight answers. This doesn't feel like a coordinated Santa effort.

That doesn't mean Santa Claus is "missing" in the criminal sense. No sleigh tracks leading deep into the Lapland forests have been found, and there is no report of a ransom note written with letters cut out from magazines as a clue to the disappearance. But one thing is for certain – Santa is definitely *gone*.

Maybe it's temporary. Maybe it's something nefarious. Regardless, Keith may have his Christmas story. After all, how often does a reporter get to chase a scoop on a missing myth? He begins to salivate at the idea of what this could mean. All he needs to do now is make it a scandal to generate worldwide attention. Fortunately, he knows the one person to start with who might know the truth about what's going on.

Chapter Fourteen

SAINT NICHOLAS

8 Days Until Christmas

The plane ride here wasn't as direct, just as the man originally promised. There was another stop after London, and it went similarly to the first. When they did finally arrive and everyone disembarked, Santa was shoved into the back of a waiting SUV. Although unnecessary, one of the two big men placed a bag over his head. It was red with a white cotton ball at the top with some sleigh bells attached. Someone has a warped sense of humor.

Forty minutes later, the SUV stops, and the "blindfold" is removed. The large mountain chalet before him is the epitome of alpine charm. It seamlessly blends rustic elegance with a degree of functionality to withstand harsh winters. This one has balconies with carved railings, flower boxes, and a steep roof with overhanging eaves to protect the façade from snow and add to the chalet's fairytale aesthetic.

"All right, Santa," his kidnapper says after climbing out of the vehicle and moving to stand beside him. "You're a world traveler. Do you know where we are now?"

Santa looks around. There is plenty of snow and countless mountain peaks. It could be one of any number of alpine villages. Fortunately, he has a sense for these things. Geography is definitely his strong suit.

"Verbier, Switzerland."

The man cocks his head. That wasn't what he expected to hear. Why would he? Verbier is a renowned alpine village nestled in Southwestern Switzerland, but it isn't as recognizable as Lucerne or Zermatt. That doesn't mean it isn't beautiful, offering panoramic vistas of the Grand Combin massif and Mont Blanc. A skier might have a fighting chance of recognizing the surroundings. Its vibrant après-ski scene and luxurious accommodations make it a premier destination for winter sports enthusiasts. Not that Santa skis.

"I'm duly impressed, St. Nick. Come."

The guards nudge Santa forward, and they enter the main residence. It has an expansive open-plan living room with a vaulted ceiling, plush seating, and a central fireplace as a focal point. The large windows offer panoramic views of the mountains and admit an abundance of natural light. There is a large farmhouse-style dining table and an open kitchen complete with every modern appliance imaginable, surrounded by cabinets with rustic finishes.

Considering they flew a Gulfstream to get here, Santa didn't expect to be secluded in a cave. He also didn't anticipate a stay in a chalet that most would consider the lap of luxury. That naturally begs his next question – the one he's been asking since he was taken from Rovaniemi.

"Why are we here?"

"Because you are my guest."

Santa checks the two beefy bodyguards standing silently against the wall. "Do you often hold your guests hostage at gunpoint and assign two large men as escorts?"

The man shrugs and raises his arms slightly. "You're the one who said that I'm on the naughty list. You tell me."

This time, it's Santa's turn to smile. He says nothing.

"You'll be staying in the guesthouse while you're here, Santa. The main house is reserved for me and my daughter."

"Daughter?"

"Yes. Fallon lives with her mother but is spending the holiday with me. She arrives here tomorrow. You are to have no contact with her under *any* circumstances. You are not to leave the guesthouse under *any* circumstances. Your food will be brought to you, and the kitchen there is fully stocked, should you want to make your own meals. Kram and Skut will see to any other additional needs you have."

"Very well."

"Understand that if you break the rules, I will have to hurt you. If you try to escape or contact anyone, especially my daughter, I will kill you. Am I clear?"

Yes, his instructions are clear, but his intentions aren't. Santa cannot decipher the meaning of any of this. He cannot fathom why a man of means, like his tormentor clearly is, would want to spirit him away from Lapland to a Swiss chalet during Christmas. If it's a joke or some special rendezvous that betrays the man's entitlement, it isn't funny or appropriate.

"You would harm Santa Claus?"

The man shakes his head. "You're not really Santa."

"No? Then you must have a problem with Finnish Santa impersonators."

The man doesn't respond. Santa only gets rewarded with a sinister grin after the statement is made. It's unnerving.

"Skut and Kram will escort you to your quarters. Go ahead and get comfortable. You're going to be here for a while."

The two men step forward, but Santa doesn't require urging toward the door. He stops after a few steps and turns to face his captor. There is one way he can think of to understand the man's intentions.

"I must return by Christmas Eve."

"Yeah, other arrangements will need to be made. That, or someone can tell the world that they can call Christmas off this year."

Chapter Fifteen

STOWE BESSETTE

Come December, the Rayburn House Office Building, the largest of the U.S. congressional office buildings, undergoes a subtle yet meaningful transformation. The Brutalist limestone façade remains unchanged against the gray, dreary winter skies. It is not adorned with lights or garlands, unlike many American homes. However, the atmosphere inside is a different story.

The typically formal halls that provide access to the legislative offices soften during the holiday season. Harried staffers are more relaxed, and public servants reduce their busy schedules. The volume of people hustling in the corridors diminishes when garlands get wrapped around marble columns and wreaths are hung outside member offices.

Building security is the only thing not slowing down and taking things a little easier. It is as tight as always, with badge checks, metal detectors, and the usual Capitol Police routine. Stowe, Ellie, and Wyatt make their way through the checkpoint and begin their trek to Stowe's old stomping grounds. What they find upon entering is one of the last vestiges of bipartisan goodwill in this city.

Members of Congress invite guests, interns, and staff into their suites for cider, cookies, and a fleeting break from the year's chaos in what is called "Holiday Open Houses." Congresswoman Pratt's suite is overrun with staff from John Knutson's office. Politics makes strange bedfellows. After being forced to work together two years ago, they actually became somewhat friendly with each other despite being on opposite sides of the political aisle.

The reception for Stowe and Wyatt is warm. Everyone was rooting for them as a couple. A couple of staffers even start chatting up Ellie until they notice the engagement ring and wedding band on her finger. Despite her marital strife, she still hasn't taken them off. The one guy who didn't seem to be bothered by her vows got a cold, hard glare from Wyatt. He's always the protective older brother, not that Ellie needs much protection.

Stowe is the first to break ranks once she is told that Angela and John are talking in the congresswoman's office. She takes a deep breath before heading in that direction. The last time she set foot in there was the day she left Washington and the staff for good. It isn't the worst of memories, but not the best of them, either.

"Well, if it isn't the ghost of Christmas past!" Angela Pratt says, standing and moving around her desk after Stowe appears at the door.

Congressman Knutson turns in the visitor's chair as she crosses the office and hugs Stowe.

"Hi, Stowe. Where is that loser boyfriend of yours?" Congressman Knutson asks.

Nobody outside of Wyatt and Stowe was more distraught at their breakup two summers ago than John Knutson. He lost a valued staff member the day Wyatt decided that he was done with the political games in Washington. Stowe thinks he may still hold that against her. She has no idea if he still harbors bad feelings toward Wyatt. In the months following Camilla Guzman's hearing to ban public depictions of Santa, Wyatt became an invaluable member of the staff. That's partly what led to the fight that almost ended their relationship permanently.

"He's right here."

The congressman stands and straightens his suit jacket as Wyatt strides confidently into the office. "You know, you are my biggest disappointment, Mr. Huffman. You displayed the rarest of traits around here – common sense. You left when you should have stayed in this town until it sucked all the humanity out of you."

Knutson smiles and extends his hand. Wyatt shakes it. It isn't the soft, limp handshake that many people use with each other. This one is shared between two men born and raised in Big Sky Country. It is robust…and meaningful.

"I've missed you on staff, Wyatt."

"And I miss you, Stowe," Angela echoes. "Christmas isn't the same around here without you singing Christmas carols in October."

Stowe has always had an abundance of Christmas spirit. It long preceded her meeting Santa Claus and was one of the reasons she was chosen for the assignment of finding the perfect one to testify at the hearing. If anything, her love for the holiday has only grown since then.

"Who is this?" the congresswoman asks.

"This is my sister, Ellie Olson. She bites, so don't put your fingers near her mouth."

Wyatt gets a slap on the chest from his younger sibling.

"Is this your first time in Washington, Ellie?"

"It is. I prefer not to tempt fate by visiting hell."

Knutson and Pratt share a smile before turning their attention to Wyatt for an explanation. He shrugs. "She's a proud Montanan and more than a little jaded about what goes on here."

"So were you, if memory serves," the congressman says with a chuckle. "On that note, what brings the two of you back to D.C.?"

"Don't tell us that Santa Claus is planning on delivering coal to the federal government or something," the congresswoman adds. "Not that we don't deserve stockings full of it."

"Not exactly," Stowe admits. "He's gone missing."

She launches into a quick synopsis of the situation. The two members of Congress listen intently, probably wondering if this is something they will get dragged into. After the hearings, they have become the go-to power brokers on Capitol Hill for anything regarding Christmas.

"You think it's serious?" Congressman Knutson asks.

"His chief elf does, and that's not a woman who spooks easily," Wyatt confirms. "She showed up in Vermont to enlist our help."

"She knows that Santa has a soft spot for you guys," Congresswoman Pratt concludes.

"It seems that way. We thought last year was the grand finale."

"You should know better. Everything happens in trilogies these days."

"Not hockey romances," Ellie mumbles, gaining everyone's attention. "There are hundreds of those."

"How do you know?"

'Oh, Wyatt, a girl needs to have a little spice in her life."

"Ew." He makes a show of gagging.

"Hockey romances, eh?" Stowe asks with a wink.

Wyatt is rewarded with another playful slap to the chest from his little sister. "When she starts reading them, you can thank me later."

"Well, if there is anyone who can get to the bottom of what is going on with Santa, it's you two. I think I can speak for John when I say that we have the utmost confidence in you."

"Thank you, Congresswoman," Stowe says, bowing her head slightly. "Only we have no idea how. That's why we're in the city – to ask for the government's help. We have a meeting in a couple of hours."

Knutson chuckles. "This is Washington, Miss Bessette. The two of you should get a couple of drinks in you to help deal with the pending disappointment. You guys should know better than anyone that the government doesn't exist to actually help people."

Chapter Sixteen

SPECIAL AGENT GAVIN KINNAIRD

The summons was unexpected. When Gavin was told to report here to receive a new assignment, his heart jumped in his chest. Maybe this was the opportunity he had been looking for to beat back the encroaching darkness and find his way back to the light. All it takes is one successful investigation to restore faith in his abilities and arrest his fall from grace.

He walks into Jenna Roth's office with pep in his step. It's the first time he's had his usual energetic gait since the incident with the CI landed him in that conference room. Maybe they realize that his dismissal is a punishment that doesn't fit the crime. They have invested a significant amount of money in his training. Why throw it away over one mistake?

Gavin is shown right into the SAC's office. This must be important. That thought is fleeting once his boss summarizes his assignment, only looking up once or twice to gauge his reaction and ensure he isn't sleeping. Now, her subordinate stands motionless, blinking slowly as Roth's words settle like an unwanted fog in his brain. This is not a plum assignment. It's worse than being benched and doing menial logistics tasks while the Bureau gets ready to drum him out. Whatever the hell this is supposed to be is a final slap in the face.

"You want me to do *what?*" he asks when she finishes, his tone flat but tinged with disbelief.

She doesn't look up from her computer screen. "Find out if Santa Claus is missing."

Gavin blinks again. "Please tell me that's a code name for a drug kingpin or foreign asset? You're using 'Santa Claus' as a metaphor, right?"

"No metaphor," Jenna replies, finally raising her eyes. "If it were a drug kingpin or foreign asset, I would be handing this case to another agent. You are getting the assignment to track down the actual Santa Claus. North Pole…well, Arctic Circle in this case. Sleigh. Jolly. Red suit. Likes to vanish from outside congressional office buildings and children's hospital lobbies without a trace and no CBP records of his exit from the country."

He stares at her, waiting for the punchline. One doesn't come. This must be some sort of sick joke. Gavin knows he made a mistake that will cost him his career. This ridiculous assignment seems like an additional punishment that he could do without.

"Ma'am, with all due respect, are you out of your damn mind?" Gavin asks, his voice edging higher. "You're putting me on a milk-and-cookie fairytale hunt?"

Agent Roth folds her hands in front of her and stares at Gavin. "Yes. Or you can sit and stare at your desk for the next few weeks while your paperwork processes. It's up to you."

"You know Santa's not real, right? It's a story we tell kids so they behave for a month. His disappearance, much less his existence, isn't a federal matter."

"And yet," she says, "this one testified in front of a congressional subcommittee and had some of the most jaded politicians in this city questioning their sanity."

"I remember."

How could he not? The country was consumed by the drama for a week, courtesy of the media, which were looking for any stories that could keep their readers, viewers, and subscribers engaged. In many cities, celebrations over the defeat of Congresswoman Guzman's ridiculous bill caused wild celebrations. The one in D.C. was akin to a Christmas rave. For the first time in a long time, America was a country that felt like celebrating something, and they did it with gusto.

"I would hope so unless you were living under a rock. You also saw what he did with the Tucker boy last year. Our government was involved with both of those events, so let's say that the powers that be have a vested interest in making sure St. Nicholas is okay."

Gavin shakes his head. "Fine. How did we learn of Santa's…what are we calling this? Disappearance?"

"His chief elf reported it."

"Of *course* he did."

"She."

"This is absurd," Gavin snaps. "You know this is probably much ado about nothing."

His boss leans back in her chair. "Then it should be a quick investigation."

Gavin opens his mouth, thinks better of uttering the words forming in it, and clenches it shut. In truth, even conducting an investigation involving Santa Claus is better than meandering around the office doing nothing until they force him out. He's not going to earn an assignment that will get him back in the Bureau's good graces. That ship has sailed. If he's going to go out, he might as well make this his swan song.

"Okay. How do I talk to this chief elf?"

"Two of Santa's representatives will be here in an hour. Book a conference room, and I will have them directed to it. You can figure out what to do once you speak with them."

"Are they from the North Pole, too?"

"You'll find out in an hour."

Chapter Seventeen

WYATT HUFFMAN

Wyatt worked in Congress, along with Stowe. Their work rarely carried them away from their representative's offices or the hearing rooms where Knutson and Pratt would attend committee meetings. It might be considered a treat to come to Washington's FBI Field Office, but it really isn't.

The conference room they were shown into isn't much more than four gray walls, fluorescent lights, a television, and a couple of neglected potted plants. Stowe sits across from him, dressed in a sweater that fits in with the attire at any Vermont ski resort. Wyatt went with a more festive option, sporting a sweater with reindeer on it. Neither of them looks like they belong in this building.

Ellie looks equally unimpressed with the field office. She decided to tag along for this meeting, showing little interest in doing any sightseeing while in Washington. What started as a trip to Vermont to get away from the drama with her husband back home is now an unexpected adventure. It's not that different from what Wyatt and Stowe experienced the past two years.

A man in a charcoal suit walks in and introduces himself as Special Agent Gavin Kinnaird. He has an athletic build and sharp eyes, but he also has an attitude. Ten seconds into this meeting, and it's already glaringly obvious that he thinks this assignment is beneath him. He drops a folder on the table and sits at its head, with his jaw tight and arms folded.

"So, one of Santa's elves says that the fat old man is missing, and you think—"

"Her name is Aurielle. You probably saw her on television a bunch this time last year. And Santa actually isn't that fat."

"And you're telling me that you think it's an FBI matter," Gavin finishes slowly, like he's reading Wyatt and Stowe their rights.

"We're not telling you anything," Stowe argues. "We're not investigators. We're asking for your help."

Gavin raises an eyebrow. "It's a local issue. Or a Finnish issue. If St. Nick is actually missing, I'm sure they can find him."

"Only they haven't," Wyatt argues. "And Aureielle wouldn't have shown up at Stowe's grandparents' Vermont cabin if it weren't serious."

"And you know that, how?"

Stowe smiles. "Call it past experience."

Gavin exhales slowly. "And you think this...disappearance...is what? An international abduction? A hostage crisis involving an old man in a red suit? I don't think we can draw those conclusions."

"Is that based on the hour or so you spent looking into this case?" Ellie asks.

"Excuse me?"

"No. I'm not going to excuse you. You just got handed this assignment, and you likely resent it. Maybe it's payback for sleeping with the boss's wife. Maybe you just suck at your job. Either way, you don't want anything to do with this investigation. Go ahead, tell me I'm wrong."

Wyatt leans back. Agent Kinnaird is getting a taste of the psychoanalysis Wyatt has dealt with since around the time Ellie learned to speak. It's good to know that her gift for reading people isn't reserved exclusively for members of the Huffman family.

Gavin shoots a glare at Wyatt's sister. It's going to take more than that to get her to wilt. "My boss is a woman, I don't suck at my job, and an hour was more than I needed to conclude that this is a waste of my time."

Ellie cocks her head. "You're that busy? I get the impression you're the low man on the totem pole around here. That's why you're so angry...or one of the reasons."

The agent cocks his head. "You are direct, aren't you?"

"You have no idea," Wyatt mumbles.

"Agent Kinnaird," Stowe interjects before this gets ugly, "we think whoever took Santa didn't do it for fun. They knew what they were doing. And if someone can kidnap a cultural figure from a secured tourist attraction with global attention...what else are they capable of?"

Wyatt understands where Stowe is going with this, but he knows it won't work. Terrorism is a selling point among America's intelligence and law enforcement agencies, but they won't connect the dots of Santa's disappearance to a larger conspiracy against the country. Kudos for the attempt, though.

"You're crazy if you think I will ever view kidnapping Father Christmas as a threat to our national security."

"You'd most likely cover it up if there was one anyway," Ellie mumbles.

"This isn't about Santa," Wyatt interjects, "at least, not really. It's about what he means. You saw that last year. You saw it the year before. He's a symbol of joy. When word gets out about this – and it will get out – you're going to have fear and panic heading into Christmas."

"And the world will find out that the FBI wouldn't lift a finger to help," Stowe piles on. "Imagine their surprise."

Ellie leans forward. "That means community activists will start pointing fingers because people will need someone to blame. Politicians will find ways to deflect it to settle old grudges. The media will demand a sacrificial lamb to eviscerate in headlines through the holiday. How long before they all channel their anger at the FBI, and the higher-ups offer the head of a lowly agent who was assigned to the investigation and thought it was beneath him?"

"Remind me to borrow your crystal ball before the next lottery drawing."

Ellie waves her hand at him. "It's human nature, Agent Kinnaird. I would have thought a highly trained federal agent would understand that."

Gavin rubs his temples. The guilt trip is working. The fear of unforeseen consequences is a powerful motivator.

"This feels like a prank from the Behavioral Analysis Unit."

"Look," Stowe says, her voice low and earnest. "We know how this sounds. But if we're even a little right, then we can't afford to laugh it off."

"Fine," he says. "You'll get my cooperation until Christmas. But if we have to travel, you need to figure out how to get us around. Maybe you can ask that chief elf to let us borrow Santa's sleigh."

Wyatt leans back. That isn't going to happen, especially since there is no evidence that Santa has a sleigh and eight flying reindeer. However, the comment raises a larger issue — how will they get around? Flying commercial is slow and expensive. There is only one place he can think of to start answering that question.

Chapter Eighteen

KEITH MEADOWS

The late afternoon briefing is humming along in its typical fashion. Some of it is fun banter, as is tradition this close to Christmas, and some of it is mired in serious questions about judicial recess appointments, a flurry of economic policy clarifications, and a few carefully worded denials about cabinet reshuffling.

Keith knows how this is going to sound. Some of the people in this room were in the press pool on Santa Sleigh One last year. Most of them cheered the metaphorical mob that formed to chase him out of town following what happened at the children's hospital. He isn't in a rush to travel down that path again, but his editor wants a Christmas story, and this could be it.

"Dana," Keith begins from his seat in the third row, "I'm seeing social media chatter and some international wire reports out of Finland suggesting that Santa Claus is missing from his village in Rovaniemi. Can you confirm whether the White House has been briefed on this development?"

A murmur ripples through the assembled press corps. A few reporters quietly chuckle at the absurdity of the question. Maybe it is absurd, but he is over the target. The press secretary doesn't mock the question. She doesn't smile or blink. Those are her usual tells.

Keith may not agree with a majority of this administration's policies, but he would be among the first to claim that Dana Bell is one of the best to ever hold the position in the modern age. Not only is she easy on the eyes, but she's smart, quick-witted, and playful, uses sarcasm effectively, and is well-versed in the government's stance on any issue. In sum, she is the complete package so far as spokeswomen go. She is going to have a bright career ahead of her when her service to the president eventually ends.

"I'm not aware of any credible intelligence regarding Santa Claus's whereabouts," she responds with a measured smile. "At this time, we have no information suggesting any involvement of U.S. interests in the matter."

Keith isn't going to let her off the hook that easily. "So, just to clarify – you're saying the White House has not been briefed about the possible disappearance of one of the most widely recognized cultural figures during the holiday season, whose annual appearance draws hundreds of thousands to Lapland and is covered by international news outlets?"

Dana shifts in her heels at the podium, her smile tightening just a hair. "Again, I have nothing to share on that front. We're focused on the business of governing, Keith, and ensuring federal operations continue smoothly during the holidays. I'm sure the Finnish government can address any concerns about tourism operations in Lapland."

"But doesn't it strike the administration as odd," Keith presses, knowing that his time is running out, "that a man who appeared before a congressional subcommittee and took a joy ride on Air Force One has reportedly failed to make a public appearance at his village in days, and nobody seems to have an answer?"

Bell's normally unflappable demeanor shifts slightly. "I understand the interest, Keith. But I'll leave folklore commentary to the experts and foreign affairs to the State Department. Next question."

The other reporters in the room aren't laughing now. Most are likely wondering if there is an issue with Santa Claus. They are about to find out.

Keith notices a member of the White House press team slip quietly out of the room. It's not completely abnormal, but the timing is suspicious. Something is happening with Santa Claus. He's sure of it now.

The press briefing wraps after Dana calls a lid, meaning there will be no more news or announcements from the White House for the day. Most of the reporters file out, their minds likely on deadlines or dinner reservations. Maybe both. Keith lingers, wondering if his hunch will pay off. It does. MacKenzie comes up alongside and escorts him to the West Colonnade, where they can have a little privacy.

"We're off the record, Keith, okay?"

"Okay."

"Yes, we received reports that Santa Claus is unaccounted for. He vanished from his village in Rovaniemi a couple of days ago and hasn't been seen since. "

Keith raises his brows but says nothing.

"It's an international matter, and we have no involvement," MacKenzie continues. "That's the official posture of the administration. There won't be an international alert or State Department advisory. He's not an American citizen but a citizen of the world. We will coordinate with Interpol and local authorities if asked, but that's the extent of it."

Keith nods slowly. "So, you received a report, which means, on some level, that the White House *is* involved."

MacKenzie stiffens. "Don't frame it that way. We are not launching a military operation to find Santa Claus."

He smiles tightly. "Funny. You didn't mind being linked to Santa last year when he arranged life-saving medication to be delivered to Antonne Tucker."

"That was *symbolism*, Keith. It was goodwill and cheer. We had the world rallying around an innocent boy and his family."

Keith nods. "All made possible by a cultural figure some would say you exploited for political gain."

"We did no such thing!" MacKenzie screeches.

"Now, you won't lift a finger for St. Nick," Keith continues, unfazed. "If he did, in fact, vanish, then people are going to want answers. You won't get a pass from me on this one. I don't want to see Dana smiling through these holiday pressers while pretending Santa Claus just took a snow day."

MacKenzie exhales sharply. "Write what you want about the situation in Finland, but don't tie it to us. This administration doesn't meddle in Santa's affairs."

Keith gives a short nod. "All evidence to the contrary, but fair enough. But fair warning: If something big breaks with this Santa story, we're going to revisit this conversation. You'll want a statement ready. The internet moves pretty fast these days."

She doesn't argue. There is no point. Games are played in this town, but the First Amendment still guarantees he can write what he wants without government interference, so long as he isn't engaging in libel against someone. And he isn't. There are facts to back his reporting.

"See you around, Keith."

MacKenzie walks back into the building, her heels clicking against the stone with each step. Keith pulls out his notebook and scribbles a single word: confirmed. MacKenzie wouldn't have bothered talking to him unless the White House had a larger role to play in this affair. Now, it's about finding out what.

Chapter Nineteen

SAINT NICHOLAS

It may not be his kitchen back in Finland, but his captor at least ensured that it was well-stocked. Santa has all the ingredients he needs: all-purpose flour, granulated sugar, brown sugar for moisture and richness, unsalted butter, eggs, baking powder, salt, vanilla extract…. The adjacent cabinet is equally filled with cinnamon, nutmeg, ginger, molasses, and a bunch of other spices and treats. Perfect!

He ties a red apron snugly around his waist. With only one set of clothing, he needs to ensure that it doesn't end up covered in flour while he shakes the rust off his baking skills. Since he's stuck here for the foreseeable future, he might as well put the time to good use baking his legendary "Wish Cookies."

These aren't just any cookies, or so he likes to say. Each one, sprinkled with magic sugar and love, grants a tiny wish to the child who eats it. At least, that's the lore. The recipe is old and was found written on a faded parchment scroll in his Arctic Circle village. Nobody even knows for certain where it came from. Fortunately, he has long since committed it to memory, even with the minor adjustments Aurielle made to the original formula.

His bodyguard is standing along the wall, having changed into denim jeans and an alpine wool sweater that must have required the fluffy coats of three sheep to weave. He watches with only passing interest as Santa lays out the ingredients. So long as St. Nick doesn't brandish a chef's knife at him, very little else will likely be of interest.

"Is Kram your real name?" Santa asks as he starts measuring ingredients and dumping them into a bowl.

The man doesn't answer. He doesn't crack a smile. He doesn't even flinch. He might have instructions not to talk to Santa, or he may simply not be the talkative type. St. Nick smiles. He's going to put that to the test.

"Let's see," the jolly old elf mutters, looking up as he tries to recall the recipe. "One cup of hope…two tablespoons of laughter…was it a dash of courage or a pinch of joy next?"

He mixes and stirs, humming a carol under his breath as he carefully drops spoonfuls of dough onto a shiny new baking sheet. The scent of cinnamon fills the air. Santa doesn't do much baking anymore. Aurielle takes care of most of that, but being in a kitchen makes him warm and nostalgic for days long since past.

"Did you know that the origin of Christmas cookies is a blend of ancient traditions, medieval customs, and European holiday rituals? Winter solstice festivals like Yule featured the baking of special treats using nuts, dried fruits, and honey to honor the gods and ensure a good harvest."

Santa glances up to find no reaction from Kram. There is no doubt he has heard of Yule. It was widely celebrated by Germanic peoples, and the man is most definitely a German.

"Expensive spices such as cinnamon, nutmeg, ginger, and cloves were introduced in medieval Europe following the Crusades. This was the time when gingerbread started becoming popular, along with Lebkuchen. Have you ever had those German spiced cookies?"

Again, he gets no response from the man. He's as still as a statue.

"Christmas cookies arrived in the United States in the late 1700s or early 1800s, when they were brought by Dutch and German immigrants. Many early American cookbooks included recipes for sugar cookies, molasses cookies, and gingerbread men. These cookies are much like snickerdoodles, only far better."

As he pulls the first tray from the oven, he holds it up to the light. The cookies shimmer faintly at just the right angle. They may be soft and taste sweet and delicious, but that's not the magic of the wish cookies.

Santa looks at the guard, who is still playing the role of chiseled marble as he stands against the wall. He offers a warm smile. "Would you like one?"

"I don't eat sweets."

Words! Finally!

"Yes, of course. You look like a man who eats lots of protein," Santa says, taking in the big man's appearance. "That wasn't always the case, was it? You ate lots of sweets as a child."

"No, I didn't."

A twinkle appears in Santa's eye as he cocks his head. "You never were a good liar, were you, Alaric?"

The man straightens and freezes like he just got hit by lightning. He blinks once…twice…a third time. He finally recovers, his jaw quivering until words finally escape it.

"How do you know that name?"

"I'm Santa Claus," St. Nick says, hands lifted from his sides, turning his palms to face up.

The man shifts his weight uncomfortably from one foot to the other. "I don't use that name anymore."

"I know. I'm sorry, but you really should. Alaric is of old Gothic roots, meaning 'ruler of all.' As far as names go, it's a great one to have."

Kram's face contorts. "I…I don't want to use that name anymore."

"Very well," Santa says with another twinkle in his eyes. "I will continue calling you Kram. I'm going to watch a nice Christmas movie. You're welcome to join me if you'd like."

Santa doesn't expect the man to do that. He's fairly certain that the beefy enforcer was warned not to fraternize with the hostage. Or he may not have a desire to. Time will tell which of those is true.

He makes some hot cocoa and slowly walks to the living area. The couch is overstuffed and comfortable. Santa nestles in and situates a throw blanket on his lap, picking up the remote to see if he can find a fun movie. Since this mountaintop chalet is fully loaded with baking ingredients, he'll be surprised if there isn't a long list of holiday films to choose from. When the menu comes up, he isn't disappointed.

Santa watches out of the corner of his eye as Kram skulks over to the counter and lifts a cookie from the platter, checking to see if his hostage is watching. He sniffs the sample before eating it. His eyes close as he savors the flavor. After another glance in Santa's direction, Kram takes another cookie before retreating to his post near the door.

Yep. There is no holiday in the world more alluring and enchanting than Christmas, and no flavors better than hot chocolate and wish cookies. If Alaric were free to interact or engage in anything resembling a conversation, he's certain that the big man would agree.

Chapter Twenty

STOWE BESSETTE

He isn't dressed for this. Wandering the halls of the Longworth Building in a sweater and jeans is awkward enough, considering that he used to wear a suit while working there. This is a whole other level. The White House isn't a place you want to show up underdressed unless you're on a tour.

After being admitted to the West Wing, Wyatt smooths the front of his sweater. Stowe looks equally uneasy about her clothing. Ellie is completely oblivious. She doesn't seem to care one iota about wearing jeans and a sweater, and probably misses the trusty hat she wears on the ranch.

A member of the press office escorts them from the foyer past the various staff offices. The place buzzes with clipped footsteps, muted phone calls, and the electric hum of power being wielded just behind closed doors. It's funny that, despite working in Washington for a couple of years, Wyatt has never once set foot in this building, even on a tour. Stowe hasn't either. Ellie has never even been to this city, despite her brother working here.

The door opens, and MacKenzie, looking sharp in a navy blazer and red blouse, beckons them in. She leans to the right to check Stowe's left hand and frowns when she doesn't find what she's looking for.

"Wyatt! What the hell are you waiting for?"

"We've been asking the same thing," Ellie mumbles.

"It's good to see you, too, MacKenzie. The annoying woman chirping behind me is my little sister, Ellie Olson."

Mackenzie reaches her hand across her desk, and Ellie shakes it. "Wyatt has told me a lot about you."

"Most of it is lies, no doubt. I never put Wyatt's favorite hoodie in the freezer, and I didn't change the ringtone on his phone to 'Let it Go' when he was in high school."

"No, it was something about you warning him that you would tell all the girls in town that he had syphilis if he didn't hear Stowe out about going on last year's adventure."

The corner of Ellie's mouth curls. "It was herpes, actually. Yeah, I did do that."

"How's Cliff?" Wyatt asks sharply, eager to move off that subject. He's lucky that Stowe already knows the story.

"You can ask him yourself. He said he would stop by when he learned the two of you were coming. Did you have any luck with the Bureau?"

"The agent assigned to the case is…how do I put this? Less than enthusiastic about investigating a missing Santa Claus."

"He's a grinch," Ellie muses.

"Well, not everyone in this city was caught up in last year's joy-fest. For some people, Santa's magic needs to be felt to be believed. Is that why you're here, Ellie?"

"Not exactly. I went to Vermont so I wouldn't give in to the urge to castrate my husband and turn him into a gelding."

MacKenzie raises her eyebrows. She waits for Wyatt's sibling to smile or chuckle or give any indication that she's kidding. None of that comes.

"Her bark is worse than her bite…most of the time," Wyatt clarifies. "It sounds like you are a believer now."

MacKenzie smirks. "What was seen cannot be unseen, and what was done…well, it's been life-changing. So, what is so urgent that you came straight here from the Washington Field Office?"

"We need help getting to Finland," Stowe says. "Government help."

"Okay, just so I'm clear – our arranging to have the FBI help investigate wasn't enough, and now you want the federal government to pick up the tab for your trip to Finland…even though you can't confirm that Santa Claus is even in distress?"

Stowe and Wyatt look at each other before responding at the same time. "Yes."

MacKenzie is about to respond when a man breezes through the door holding a coffee. He stops, looks at the faces in the small gathering, and frowns. Marco Ramirez isn't the type who searches for drama. There must be enough of that in this part of the building, as there is.

"Oh, no," the White House chief of staff whines. "Why do I get the feeling I just walked into another Santa Claus Christmas nightmare?"

"It worked out pretty well for you last year," Stowe sweetly says.

"Humph," Marco groans. "That doesn't mean I want a repeat performance. I single-handedly created a recipe for Pepto Bismol eggnog while waiting for you guys to make it to St. Louis."

"You aren't marketing that?" Stowe asks.

"The color isn't quite right for Christmas."

"Works for Valentine's Day, when it's really needed," Wyatt offers.

Marco gives him a nod as he chuckles, but it's Stowe and Ellie who land slaps on his chest and arm.

"They only want a ride to Finland," MacKenzie says, eager to move off that subject. "For reasons we have already discussed, I think we should authorize it."

"Oh, of course. Why don't you take Air Force One again?"

"Are you serious?" Wyatt asks.

"Hell, no!" Marco exclaims with a laugh. "I'm not letting the White House get within a hundred miles of whatever circus you guys have planned. I learned my lesson last year. I support your investigation if that's what this is, but you'll have to get to Lapland the old-fashioned way."

At that moment, Cliff Sutton leans in through the open doorway. His black overcoat is still on, and he has a sprig of holly pinned to the lapel. He gives MacKenzie a broad smile before addressing the room. "It looks like we're getting the band back together."

"Okay, it's getting crowded in here," Marco says, rolling his eyes before stealing a candy cane from MacKenzie's desk. "Let me know how it goes. Or better yet, don't. I don't think I want to know."

"Hope I'm not interrupting anything important," Cliff says, shaking Wyatt's hand and hugging Stowe after the chief of staff spins and strides out of the office. "I think you need to excuse the chief of staff. Mac says that he still has PTSD from last year's escapades and maybe even an ulcer or two."

"I didn't say that!" MacKenzie argues.

Cliff purses his lips and nods a few times before introducing himself to Ellie. "I heard something about needing a lift to Finland."

"You heard right," Wyatt confirms.

"Well, you're in luck. Thanks to Malcolm Chapman, my non-profit, Horizon Circle, landed a huge contributor who happens to be the CEO of JetLynk. He has given us access to any plane we need when we need it."

"They'll lend us a plane?" Stowe asks.

"You can be wheels up out of Dulles with two hours' notice. I can make the call right now if you'd like."

"Well, this visit to Washington is coming together nicely," Wyatt muses. "We scored a federal agent and a plane."

"You guys have more plot armor than a Liam Neeson character," MacKenzie observes.

"Thank you, Cliff."

"No, thank you, Stowe. And you, Wyatt. I met Malcolm because of you guys. He's done an amazing job for us. We would never have achieved this level of success so quickly without him. I also wouldn't have reconnected with the love of my life. Offering you use of a jet for both doesn't begin to repay that debt."

MacKenzie places her hand over her heart as her face softens. "Then you guys should get going. Try not to cause an international incident while you're there."

Wyatt just grins. "It's Santa Claus, Mac. No promises."

Chapter Twenty-One

SPECIAL AGENT GAVIN KINNAIRD

The wind cuts across the National Mall like a blade, sharp with the bitterness of mid-December. Despite the cold, Gavin Kinnaird finds himself sitting on his favorite bench beneath a bare sycamore, his coat collar turned up against the cold, biting air. His hands are shoved deep into the pockets of his overcoat as he watches bundled-up kids while gawking at the monuments.

He must be a pathetic sight. There is no doubt in his mind that he looks like a man who's been run through the wringer and wasn't sure which way was out. Too much of that is true.

Gavin hadn't meant to end up here – not in the city, not on this bench, not in this life. He's unengaged, unwanted, and about to be unemployed, with homelessness and financial ruin sure to follow. His only bright spot, if someone could call it that, is a ridiculous assignment to find Santa Claus. Yeah, Merry Christmas. This holiday has completely gone to hell.

Jenna Roth sits beside him with two paper cups of hot chocolate in hand. She hands him one without ceremony. He accepts it, nodding a quiet thanks. She has always been more like a close friend than a boss. They sit in silence for a moment, admiring the museums lining the National Mall like stern chaperones.

"Hot chocolate?" he mutters after taking a sip. "I didn't expect you to bring a peace offering."

"Well, what can I say? I'm a softie. I figured you could use something with a little sugar and less bitterness. Mark told me about Jules. That's the worst possible timing. I'm sorry."

Gavin exhales, a plume of breath visible in the cold air. "She left a note explaining that the Bureau got more of me than she ever would. This has been brewing for a while. I guess she couldn't do it anymore. The long nights, the danger, the silence about my day. The whole thing is kinda tragic since I would have told her that she was getting her wish of not having to deal with that anymore."

"Breaking that news to you was the last thing I wanted to do," Jenna says, staring straight ahead. "We have been good friends basically since the moment you walked through the doors. It crushed me to have to do that, but in the office, I have to be—"

"I get it," Gavin interrupts. "Orders, appearances, structure. That doesn't mean it didn't sting."

"I know. I'm sorry. All I really wanted to do was give you a hug. I don't want you ousted from the Bureau. Nobody there wants to see you go. That decision came from above."

He wants to believe her. They have been close…very close, although not in a romantic way. More like brother and sister. But after the way she delivered the verdict that would eventually lead to his demise without warmth or humanity, he wasn't sure she was capable of softness anymore or if there was still a strong bond between them. And yet, here she is, shivering on the same bench that he is when she doesn't have to be.

"Politics and optics. People are protecting their careers. I get it."

"It's more than that, and you know it. We've talked a hundred times about the Bureau. You aren't happy there. This could end up being a blessing in disguise."

"It's quite the disguise," Gavin mutters.

"Are you going to work on the Santa investigation?"

He scoffs lightly. "Do I have a choice?"

"You do," she says, turning to face him. "You could walk away. Right now. There's no shame in it."

He doesn't respond, opting to sip the hot chocolate instead. It's too sweet for his tastes, but the warmth is not unwelcome. Another half an hour on this bench and people may start mistaking him for an ice sculpture.

"But I hope you don't," she continues. "I hope you follow it. Something's *off* with this story about Santa, and I think you're the perfect person to find out what. If St. Nick really is missing in action, you'll find him."

Gavin shakes his head, disbelief worn into every line of his face. "You believe in Santa Claus now?"

Jenna offers a laugh. "When I was six, my mom lost her job. She was a single parent, and we had nothing. I didn't expect presents. I just hoped we'd have heat in the house to stay warm. But on Christmas morning, there was a coat for me under the tree – not a secondhand one, but a new one with my name stitched inside. My mom swore up and down that she didn't buy it. I believed her. An Oscar-winning actress couldn't pull off the look of surprise on her face. We never did figure out where it came from."

Gavin doesn't think that's empirical proof of Santa Claus's existence. It's anecdotal evidence at best and not overly compelling. However, that's not the point of Jenna's story. At least, he doesn't think it is.

"I'm not saying Santa came down the chimney," she said. "But I've seen plenty of things about this guy that don't make sense. You watched the hearings. How could he have known those things about the representatives sitting there? And last year…that was one of the most amazing things I have ever witnessed. Whether we want to admit it or not, this Santa is special."

Gavin stares down into his hot chocolate, the steam curling from the hole in the lid. What if this absurd assignment *actually* led somewhere? He hasn't believed in Santa

Claus since he was six. But he believes in truth. If something is *wrong* in Finland, he may be the perfect man to find out what.

Jenna swallows the rest of her hot cocoa, stands, and offers a final nod. "I know you're broken right now. You made a mistake, but I think you're still a good agent because you're an even better man. If there's even a shred of something real in this Santa disappearance rumor, I'd trust no one other than you to find it. But ultimately, the choice is yours."

It's not much of a choice. New career plans will need to be made. Hell, new life plans will be on the agenda once the ball drops in Times Square. But, until then, he needs a paycheck. If this is the only assignment he's going to land, he might as well give it a go.

"I'll find out where Santa went," Gavin concludes. "Maybe I'll find a guy in a red suit who knows if children are naughty or nice. Maybe I'll find a complete fraud."

Jenna looks down at him and offers a weak smile. "Or maybe you'll find a little bit of Christmas magic."

Chapter Twenty-Two

WYATT HUFFMAN

Washington Dulles International Airport serves as a premier hub for private international flights for the capital region, offering world-class facilities and services tailored to discerning travelers. Wyatt and Stowe appreciated having dedicated customs and immigration services at their disposal, as well as a private lounge where everyone could wait. It beats the hell out of dealing with a commercial aviation terminal.

Flying on one of JetLynk's Gulfstreams, Citations, or older Learjets won't be quite as impressive as hopping around the world on a modified 747 used by the president. It will still be far more comfortable than flying in an economy-class seat on a commercial carrier. That, and there is no need to connect through Helsinki.

Ellie has been conspicuously quiet since leaving the White House. Wyatt is surprised that she wants to tag along on this trip. He was more surprised that she brought her passport until he learned that she had never bothered getting a REAL ID. He was most surprised to learn that she had a passport at all.

His sister is biding her time, staring at the overwater huts featured on a poster of Bora Bora. This lounge is filled with promotions for various travel destinations, including Capri, Santorini, Morocco, Paris, Vienna, Ireland, Bavaria, Seoul, and Bali.

"Dreaming of a warmer climate than the one we're heading for?" Wyatt asks, coming alongside her.

"I've always wanted to go there. You know that."

"I know – since you were twelve. You're an adult now. Why don't you?"

Ellie turns to him and shakes her head. "I'm a rancher's wife in Montana. Unless we mortgage the ranch to the hilt, I don't have the cash for that trip. And Billy didn't like to fly. I have as good a chance of visiting the moon as setting foot in Bora Bora."

Wyatt immediately notices her referring to her husband in the past tense, but says nothing. It's not something he wants to bring up now. If she wants to talk about it over the Atlantic, he'll lend a sympathetic ear. Something tells him that she is on this trip because she doesn't want to talk about Billy Olson's alleged extracurricular activities. Nothing screams escapism like a journey to the winter wonderland of Lapland.

"Where's Stowe?" his sister finally asks.

"Ladies' room, I think."

"Good. Then I can finally ask this in private: Did you bring the ring?"

Wyatt cocks his head at her. "What?"

"You heard me."

"What makes you think I bought her a ring?"

He shouldn't be surprised that she knows he bought one. He wouldn't even have to tell her. She psychoanalyzes pretty much everyone she meets, so she no doubt sleuthed that out on her own. She knows that he loves her. She knows that Stowe loves him. Why wouldn't he have bought a ring?

"Because, despite your being a moron on occasion, you aren't stupid. You are never going to meet another woman as amazing as Stowe. And I don't want you coming back to Montana singing, *"If you like it, then you shoulda put a ring on it."*

"What are the odds I would be singing anything by Beyoncé?"

"Pretty damn good if you don't take her advice. Stowe's your person, Wyatt. A blind man can see that. If you have cold feet, put on some wool socks and man up."

"Given your current predicament, I didn't think you would be promoting the institution of marriage."

"*Whoa, oh, oh, oh, oh-oh, oh, oh, oh, oh, oh, oh. Whoa, oh, oh, oh, oh-oh, oh, oh, oh, oh, oh, oh,*" Ellie says, complete with the hand gesture from the music video.

"I…get…the…point."

Calling Ellie out about her marital problems was out of bounds. For some reason, she let it slide without ripping his head off. He would have deserved it. Wyatt knows that she is hurting inside despite not showing her pain to others. That's Ellie's way. That's what the women he knows in Montana do.

"As for marriage, what can I say? I'm a complicated woman. Now, answer my question."

"The ring is safely stored back in Vermont."

If you can call a sock drawer "safe."

"Wait…you're going back to Finland, where you shared your first real kiss at the bottom of a hill and realized you were in love under the Northern Lights, and you aren't planning to take this opportunity to propose? Maybe you are stupid."

"In my defense, I didn't know we were going back there."

"Yes, because you thought we would find Santa in his hidden workshop under the Pentagon," Ellie says, shaking her head.

Wyatt is about to respond when Gavin walks into the lounge and drops a duffel bag on the chair. He's lost the suit and has dressed down, but still has a federal agent's swagger. He also looks miserable. It's the face a patient has when they show up for their colonoscopy. They know it's necessary, but understand full well that the experience isn't going to be fun.

"Well, if it isn't Agent Scrooge McGrinchipuss."

"Does your mouth have an off switch?" he fires back.

"Not one that you'll ever find," Ellie responds.

"You don't look overly enthusiastic to be here, Agent Kinnaird," Wyatt says. You don't need to be trained to read body language to see that the man would rather be watching a Barney the Dinosaur marathon than getting on this plane.

"Because I'm not. I don't do fairy tales," he says. "I do facts."

"Well, here's a fact for you, bucko. Santa is missing."

"So you say."

Stowe returns and picks up her bag. "This looks like a fun group. The pilot says the plane is ready, and we can board."

The four of them make their way to the hangar and the gleaming Cessna Citation Longitude jet. Wyatt would be impressed if he hadn't spent last Christmas flying around on the president's plane.

The flight crew briefs them on the flight plan, which may require a refueling stop in Keflavik, depending on the winds. Wyatt is okay with that so long as they don't lose an engine like the first time they diverted to Iceland. The flight attendant discusses the aircraft's amenities, which include a stand-up cabin, fully adjustable seats that convert into lie-flat beds, and high-speed internet.

Aircraft like this cost tens of millions to buy and hundreds of thousands of dollars to operate. It's incredibly generous of the JetLynk CEO to let them use this. Wyatt must remember to ask Santa to put a little something special under the man's tree this Christmas. If they can find him.

Stowe smacks him on the shoulder a couple of times to get his attention. She points at the nose of the sleek jet, where the words Polar Star are painted in cursive. That's fitting. Wyatt turns to her and smiles.

"Let Operation Polar Star begin."

Chapter Twenty-Three

KEITH MEADOWS

Two decades ago, the newsroom would have been humming with the usual pre-holiday chaos. Editors would be bickering over word counts, phones would be ringing off the hook, and overweight reporters would be scrambling to finish stories while gripping half-eaten sugar cookies. No more.

The office is even quieter than it was the last time he was here. The Digital Age has changed almost everything about reporting the news. There are no cycles anymore. It is now a continuous stream of events reported in real-time, perpetually. The days of holding an article right until the print deadline for the morning newspaper are over.

The new paradigm is that the organization that breaks the story first wins. They are the ones cited in reports worldwide. That amounts to prestige for the reporter and clicks for the outfit, which justifies their advertising costs and pads their profit margins. It's a win-win. That's what Keith is counting on.

The one thing that hasn't changed is that Haverson is still at his desk, his face buried in his laptop. He is a legacy of the past. There could be nobody in this office, and he would still come here to work. Keith isn't even sure if the man changed clothes.

The senior White House correspondent marches straight into the editor-in-chief's glass-walled office and drops a slim manila folder onto his desk. He actually printed this request out in addition to submitting the request via the form on their web portal. Again, his editor is old-school. Ben doesn't look up.

"That had better be either a Christmas story you're pitching me or a copy of your resignation for failing to follow instructions."

"I'm not pitching a Christmas story…I *found* one. I'm going to Rovaniemi, Finland."

"The hell you are. You are the senior White House correspondent. That's what we pay you to be. Unless they picked that building up and moved it to Scandinavia, I'm not sending you to a place that sounds like a type of cheese."

"You're going to want to reconsider. The Santa Claus who testified at the hearing two years ago and traveled to St. Louis last year is missing," Keith says, sliding into the chair across the desk from his editor.

"So?" Ben finally looks at him and leans back in his chair with a sigh. "I'm not about to send you to the Arctic Circle for some puff piece about Santa taking a vacation."

Keith leans forward, voice low and urgent. "Santa. Claus. Is. *Missing*. He hasn't shown up at his office there in three days. The Finnish press isn't providing many details. The staff at Santa Claus Village is stonewalling, but the locals are talking.

Something is wrong. Tourists are posting about it on social media, parents are beginning to panic—"

"Maybe there was a mishap with the elves at the toy factory. Maybe they unionized. Maybe Santa's sleigh broke down, or Rudolph was diagnosed with hoof and mouth disease."

"I know you're naturally glib, but you asked for this. It's not only a good Christmas story, it's going to be *the* Christmas story this year."

Ben waves a hand. "Not for a senior White House reporter."

He wants drama from within the government. They usually oblige in the toxic and partisan world of politics we live in, even this time of year. Last year was special, and the year before that was equally compelling. Now, Ben wants more, and if recess appointments aren't going to get it done, this is the only thing that's left.

"I think the White House is involved," Keith says without blinking. "MacKenzie Walsh practically sprained her jaw trying to convince me that they weren't."

Ben's face twists in skepticism. "You're telling me the U.S. government is investigating the disappearance of a mythical figure... in Lapland?"

"No. I'm telling you that *if* the White House knows about it, it falls into my purview. I'm telling you, Ben, this story will get the clicks you are looking for. If this administration isn't willing to search for a missing Santa who brought so much joy to the world, it will get even more clicks. Millions of them. Christmas, mystery, geopolitics—whichever way this story breaks, it will be gold, just like it was last year. And if the White House *isn't* involved yet, I can promise you, they will be by the time I'm done writing."

It's a bold promise, but one Keith knows he can make good on. He wants to press for a decision, but bullying his editor isn't going to have the desired result. The man is as immovable as Mount Everest, so it's better to let him reach the right conclusion on his own.

Ben rubs his temples. "It's not in the budget. There is no travel allotment money for you unless you're in the press pool."

"Find some. I'll fly coach. Stick me in a hostel up there for all I care. You want more website and social media traffic before year-end? This gets us traffic. I promise you, there is going to be no story bigger than this one."

He sighs and then points a finger. "You'd better bring me back more than a picture of a sad elf and a puff piece about missing Christmas cheer. After last year's debacle, I'm only giving you one shot at this."

Keith nods and bails out of the office as fast as he can. There is an old axiom that he lives by – once you get the answer you want, leave. There is no point in sticking around and giving someone time to change their mind.

The game has started. Once in Finland, he can confirm that Santa is, in fact, gone. Once he does, it's a matter of finding out why. Someone knows the truth – someone is going to be tied to St. Nick's disappearance. While he searches for answers, he plans on turning this into a global story. The world was caught up in his escapades last year. They will tune in to the mystery this year.

It's not going to be an easy journey. Keith's investigative journalism days are long in the rearview mirror. He is going to need to employ old-school, shoe-leather reporting, intelligence gathering, and schmoozing to find out what happened to Santa and whether the U.S. government is more than casually interested in his apparent disappearance.

Once he gets that, the headlines will write themselves.

Chapter Twenty-Four

SAINT NICHOLAS

7 Days Until Christmas

This place is actually dreamy. Snow falls in soft, fluffy waves, cloaking the Alps nightly in a fresh white blanket. From the window of a cozy guesthouse nestled beside the grand chalet, Santa sits quietly in a leather armchair facing the oversized window. He has a thick wool blanket over his knees and a steaming mug of cocoa in his hands. He almost went with coffee instead. He is far too accustomed to the cocoa Aurielle makes, and nothing compares to it.

He has been missing for three days. Surely, Aurielle has sounded the alarm. They are probably scouring Lapland looking for him. How would they ever know he is in a mountain chalet hundreds of kilometers away? How long before they even think to look for him here?

Outside, a small girl is dancing alone in the snow. She's wearing a pale blue ski parka with a fur-lined hood and tiny white mittens. Her boots leave staggered tracks in the powdery snow as she spins in circles and flops into it, making snow angels. She giggles to herself after admiring her latest work, then begins tossing snow into the air like confetti.

Santa's eyes droop with a deep, weary sadness. He misses the children. This is a magical time in the village. Young faces full of wonder line up outside his door, eager to meet the man who can grant their Christmas wishes. Even the parents are at a loss for words when they step into his domain. It's something Santa looks forward to every day…and that has been taken away from him.

There has been no sign of his kidnapper since the night he was swept away from Rovaniemi. The man hasn't been cruel. There has been no abuse – just warnings about consequences for not following simple instructions. There is also a complete lack of reasons for why this is happening. Santa is going to miss Christmas. That much is certain. But there is no indication of why or what happens after that.

The man hasn't chained him up. He is not being kept in some basement or hidden away in a secure room with no windows. Instead, he is in this immaculate alpine guesthouse, with plenty of wood stacked next to the fireplace, a fully stocked pantry, and meals brought to him at the appropriate time. Breakfast this morning was delicious.

And now, the girl has arrived, just as his captor said she would. Santa watches her laughing at the sky as she builds a tiny snowman with an acorn cap and pine needle arms. The wonder of small children. Their joy. Their belief. Their innocence. Their complete disregard for the dangerous world around them.

He leans forward, pressing closer to the glass. Is this child the reason he's here? It must be about her. But why? She isn't depressed or traumatized. Her eyes are clear and wide, and her cheeks are flushed and rosy red. There is life and love and magic in her.

"Don't get any ideas," Skut mutters from his spot near the fireplace. "You know the rules, and I don't want to have to hurt you because you didn't follow them. The boss is serious about his demands."

"I'm sure he is."

Skut isn't like Kram. He's colder, more hardened, and maybe even more physically imposing, with broad shoulders and bulging muscles pressing to break free of his black turtleneck. A bully who remained a bully long after he finished his schooling. He also has a gun casually affixed in a holster at his hip, but he hasn't touched it once.

Santa closes his eyes. He can hear the young girl's laughter from the other side of the windows. If this abduction is somehow about her, then he needs to find out.

"Tell me something, Skut…why is your boss holding me here?"

The blank stare he receives isn't hostile. It isn't aggressive. It's indifferent and unfeeling.

"I follow orders. I don't ask questions."

"Mmm. And I suppose I'm not meant to ask questions, either?"

The big man folds his arms across his chest. "You'd be better off not to."

Santa leans forward slightly, his eyes twinkling. "But I ask questions all the time. It's how I get to know people…their wants, wishes, and dreams. It's how I know that you have always been tough, but you weren't born an unmovable wall."

"I learned my place. Right now, that place is to watch over you, not get therapy."

Santa quietly nods. "No, you're just here to guard a myth you don't believe in on orders you don't understand."

There's a long pause. The fire snaps as a chunk of snow slides off the roof and crashes into the ground beside the guesthouse. Skut looks away, remaining silent. But something behind his eyes has shifted ever so slightly.

The girl is staring at the main chalet from beneath her snow-crusted hood. She raises her hand and waves at the window of the main house. Santa can't see if anyone is waving back, but he assumes so. Whatever this is, she is the key. This must be about her. Now that she has arrived, the time has come to find out why.

Chapter Twenty-Five

STOWE BESSETTE

Snowflakes dance like feathers over the rooftops of Santa's Village as Wyatt and Stowe crunch across the fresh powder toward his office. The line that demarcates the Arctic Circle has been cleared with a shovel, but the rest of the square has about four inches of freshly fallen snow on it.

They were worried that a crowd would have gathered by now, perhaps expecting Santa's absence to be temporary. But nobody is there. There are lines of fresh tracks in the snow leading to the door, but then they peel off and head away from it.

The two of them stop in front of Santa's Office and read the handwritten note on a standard European sheet of A4 paper taped to the door explaining that Santa is not available at this time. Wyatt jiggles the handle and then knocks. Finally, Aurielle comes and lets them in.

"He's still not here," the chief elf says, her face still contorted with worry.

That much is evident. The workshop office, usually aglow with warmth and cheer, is gripped by an uneasy silence. Faint traces of cinnamon and peppermint linger in the air, but they feel like memories rather than presence. The whole vibe is almost spooky.

Wyatt moves around the wall and sees the stained bench, worn from decades of use, empty. A red velvet cushion flattened slightly by time has been tossed to the side. Everything else looks largely like it did the first time Wyatt and Stowe walked in here two years ago. The office is as timeless as its owner, but without his being here, the space feels less magical and more like a shrine frozen in the moment he vanished.

"He never leaves it like this," Aurielle whispers. "Even when he travels, like the past two years, he tidies up first."

Stowe sighs as she looks around. It has the clutter of an old workshop, but everything seems to have its place. If the elf thinks this isn't tidy, she should have seen Stowe's room as a child.

"Hey…what's this?" Wyatt asks after a glint of red catches his eye on the old bookcase.

He retrieves a small, red envelope from its spot next to a wooden truck. It's the same type of envelope they were handed during their journey with Santa last year. He flips it over and shows Stowe their names in the gold-embossed lettering. That part is unexpected. A red envelope is one thing, but one addressed to them is quite another.

Aurielle steps forward, frowning. "That wasn't there before. I'm certain of it. I dusted that shelf when I got back to Finland."

"Convenient," Stowe mutters.

Wyatt opens the envelope and reads aloud:

> *Time is growing thin. Follow the music in the City of Light. Meet her at the Christmas Rose, where a flower glows next to a soul weighted with solitude.*

The three of them stare at each other in silence until Stowe breaks it. "Santa expects us to follow riddles now?"

Wyatt spins to face Aurielle. "You need to level with us. Is this another of Santa's crazy publicity stunts?"

"No."

Stowe folds her arms. "You need to come clean, Aurielle. We aren't interested in playing games—"

"This isn't a game," Aurielle says, stiffening. "Stowe, Wyatt…something's wrong. I swear it. He left without telling me. He *never* does that."

Wyatt holds the card up. "Then how did this get here? He either dropped it off himself or had someone do it for him. Either way, it doesn't look like he's in any danger to me."

"He hasn't been here. Nobody has, except me. And now, you two."

"Then how?" Stowe demands.

Aurielle shrugs. "He's Santa Claus."

Stowe presses her lips together. That's really the only explanation that she needs. Two years ago, it wouldn't have been enough. After a pair of Christmases experiencing a magic that cannot be easily explained away, it is now. She doesn't understand how Santa knows what he knows. She doesn't understand how he comes and goes without a trace. The only thing she is convinced of is that he's special, and special people can do extraordinary things.

Wyatt slips the card slowly into his coat pocket. "All right. Either he's trying to get found…or someone else wants us to find him. Either way, it looks like we're going to Paris."

"He was a little light on the details," Stowe cautions.

"That's a theme with him, isn't it? Somehow, I think we'll figure it out."

Aurielle's eyes shimmer. "You'd better hurry. I'll stay here in case more envelopes show up."

The wind is picking up as Wyatt and Stowe step back into the snowy square and steer themselves in the direction of the security cabin. She eyes him as he shifts his hand in his coat pocket, likely feeling the rigid envelope. It's real and not in his imagination, meaning they have another Santa-fueled adventure in Europe in store for them.

"Wyatt, do you think we're getting played?" Stowe asks as she kicks a clump of ice on the ground left over from the previous snowfall. "I mean, I believe this, but I don't know if it's because it's the truth or I just want to."

"Santa is involved. Normally, I would say yes. But if we are being bamboozled, then Aurielle deserves an Academy Award. It's an Oscar-worthy performance."

"Bamboozled? Good word. I don't think she's faking it, either, for what it's worth," Stowe confirms before pausing. "What the hell is in Paris?"

"The Christmas Rose, apparently."

"Okay, what is that? Bar? Café? Christmas Shop? Nightclub?"

Wyatt shrugs. "We're going to find out. What are the odds our friendly FBI agent will tag along?"

Chapter Twenty-Six

WYATT HUFFMAN

The security office is in part of the main building. The term "office" may be generous. The main counter area is for guests reporting missing children or some other unwanted encounter. Not that much of that happens here. There are few, if any, places Wyatt has ever felt safer.

Stowe peels off and stops to talk to a woman manning the counter. Wyatt proceeds into the adjoining room, where his sister, Special Agent Kinnaird, and a guard are reviewing video footage. The space is warm but claustrophobic, the air thick with the hum of outdated computers, the glow of old CRT monitors, and the pungent smell of stale coffee. Outside the one small window, sleigh bells jingle faintly in the distance.

The FBI agent leans against the desk with his arms crossed, eyes scanning the grainy black-and-white footage flickering on the screen. He rubs his eyes and then his temples, sighing deeply. Ellie scowls and shakes her head at Wyatt when he enters the room. He knows that look.

"This can't be all you have," Gavin moans.

"I tried telling you," the stocky security guard with wind-chapped cheeks and a lumberjack's beard says, "we don't have many cameras in the village. Mainly the entryway, a couple of angles in the post office, and a smattering of them over near the reindeer barn. There are none in or around Santa's Office. This place isn't exactly Fort Knox. Folks come here for magic, not metal detectors."

"Of course not. Why would Santa Claus even have basic security measures? It's not as if he's one of the most *iconic* figures on Earth." Gavin spins to face Wyatt. "We're not going to get anywhere with this."

Wyatt sits in a swivel chair beside him. "Don't give up now. You're so close to almost trying."

"I don't need your sarcasm, too," Gavin says, sighing heavily as his eyes do an arc in their sockets. "I get enough of it from the queen here."

"Don't pull a hamstring from all that eye-rolling, Agent Scrooge McGrinchipuss."

"Will you stop calling me that?"

"Sure," Ellie says, her tone harsh and unwavering. "When you stop acting like one."

Stowe slides into the room, immediately recognizing the thick tension. How could she miss it? The air in here is so heavy that it almost hurts to breathe.

"What did I miss?"

"Our government lackey is tapping out because he isn't being spoon-fed leads on finding Santa," Ellie muses.

"I'm not quitting! I'm…reevaluating my life choices. I never thought I'd be trying to chase down a mythical figure with a sarcastic travel companion for a partner."

Wyatt raises an eyebrow. "If you think my sister is bad now, wait till she starts spreading rumors that you have herpes."

Gavin gives him a puzzled look before Ellie changes the subject. "Did you guys find anything?"

Wyatt holds up the red envelope with gold lettering. "Yeah. It looks like we're going to Paris."

"Is that from Santa?"

"Apparently."

"So, he is here!" Gavin exclaims, all too eager to put a bow on this case and return to Washington.

"No, he isn't," Wyatt assures him.

"Okay, then, how did that envelope appear?"

Stowe shrugs and then grins. "Christmas magic. How else?"

Wyatt can't think of a better description of it. He stopped trying to figure out how Santa does what he does long ago. There are YouTube videos that explain how magicians pull off the tricks in their acts. Nobody has been able to explain how Santa can disappear without leaving a trace of his having left the country. And that's the tip of the Christmas magic iceberg.

"You people are insane," the agent says with a sneer.

"Oh, my God!" Ellie says, throwing her hands up. "Then leave! Nobody is holding you here against your will, and you're bringing the mood down."

He turns back to the screen, resigned. "I would, but someone has to represent rational thought in this group."

Ellie gestures toward the monitor. "Fine. Then be rational, stick a candy cane in your cake hole, and get your eyes back on that footage. Wyatt, you, and Stowe should go. I'll stay here with Scrooge McGrinchipuss to make sure he goes through all this footage instead of leaving to have improper relations with a reindeer."

"Excuse me?" the agent asks incredulously.

"Not a chance of that happening, buddy. Eyes…screen…now."

Wyatt has to force himself to stifle his laughter. He had thought that Ellie only treated him, their brother, and her husband with that level of disdain. Apparently, that's not the case. Agent Kinnaird better start toeing the line, or he's going to be in for a world of hurt. He almost feels bad for the guy.

"Are you sure, Ellie?" Wyatt asks.

"I'll be fine. You know I'm not the traveling type."

"Wait a second," Gavin says. "Hold on. Those guys are too big to be children."

"Friends? Adult children?"

"Or yetis. That seems to be the vibe here. Look how they move. Watch their heads. They are on a swivel. Do you keep records of who visits the village?"

"No," the guard says. "You don't need a background check to visit Santa."

"We should check and see if these guys are seen leaving," Ellie says before turning to Wyatt. "Keep us informed about what you find in Paris. We'll track down whatever leads we can here."

Wyatt reaches down and hugs his sister. "Thank you," he whispers.

The pair heads out as Stowe calls the pilot and tells him to file a flight plan to Paris and prepare for departure. Having a private jet at their disposal is proving to be useful. Wyatt could get used to this.

"We're all set," she says. "Let's get a lift to the airport."

"What do you think we'll find in Paris?"

"The Eiffel Tower, the Louvre, the—"

"What do you think *Santa* wants us to find in Paris?" Wyatt corrects.

Stowe smiles. "More than a bag of soccer balls or an old mantel clock. Whatever Santa has in store for us this year is bound to be even more epic than last year."

Chapter Twenty-Seven

SPECIAL AGENT GAVIN KINNAIRD

Inside the dim security office, the only light comes from the glow of the monitors. Ellie killed the overhead fluorescent lighting after rising from her chair, and right before she began pacing behind Gavin. Her eyes hurt, her muscles were screaming for movement, and ten minutes later, the nervous energy is only now beginning to dissipate. Her eyes narrow as she gazes at the screen, where the footage is fast-forwarded at 4x speed.

She leans in and points at the monitor. "We're getting close to closing time, right?"

Gavin nods, his eyes scanning. "I still haven't seen the two big men leave."

"There," Ellie says. One of the targets they are looking for strides through the main entrance alone. There is no sign of the other two.

"Is there any equipment here we can use to enhance the resolution?"

The guard chuckles, shaking his head. "This ain't your NSA, Agent Kinnaird. The computers here barely run Solitaire and Minesweeper."

Gavin frowns and continues scrubbing through the rest of the footage. Very few other people have left through that entrance to reach the main parking area. None of them was the two men he walked in with. There is no sign of his comrades at all.

"This doesn't make sense," he mutters. "The other guy's also a walking tree trunk. There's no way he slips past these cameras without us spotting him."

"Unless they didn't go out that way."

Ellie gets on a computer that wasn't new ten years ago, and she waits for the Santa Village website to load. They will have a map of the place that they may use to see how easy it is to avoid those cameras. That's when she spots something she hadn't noticed before.

"Is this webcam always on?"

"The Arctic Circle Visitor's Cam? Yeah, 24-7-365," the guard says.

Gavin leans in. "Why didn't you tell us? The camera is pointed right at Santa's Office!"

The man shrugs as Gavin goes to work on his laptop. The camera is a live feed, and he doubts that they record it here. That doesn't mean nobody else does, and he happens to know just the place. After five minutes, he finds the video store on a website and searches for the footage using the timestamp. There are two possible candidates. He clicks on the first as Ellie slides over to him to watch the footage play on his small laptop screen.

"There," Gavin says, jabbing a finger at the monitor. "That's them."

Three men move through the village plaza, beelining straight for Santa's Office. Two of the men look more massive than they did on the security video. They have thick, broad shoulders and would be unmistakable in any crowd. The third man is much smaller and impeccably well-dressed in a black overcoat. It's almost shocking that a live webcam broadcast of the Arctic Circle line that runs through the village is better than the cameras that security uses in the rest of the village.

The three men walk through the square like they own the place. They see one of the big men reemerge and walk back across it toward the entrance. Ellie and Gavin grow impatient, and he speeds up the footage to twice the normal rate. Then, four times. The other two men never reappear. At the point where the timestamp counter above the video reads eleven p.m., it's clear they won't reemerge. Nobody's Christmas list is that long.

"Hey," she says. "Is there another way out of Santa's Office? Some back exit or hidden road?"

The guard scratches his beard. "Yeah. There's a service road behind it. Since there is no admission to get in, there are no fences. People can enter and leave from almost any direction."

Gavin and Ellie exchange a look.

"That's where they went," she says. "This guy went to retrieve their vehicle and pull it around to the back of the building. They didn't want to be seen leaving the office."

"They must still be in Lapland," Gavin concludes.

"Mmmm…wouldn't two men like that stand out in this part of Finland?"

The security guard laughs. "They're the size of trucks. If somehow the entire city went blind and didn't notice them, their grocery bill would still stand out."

Ellie shakes her head. "They wouldn't take that risk. What are the options for getting out of the city?"

"Car, of course," the guard says, stroking his beard. "Finnish Railways operates between Helsinki and Rovaniemi. They have an overnight train. Buses run between Rovaniemi, Helsinki, Oulu, Levi, Inari, and other Lapland towns. The most popular way is the airport, which I'm sure you already know."

"We should try the airport first," Ellie concludes.

"To what end? A bunch of guys on the ground crew aren't going to remember anyone," Gavin says, waving a hand dismissively.

"Call and find out."

"I'm not going to bother. It's a waste of time."

"Fine. I will."

Ellie pulls out her phone, dials a number that is on the airport's website, and presses it to her ear. Gavin looks unamused but goes back to scanning footage.

"Rovaniemi Airport, how may I direct your call?" he hears through the speaker.

"Yes, hello. This is Special Agent Ellie Olson with the American FBI," she says, causing Gavin to straighten in his chair like he's been hit by a taser. "My partner and I are helping investigate Santa's disappearance from the village as part of the Polar Star Task Force. We have identified three persons of interest we'd like to speak to and are checking to see if they may have passed through your airport."

"What are you doing?" Gavin asks, reaching for the phone. She slaps his hand away.

There is a beat of silence on the other end of the line. "You said FBI?"

"Yes, ma'am," Ellie repeats firmly. "I need to speak with someone who handles departures – and possibly someone who handles private flights in and out of the airport."

"Impersonating a federal officer is illegal!" Gavin whispers loudly.

"Glad I'm not in the U.S. for you to arrest me. Now, shush!"

"Uh…well, I can get you the commercial ticket agents, maybe a gate attendant or two," the woman replies, her voice tinged with confusion. "The private flights are easier. Fewer of them to keep track of. Let me transfer you to Operations. They log every private takeoff. You can start there."

"That's helpful. Thank you."

A click is followed by hold music—some instrumental version of "Jingle Bells" that feels more mocking than festive. Ellie hazards a glance at the distraught FBI agent. He is very unamused by this antic.

"Let me talk to him," Gavin says, gesturing for the phone.

"Not a chance. You didn't even want to make this call, remember?"

"Give me the phone."

"No. Suck it up, buttercup. Sit there and listen. Maybe take some notes."

"Ellie…give me the damn phone!"

She shakes her head. "Do you really talk to women that way? Gee, I can't imagine why you're not married."

His face turns bright red. After a moment, a man comes on the line. "Rovaniemi Ops, this is Pekka Rantanen."

"Hi, Mr. Rantanan. I'm Agent Olson, FBI. I'm here with my *junior* partner, Agent Kinnaird. I need to ask about any private aircraft departures within the last seventy-two hours. Particularly ones with minimal notice or an unusual manifest."

"Did you say FBI?"

"Yes, sir. You've heard the rumors about Santa Claus by now. He may not be an American citizen, but he belongs to the world. We've been assigned to the Polar Star Task Force to get to the bottom of his disappearance. I'm hoping you can help with that."

"Okay…yeah, sure. Uh, nothing unusual that I recall."

Ellie frowns. "What about passengers? We're looking for three men. Two of them are the size of polar bears. They may have had a fourth with them when they departed."

"I'm sorry. I'm stuck in this office all day. If the men are the size you say they are, someone on the ground crew who works shifts at those hangars might know."

"I understand, Mr. Rantanan."

"Pekka, please….call me Pekka."

"Thank you, Pekka. Can I arrange to speak with them?"

"Well…they're currently out on the flight line. We have one departure left tonight, and then they're heading home for the evening."

"Good. We'll be there in half an hour. Can you arrange an introduction?"

"Absolutely. I'll be waiting outside the Ops building. Can you find it?"

"We'll find it. See you then, Pekka."

Ellie stands and grabs her coat off the back of the chair. Gavin scoffs and reluctantly does the same.

"All right. I have to admit that was actually impressive."

"Why, thank you, Special Agent Scrooge McGrinchipuss."

"Call me that again, and I will cuff you to a reindeer. Come on, let's get to the airport before those guys go home for the night."

Ellie claps him on the back. "That's the spirit. Well…you know, maybe not the *Christmas* spirit, but you're getting there."

Chapter Twenty-Eight

KEITH MEADOWS

Title: Christmas is canceled

By Keith Meadows, Senior White House Correspondent

The dull hum of the jet engines fills the cabin with a steady white noise as I write from seat 12A, somewhere high over the North Atlantic. The drink cart has just passed to be returned to the galley, the lights have been dimmed by the cabin crew, and the man beside me is asleep with his mouth open. It's the kind of setting where war stories are usually filed or long-delayed novels are finally written. But tonight, I'm writing an obituary – not for a person, but for a myth.

"Christmas is canceled," Keith mutters to himself.

"What?" the guy next to him in the middle seat snaps.

"Nothing. I'm working."

"Work quieter, then. Having the light on is bad enough. I don't need to hear you yappin' to yourself."

He shifts in his chair and pulls the blanket over his head. Well, if he feels that way about it, Keith will just have to find more ways to annoy his testy seat neighbor. Maybe a lavatory break, just as the man dozes back off, is in order.

The reporter returns his eyes to his laptop's screen. He initially typed that headline with a heavy heart. It's not because of the subject matter but because he has harbored a disdain for sensationalized headlines since he graduated from journalism school. Now, it's not only a part of the news business, it's a necessity.

Somewhere ahead of me lies Rovaniemi, Finland, and Santa Claus Village, the "official hometown of Santa Claus." Or at least, it used to be.

I have learned what locals have been whispering for a few days now: Santa Claus, the beloved symbol of seasonal wonder who has enchanted us with congressional testimony and a memorable global journey, has vanished without a trace. There are no hints of his whereabouts and no note explaining his absence. There is also no indication of foul play – at least not publicly.

The village remains open to tourists, even without its main attraction. But St. Nicholas's absence has cast a pall over the normally magical city nestled on the Arctic Circle. And, despite the denials of a problem and hollow assurances to the contrary, something is terribly wrong.

Before reporting from the White House, I've covered protests in Paris, coups in Myanmar, and even celebrity divorces in LA. But nothing – nothing – has prepared me for the surreal emptiness of writing about the disappearance of Santa Claus.

He smiles. Nobody cares less about Santa Claus than he does. Sure, last year was interesting despite the fallout that nearly cratered his career. The testimony in front of Congress the year before made for great stories. And that's what he sees now… a story.

Parents must be struggling to explain this. How can you take your kids all the way to Northern Finland to see Santa Claus only to find out he's not there? Maybe they're trying to cover it up. Most adults think that children aren't capable of recognizing the lie for what it is, but the observant ones will eventually realize something is wrong. They will draw pictures of empty sleighs or broken gifts, and some will ask if something bad happened. Their parents will become increasingly desperate to shield them from the truth.

Keith's fingers touch the keys before he pauses. A phrase from J-school keeps repeating in his mind: *Sometimes it's better not to say too much.* One of his professors was a master at building a narrative. He said the key to keeping people's attention was to drip information to them, not open it up like a fire hose. He needs to build interest and fear. Reactions can come later.

No one is saying it aloud yet, but the implications are chilling. If Santa, whether you believe he is real or not, isn't there come Christmas Eve when the world most needs its symbol of joy and generosity…what will it mean for the holiday season?

I'm flying to Rovaniemi to speak with the locals and walk the snowy paths. I will dig where others won't. Because someone has to ask: What happened to Santa Claus, and what happens to Christmas without him?

Keith smiles. He hasn't done investigative work in a long time. His assignment to cover the White House means poking holes in political narratives and agendas, not finding mythical figures. But it's like riding a bike – you never really forget how to do it, no matter how long it has been.

Santa Claus could have been taken by a foreign intelligence operation in an attempt to sabotage Western joy. He could have left voluntarily in what would be the world's greatest burnout story. It could also be a PR stunt to garner even more attention than last year. Whatever the reason, Keith is going to find and expose it.

> There's still time. Maybe it's all a misunderstanding. A publicity stunt. Or maybe Santa got tired of centuries of thankless labor and is sipping hot cocoa on a remote beach in Tahiti. But the clock is ticking.
>
> And if he doesn't show up? Then, the title of this article won't just be a flashy headline. It will be the first in Santa Claus's eulogy.
>
> *Keith Meadows will be reporting live from Rovaniemi, Finland. Follow his continuing coverage on The Observer and @KeithMeadowsWH.*

Keith ensures the document is saved and shuts his laptop. That will make the cranky passenger next to him happy. He kills the overhead light and stares out the window into the inky darkness. Answers are coming. So are clicks and readers.

Chapter Twenty-Nine

SPECIAL AGENT GAVIN KINNAIRD

The road out of Rovaniemi is dusted in snow, and the headlights of their SUV are carving twin paths through the darkness. Pines along the way stand strong like silent sentinels, and the only signs of civilization are the Christmas lights that twinkle faintly on distant rooftops. Inside the vehicle, the silence has grown thick – too thick for Gavin's liking.

At least Ellie isn't insulting him. That's a nice departure from the norm. He's tired, a little jet-lagged, and still not completely convinced that this trip to the airport isn't a waste of time. But, since he's here to investigate Santa's disappearance, he might as well do some investigating, fatigue be damned. With that thought, Gavin tries to stifle a yawn and fails.

"Aw, are you getting a little sleepy? Does Mr. Secret Agent Man need a little nappy poo?"

He clears his throat. "You know, for someone who guilted me into coming to Finland, you've been pretty hostile. Are you like this with everyone, or am I special?"

Ellie doesn't look at him. She clenches her jaw as she stares out at the nothingness beyond the frosty window. "Maybe I just don't like federal agents who act like they know everything."

Gavin exhales slowly. "I don't think that's it."

"Don't profile me."

"I graduated from Quantico. I profile everyone."

"You must be *a lot* of fun at parties. Look, unless you want me to grab your lower lip and pull it over your face, keep your comments to yourself."

Gavin shakes his head slowly before deciding to tempt fate. "Your husband must wake up screaming, being married to you."

The silence that follows is instant and sharp, like the snap of a wire pulled too taut. Ellie turns her head even farther to the right, making it a point not to look at him. He can sense the awkwardness. The warmth in the car provided by the heater is overpowered by a cold tension that settles in the space between them. His comment landed like a punch to her jaw, and for the first time since he met her, Gavin now wishes he could take the words back.

Ellie starts to speak, then hesitates. Then, in a near whisper, she says, "That would explain why I think he's cheating on me."

That catches him off guard. Gavin doesn't know Ellie well, but he pegged her as the bunny-boiling or ice pick under the bed type from *Fatal Attraction* or *Sliver* after their first meeting. If that's remotely true, her husband still having his scrotum attached is a small miracle.

"Your husband is cheating on you?"

"With Missy Petersen," she says bitterly. "Who, ironically, had the hots for my brother until he got back together with Stowe."

"She moved on from your brother to your husband?"

"Montana is Big Sky Country, but small-town America. There aren't a ton of dating options where I live. I guess she got tired of waiting for her Prince Charming and decided to play homewrecker."

Gavin stays quiet, gripping the steering wheel tighter. He may have his own relationship issues, but he can be fairly certain that Jules cheating on him isn't one of them.

Ellie lets out a humorless laugh. "Guess I've just been waiting to take my anger out on someone, and you're a convenient target. I'm sorry."

"I get it," Gavin says, glancing over at her. "The pain…the suspicion…the not knowing."

She finally looks at him, the fight against breaking down into tears well underway in her eyes. "Do you? Have you ever been married?"

"Engaged. I was engaged."

"Was?"

He nods. "My fiancée broke off our engagement the day before I was assigned to this case. She was always supportive and said she understood the demands of my job. Then, I guess she decided that she didn't. I came home to an empty apartment, a letter, and her ring inside the envelope with it."

Ellie raises an eyebrow. "Okay…well, that explains why you're so grumpy."

"Merry Christmas to me, right?"

"What is her name?" Ellie asks, turning more fully in her seat to face him.

"Jules."

"Do you still love her?"

Gavin can try to bury the truth, but it will latch onto him with an iron grip. He knows that no matter how much time and distance he puts between himself and the life he once imagined, her absence will follow him like a shadow. Even the quietest moments alone cause his heart to ache. He wasn't given a choice. Jules handed it down to him like a death sentence. But despite all the pain, heartache, and lingering confusion as to why now, there is only one answer to her question.

He forces a smile. "I will always love her. I wouldn't have proposed if I hadn't. I take vows very seriously."

The runway lights of the Rovaniemi Airport shimmer in the distance as Ellie sighs and leans back in her seat. "Guess we're both just trying to figure out what comes next.

What are the odds that two damaged souls would find each other on a Santa adventure right before Christmas?"

"It's a coincidence," Gavin concludes. "Nothing more."

"Maybe. But I heard all the stories about my brother's interactions with this Santa. The Finnish St. Nick may not fly around the world in a sleigh, but he *is* different. He changed my brother…he changed his entire life forever. If there is any lesson I can draw from that, it's that you never underestimate the power of Christmas magic or this Santa's ability to conjure it."

Chapter Thirty

SAINT NICHOLAS

The digital clock on the bedroom dresser glows "12:17 a.m." in soft blue light. Santa can hear the winter wind from the Alps whispering through the trees outside, and light snow gently taps against the windowpane. It's the only noise in the otherwise still house.

From a cursory look around this alpine bedroom, she favors cozy things – fuzzy socks, plush stuffed animals, wool sweaters with tiny reindeer or stars, and warm knit hats. The decor of this room is a testament to its lack of use. The dolls piled on an overstuffed chair in the corner look fresh out of the box. Plush stuffed animals on the bed have never been cuddled with. The crayons lying next to their box on the desk are barely worn, and there are no pictures taped above the desk or coloring books stacked up. This is the room of a little girl who doesn't spend much time here, if any.

Santa quietly inches closer to the small bed. The girl is about eight years old with long, tangled chestnut-brown hair. The front is cut shorter, forming a natural wave that frames her round face. She stirs, as a child does, rubbing the sleep from her eyes as she lifts her head from the pillow. She must sense something unusual.

When her eyes focus on him, she gasps and sits bolt upright. "Wha—"

"Shh," Santa hushes, putting a finger to his lips, his eyes gentle and understanding. "We mustn't wake your father."

Her eyes are as wide as saucers, the white of them framing stormy gray-blue irises, like winter skies just before snowfall. He can see her chest heaving as her little heart pounds inside it. She clutches her blanket.

"Are you…who…who are you?"

He smiles, steepling his fingers next to his chest. "I think you know."

"Santa?" It's a question posed with the innocence that only a child can muster.

"It's nice to meet you, Fallon," Santa whispers.

"How…how do you know my name?"

"Santa knows," he says with his warmest, most gracious smile.

"Yeah, but how?"

"Do you mind if I sit?" Santa asks, getting a nod as she makes room for him next to her. "Well, in my village, there is a chamber carved from ice and starlight where a magical scroll writes itself. It doesn't track behavior like the naughty or nice list – it tracks what is in people's *hearts*. Every person who believes has their name written on that scroll, and it allows me to know who everyone is."

There is nothing in this world that matches the amazement and wonder in a child's eyes. At her young, tender age, everything about life is still so new and awe-inspiring. While they absorb their surroundings with a certain innocence, they still challenge what they are told.

"That sounds made up," Fallon whispers, still clutching her blanket. "Why are you here?"

"I was brought here to talk to you, my dear."

"Why?"

It's a good question and one that his captor still hasn't explained to him in three days. This is about her. It has to be. He just doesn't know why yet.

"I don't know," he says softly, "but I know you're special."

"Are you really Santa?" Fallon asks, crossing her arms over her pajama top.

"Yes."

"Prove it."

Santa's eyes twinkle. "Do you remember last year when you made a drawing of your mom, tied it with a red ribbon, and hid it in the back of your closet so no one would find it?"

Fallon gasps, her eyes growing wide again. "How do you know about that?"

Santa simply smiles. "You like to draw. Sometimes, what you draw even appears in your dreams. You once drew a winged fox soaring over a hill with big purple and red flowers. You had a dream about it that night. You told your father, and he only said—"

"Foxes can't fly. They can't."

Santa leans in and winks at her. "They say the same thing about reindeer."

"You really are Santa!" she says, almost too loudly. "I can't wait to tell my daddy that you came to visit me!"

After a glance at the door, Santa shakes his head. "I'm sorry, Fallon. You can't tell anyone, especially your father."

She lowers her eyes, and her mouth contorts into a pout. "Why not?"

"Because Christmas magic only works when it's kept a secret. Will you keep this between us?"

She nods solemnly. "Okay. Do you want my Christmas list?"

"Have you made one?"

She shakes her head. "No, but I will. Will you come back to get it?"

"Tomorrow night," he says, rising from his seat at the end of her bed and stepping backward into the dark room. "And then we can talk about your Christmas wish."

"I get a Christmas wish?"

"We will talk about it when I return. Now, close your eyes, dream your dreams, and sleep well, Fallon."

The girl gets back under the covers and closes her eyes. She won't fall asleep quickly, but she doesn't need to. It's long enough for him to get back to his room before Skut realizes that anything is amiss. With that, Santa touches his nose.

Chapter Thirty-One

STOWE BESSETTE

Stowe is caught up in the moment. The touristy areas of Paris along the Seine rank among the most iconic and picturesque in the world. It is a breathtaking ribbon of history, art, and romance, beginning with the Eiffel Tower and the Trocadéro's sweeping views. The river winds past the elegant Musée d'Orsay, the world-renowned Louvre Museum, and the lush Tuileries Gardens.

At its heart lies the Île de la Cité, home to the majestic Notre-Dame Cathedral and the stunning stained glass of Sainte-Chapelle. Across the bridges are the charming bouquinistes – green bookstalls selling vintage prints and literature – and the quaint streets of the Latin Quarter and Le Marais. With each step along the river, Paris reveals its soul through grand landmarks, hidden gems, and views that have inspired generations. And, now, she's finally here.

For her, Paris during Christmas feels like stepping into a storybook. The city glows with golden lights strung across boulevards, and shop windows dazzle with whimsical holiday displays. Like in many European cities, Christmas markets pop up in neighborhoods like one near Notre Dame. Wooden chalets sell handcrafted ornaments, local treats, and warm drinks as festive music creates a sense of quiet, undeniably Parisian enchantment. It's a city where old-world charm meets the magic of the holiday season, and it's unmatched by anything in the United States.

"You okay? You're uncharacteristically quiet."

Wyatt doesn't answer right away. He stares at the twinkle lights and crowd milling about the Christmas market before sighing. "I'm worried about Ellie. I know she's hurting. I don't think she knows where to go from here. I'm afraid she'll give in to her impulsiveness and do something stupid."

"Like what?" Stowe asks gently.

He shakes his head instead and lets out a hard exhale through his nose. "I just…she wanted to stay with Gavin. He's probably not a bad guy, but Ellie's vulnerable."

"You think she'll hook up with him?" Stowe asks, more curious than judgmental.

"I don't know. Maybe. I mean, he's…." Wyatt cuts the sentence short.

Stowe smirks and cocks her head. "Not a bad-looking guy."

It was a statement, not a question. Wyatt gives her a disapproving look. "That's not the point."

"I know," Stowe says, raising a hand. "I get it. She's married, but do you think that still matters to her if she thinks her husband cheated?"

"I just don't want her to do anything she'll regret…anything that might mess her up more. Look, I don't want to talk about it," Wyatt says quickly, turning away, the muscles in his neck tensing.

Stowe nods slowly and doesn't press. She knows better. "Okay. But know that you don't have to carry this by yourself. I'm here if you want to talk about it."

Maybe he will, and maybe he won't, but she's resolved not to push, even if she wants him to talk about it. She breathes deeply. The air is crisp and carries the faint scent of roasted chestnuts and mulled wine drifting from the wooden stalls near Notre Dame. The string of lights twinkles overhead like stars caught in a net, and the Seine shimmers as it catches their reflection. Stowe tucks her gloved hand into the crook of Wyatt's arm as they stroll slowly past a stand selling hand-carved nativity scenes and delicate glass ornaments.

"This city feels like it was designed to make people fall in love," she says softly, a smile playing on her lips.

Wyatt chuckles under his breath. "You really think Paris is that magical?"

"I do. Not just magical…enchanted. Paris is a city that remembers dreams, even if you forget them yourself." Stowe lets out a wistful chuckle. "I had hoped Santa would stop here last year."

Wyatt tilts his head, curious. "Why here?"

She doesn't answer right away. Her gaze lingers on the slowly turning carousel at the center of the market, lit up and playing a Christmas tune as the horses glide up and down. It's filled with bundled-up children and nostalgic adults.

"Because Paris makes you believe," she replies, her voice even softer now. "In love. In the possibilities of the future. In life."

If there was ever a city she would want Wyatt to propose in, this is it. Right here and now works, although he isn't nervous enough to be considering it. Too bad. It would be magical.

"Paris has never been on my travel list," Wyatt admits, rubbing the back of his neck. "But… I get it. The question is, why are we here now? Why did Santa send us to the City of Light?"

Stowe shrugs, in part at the question and in part to shake the dream of an impromptu proposal. "He's been vague before."

"Not this vague."

Under the watchful gaze of Notre Dame's grand silhouette, a large group of carolers begins singing, "O Holy Night." Stowe and Wyatt stand perfectly still, soaking in the music as it pleasantly rises above the din of the crowd and the hush of the city's ancient, romantic magic.

They move off once the final lyrics are sung, and the applause from the families in the market dies. They don't get far before a smile creases Stowe's lips as the "a-ha" revelation pops into her head.

Wyatt turns to her. "Okay. Now what?"

"We take Santa's advice and follow the music."

Chapter Thirty-Two

SPECIAL AGENT GAVIN KINNAIRD

Gavin and Ellie hustled back to the airport's operations center. What started off as a rather desperate gamble and a likely waste of time has paid big dividends. Rovaniemi Airport isn't JFK, LAX, or Atlanta. The private jet terminal doesn't receive the same level of traffic as places like Vail, Colorado, or Jackson Hole, Wyoming. Lapland is nice, but it isn't the playground of the rich and famous.

The ground crew remembered the two big men all too well. It wasn't because they were rude, obnoxious, or even threatening. It's that they didn't know men could be that big. So, they drew eyes, the crew paid attention, and now Gavin has a lead to work with. That's a double-edged sword.

On the plus side, they have a lead, and the apparent disappearance of Santa Claus can now plausibly be called a kidnapping. The three men who disembarked the aircraft were wheels up less than three hours later with an additional passenger. While there is no confirmation about who it was, a reasonable assumption can be made. Now, it's a matter of confirming the information and tracking the jet.

The bad news is that he will never hear the end of it. There is no way that his new "partner" is ever going to let him live this down. Ellie doesn't strike him as the kind of woman who won't bludgeon him with that fact. This was her idea. He objected. That will come up in every disagreement he has with this woman for the rest of the time they are here. If he thought his fiancée was bad, this hardass Montana rancher will be a hundred times worse.

"All right. Well…" Pekka says, hesitating as he stares at his computer screen. "The tail number is…here it is…November Seven Five Zero Echo Lima. I don't have much information on the plane. It's a charter that arrived here from Helsinki. The manifest lists three passengers…all men."

He scribbles the names onto a notepad and hands it to Gavin, who glances at Ellie. "I can run the names, but they're probably aliases. Were passports checked?"

"It was a domestic flight," Pekka informs them, "so there was no need. That's probably why they went to Helsinki first. Their luggage was left on board, so they didn't plan to stay the night. The plane was refueled, but there were no additional services like catering or cleaning provided."

Ellie's heart pounds. "Is there a flight plan for the jet's destination after it departed?"

Pekka refers to his computer. "Filed for London, England."

"Do you have a spare office we can use?"

Pekka leans back in his chair. "People around here are a little possessive of their personal spaces. There's a desk in the lost and found you can use without much fuss, though. It's just down the hall on the right."

The pair thanks him and makes their way to the room dominated by metal shelves with boxes of what can generously be described as "stuff" perched on them. Gavin opens up his laptop and accesses the FBI's backend systems. "Let's see who's flying private in and out of the Arctic with something to hide."

He enters the tail number and waits as the database does its search. A moment later, the screen flashes with a hit, and Gavin frowns. "The registered owner is a corporate entity called 'Quorvium.' It's a crypto firm and a very successful one, from the looks of it. They're headquartered in Switzerland but have offices all over the EU and a couple in the States."

"That's not a company you would expect to be involved in a kidnapping, is it?"

"No, it isn't," he moans.

Ellie's fingers brush over a small woven keychain lying forgotten on the edge of the airport office desk. It's turquoise, sun-bleached, and unmistakably marked with the words *Bora Bora*. The bright colors and delicate craftsmanship are completely out of place in the stark, functional space surrounded by winter coats, reindeer tourism brochures, and snow boots.

"What's up with the keychain?" Gavin asks, glancing at her before studying his laptop screen.

"Just a thing," she says, startled by the observation. "I've always wanted to go to Bora Bora. Finding this here just feels…surreal."

"How so?"

Ellie holds it up and lets it dangle by the keyring and chain. "This isn't some random lost tourist trinket. Someone had been there. Someone stood beneath swaying palm trees and is now living under the Northern Lights. Whatever that story is, this keychain doesn't belong here."

She tucks the keychain into her coat pocket. "What are you doing?"

"Looking for the current location of that Gulfstream."

Ellie leans in, closer than she has ever gotten to him. She smells good. "Where is it?"

"I don't know. It's not on any of the flight trackers, so it isn't airborne. I can get some people back in D.C. on it to find out where it ended up."

"How long will that take?" she asks, getting a shrug.

"This isn't exactly a high-profile assignment, even if it was the White House that pulled the strings. It will take a few hours, at least."

Ellie purses her lips. "Then we should get some rest. There is nothing more we can do without that information."

They pack up, thank Pekka for his help, and make their way to the car. Gavin looks up. The cloud cover will prevent them from seeing the Northern Lights tonight. Too bad. He's hoping to see them once while they're here. He fires up the engine and pushes the gear into drive.

"Tell me about your husband," Gavin says as he steers the car out of the airport on Route 951 for the ten-minute drive into the city.

"Why?"

"I'm curious."

Ellie scoffs. "Are you going to profile him?"

"I told you – I profile everyone. Why do you think the moron is cheating on you?"

"Billy is his name…and that's kinda personal, don't you think?"

"Yeah, it is. But I also think a part of you wants to tell me. So, out with it."

Gavin isn't sure of that at all. But that's what she does. It's clearly the abridged version, and if this were a deposition, she would be forced to provide a lot more detail. But he gets the gist of what she's saying. The story's climax was Billy admitting he was with the hussy, although she didn't wait for him to say why. That was a key piece of information.

"What do you think?" Ellie says once she finishes.

Gavin's head bobs from side to side. "It's suspicious, but there's not enough evidence to make a determination."

"Are you serious?"

"Yes. You have plenty of cause to be suspicious, but if I were to hand what you told me to a prosecutor, they would shake their head and tell me to keep digging. I don't think you can make the leap to infidelity based on what you told me."

"So, you think I overreacted?"

These are dangerous waters. He may never have been married, but he was engaged. That's the kind of question Jules would ask. He made the mistake of answering honestly and rather diplomatically once. It took a tennis bracelet, a dozen long-stemmed red roses, and an expensive dinner just to begin undoing the damage.

"I think you reacted like any proud woman would when she thinks the man she married is being unfaithful."

"But?"

"Who says there's a 'but?'"

Ellie drops her head and stares up at him. "But?"

"I don't see a motive," Gavin admits after sneaking a peek at her from the corner of his eye. "You are sassy and maybe a touch impossible and definitely kinda scary, but you're also smart, beautiful, independent, and strong. I don't think there's a man alive who would willingly walk away from you."

Her face softens. Whatever she expected Gavin to say, that wasn't it. The best part is that he was being truthful. Although his words sounded flirtatious, partly by design, it was an honest assessment of what he sees in her. If Billy is stepping out on her, he absolutely is a moron. Gavin loved his fiancée and lost her. What are the odds that he would find another woman like her so soon?

The agent steers the car down a street and pulls up alongside the hotel. It looks comfy enough. Ellie smiles when she sees the name "The Arctic Sky" before letting out a laugh.

"Gavin, please tell me you booked two rooms before you drove here."

"Of course. Why wouldn't I?"

Ellie smiles, remembering Stowe and her brother's first trip to Lapland. "No reason. I'll tell you another time."

Chapter Thirty-Three

WYATT HUFFMAN

The distance from Notre-Dame Cathedral to the Tuileries Garden in Paris is approximately one and a half miles, and may have been one of the most romantic strolls Wyatt has ever taken. Stowe enjoyed it immensely. It was more than the scenic walk along the Seine River as they passed Île de la Cité, the Louvre, and the Pont des Arts. It was the feeling.

The carolers were a school choir just out to have fun and spread Christmas cheer. They were a big hit. Stowe sang along with the English versions as they walked, but was most enchanted by *"Douce nuit"* and *"Vive le vent,"* the French versions of "Silent Night" and "Jingle Bells." When they broke into the modern classic *"Petit Papa Noël,"* or "Little Father Christmas," dozens of children came running up to them and started singing along. Wyatt has no doubt that the sight would have made Santa smile from ear to ear.

The carolers stopped at the entrance of La Magie de Noël in the Tuileries Garden, near the Louvre. They followed the music, and it didn't surprise either of them that it led them here. Santa has a thing for Christmas Markets.

This historic park has been transformed into a festive wonderland. The holiday village, with its rows of wooden chalets selling handcrafted gifts, regional specialties, and seasonal treats, feels like a physical manifestation of joy.

Stowe dragged him from chalet to chalet, and they sipped mulled wine and ate roasted chestnuts as they watched some skaters gliding and others falling on the large ice rink. He took her for a ride on the towering Ferris wheel, but she refused to go on some of the other traditional carnival rides on a full stomach. He has never seen her so happy.

And that is where guilt has come in. Wyatt knows he should have brought the ring. His sister was right, even if he will keep that revelation a secret until the day he dies. If there was ever a place to propose, this was it. The mood, the sights, the smells, and the throngs of happy people would have made getting on one knee and asking the love of his life to spend the rest of her days with him absolutely magical.

"Joyeux Noël," a woman dressed in festive clothing and carrying a basket full of flowers says to Stowe. "Would you like a Christmas Rose?"

"A Christmas Rose?" Wyatt asks, glancing at Stowe.

"Yes! It's a winter-blooming flower that seems almost too fragile to bloom in the cold," she says, pulling one out of the basket to show them. "Yet it does, often peeking through the snow. The petals are typically pure white, but sometimes they blush with pink or green as they age."

The woman hands Stowe the flower, and she holds it up, almost with reverence. The petals look like silky, open cups with gently ruffled edges. In the center, a ring of bright yellow stamens vividly contrasts with the white petals. To Wyatt, it almost looks like a handful of candles in the snow. The leaves are dark green, leathery, and shaped like a hand with spread fingers. It's not like the long-stemmed red roses he buys for Valentine's Day back home – this flower is only about nine inches long.

"Does this rose have any magical properties?"

She stares at Wyatt like he just asked the stupidest imaginable question. He can see why, but at the same time, she doesn't know they were sent here on a mission for Santa Claus, and he doesn't want to take the time to explain it. So, living with the humiliation is the price of that information.

"Uh…not that I know of. There is a legend that says the Christmas Rose is faintly luminescent under moonlight or candlelight. But that is only a myth."

Wyatt shares a knowing look with Stowe before she turns back to the woman, who is repositioning the basket of flowers on her arm.

"May I ask you why you are handing these out?'

The young woman smiles. "We couldn't think of a better way to get people to visit our chalet."

She points off to her right, and Wyatt wants to kick himself for not noticing it sooner. Over the counter is a sign that reads "The Christmas Rose." It's a little on the nose for Santa, but at least that part of the riddle is solved.

They thank her, and she moves on to distribute the rest of her flowers to the passersby. The Christmas Rose chalet is nestled slightly off the beaten path, and thus, the tactic is to entice more foot traffic. It's smart. The warm, inviting aromas of seasonal delights, such as buttery crêpes, tartiflette bubbling with cheese, golden churros, and spiced gingerbread shaped like stars, act as a beacon once Wyatt and Stowe get a little closer. Friendly vendors are serving steaming cups of vin chaud and rich hot chocolate, topped with whipped cream, that patrons enjoy next to large oak barrels used as tables.

"Okay, we're here. Now what?" Stowe asks.

"Beats me. We find a glowing flower next to someone lonely, I guess."

"Like her?"

Wyatt follows Stowe's finger to a lone woman standing next to one of the barrels in the far corner. She is alone but doesn't look "lonely." Then he sees it. It may be the way the light from a lantern is hitting the flower resting on top of the barrel, but it'd be hard to refute that the rose looks like it's glowing. So much for myth. Like Santa Claus, there may be more truth to the legend than fiction.

"You've got to be kidding me," Wyatt says, exhaling loudly. "Do you want the honors?"

"I think I'm going to let you take the lead on this one."

Stowe smiles broadly and loops her hand around his arm as they walk over. The woman is attentive to her surroundings, but her dour face stands out among the smiling families and gleeful children milling around the barrels with steaming cups of hot cocoa. Wyatt takes a deep breath. He knows how this is likely to be received.

"Excuse me. Hi, I'm sorry to bother you. This is going to sound strange, but—"

"Are you the couple that I'm supposed to meet?" The woman smiles weakly, searching Wyatt's face before turning her eyes to Stowe and then back to Wyatt.

"I'm sorry?"

The woman digs a red card with gold lettering out of her purse and shows it to them. Neither one of them needs to examine it closely to know who it's from. They were handed enough of them last year.

"I got this strange card at my hotel after I arrived. It directed me to meet two people here. I thought it was a prank and wasn't going to come, but my curiosity got the best of me."

"Well, we can assure you that it's not a prank," Wyatt says, causing the woman's brow to furrow.

"Wait until you find out who sent it. I'm Stowe. This is Wyatt."

"Nice to meet both of you," she says, shaking their hands. "I'm Julie."

Chapter Thirty-Four

KEITH MEADOWS

Keith Meadows sits hunched at a low wooden desk inside Santa's Post Office, the scent of pine and old paper thick in the air. Around him, parents watch their children write letters to Santa and deposit them in the red mailbox near the entrance for him to read before Christmas. Too bad he isn't here to do that. The world may very well be waiting for someone who might not be coming.

Keith goes back to checking his phone and smiling at the headlines he sees. Each one leaves him more breathless than the last:

"Santa missing? Chaos in Rovaniemi!"
"Santa Claus Village closed to visitors—no sign of St. Nick"
"Has Christmas disappeared from the Arctic Circle?"
"Elves deny involvement in Santa's whereabouts"
"Finland faces a Claus conspiracy"

He lets out a quiet chuckle. "A Claus Conspiracy." Keith wishes he had thought of that one, even though there is no evidence of a conspiracy…at least, not yet. His devilish grin is the kind only a seasoned journalist can muster when watching the rest of the world catch up to a story he's already broken. *Christmas is Canceled*, his article declared just this morning, was bold, clear, and way ahead of the pack. Let them chase the smoke because he's determined to find the fire.

His notebook lies open and untouched on the desk. There is darkness outside the windows. That's not a shock since there is no sun during the winter solstice at the Arctic Circle. It could be eight a.m. or eight p.m., and nobody would know the difference. How can anyone live here?

Across the plaza, Santa's Office remains locked and dark. There is still no light in the windows. There is still a sign on the door. There is still no Santa. When he cornered the spokesman from the village earlier, the round-faced man with an elf hat and a rehearsed smile simply said, "No comment" to Keith's questions. And then, more firmly, he stated that, "Santa will return soon." That isn't very likely.

Keith has worked in Washington for a long time. He deals with the White House press secretary on a daily basis. He has interviewed dozens of politicians. He knows artful dodges when he hears them. The guy has no clue what's going on.

He pockets his pen and notebook and heads outside. Tourists are still milling about, snapping the last selfies at the Arctic Circle before heading to their cars as the village closes for the night. There is no panic among them over not seeing Santa. No outward displays of fury over a wasted trip to Lapland. Just the distracted contentment of people who came for magic and settled for photo ops.

There is no story here that would beat out the flood of shallow headlines already leaching into the world. He needs a new lead to expose the problem. Something the others haven't seen.

Keith zips his coat and makes his way to the small security office. He pushes open the door to a blast of warm, stale air and the hum of monitors.

Inside, a stocky security guard with a thick gray beard sits behind a cluttered desk, sipping lukewarm coffee. He doesn't look up right away.

"I was hoping to ask a few questions," Keith begins, flashing his White House press badge that holds no real sway here but looks official. "Maybe take a look at some of the security footage from Santa's Office?"

The guard looks up with a grunt. "Are you with the FBI too?"

Keith blinks. "I'm sorry…what?"

The guard sets his coffee down and leans back in his chair, eyeing him more carefully. "Some agent was here most of the day."

"From the American Federal Bureau of Investigation?"

"He didn't show a badge but acted like he owned the place. He was sifting through footage and asked a lot of questions about our camera locations. He was with another woman."

"Was she FBI?"

The guard shrugs. "No idea. They found what they were looking for about the time their two comrades showed up."

"Do you know their names?"

"Actually, I do, but only because I've seen them for the last two years. Wyatt and Stowe. Santa has a soft spot for them. I don't remember their last names."

Keith offers the guard a thin smile. "I do. Thank you."

He beats feet out of the office, his heart already racing as he steps back into the frigid arctic air. FBI agents were in Santa's Village with two of the most recognizable names from the past two Christmases. That isn't a coincidence. Pulling out his cell, he places the call he's been putting off since he arrived in Rovaniemi.

"Haverson."

"Ben, it's Keith."

"How's the North Pole?" his editor grumbles more than asks.

"It's the Arctic Circle, but still cold. The White House knows."

"Knows what?"

"The truth about Santa's disappearance. The FBI is in Rovaniemi. So are Wyatt Huffman and Stowe Bessette."

He can hear Ben lean back in his chair. "Did you see them?"

"No, but they were here. A security guard at the village confirmed it. I'm going to keep digging."

"Is Santa Claus really missing?"

"Yeah, and it's looking more and more like foul play to me. If the government is involved, we could be talking about a non-state actor, a terrorist organization, or another hostile group. We could be looking at an international incident of massive proportions right before Christmas."

"Get me sources that will go on the record, Keith. We can't afford a repeat of last year's debacle."

"There won't be one."

Keith hangs up. He did his job by checking in with his editor. Now, he needs to get some rest and then get back to work. Other news outlets are chasing rumors. Keith knows that he has just found the story.

6 Days Until Christmas

The cafés near the Seine in Paris are charming, timeless pockets of life where the city seems to exhale. They pass dozens of them nestled along the riverbanks, most with postcard views of Notre Dame, the Eiffel Tower in the distance, and the bridges arching gracefully over the water.

The one Wyatt, Stowe, and Julie selected has wrought-iron chairs and small round tables arranged to face outward for people-watching – something that appears to be a favorite Parisian pastime. The interior, with its carved wood and smoky mirrors, has a faded, old-world charm. Waiters in crisp aprons move briskly between tables, balancing trays with various meals and glasses of French wine. Nobody is hungry, but alcohol isn't a bad idea right now.

Wyatt doesn't want this to be an interrogation, but they need to learn all they can about Julie Cooke. Santa sent them here for a reason, although neither of them has the faintest clue why. Fortunately, she's just as curious about them and asks about their adventures with St. Nick. Stowe does most of the talking, with him filling in details or relaying things about the congressional testimony and the journey last year.

"That is such an amazing story," Julie says when they finish. "I watched the hearings and the trip with Santa intently. I thought I recognized you from somewhere."

"You watched the arrival at the children's hospital?"

"Along with most of the world," Julie says with a chuckle. "Santa is real?"

Stowe looks at Wyatt. It looks like he needs to take this one. "Maybe not in the flying around the world in a sleigh pulled by reindeer kind of way, but he's definitely special."

"And that's why you're here?"

That part of the story takes another ten minutes, starting with Aurielle showing up on Stowe's grandparents' doorstep in Vermont, the trip to Washington, them receiving the card, and then traveling to Paris. He's glad Julie doesn't ask how the card got in Santa's Office if he is missing. There is no answer to that question.

"So," Wyatt says gently, leaning forward. "We're trying to understand why Santa wanted us to meet you."

Julie offers a small, uncertain smile. "That makes three of us."

Stowe glances at her. "You're from Virginia, right?"

"Northern Virginia. I live in Fairfax County, just outside of D.C."

Bells ring in Wyatt's head. Not the shrill ones sounding the alarm about something amiss. More of the type that indicates a revelation. The area that she's from has to be related. This has to be the link.

"You don't happen to work for a non-profit, do you?" Stowe asks. She picked up on it, too.

She shakes her head. "No. I teach third grade."

"Do you happen to know a Cliff Sutton or Malcolm Chapman?"

Julie shakes her head. "No, I don't think so. Malcolm…is that the pharma guy from last year?"

"The very one."

"I'm sorry," Julie says with a frown. "I don't know him."

Stowe and Wyatt pause. That's not what they were expecting…or maybe hoping for. A connection back to Cliff or Malcolm would have made a lot more sense. Now, they are back to square one.

Wyatt furrows his brow. "Then…why Paris? How did you end up here right before Christmas?"

Julie studies her glass of red before picking it up and draining it. It's the universal symbol that someone is about to relive something painful. Wyatt has done that before, especially in the aftermath of breaking up with his high school sweetheart, Jessie Stills. Only his drink of choice was whiskey, and he didn't settle for just one shot.

"I needed to get away," Julie says, her voice soft and unsteady. "I just broke things off with my fiancé. It was a snap decision. I'm not proud of the way I did it, and I regret…. Well, let's just say I didn't want to be home for the aftermath. I didn't want the constant reminders of what I lost."

"Yeah, we've had some experience with that ourselves."

Wyatt offers Stowe a knowing nod. She admitted over the winter that the reason she came to get him in Montana was more about needing to see him than about fulfilling her mission for Congresswoman Pratt. She could have faked that. Even though it was painful, her heart pushed for it. She expected a bad reaction. She expected final closure and a lifetime of wondering what could have been. Instead, they got the most amazing adventure two people could ever hope for.

"It seems to have worked out for you two," she says with a faint laugh. "I won't be that lucky with…my ex. So, I hopped on a flight and came here. I wanted to feel Christmas again. The real kind. The lights, the music, the wonder… I figured if it still existed anywhere, Paris was a good place to start."

Stowe and Wyatt exchange another glance. Julie is a third-grade teacher on a heartbroken holiday escape. There's nothing obvious about why they were sent to get her. No motive for the card is easily discernible. But, for some reason, Santa knows she matters. And that means she does, even if they don't know why yet.

"This is going to sound like a stupid question," Stowe says, "but do you have any connection to Santa Claus?"

"Not really. I waited for Christmas morning like every other kid growing up," Julie confesses. "I once wrote a letter to Santa as a little girl – one that was never answered. I honestly stopped believing in him not long after that."

"You didn't get your wish?"

She smiles. "It wasn't something that Santa could grant on the spot. I was only six…or maybe seven. I thought it was granted once, but I don't think that's the case now."

Wyatt rubs his chin. That letter could be relevant, or it may have nothing to do with Santa's disappearance. Probably the latter. That means they are stone-cold stumped as to what to do next.

"It's getting late, and we need to crash. Would you be willing to meet us tomorrow morning?"

"This is too surreal for me not to. I have no agenda here, so I'm absolutely willing to help figure this out. It will help me keep my mind off things. Worst-case scenario, I'm going to have a heck of a story to tell the kiddos in my class in the new year."

Chapter Thirty-Six

SAINT NICHOLAS

The night is bone-deep cold, silent, and still. Inside the chalet's guesthouse, the warmth stubbornly clings to the fireplace hearth. Santa Claus sits with his hands folded in the comfortable chair he has claimed in front of the fire as the logs hiss and pop, and the flames cast tall, crooked shadows along the wooden walls. Kram keeps vigilance from fifteen feet away, as silent and untalkative as ever.

The door bursts open with a bang, the cold wind forcing its way in like an uninvited guest. His captor stomps inside, boots heavy against the floorboards. His jaw is set tight, and his eyes, dark and sharp, scan the room for anything amiss.

"I trust you are comfortable here, St. Nick," he says, his tone laced with disdain. Beside him, Skut, stone-faced and hulking, stares at him through unblinking eyes.

"Why am I here?" Santa asks, continuing to stare at the fire without acknowledging the man's comment.

"You still haven't figured it out yet?" he says, warming his hands against the heat of the flames. "You're here, locked in this guesthouse instead of gallivanting across rooftops or whatever it is that you have the world fooled into believing you do, because I *want* you here. That's the only reason you need to know."

"You always were impetuous and selfish as a child, Trent. I see adulthood hasn't changed that."

The mood in the guesthouse instantly shifts. Trent's look of surprise at the use of his first name is unmistakable. He turns to glare at Skut and Kram, both of whom look as shocked as their boss is.

"You told him."

Skut stiffens. "We didn't say a word."

"We didn't, I swear," Kram adds.

"You're lying! Trent barks.

Santa shakes his head, almost sadly. "They didn't tell me anything. They don't say much of anything, actually."

"Then how?" his captor demands, stepping forward, hands balled into fists at his sides. "How else could you know my name?"

"I *am* Santa Claus."

There is no mockery in the way the words escape his mouth. They aren't accompanied by bravado or the usual twinkle in his eyes. Just quiet certainty. The kind that doesn't require permission to be believed.

Trent stares at St. Nick as if looking at him harder would peel back the layers and reveal the trick. But he only finds deep, profound old eyes that have seen so much. There is no fear in them – only knowing.

"You're just a man in a red suit playing make-believe," Trent finally says. "You aren't real. You're the physical manifestation of a story told to children to make them behave. The world needs to understand that no person can bring them joy, especially one as *fake* as you."

Santa says nothing at first, causing Trent to scoff. Then, the jolly elf leans forward in his chair and says in a slow, sympathetic tone, "Losing a child is hard."

The words land like thunder in the quiet of an Arctic forest. Trent freezes. His jaw slackens. He looks as if he is about to launch into a verbal assault on his two bodyguards.

"But your wife blaming you for the loss is even harder." Santa's voice is softer now, laced with something raw and infinitely human. "His death was painful, but the blame…you carry it with you. That night. The argument. The fact that you were there when it happened and were powerless to stop it."

"Shut up!" Trent's voice cracks like ice.

"Now, you are trying to outrun it. All of it. The blame your wife casts on you. The blame you cast on yourself. But punishing the world for its joy and happiness won't bring your son back. It won't reconcile things with your wife. It won't make your family whole again."

Trent lunges suddenly, grabbing the back of the chair, his face inches from Santa's. "You don't *know* me. You don't know what I've been through!"

"I know Fallon," Santa says quietly, unflinching from the aggressiveness. "She has a heart the size of an ocean, and she's trying so hard to be strong for you. For her mother. But she's still a little girl. She misses her brother, and she misses *you*, Trent – the version of you who smiled. The father who carried her on his shoulders and read to her at night."

Trent steps back like he's been struck with the back of a shovel. For a long moment, the only sound in the guesthouse is the fire whispering between the logs. Trent looks away, blinking fast with his lips pressed into a hard line. He doesn't respond. Doesn't argue or threaten. He just turns, moves to the door, pulls it open, and stomps out into the night.

* * *

Fallon fell asleep on the edge of her bed, her knees pulled to her chest, her head resting upon a pillow perched on the windowsill. Santa wonders how long she waited up for him. A while, probably. Children have almost limitless energy during the day, but few can maintain that at night.

With the drama from earlier still fresh, Santa knows this visit will need to be short. Kram and Skut are on high alert after being accused of oversharing. Despite the assurances, Trent isn't going to believe in Santa magic. He is going to think that the two big men betrayed his confidence, because that is the only logical explanation.

Santa takes a step, and there is a soft creak of wood below his foot. It's enough to rouse Fallon, who opens her eyes and spies his broad frame wrapped in a simple woolen red robe. A smile stretches across her face as her eyes light up.

"You came back!" Fallon exclaims, her voice high, yet still at a whisper.

Santa lowers himself onto the bed just like last time. "I promised I would."

There is a flicker of wonder in her eyes. "How do you do it? The presents? The sleigh? Going around the whole world in one night?"

"Santa magic."

Fallon raises an eyebrow. "That's not a real answer."

She's sharp and inquisitive. Even at her tender young age, she is questioning the world around her and chiding him for answers she thinks aren't completely truthful. This young girl is going to grow up to become a remarkable woman. Of that, he has no doubt.

"No, I suppose it's not," Santa admits with a chuckle. "But it's the best one I have. Did you make your Christmas list?"

Fallon looks away, her voice quiet. "I could only think of one thing I wanted."

"That's all right. Let me see it."

She slides off her bed and toddles over to the small writing desk on her bare feet. She retrieves a folded piece of paper from it and hands it to Santa. He accepts it gently, unfolding the note with care. His eyes move slowly across the page. It's just one line, written in small, careful letters with a purple crayon:

I want my brother back.

Santa looks up. Fallon's eyes are brimming now, but she doesn't cry. She just stares at him, waiting. He holds the letter as if it were a sacred ancient scroll. For her, it is one.

"Fallon," he says, his voice even and consoling, "there are some wishes that even Santa can't grant."

"Why not?" Her brittle voice cracks as she asks. "You're magic."

"I am. But not *that* kind of magic," he explains. "I can't undo what's been done. I can't change the course of life and death. If I could...the world would be a very different place."

She looks down at her hands, fingers twisted in her pajama sleeves. "Then my wish is no good."

He reaches out and gently places her note on the desk beside them. "No, my dear. Your wish is made out of love – pure, deep, powerful love. That doesn't go unnoticed."

Fallon swallows. "But it won't bring my brother back."

"No," he says, "but love can do other amazing things. It can bring people *closer*. It can heal wounds and soften hearts. It can create a lifetime of memories."

Her lip trembles. "That's not what I want for Christmas."

"I know," he says, reaching over and squeezing her hand. "But is there anything else? Even something small?"

She is quiet for a long time. Then she leans forward and whispers into his ear. Santa pulls back, his eyes twinkling – not with mischief, but with something warmer. He slowly nods.

"I will do everything I can to make that happen."

Fallon stares at him, a smile growing on her face that could light up a room. "Really? Thank you!"

Santa stands, smoothing his robe. "Sleep well, Fallon. You're much stronger than you know."

She moves to the head of the bed and nestles into her pillow. Thirty seconds later, she is fast asleep. It's time for him to go. He has a mission now, and more arrangements need to be made.

Chapter Thirty-Seven

SPECIAL AGENT GAVIN KINNAIRD

In addition to his office, Santa also greets visitors at the Christmas House in his village. Set outside the main plaza, it was the place where the administrators of this landmark thought Gavin and Ellie could get some privacy for their investigation. The wi-fi is fast, the fire is warm, the space is cozy, and the hot cocoa is out of this world.

"This company is a beast," Ellie muses from her overstuffed chair as she stares at her cell phone browser. "Quorvium is headquartered in Switzerland and made $1.6 *billion* last year. Not bad for only being around ten years and having fewer than six hundred employees."

"Thanks for the profile," Gavin says, running his hand through his hair from a sofa on the opposite side of the room.

"Quorvium is a decentralized platform renowned for its innovative blockchain technology used to build and deploy smart contracts and decentralized applications without intermediaries."

Gavin looks up. "You know about crypto?"

"Don't you?" Ellie asks with a grin. "Its flexibility and robust infrastructure have made it a cornerstone of the blockchain ecosystem."

"That's all good background to know, but it doesn't help us find Santa."

"I love their slogan: *Code is truth. Currency is freedom. Trust is dead.* That has a really nice ring to it."

"You're killing me here," the agent whines.

"The owner is a bit of a weirdo. Trent Quinlan was born in Palo Alto, California…naturally," Ellie says, ignoring Gavin. "He grew up in the shadow of Silicon Valley. A computer wizard by thirteen, he was accepted at MIT and expelled during his second semester for unauthorized access to sensitive faculty research. Then he went off the grid for five years.

"It says here that he was rumored to have worked as a cybersecurity mercenary, darknet cryptographer, and private blockchain architect for wealthy investors. He returned to the public eye with the launch of Quorvium, and it took off. The company has evolved from a radical fintech startup into a global powerhouse with users in over seventy countries, powering unbanked economies and speculative hedge funds."

"Ellie—"

"Quinlan is a recluse. This doesn't say whether he has a family. He rarely gives interviews, avoids social media, and hasn't attended a live event in over three years." Ellie taps her screen. "This could be our guy."

"A crypto dork? Why would a guy with more money than God kidnap Santa Claus?"

"Well, since there has been no ransom demand, maybe this isn't about money."

Gavin bobs his head from side to side as he bites his lip. "Okay, that's true."

"Think about it," Ellie says, standing. "Who else would have unfettered access to the company jet?"

"Other executives could. This plane has been everywhere. London, Paris, Madrid, Geneva, Vienna, Stockholm—"

"Where is it now?" Ellie interrupts.

"Berlin," Gavin says, staring at his laptop. "At least according to their last filed flight plan."

"So, if they abducted Santa—"

"There's no real evidence of that. Only a hunch."

"*If they abducted Santa*," Ellie continues, glaring at him, "they could have dropped him and his abductors off at any of those airports. Wanna roll the dice and play some Monopoly? Which square has the hotel that Santa is staying at?"

"We can't check all these places," Gavin argues.

Ellie folds her arms. "I don't see you trying."

"Oh, you must think I'm Superman or something."

"Not really," Ellie mutters, rolling her eyes.

"I'm one guy! I don't have a task force behind me to do the grunt work. I have nobody helping me on this assignment."

"You have me," Ellie softly says.

Tone is everything in verbal communication. Words matter. They are the foundation for communication, but tone is what really conveys the sender's message. The words "you have me" are innocent enough. And they are true. Ellie is in this room with him. But the tone…that is conveying a completely different message, unless Gavin is misinterpreting it. Which he may be. On that mental note, he decides to ignore any implications of the words or the message.

"And I appreciate that," the agent says, his voice returning to a normal volume, "but the two of us can't check all these places either."

Ellie hangs her head for a beat before lifting it quickly. "Maybe we don't have to. You said the plane is in Berlin, right?"

"Theoretically."

"Call the authorities there and have them detain the flight crew. Question them about their passengers. They will spill where Santa was dropped off."

"They're not going to talk."

"Are you telling me the Germans, of all people, can't get that information from them?"

"You've been watching too many movies. Life isn't like that. The flight crew won't talk, and the Germans aren't going to pull their fingernails out until they do. I'd be surprised if they even cooperate with us."

"How did you make it through Quantico?" Ellie questions. "You're in the *Federal Bureau of Investigation*. Ask them nicely. If that doesn't work, ask them not-so-nicely. Their children believe in *Weihnachtsmann*, too. Remind them of that."

"You know who the German version of Santa is?"

"You've met Wyatt. He talks a lot."

The agent shakes his head. "This isn't going to work."

"I thought we were making some progress, Agent Scroge Mc—"

"Stop! Don't say it."

"Fine. Then stop being such a wuss. Get on the phone and use your shiny gold badge for the greater good, or I'll use it for you...*again*."

Ellie marches out of the room with her cell phone in hand, ostensibly to call her brother with a progress report. They make people different in Montana. It's equal parts infuriating and enchanting.

He grabs his phone and begins searching for contacts in Germany. He may have to call back to the mothership to get one. He's a low-level agent with only a couple of years of experience. He has trained with Germans before, but doesn't have an extensive network there.

His thoughts drift back to Ellie and what she told him about her husband. She's a handful, but she's also loyal, driven, and confident. Now, he's convinced Bill Olson isn't cheating on her as she believes. No man has balls that big.

Chapter Thirty-Eight

STOWE BESSETTE

There are times in life that are equal parts fun and frustrating. Visiting Christmas markets in one of Europe's most iconic cities certainly qualifies as "fun." Not knowing what to do next to find Santa is the frustrating part. They aren't here to sightsee, as alluring as that might be. They have a task, and the lack of progress is taking its toll.

There have been no more cards. They successfully found Julie but have nothing of use to tell her. There is no explanation as to why or what to do next. All that remains is time to kill – precious seconds that they don't have to spare as the clock marches on toward Christmas Eve.

Her card is equally mysterious, and no answers are coming. At least she's being a good sport about this. Part of that is the distraction it provides. Stowe doesn't know many details about her failed engagement and what led to it. She's afraid to ask because it's really none of her business. But she knows what a broken heart feels like all too well.

All they can do is explore the city and wait. Nobody in their trio wants to think about the most likely reason for the lack of instructions from Santa – that something terrible could have happened to him. It's not the only plausible explanation, but it is the most unsavory one.

She spots a cluster of children huddled near a reindeer carousel, their faces pink from the cold and their cheeks wet from tears. It's an odd sight. Stowe could understand if it were one child, but they all have their waterworks turned on as a couple of mothers try to console them.

Julie, a third-grade teacher who is likely more in tune with the children than Stowe or Wyatt are, is already striding over to them with a purpose, her scarf fluttering behind her like a red ribbon of purpose.

"What happened?" she asks gently in English, crouching beside a frazzled woman and touching her on the sleeve.

The woman sighs heavily. "Some teenage boys were mocking the children. They kept saying that Père Noël isn't coming this year because he's gone missing or something. I told them it was nonsense, but…I've seen the articles in the news. I didn't want to lie to the children."

Julie continues to console the woman and help her with the children as Wyatt and Stowe exchange a look behind her.

"Articles?"

Stowe already has her phone out. She hasn't been checking the news sites. Her fingers fly across the screen, eyes scanning articles. They are everywhere, and most point back to the reporting of one journalist.

"Keith Meadows."

Wyatt's jaw tenses. "That figures."

He leans over Stowe's shoulder and watches her search for more articles on the news tab of her browser. They aren't good, and most are variations of the same three headlines:

"Global Concerns as Rumors Swirl About Santa's Disappearance"
"Père Noël Missing? His Shocking Absence in Finland"
"Keith Meadows Claims Exclusive Source: 'Christmas May Not Come This Year'"

Wyatt presses his lips together and stretches his neck from side to side. "Meadows is a provocateur. We saw that in St. Louis. He likes to make a big splash, and this one is rippling across the pond."

Julie returns from chatting with the mothers and their children. She looks back at them, still wearing a distraught look. The woman has a smile that can light up a pitch-black room. She hasn't flashed it much, but any hint of it is gone now. The interaction is definitely bothering her.

"Are they okay?" Stowe asks.

"They're upset. If the world starts believing that Santa is missing – I mean, really believing it – what does that do to Christmas? Believing in him is part of the magic of childhood."

"They lose faith," Stowe said quietly. "And that has real consequences. Especially since Santa *is* missing."

Stowe scrolls through the headlines again, scanning for more. This has become a global story. While it may not yet have reached the interest and urgency of their journey last year, it could easily get to that level as Christmas draws closer.

"This doesn't make sense," Wyatt mutters. "We've followed the instructions on the card. We found Julie. We must have missed something."

The comment lands on them like a snowball to the face. Stowe looks at him, her eyes wide and full of a rare vulnerability.

"No. We couldn't have." But even as she says it, her voice wavers.

"Maybe we missed something else…some instruction we didn't recognize for what it was. Santa is speaking in riddles."

Silence lingers between them. The sound of distant carolers outside only makes the moment heavier.

Stowe rubs her temples. "This isn't just a PR nightmare or a seasonal myth falling apart. Santa has the world believing in hope and joy again. Whatever forces are behind this – if they're trying to extinguish everything that makes Christmas magical – they're doing a damn good job."

Wyatt's voice is calm, resolute. "Then we give it one more day in Paris. If we don't get any other cards, we head back to Rovaniemi."

"To do what?" Julie asks.

"You're a teacher. You know how to talk to children. You can help us explain to them the real magic of Christmas and how it's still there without Santa. Maybe that is why Santa sent us to find each other."

"How do we do that? It's not like Keith Meadows will interview us," Stowe argues.

Wyatt shrugs. "We have a day to think about it and figure something out. All I know is that I'm not about to let Christmas get ruined for millions of children on our watch."

Chapter Thirty-Nine

KEITH MEADOWS

Santa's Village is usually a kaleidoscope of light and laughter, or at least it was last year. Now, it has an uneasy stillness. The lampposts that mark the line the Arctic Circle traces through the village stand like lonely sentries at an unvisited monument. There are no tourists or families taking pictures straddling the line. Nobody is walking toward Santa's Office. The restaurant is nearly empty, as is Santa's Post Office. The word is out that the main attraction isn't here.

Questions need answers. That's the way it works. Unfortunately, he won't find them in this barren tourist attraction. Santa is gone. That much is obvious. He isn't going to uncover who took him by aimlessly milling around Santa's Village. The answers lie elsewhere, but he doesn't have the resources or support to find Santa on his own, and if Wyatt, Stowe, and the FBI are here, he hasn't found them. This story needs to be taken in another direction.

That is yet another issue. The media are assembling in Lapland like they are the Avengers. He got his wish to make this an international story and has put himself squarely as the reporter who uncovered it first. Now, the real challenge begins. The hardest part about living in the limelight is staying there.

"Keith Meadows?" a voice calls out.

He turns to see a news crew setting up opposite the plaza from Santa's Office, likely to angle the shot to include it in the report. The reporter in his mid-thirties is instantly recognizable as Evan Tasker, a prominent cable news field reporter. He's a veteran of countless conflicts and crises, making a name for himself by reporting from some of the most dangerous parts of the world. He is always where the big stories are. This is a good sign.

Evan walks over as his cameraman finishes setting up the tripod and lighting. "I thought that was you. You're a long way from the Beltway."

He extends his hand, and Keith shakes it. "What brings you to sunny Finland?"

"You know why we're here," Evan says, grinning at the obvious sarcasm. "You have half the world talking about Santa's disappearance. If it's true, it's a big story right before Christmas."

"Well, the rumors are true. You are seeing the results. Outside of media types, the village is practically shut down."

Evan's expression sharpens. "Can we get that on the record?"

Keith hesitates. Technically, Evan's outfit is a competitor, but not a direct competitor. He has appeared on his network and others before to comment on stories.

Besides, if he wants the flames on this story to grow, he needs video reporting to stoke the fire. He gives a slow nod.

The pair makes their way back to the setup, and Evan gives some quick instructions to his cameraman. There is little discussion over what questions will be asked, but Keith has a decent idea of what direction this will go. When the camera light flips on, it's showtime.

"I'm standing outside Santa's Village, where the usual holiday magic has given way to whispers and worry," Evan says into the lens. "With me is Keith Meadows, Washington D.C. senior White House reporter and now…tourist?"

Keith smirks but doesn't answer the question as Evan turns to him. "Keith, what can you tell us? Has Santa disappeared?"

The journalist keeps his eyes on the camera. "I have confirmed that he has, but the real question we should be asking is 'why?' I've been asking since arriving here, and no one is talking. Not to the press and not even to each other. That leads me to believe there is something nefarious about Santa's absence and that people here are covering it up."

Evan raises an eyebrow. "Nefarious? You're saying someone took Santa Claus…kidnapped him?"

"I'm saying," Keith replies carefully, "that's what authorities are quietly investigating."

"Authorities…from here?"

"And possibly from elsewhere."

Evan cocks his head. "But why the cover-up?"

"That's the question," Keith says, a dour look seizing his face. "It could be innocent, like the fear of mass panic among children if the truth comes out. There is a consideration of the emotional and psychological toll on them during the most sentimental season of the year. It could also be economic. Tourism is one of Lapland's primary industries.

"But the scariest reason is that someone is aiming to destroy the spirit of Christmas. That he was taken to destroy the myth, and everyone here knows that Santa won't be coming back. It's better to pretend he's 'just missing' or 'needs a break' than to confirm that the holiday is canceled for millions of children."

"Aren't you concerned that your reporting could just be alarmist? That there may be nothing wrong at all?"

Keith leans in to the mic. "Of course. But Santa is not here. I have sources telling me that criminal activity not only could be but is likely involved. It is our responsibility to report if Santa isn't coming this year. The world's children deserve answers, not fairy tales or PR spin. We deserve the truth, and we need it before Christmas Eve. I am hoping the world will be vocal and join me in demanding answers."

"A strong challenge from the man who has been covering this story from the beginning. Thank you, Keith. We will all wait to hear from the jolly man in the red suit and continue asking two big questions: Was Santa taken, and who's going to save Christmas if he was?"

Evan signs off, and the segment cuts. The reporter is thrilled with the result and thanks Keith profusely for the chance to interview him. The journalist walks back through the plaza with a smile on his face. After seeing that, it won't be long before Keith gets interview requests from other outlets. He can shape the Santa narrative. All he needs now is more information to help mold it.

Chapter Forty

WYATT HUFFMAN

5 Days Until Christmas

They'd spent all of yesterday drifting through the city's various Christmas markets with cocoa in one hand and a shopping bag filled with ornaments and trinkets in the other. Despite the experience, they weren't merely celebrating the holiday – they were chasing the next clue that would direct them as to what to do. It never came.

At a complete loss, it was a matter of someone deciding what to do next. So, when Julie suggested they get up early to beat the crowds at the Louvre, it felt like a worthwhile plan. At least it gives their Santa-inspired visit to the city a small semblance of purpose.

The walk to the museum from their hotels was relatively short. Sublight glints off the iconic glass pyramid in the pale blue morning. As they entered the ticketing area, it was busy but not overly crowded. Wyatt wasn't in love with the idea of fighting crowds in the marble halls.

The Louvre at Christmas felt quieter than any of them expected. They drifted through galleries of marble statues and winged goddesses, and through gilded rooms with art in gold frames. They enjoyed the sights, but none of them said much. The wonder of the art was real, but so was the unspoken weight of the feeling that they were somehow failing.

Stowe walked a few steps ahead, hands in her coat pockets, shoulders slightly hunched. Her eyes moved over everything – the way the light fell on ancient sculptures, the folds of painted robes, the faces brushed in oil and frozen in time. Julie lingered at each painting longer than Wyatt or Stowe, her breath sometimes catching when a particular brushstroke or expression spoke to her.

Wyatt stopped often to look through doorways into other galleries. He wasn't trying to take it all in – he knew that was impossible – but rather to find *something* that led back to finding Santa. It was all for naught. There were clues here. No red cards were resting in the hands of a statue or lying on a bench. The question is, are more even coming?

Every so often, Christmas whispered itself back into the museum: The faint tune of "Silent Night" echoed softly from a nearby room where a string quartet rehearsed; a child in a puffy red coat skipped down a corridor, tugging her parent toward a statue she called "the angel lady." But nothing of Santa.

Now, they have found themselves sitting on a stone bench near the Louvre's inner courtyard, paper cups of hot chocolate warming their hands as the gray sky hints at snow. The city buzzes faintly beyond the museum's walls, but inside the courtyard, it feels like time has slowed down again – it is just the three of them, the echo of footsteps in nearby corridors, and the quiet reflection they share.

Stowe is the first to break the silence. "I thought we'd get another card by now. I'm scared to death that something bad happened to Santa."

Wyatt glances up, not surprised. He's been thinking the same thing but hasn't wanted to say it out loud. Saying it makes it real. The weight of that admission hangs in the air like fog.

He leans forward, his elbows on his knees. "I don't want to think about that."

The red envelopes were like whispers from fate ever since Santa began handing them to Stowe and Wyatt last year. Each led to an adventure more amazing than the last. Some moved people. Others changed lives. When he found the one in Santa's Office, he thought, "Here we go again." Now, they've stopped coming.

Even as doubt settles in, Wyatt finds himself reaching into his coat pocket, hoping to find that a red card has materialized there. If this is a test, it's a horrible one. They have no idea what to do next, other than continue their exploration of one of the world's greatest museums.

They set out and find their way to the one room that everyone who visits Paris comes to see. There she is. The Mona Lisa. It's much smaller than he expected, yet still undeniably magnetic. A velvet rope stands between the painting and the early visitors, but there aren't that many, which is surprising. Julie leans forward, whispering something about the smile. Wyatt tilts his head, seeing if the change in perspective alters her grin. Stowe just stares.

Then, there is a tap on his shoulder.

"Johan?" Wyatt asks, blinking as if not believing his eyes. "What the hell—?"

Stowe's head shoots around. Behind Johan, a woman with red cheeks and wide eyes beams. Hanna. His wife. The last time Wyatt and Stowe saw the Swedish couple was at their wedding in April. It was a magical event full of lilacs, family, laughter, and wine.

"Oh, my God! What are you doing here?" Stowe asks, dumbfounded.

"Looking for you, apparently," Johan says, shrugging with a grin as Hanna's head bobs up and down.

She steps forward and pulls something out of her purse – a red envelope. She hands it to Stowe, who opens it slowly. The card inside is the usual simple paper with gold lettering embossed like a secret.

*Go smile at the Mona Lisa, and you
will find old friends smiling back.*

Chapter Forty-One

SAINT NICHOLAS

The fire crackles in the cozy guesthouse, casting flickering shadows across the wooden walls. Santa sits in silence on a worn armchair with his hands once again folded calmly in his lap. On the outside, he is a picture of contentment. On the inside, he is going stir crazy.

This is his busiest time of year. He should be greeting children or their families. Being away from the village last year was hard enough despite being able to spread cheer in Viennese and Italian Christmas markets and in the remote Atlas Mountains of Morocco.

Now, he is a prisoner. His cell may not be iron-barred walls with a toilet and a thin mattress, but it is a prison nonetheless. His captor may not be a sadistic warden bent on abuse and malfeasance, but the isolation is torture enough. The only silver lining is the understanding he has about what must be done to end this tribulation.

Across the room, the broad-shouldered and barrel-chested Kram sits stone-faced against the wall with his arms crossed. It's his turn to watch Santa, having switched places with the more uptight and brooding Skut around midday. Kram isn't much friendlier, though the air between them is less hostile now and more… uncertain.

The silence has spanned a couple of hours until Santa looks at him and decides to break it. "I'm sorry, Kram. I didn't mean to cause Trent to lose trust in you. I hope he wasn't too angry."

Kram's brow furrows. "I didn't tell you his name. Neither did Skut. How did you know it?"

Santa rewards him with a soft, almost paternal smile. "I know a lot of things. About people. About you, and why you stopped using your real name. Why the name 'Alaric' hasn't left your lips in years."

Kram stiffens. His eyes narrow and study Santa for deception. He must think this is a trick. Most people do.

"You don't know. You *can't* know. Stop lying," Kram says, his voice low and skeptical.

Santa's eyes soften with a deep well of compassion. "You were ten years old the day your father walked out. The fight he had with your mother was bad, but you and your brother had seen them argue before. He always came back.

"You spent days behind the shed building a sled after he left. You thought you could both ride it down the big hill in town when he returned. When it was complete, you painted it red with leftover barn paint, thinking that it would look like flames racing down the slope. You called it *'Schneefeuer.'* "

Kram's mouth parts, but no words come.

"Snowfire. That's a great name for a sled. You held onto it for years, unridden, hoping your father would return to ride down the hill with you. When your brother broke the runner, you fixed it with a scrap of pine. You had hope – hope that your father would return to the family he abandoned. Hope that things could be as they once were. Hope that there was a second chance for you, just as you gave to Snowfire.

"But your hope dwindled over time. You stopped using the name Alaric because you associated it with a young boy who once believed in magic and second chances. You became 'Kram' because the tough-guy name felt safer. Simpler. Stronger."

The hulking man turns away, his jaw clenched. Santa knows that he is shaken, but not to the point where he orders silence. He's a man who's built walls around his past to hide the pain. Those walls are crumbling.

His face betrays the swirl of confusion and disbelief in his mind and the vulnerability in his soul. The name *Alaric* hasn't been spoken in well over a decade. It must be like hearing a ghost whisper his name. The story of a boy's lost innocence, long buried under layers of emotional armor, must be jarring to hear uttered for the first time.

"No," he says, standing abruptly. "You *can't* have known that."

Santa looks up, his expression unchanged and as serene as an alpine lake. He doesn't respond to Kram's disbelief. He's heard it thousands of times before. The stoic demeanor of the guard is still there, but Santa can sense the hopeful boy still stirring beneath the surface.

"That sled. The paint. The runner. No one knew about that. Not my mother. Not even Trent. I never told *anyone*. So, how do *you* know?"

"Because it mattered to you. Because it is *true*. You are more than the imposing man who does the bidding of his employer. You are the boy who built a sled and believed it could fix everything wrong with your family. That boy didn't disappear – he just got tired of being disappointed."

Kram's shoulders tense, and his breath shallows. The room suddenly feels small. The guard turns back to his captive, eyes glassy and wide.

"Why are you telling me this?"

"Because," Santa says, "you're not as lost as you think you are. And because people don't stop deserving joy in their lives just because they've forgotten how to believe in it."

Kram sits down heavily in the chair. "You think just because you *say* things no one else knows, it gives you power over me?"

"No. You asked me how I knew Trent's name. The answer is the same as how I know the story about Snowfire," St. Nick says, turning back to watch the fire. "I'm Santa Claus."

Chapter Forty-Two

SPECIAL AGENT GAVIN KINNAIRD

The agent returns from the other room and collapses into the sofa. His series of calls led from one revelation to another. That's not a bad thing, other than what it means for this conversation. Hot cocoa is so good here that it should be its own food group. Now, he wishes it were spiked with something harder.

"Go ahead and say it."

Gavin sighs. "You were right. The Germans were more than willing to help, and the pilots rolled over on their boss after thirty seconds of questioning. They did have a man with a white beard with them when they left Rovaniemi. After a couple of stops, the four of them were dropped off in Geneva, Switzerland."

"Mmm-hmmm," Ellie says, a grin creasing her lips. "Maybe I missed my calling."

"I'm beginning to think that myself," Gavin admits.

"All right. That narrows it down. Now what?"

"Geneva is a decent-sized city, and there are plenty of quiet places to hide within driving distance in both Switzerland and Southern France. I have an agent at the Bureau trying to track down an address for this Quinlan guy. Unfortunately, he's a black hole. He doesn't even have a primary residence listed. If they do find his house, we can't assume he's there. Wealthy people like to lease places using shell corporations to hide money and expenses and to maintain anonymity. It's also plausible that they took a train to Zurich or somewhere else. They could be in France, Germany, Italy, Austria…"

Gavin braces himself for a verbal bashing over his schooling her on European geography. Too many Americans can't find China on a world map, but she doesn't strike him as the uneducated or ignorant type, even if overseas travel is new to her. Instead, she aims her eyes skyward at the invisible map she is drawing in her mind.

"Germany and Austria are too far of a drive in winter conditions, and they won't take Santa by train. A jolly man with a white beard is going to stick out. Maybe France or Italy, but then why not fly into Milan or Lyon and save the windshield time?"

"My thoughts exactly."

"We should go there," Ellie concludes. "To Geneva."

The agent smiles. "I already made the call. Unfortunately, the jet is still in Paris, and the crew is resting. They will fly it up here as quickly as they can, but it won't be until tomorrow at least."

"That's inconvenient," Ellie says, grabbing her coat, "but I guess there's nothing we can do about it. We should see if we can find Aurielle and tell her we might have a lead. I need to stretch my legs anyway."

"Great idea. Let's stop by the security office first. I want to give them a heads-up that we're leaving and have a question to ask them. "

The pair grabs their things and exits the Christmas House, heading for the village plaza. Gavin doesn't want to poke the bear, but he can't let this observation rattle around in his head any longer.

"Are you sure you aren't a cop or a fed?"

"Positive. I'm a rancher…and if you believe my family, a part-time psychologist," Ellie adds.

"How does a rancher from Montana know so much about people?"

She shrugs. "People are easy. They have agendas. Cows and horses can be harder to understand when they act up."

"Do you armchair profile your family?"

"Every day."

"I bet they love that," Gavin concludes in an unmistakably sarcastic tone.

"You have no idea."

"Yeah, I do," he mutters under his breath.

Ellie and Gavin make their way over the snow-dusted paths of Santa's Village to the small security office. It's just as empty as it was last time they were here. The village isn't completely devoid of visitors, but there seems to be more media here than families.

Inside, the woman is nowhere to be found, and the bearded guard is sitting behind the counter and typing on a computer keyboard that looks straight out of the 1980s. Gavin informs him that they are leaving and no longer require the use of the Christmas House.

"I'm also wondering if you've ever had a report filed involving someone named Trent Quinlan," the agent asks.

The guard gives Gavin a curious look but nods. "I can check."

As he taps away at the keyboard, the door creaks open behind them, letting in a blast of cold air. A man steps in and brushes snow from his coat. He's tall, in his late thirties, with sharp eyes and a somewhat familiar face. Gavin can't place it, though.

The guard glances up from the screen. "Nope. No record of that name in here. But unless he lost a kid or got bitten by a reindeer, he wouldn't be."

Gavin nods. "Thanks. Appreciate the help."

"Always happy to help the FBI," the guard says with a casual grin.

The man who just entered raises an eyebrow, and his gaze shifts to Gavin. "FBI? You're in the Bureau?"

Gavin straightens. "Special Agent Gavin Kinnaird. And you are?"

The man extends a hand, but with something more akin to a sinister smirk rather than a smile. "Keith Meadows."

"Ah. I recognize you now. You sit in the press briefing room at the White House."

Keith gives a mock bow as Gavin senses Ellie immediately tense. "Guilty as charged."

"What are you doing so far from the Washington cesspool?"

Keith presses his lips together and looks around the office. "Same as you, I'd guess. I'm looking for Santa and trying to determine if his apparent disappearance is a kidnapping, terrorism, or something else. Since you're here, it's looking like something nefarious."

"I'm just advising local authorities," Gavin snaps.

Keith raises an eyebrow again. "Yet, the local authorities aren't here with you. And since you are making inquiries about incident reports, you must have a lead. Care to share?"

Ellie, who has been quietly observing, steps forward. "When we are ready to share anything with the press, it will be with someone with more credibility than a man who thinks clickbait is real journalism."

Keith turns to her, smiling thinly. "And you are?"

"Ellie Olson."

"Not a fan of *mine, huh*?"

"No," Ellie says flatly. "I remember your reporting from last year. You tried to ruin Christmas with that garbage you pulled at the children's hospital in St. Louis."

Keith straightens a little. "That wasn't garbage. That was investigative journalism. And for the record, I wasn't *wrong* about Malcolm Chapman being a Heilung exec."

"Sure," she fires back. "You were just wrong about every other aspect of the story and tried to ruin a beautiful moment of Christmas magic in an ambush."

"You think Santa's magic? Interesting." He tilts his head. "If that were the case, how did he allow himself to be kidnapped?"

"That's a question I'm sure you will pose to your readers," Gavin interjects, sensing that Ellie is about to rip the reporter's head off. At this point, he'd let her, but isn't in the mood to fill out the subsequent paperwork.

"Count on it. And thank you for giving me a new twist to the story," Keith says with a cool smile.

Wyatt's sister looks as if she is going to say something, but decides against it. She bolts for the door with Gavin following. Keith eyes them with a glimmer of intrigue in his eyes. Gavin didn't need instruction at Quantico to know the guy is up to no good.

"Merry Christmas, sweetheart," he sings out just as they step out the door.

Ellie turns around. "Call me sweetheart again, and you'll need a good dental plan for New Year's."

Gavin gently guides her away from the office and deeper into the Arctic cold. He turns to make sure the reporter isn't following them and is relieved to see that he isn't.

"You know him?"

"*Of* him," Ellie confirms. "He was on Santa Sleigh One with the press corps last year. Stowe had more than one confrontation with that jackass during their journey, and she told me all about them. And everyone knows what he did in that hospital lobby. We need to find Santa before that asshat tries to write himself into the ending of this story."

Chapter Forty-Three

STOWE BESSETTE

The late afternoon sun glinted off the glass pyramids of the Louvre as the five friends, new and old, spilled out of the bustling museum. There is a lot to catch up on – and a burning question to answer about the mysterious red card the Swedes received.

Stowe tugged lightly on Wyatt's arm and pointed across the street to a charming café tucked beneath the shadow of leafless trees. They made their way over to it and were seated at a corner table. The five of them settled in over steaming coffees and flaky pastries, and it didn't take long before the conversation was buzzing with stories and smiles.

It had been just over eight months since Wyatt and Stowe last saw Hanna and Johan outside of Stockholm at their wedding. The weather was perfect, the ceremony was beautiful, and it was the one time that Johan managed to hang onto the ring. The ease between them returned as if no time at all had passed.

Wyatt excused himself to take a call from his sister as Stowe leaned back in her chair. Three Christmases in a row. Seeing the Swedish couple is getting suspiciously close to tradition. But Stowe simply smiled at this moment – a gathering of friends, old and new, in the City of Light on a mission to find Santa Claus. Yeah, the Hallmark Christmas movies now have their trilogy in the making.

"That was Ellie," Wyatt announces, returning to the table.

"Has she killed our FBI agent friend yet?" Stowe asks, only half-kidding.

"No, but apparently, she's managed to verbally beat him into submission."

"The FBI is with you?" Julie asks, perking up.

"Yeah. The agent is an arrogant ass who thinks he has better things to do than investigate the disappearance of Santa Claus."

"Most of the agents at the Bureau are arrogant asses, so that sounds about right," Julie says. "Trust me. I have some experience with that."

Stowe is about to ask how when Wyatt touches her on the shoulder to get her attention. "They ran into an old friend of ours up at Santa's Village."

"Who?"

Wyatt tries and fails to stifle his scowl. "Keith Meadows."

Stowe scoffs and rolls her eyes. If there is ever a movie made about their adventures, he's the perfect villain. She has spent too much time thinking about what actor could play that egotistical moron in the film, settling on Christopher McDonald channelling Shooter McGavin from the movie *Happy Gilmore*. It doesn't matter that Keith Meadows doesn't look like that. The attitude is about right.

"Who's he?" Johan asks.

"It's a long story," Stowe moans.

"Wait, isn't he the White House reporter?" Julie asks. "The guy who tried to ambush the pharma guy at the hospital last year?"

"That's him. Only that was just the last in a long list of reasons why Keith Meadows deserves a dump truck's worth of coal in his stocking."

"Well, he almost found out the hard way what happens when you cross Ellie Huffman Olson."

It's something Stowe doesn't want to find out firsthand. She owes her getting back together with Wyatt to his sister, but the consequences of her breaking his heart were made crystal clear: two broken legs made to look like a skiing accident. When Ellie made the threat at the Huffman ranch, Stowe didn't know if she was kidding. In the time she has gotten to know her since that trek to the barn, she has learned that his sibling absolutely was not joking.

"Other than a run-in with Ebenezer Scrooge Cronkite, please tell me they've made some progress in the investigation."

"Yep, they have a solid lead. Santa was loaded up on a private jet at the airport and taken from Lapland. They traced the tail number, and the flight plans have taken it to half the cities in Europe. They think Santa may have been dropped off in Geneva."

"As in Switzerland?" Julie asks.

"Yup."

"Why there?" Hanna questions.

Wyatt's shoulders move up to his ears before dropping. "They have no clue."

"Whose plane is it?" Stowe asks.

"Some crypto company, I guess. Quorum, or something like that."

Johan's head jerks so hard that it nearly rips off his shoulders. Hanna covers her mouth with her hands and stares wide-eyed at her husband. Both reactions seem wildly out of place for the conversation.

"Quorvium?"

"That's it," Wyatt confirms for Johan. "You know them?"

He chuckles. "You're not going to believe this. Remember when I told you before the wedding that I worked in finance?"

Wyatt nods.

"That's the company I work for."

Stowe leans back in her chair again. The odds of this being a coincidence are incalculable.

"That explains the card," she concludes. "Now we know why Santa brought you here."

"Wait a second," Julie interjects. "How could Santa possibly make this happen? I mean, even if he knows what he knows, how could he guess that Johan and Hanna would even come to Paris, much less be in the exact room at the Louvre at the exact moment we were?"

A smile creases Stowe's lips. "We don't try to guess or explain the 'how' anymore. It's easier to focus on the 'why.'"

"Do you know why the owner of a crypto company would have taken Santa?" Wyatt asks. "Or where?"

Johan shakes his head. "No to both. Trent Quinlan is a financial and computer genius, not the underboss of some criminal enterprise. He may be eccentric, but he isn't a Bond villain. He has a fortune he wouldn't want to lose over…this."

"Assume he did," Stowe argues. "Where would he go?"

"I don't know. Trent has a reputation for being a recluse. I've never met him in person, and I'm not even sure I know anyone who has. When he holds meetings, it's over video or the phone. He leases properties all over the world, and usually multiple at a time."

"Why would he do that?" Julie asks.

Johan grins. "Because he can. We didn't even know he was married until an office rumor began circulating a while back that he and his wife had split. So, I don't think he has a real place to call home. He just moves around now."

"That doesn't sound helpful," Julie admits.

"Lucky I know the guy who handles his real estate leasing operation. I can make a call, but we would have to narrow it down a little. Trent Quinlan has dozens of properties and apartments leased or rented just in Western Europe."

Wyatt grins. "Tell him to start with any property near Geneva, Switzerland. Would there likely be addresses there?"

"Probably four or five of them, knowing what I do about Trent Quinlan, and given that our headquarters is in Zurich. But yeah, I can get them in the morning, assuming I can reach my friend. If he's playing his video games, it may take him days to pick up the phone."

Chapter Forty-Four

KEITH MEADOWS

He has it. Just when he thought milling around Santa Village was pointless, it paid the largest possible dividend. Now, it's time to take it to the bank.

Keith adjusts his Bluetooth earpiece and ensures that it's connected to his cell phone. The question he had before coming here was whether the White House and U.S. government were involved. Learning that Stowe Bessette and Wyatt Huffman were here partially answered that question. Meeting an FBI agent fully answers it.

He presses the call button. There is a better than even chance that this call isn't permitted to go through. Gatekeepers at the White House communications office are notorious for stymying reporters. He's almost surprised after making his request to speak with his nemesis to hear the line activate and a familiar voice speak.

"Keith," MacKenzie says in a tone that can charitably be called cool and clipped. "What's going on? How's the Arctic Circle?"

He gets right to the point. "Is the U.S. government investigating the disappearance of Santa Claus?"

"I think we have already covered this."

"Answer the question."

She sighs. "Why would we be?"

"Don't answer a question with a question."

"I have no idea," MacKenzie argues.

"I don't believe you."

"Keith, despite your ardent belief to the contrary, not everything is a conspiracy. Why would I lie?"

The corner of the reporter's mouth curls. "Let's start with the obvious reasons. You want to avoid any responsibility for whatever is happening in Rovaniemi. By stonewalling me, you think you can maintain control of the narrative and avoid political fallout."

"There is no narrative," MacKenzie interjects.

"Santa's disappearance is now the number one topic of conversation at dinner tables across the world. With that comes public outrage, a media frenzy, and the president who championed this Saint Nick last year will become the one who couldn't find him in time for Christmas."

"I marvel at your imagination, Keith. Really, I do."

"I think the White House may know something the public doesn't. So, tell me now – did a bad actor kidnap Santa?"

MacKenzie chuckles. "You must be desperate for ratings. Are you suggesting that his disappearance is some sort of terrorist attack?"

"No, I'm asking you. On the record."

"The White House has no knowledge of any plot, past, present, or future, against Santa. If he disappeared, we have no information as to why, nor have we been asked by any authority to assist in any investigation into his whereabouts. Happy?"

Keith smiles. He's very happy. "Stowe Bessette and Wyatt Huffman are here. Considering their involvement with the hearings and last year's multi-country adventure, don't tell me that's a coincidence."

MacKenzie sighs. "Look, Keith. Neither of them has a role in the government anymore. You know that. It's December, and Stowe and Wyatt have a close relationship with Santa. Do the math."

"Is the FBI involved? Are they investigating Santa's disappearance?"

"You'd have to ask them. I don't speak for the Bureau or the DOJ."

That's classic deflection. He doubts that anything MacKenzie is telling him is an outright lie. She's too good for that. But her statements are likely half-truths, at best, and missing plenty of context. Under these circumstances, if Wyatt and Stowe are here, the White House communications director likely knows why. And, if they have help from the Bureau, she would know that, too. The Department of Justice wouldn't hide that information from her.

"I plan to ask them," Keith says. "I'll start by asking a man I just met by the name of Special Agent Gavin Kinnaird. I wonder if he'll tell me whether the White House told him to come here."

There is a long silence. Too long. "I wouldn't know what he'd say, but to my knowledge, there is no White House involvement and *no* FBI deployment in Finland. Officially. None. Period."

Keith nods to himself, even though she can't see him. "Got it. Do you want to tell me the truth off the record?"

"Goodbye, Keith," she says before the line goes dead.

Keith slowly pulls the phone from his ear and looks out at the snow-covered village. It truly is a sight that belongs on a Christmas card.

The White House is involved at arm's length, being careful to distance itself from any fallout. The FBI's presence here is nominal and unofficial, guaranteeing the same. That means something is very wrong, and they don't want any part of it. If it were an easy fix, they would have swooped in to save the day, just like last year.

That means that the cover-up is real, and his reporting is spot-on. Christmas is going to happen this year without Santa, or at least the one the world knows the best. That's news, and it only means one thing.

"It's beginning to look a lot like Christmas," Keith sings out as he makes his way to the parking lot for the drive to his hotel.

Chapter Forty-Five

SPECIAL AGENT GAVIN KINNAIRD

4 DAYS UNTIL CHRISTMAS

They are back in the Christmas House. After returning to the hotel, Gavin didn't sleep well. Maybe it is the assignment, and maybe it is the woman sitting on the sofa next to him as they wait for the jet to be ready. He is growing closer to her. Every time they talk, the connection seems to grow. She must feel it, too.

Ellie bites her lower lip after slinging her last comment in his direction. Flirting is a skill she probably never developed. She previously mentioned that she has been with her husband almost exclusively since high school, so there has never been a need to do it. That said, she isn't bad at it. Not bad at all.

Gavin shouldn't be this comfortable with her advances. Part of him isn't. His mind constantly wanders back to Julie. She was the love of his life and the woman he was ready to spend the rest of it with until destiny made other plans. Now, he has been tossed back into the deep end of the pool.

Ellie has her own relationship baggage. He thinks she may be looking at him as a potential rebound target…or a way to get back at her philandering husband…assuming that's what happened. Gavin still isn't completely sold on that. It's not to say he isn't interested in her…not by a long shot. He just doesn't want to be part of a regret if it comes to that. And he is still in love with Julie. That's going to take a long time to get over, which isn't fair to anyone.

He is about to respond to her latest flirtation when Ellie's phone buzzes on the coffee table. The sudden vibration jars the quiet stillness of this makeshift office with the subtlety of a 6.5 magnitude earthquake. She sighs and picks it up, showing him the caller ID. Wyatt. He was saved by the bell, or more accurately, the call.

"Hold on," she barks, steps away from the warmth of the cabin into the cold Arctic air outside. The amber glow of the Christmas lights strung across Santa's Village pierces the still dark night sky that sees only the muted colors of early dawn and late dusk this time of year.

"Hey, Wyatt," she says, setting the phone to speaker so she doesn't need to hold it to her ear.

"Hey, Ellie. Where are you?"

"We're still in the magical snow globe that is Santa's Village. Why are you calling so early? Making sure I went to bed alone last night?"

"You're a big girl, and you wouldn't tell me if you didn't anyway."

"That's true," Ellie admits with a smile.

"You sound...exhausted."

"I am," she admits. "Just not for the reason you're probably thinking, horn dog. Gavin and I are still chasing down the elusive CEO of Quorvium. The guy is a ghost."

"Look at you go, *Agent Christmas.*"

She laughs, maybe for the first time since leaving Montana. "It's a bad game of *Where in the World is Carmen Sandiego?* Trent Quinlan is an international man of mystery. There is no consistent route or clear destination in his travels. The crew said they dropped him off in Switzerland, but they could have been lying...he could be anywhere. Even if he is in Geneva, we have no idea where to look for him."

"Unless I give you some possible locations," Wyatt says smoothly, sounding all proud of himself.

Ellie stares at the phone. "Wait. How do you—?"

"This is a long story for a stiff drink around the fire pit, but the short version is that Stowe, our new friend, and I ran into Johan and Hanna yesterday at the Louvre."

"Ran into?"

"They got a red card from Santa instructing them to meet us there. Well, meet someone...again, long story."

"You have to be kidding me!" Ellie says, exasperated. "How...?"

"Wait, it gets better. To get straight to the point, Johan works for Quorvium. He knows the guy who handles Trent Quinlan's property leases. There are nine properties in the Geneva area of Switzerland alone. They range from apartments to houses to ski chalets. He has another five up near Zurich, where their headquarters is located."

"Nine in Geneva?" Ellie repeats, making certain she heard her brother correctly. "Who even *needs* that many?"

"According to Johan, Quinlan is a recluse. He cherishes his privacy and has plenty of money to burn."

"Must be nice. Rich people are so weird."

"No argument from me on that. I thought our first dog was weird. Then we got hooked up with Santa Claus. Nothing approaches his level of weirdness."

"Cheddar," Ellie says with a snort. "He was afraid of ducks...and water."

"Ironic for a Golden Retriever."

"I will tell Agent Scrooge McGrinchipuss to get the pilots busy on prepping the jet. They should be back from Paris and at the airport by now."

"Do you need any help motivating him?"

"No, like I told you earlier, he's beginning to warm up to things."

"Okay. Please be careful, Ellie, and try not to do anything stupid."

"Who, me? I thought doing dumb things was a male Huffman family trait," she says with a grin. "Talk soon."

She ends the call and stands in the falling snow for a long moment. The cold bites at her cheeks, and she shivers slightly without her coat in the Arctic air. But she doesn't move. Her brother's words echo in her mind. Nine places. All in the Geneva area. Trent Quinlan has covered his tracks, but not well enough.

She pulls the door open and steps back into the warmth of the Christmas House. Inside the lodge, the agent ends a call and watches her step through the door.

"Gavin," she says, pulling off her gloves. "We need the jet. Now."

He raises an eyebrow. "Already called it in. It's being fueled, and the flight crew says we can be wheels-up in ninety minutes."

She blinks. "Wait, you…how did you…?"

"I overheard your conversation with Wyatt."

Ellie puts her hands on her hips. Jules used to do that to him. It's how he knew he was in real trouble.

"You *eavesdropped?*"

"Hardly. You weren't exactly whispering out there," Gavin informs his partner with a half-smile. "It's called situational awareness."

Ellie arches a brow. "So, you took it upon yourself to make our travel arrangements before I even finished the call. You're really leaning into this 'man of action' thing."

"Good." He stands, sliding his phone into his jacket. "I was aiming for shedding the 'Agent Scrooge McGrinchipuss' moniker once and for all. How am I doing?"

She steps closer, folding her arms and tilting her head. "The jury is still out, but I'm starting to think you're beginning to enjoy this assignment."

"Jet-setting across Europe? Cracking a Santa Claus kidnapping conspiracy? Getting torn to shreds by a lovely woman with a heart the size of the state she lives in?" He shrugs. "I've had worse weeks."

Ellie desperately tries to ignore the heat that is creeping into her cheeks. "You know that I would have gone alone if you insisted on staying here."

"I know. Although it's more likely that you would have put a shock collar on me and made me carry your bags and look intimidating."

"You *do* have the brooding stare with those eyes of yours," she says, her face softening. "Did they teach that at Quantico?"

"Staring 101. It's the block of instruction we receive right after bulletproof banter and how to drink bad coffee."

Ellie laughs softly. He thinks of pointing out that she has a nice laugh, and he takes a pass, opting to let the silence settle between them. Outside, the snow dances down from the sky like ash from a slow-burning fire. Something warm stirs behind his ribs. Maybe it's a flicker of appreciation. Maybe it's more. But he can't fight the reality of this situation any longer. He is enjoying this assignment, and it's because of her.

"Okay. Let's go crash some Swiss chalets and make some Christmas magic happen."

He smiles. "That almost sounds like a date."

She smirks, brushing past him as she grabs her coat and bag. "Don't get too cocky, Agent Kinnaird. You don't want to end up on my naughty list."

Chapter Forty-Six

WYATT HUFFMAN

The stairwell of the Hôtel Madeleine is narrow and softly lit, with the worn red carpet muffling their footsteps as Stowe and Wyatt slowly climb to the third floor. A chandelier flickers above them like a candle struggling against the dark. Outside the window at the landing, Wyatt can see the Parisian rooftops under a velvet sky and glimmers of light reflecting off the Seine.

There are a lot of hotels for tourists in this area, and Wyatt is only partly surprised that Julie, Hanna, and Johan aren't staying at the same one. It would be a feat that he could imagine St. Nick managing to pull off. They are only blocks away, though.

"What's bothering you?" Stowe asks from behind him.

"Nothing."

"Pssh," she says, catching Wyatt's arm as he absently runs his hand along the railing. "I know you better than that. You're the strong and silent type, but this mood is closer to brooding."

He stops and turns. "All right. I can't shake the feeling we're failing him. The world's beginning to panic thanks to Keith Meadows and his irresponsible reporting. Santa is gone, and we're in Paris chasing the clues on red cards that have no meaning."

"Unless they do," Stowe whispers.

Wyatt lets out a humorless laugh and leans against the wall, his arms folded. "Maybe that's just it. We're chasing ghosts. Each of the cards we got last year was specific. These feel more like clues to a puzzle, like we're part of someone's elaborate little game."

Stowe tilts her head. "You think Aurielle's behind this?"

"I don't know. Maybe. I just keep thinking about last year. Each one of our stops gave us a mission. Some were about us. Others were about Antonne Tucker. But whether we were in Vienna, Florence, or Marrakech, every card had felt random until suddenly it wasn't. These just feel random."

Stowe's gaze softens. She has to be feeling the same way. They have spent hours reminiscing about the cards turning into revelations. How each discovery brought them closer to a goal – and each other. None of it had made sense until the final pieces clicked into place.

"You're right about one thing – they felt random then, too," she quietly says. "Every red card had to land in the right hands, at the right moment. We only see the pattern because of the benefit of hindsight. It always could have gone wrong – one delay would have unraveled everything. But it didn't. It was like a choreography where we didn't know the steps until after we danced them."

Wyatt starts to speak and stops. Instead, he nods.

"That's how Santa works," Stowe continues. "It's not about control. It's about trust."

He looks at her, his eyes searching. "But don't you think…if Santa's okay…wouldn't it be easier to just tell us? If he can get us red cards, why can't he just tell us his location? Why not let us know that he's okay so the world can breathe easier again?"

She takes a breath and climbs to the stair tread Wyatt is standing on. "Maybe. But Santa always has a plan. Maybe the world isn't supposed to just breathe right now. Maybe it's supposed to *believe*. There's a difference."

"I just wonder if we're doing the right thing. What if we're walking in circles while Christmas falls apart behind us?"

She touches his face. "I don't think we're walking in circles. We're following a path we can't see yet. That's faith, Wyatt. And last year, that faith led us exactly where we were supposed to be."

A silence passes between them, long and gentle. He bends down and kisses Stowe softly on the lips. It's the same affectionate kiss he has shared with her hundreds of times before. No matter how many times he does, he still gets a tingle.

"Okay. Let's get some sleep and see what tomorrow brings."

Wyatt resumes climbing the stairs with Stowe following. The third-floor landing creaks beneath their feet when they reach it. Somewhere down the hall, a door closes with a thud. When they reach their room, Stowe immediately turns and heads into the bathroom. It's been a long day, so Wyatt collapses face-first into the bed without even taking his shoes off. He stays there for a few long moments before rolling onto his back.

"You okay?"

"Yeah," Wyatt says, lifting his head off the mattress to ensure his voice carries into the bathroom. And then he sees it.

Perched against the bottom of the flat screen television on the dresser is a red card with shimmering gold lettering. It's not something housekeeping or hotel management would have left. It's something Santa would have given them had he not been missing. Which he is. How it got here will be a mystery to unravel another day.

"Hey, Stowe?"

"Yeah?"

"Get in touch with the gang. I think we have work to do."

Chapter Forty-Seven

STOWE BESSETTE

The gang was quick to respond to the group text that Stowe set up. Five minutes later, everyone met down in the lobby of their hotel. They decided to have this conversation in a nearby café. She knew they would need to be seated when they heard this.

Wyatt is about to order an espresso when she reminds him that it is nearly eleven o'clock. Thanking her for preserving his ability to sleep tonight, he orders a glass of wine. It's not what she expected him to select, but when in Rome…or, in this case, Paris…do what the locals do. The rest of the group does the same and then turns their attention to Stowe. She pulls out the card and reads the note written in gold lettering:

> In morning's hush and winter's chill,
> She'll climb the steps with quiet will.
> A camera raised, she finds the light,
> The Tower captured in her lens just right.
>
> No crowds, no noise, just pink-hued skies,
> and a forlorn woman with weary eyes.
> This second card is not a gift,
> But a tool to mend the rift.
>
> Her eyes will weep, her breath will slow,
> A heart, once heavy, will start to glow.
> With heartfelt words, she'll make her peace.
> Once this is done, you are released.

"What in the absolute fu—"

"Don't finish that sentence, Johan," Wyatt advises, nodding at the family a few tables away with the sleepy children who probably should have been in bed hours ago. "There are kids around. But, yeah, we thought the same thing."

"Wyatt said the same thing when we opened the card," Stowe admits. "I'll be honest. I think Santa had better not be found because I'm going to throttle him when we do."

"She's joking," Wyatt advises. "At least I hope she is."

"I love riddles," Hanna says. "We can figure this out!"

Johan takes the card. "*In morning's hush and winter's chill*…that must be morning. That's easy enough. *She'll climb the steps with quiet will.* Are there any famous staircases in Paris?"

"The Spanish steps?" Wyatt asks, knowing next to nothing about this city.

"That's in Rome, silly," Hanna chides playfully.

"Sacré-Cœur has steps. I saw them in *John Wick 4*," Johan states proudly as Hanna rolls her eyes. "What? I did."

"The Eiffel Tower, Notre Dame, the Montmartre neighborhood has a lot of staircases, even the Arc de Triomphe has a bunch to the top—"

"Let's put a pin in that one," Stowe advises. "It could be anywhere. *A camera raised, she finds the light…The Tower captured in her lens just right.*"

"Someone taking pictures of the Eiffel Tower at sunrise," Wyatt deadpans. "Probably with the sun right behind it, so she will be on the west side."

"Are you sure?"

"I may not write for Condé Nast Traveler, but do you know of another iconic tower in Paris worth visiting?"

"Notre Dame has two bell towers," Hanna argues.

"But it would have said 'church' or 'cathedral' on the card instead of 'Tower,' Johan correctly points out.

"Okay, so taking pictures of the Eiffel Tower at sunrise," Stowe concludes. "How will we know her?"

"She'll be alone and very unhappy," Wyatt deadpans again.

The other four look at him blankly, and he gestures at the card. Johan takes up the task.

'*No crowds, no noise, just pink-hued skies and a forlorn woman with weary eyes.*"

"You're good at this, Wyatt," Hanna confirms.

No, he isn't. At least, Stowe knows that he doesn't think so. Wyatt told her once that he despises riddles because he has never been able to figure them out. This one seems obvious because it's written right on the card. And that's the problem. She also thinks they are probably missing something.

"The rest is just what happens next," Johan says. "I guess that's how we'll know the right person got Santa's card."

"Or it's a code we don't yet understand."

"Speaking of which," Stowe says, folding her hands on the table and leaning forward. "It doesn't mention anything about the three of you. Mine and Wyatt's names were on the card. We're committed to this. You guys don't have to tag along with us if you don't want to."

The three of them exchange glances. Stowe almost made it sound like she didn't want them to come. It wasn't her intention at all, but that's how it came out. She just doesn't want them to feel obligated. Julie is the first to pipe up.

"I came here for a distraction. I can't think of a better one than this. I'm in this for the long haul. I want to know if we are right."

"Same here," Hanna seconds. "After hearing all the stories about your Christmas adventures with Santa, we never actually thought we'd get to participate in one."

"Plus, consider it payback for rescuing Hanna's ring," Johan adds.

"I rescued yours last year, too," Wyatt says with a smirk.

The memories of retrieving the diamond engagement ring after the botched proposal come flooding back to Stowe. She can't suppress the smile. That was the moment when she really began to trust Wyatt. In some respects, it was the moment she realized that she may have started falling in love with him. She can't imagine climbing on someone else's back like she did his that day. She can barely believe she did it then.

That was all punctuated last year when they bumped into Johan and Hanna in the restaurant in Rovaniemi. Johan was looking for his own ring that he had dropped, and Wyatt found it after it rolled away. That Santa-arranged meeting is how they ended up at their amazing wedding in Sweden.

"All right, that's settled," Stowe says. "What time is sunrise in Paris tomorrow?"

"8:15 a.m.," Hanna says, checking the weather app on her phone.

"We can meet in the lobby here at seven and head over. That should give us plenty of time to find a woman with a camera."

"In a sea of a thousand tourists, all doing the same thing," Wyatt moans, adding to Stowe's sentence. He frowns. "This ought to be fun."

Chapter Forty-Eight

SAINT NICHOLAS

3 Days Until Christmas

Santa knows that he's playing with fire. Even while keeping his visits brief, all it would take is Skut or Kram cracking open the door to the guesthouse bedroom and finding him not there to…well, he doesn't want to think about what would happen. But Fallon is the key to everything, and Santa needs her to know that he's still looking out for her.

She lies on her bed, clutching a stuffed bear close to her chest. Despite her slumber, her eyes open as they have previously when she senses his presence. She smiles – not a forced smirk, but one of genuine surprise and joy that he returned.

"Hello again, Fallon," Santa whispers, his voice like a lullaby wrapped in velvet.

"You came back," she says, blinking away the sleep.

"I did. I wanted to check on you. May I sit?"

She nods and motions to the foot of the bed. The mattress sags slightly under his weight. For a moment, they sit in silence, watching the moonlight reflect off the alpine snow.

"I've been thinking about your wish," Santa says at last, "and about the love in your heart. I know you miss your brother. Do you think of him often?"

Fallon's small voice catches in her throat. "Every day."

Santa reaches out and holds her hand gently, saying nothing. He simply waits as Fallon takes a deep breath.

"I know it's painful, but can you tell me what happened to him?"

She nods. "We were playing in the front yard. It was a sunny day. I went inside for a minute to get a snack." Her grip on the stuffed bear tightens. "When I came back, he was gone. He…he ran into the street."

She looks down, and Santa can see that her cheeks are damp with the tears flowing from her eyes. The pain is real. The images of that day are seared into her memory. The loss is still fresh, but the aftermath of the accident is what haunts her.

"Mommy blamed Daddy," she admits. "She said he should've been watching. But Daddy was getting something out of the car. He wasn't being bad. It wasn't his fault. It was just…."

"An accident," Santa says, nodding slowly with the patience of someone who has heard every kind of sorrow the world could offer. "The hardest things to deal with don't have anyone to blame. No one to point a finger at. They just happen. And they hurt so much because love – real love – gets left behind."

Fallon sniffs and wipes at her eyes. "Daddy hasn't smiled in a long time."

"Grief is love with nowhere to go. Your daddy still loves your brother. And he still loves you. That kind of love doesn't disappear. It just gets quiet…until someone brave like you brings it back into the light."

Fallon looks at him, eyes wide and searching. "Do you think Daddy will ever be happy again?"

Santa offers her a smile. It's not the big, jolly smile from the songs and stories, or even the ones he shared with children in the Christmas markets in Italy and Austria last year, but a smaller, warmer one. The kind that engenders trust.

"I think he already is…because of you."

Santa now understands what is happening and why. He was right that this kidnapping had to do with Fallon, but he was wrong about the reason. The world loses its color when grief takes over. Tears flow, and silence is heavy. The feel of living life is like a storm that has passed but isn't quite over.

There is an ugly truth about grief that most people won't admit – it's not something you get over. Ever. Instead, you learn to carry it with you. Over time, the heart makes room for love by filling in the hole from loss. Trent loves his daughter. He misses his son. With his wife now absent from his life, it falls on Fallon's love to fill the void.

And that is the key to unlocking the mystery behind this kidnapping. One simple question. One innocent answer. A single response that aggravated the wrong nerve, setting all the events that have transpired since into motion.

Not that it matters. Plans can be adjusted, but it means risks will need to be taken. For the first time since arriving here, Santa sees his purpose with great clarity – and the key to his leaving and returning to the only home he knows.

"I am still working on your Christmas wish, Fallon. I promise to do everything I can to deliver it."

She leans against him and wraps her small arms around his body. He rubs her back gently, assuringly, as she whispers a thank-you into his ear.

There's something timeless about a child's Christmas wish, especially one that is selfless. Sometimes, it's a mere whisper wrapped in hope and wonder, and sprinkled with a touch of belief in something more than can be seen in the physical world. It doesn't need to be spoken aloud or even written on a folded note. It just needs to exist.

The magic lies not in the wish itself, but in the unseen way the world sometimes listens. Last year was an example of that when a single miracle moment inspired the entire planet. It just requires the right person to make it at just the right time. Even in a world defined by logic and deadlines, there's still room for mystery. Santa has proven that. Now, this may be his encore, showing the world that hearts can heal, dreams can come true, and love can find its way back.

Because at Christmas, the line between the ordinary and the extraordinary disappears. And for just a little while, anything feels possible.

Chapter Forty-Nine

WYATT HUFFMAN

Before the sun rises over Paris, the Eiffel Tower stands in serene majesty against a quiet, darkened sky. Wyatt, Stowe, Julie, Hanna, and Johan arrive to find the streets around Champ de Mars hushed, save for the soft hum of distant traffic. Streetlamps still cast golden pools of light on the cobblestones, and the iron lattice of the tower glows beneath its own lighting.

Despite this being one of the most visited landmarks in the world, there are relatively few people here at this hour. There is a sense of solitude and grandeur in the early hours of the morning, as if the city has briefly forgotten its pace and surrendered to stillness. It makes the tower, usually surrounded by crowds of camera-wielding tourists, appear more intimate as it stands proud over a sleepy city.

Dawn is quickly approaching as soft strokes of lavender and gold begin to appear in the eastern sky. The appointed time has nearly arrived to satisfy the next Santa riddle, but their quarry is nowhere in sight. Nobody matching the description on the card is anywhere nearby. Then again, why would she be? There is no guarantee they are even here on the correct day.

"This is wrong," Julie says.

"I thought we agreed on the Eiffel Tower," Stowe says, her face scrunched in the look she gives when she's utterly confused. Wyatt understands where she is going with this.

"We did, but Julie's right. We didn't climb any steps to get here."

Johan looks around. "He's right."

"Besides, if you wanted to take a picture of the tower at sunrise, why would you be standing right next to it?" Julie states.

Wyatt looks up at the top of the tower that was built for the purpose of being the main gate to the World's Fair. Their new friend has a good point, not that Wyatt knows anything about photography. That's why he lets Stowe take selfies of them.

"So, where would you take it from?" Hanna asks.

"There," Stowe says, pointing. "The Trocadéro. I should have known. It's one of the best places to see the sunrise in the city."

"How do you know that?" Wyatt asks.

She grins. "I told you. I love Paris."

"Clock's ticking, guys," Hanna warns.

The five of them cross the Seine River via the Pont d'Iéna, the closest bridge to them. Despite being in a rush, they each look back at the spectacular view of the Eiffel

Tower rising behind them. Once across, they arrive in the Trocadéro Gardens. When they reach the Esplanade Joseph-Wresinski, they know they are in the right place.

"I guess we found the stairs."

"C'mon!" Johan urges, more excited about this than he should be.

Two stairwells come down on either side of the Trocadéro. One is a little more crowded than the other, with photographers and couples taking selfies on both. This place isn't as empty as Wyatt thought it would be. There are plenty of other sunrise watchers out here, although, given the view, it must still be much less busy than any other time of day.

Stowe immediately pulls out her camera. A picture of the beautiful colors crossing through the Iron Lady is a shot that nobody should miss. Johan and Hanna rope a tourist into taking pictures of them as well. Wyatt wants to join in, but he also doesn't want to lose sight of why they are here.

"Uh, Wyatt?" Julie says from next to him, pointing. "I don't think you get much sadder than that."

Well, that's not entirely true. Julie never saw his sister when they were kids after the family dog died. She moped around the house for three months after losing Cheddar. But in terms of seeing a forlorn woman framed by the soft golden light beginning to spill across the Parisian sky as she takes pictures in the City of Light, she's certainly a candidate.

The woman is no tourist. If she is one, she has money in spades. She is dressed in a long, elegant white coat, her high heels clicking softly against the stone, a red woolen scarf fluttering slightly in the early morning December breeze. Her hair is neatly styled, and her makeup is pristine at this early hour, except for the streaks of mascara tracing faint lines down her cheeks that trace the march of tears from her eyes.

With one hand, she lifts a vintage camera, capturing the Eiffel Tower as it emerges from the shadows, regal and unbothered by the people milling around below. Her other hand trembles slightly, brushing another tear from her cheek before it falls. There is a quiet desperation in her expression, as though the act of taking photos is her only way to hold onto something slipping away – memories, perhaps, or someone she once stood here with. Around her, a smattering of tourists stirs, unaware of the grief cloaked in elegance standing at the edge of morning.

"Do you want the honors?" Stowe asks.

"I took the last one. It's your turn."

Stowe inhales deeply and approaches the woman cautiously. "*Excusez-moi, madame?* Do you speak English?"

She hurriedly wipes more tears from her cheeks as she stares at Stowe. "*Oui.* Can I help you?"

"This is going to sound very odd, but we have a card for you."

"At least, we think it's for you," Wyatt adds, hedging their bets.

Stowe retrieves it from her pocket and hands it to her. Julie, Johan, and Hanna join them as the woman looks at all five of them apprehensively. Wyatt can't blame her for that. Considering the number of scams in this world, it's not unreasonable to think this is one.

"Who is it from?"

Oh boy. Wyatt grimaces. Telling this woman that the card is from Santa Claus may sound like a whimsical and enchanting gesture, but she is going to think the five of them are crazy. Who wouldn't, even in light of what happened last year? If she becomes evasive or dismissive, she may decline to open it at all, thinking they are trying to scam her.

"It might be better if you just read it and judge for yourself."

She slowly turns the envelope over in her hands several times as if thinking it has Anthrax in it. Finally, she must figure that it's harmless enough to open. When the woman pulls out a sheet of paper, it isn't the typical note from Santa. That much is certain. Every red card they have ever received was a short missive, even if the jolly old man is dabbling in riddles these days. This is more like a letter.

Her intensity and interest grow the farther down the page she reads. Before moving to the second page, she places her hand over her mouth as her eyes glisten with fresh tears. By the time she finishes, she's gripping the paper with both gloved hands as she fights back her emotions. She finally peels her eyes from the paper.

"*Merci*. I have to go."

Without another word, she tucks the camera and Santa's letter into an oversized designer pocketbook and hustles back across the Trocadéro as fast as any woman wearing three-inch heels could. She didn't ask any questions. There were no inquiries about the note, who wrote it, or why the five of them were entrusted to deliver it. Just a quick thanks and a hurried exit.

They watch her go until looking at each other, dumbfounded. Whatever was in that letter clearly rattled her. Her reaction was raw and emotional. At least Wyatt can be fairly certain that they found the right person. Too bad they'll never find out what was written.

"Well, that was anticlimactic," Johan concludes, earning a slap to the chest from his wife.

"How did Santa Claus know she would be here?" Hanna asks.

"I told you. We learned to stop asking that question long ago," Stowe admits.

"Christmas magic is as good an explanation as anything."

Julie nods at Wyatt before looking around. "Now what?"

"Well, the card said that it was our last task, so I guess we're done."

Everybody stares at Stowe. It wasn't because of what she said or even how she said it. There is a finality to completing this task that nobody wants to admit. All that's left to do this morning is to continue watching the beautiful Parisian sunrise. They can talk over breakfast about what comes next.

Chapter Fifty

KEITH MEADOWS

Keith moves through Santa's Village with a purpose. All morning, he has been like a conductor in a symphony, directing his colleagues about what part they should play in the performance he is planning. Journalism may be a cutthroat occupation, but they are grabbing their instruments and taking seats on the stage…at least, for now.

The twinkling lights around the plaza flicker as if unsure whether to shine. The few tourists still visiting move stiffly, their cheerful demeanors repressed by learning the truth that the main attraction – and symbol of Christmas itself – is nowhere to be found. The employees are walking around in absurd costumes and doing their best to bring joy, but it's clear that this place is rapidly shedding its magic.

Keith's wool coat flares with each brisk step, his meaningless press badge swinging on a red lanyard around his neck. His phone hasn't left his hand in hours. His fingers have been tapping messages, drafting emails, and jotting notes for the planned press conference. He already has a lot of buy-in for the event. Now, there is one more big group to tackle, so he planned this meeting.

He stops in front of a knot of international reporters who have clustered just outside the gift shop. Most of the major news outlets have reporters here, including Al Jazeera. Keith supposes that there is a lot of interest surrounding this Santa in the Muslim world following last year's stop in Marrakech and the trip to the Atlas Mountains.

Most of the reporters wear puzzled frowns. All of them have dressed for the Arctic, donning down coats, wool hats, and gloves. Some are looking around while others are speaking into phones or tapping impatiently on tablets. Most turn to face him when he walks over.

"Ladies and gentlemen," Keith says smoothly, holding up a hand like he's the president addressing a press pool outside the White House. "As most of you are now well aware, Santa is gone. We need to stop tiptoeing around his disappearance. The world deserves to know the truth without the PR spin you are all undoubtedly being fed. Everybody must understand that this isn't some cruel rumor."

"I heard you're talking about holding a press conference?" one of the German correspondents asks, his arms folded. "Is that true?"

"Christmas Eve morning," Keith confirms. "Right here in the plaza. While the cameras roll, we will stand here and demand that authorities confirm what we already know. That he *hasn't* been here and may have been taken against his will. That there is no Christmas miracle coming to save the day."

"But what if he shows up?" a British anchor asks, half-sarcastic, half-hopeful. "Won't we look foolish?"

Keith raises an eyebrow. "If he shows up, the world will cheer, and we'll all go back to wrapping fluff pieces in tinsel, knowing that we did our jobs. But if he doesn't? Because I don't think it's likely. We'll be the ones telling the truth first and proving that this story matters at a time when people are finally *watching*."

There is a long pause. Every reporter standing here understands the point of the comment. Views mean ratings, and journalists and news outlets around the planet want the clicks and attention this is likely to bring. The journalists glance at each other. Some nod, and others look a little unsure. That's easy enough to fix. Even if there is apprehension, none of these journalists will refuse to report on a story that all their peers are covering and risk uncomfortable questions from their editors back home. Keith knows it's time to put a bow on this.

"The world's in a state of suspended belief," Keith presses. "Millions of kids are already beginning to ask their parents what's going on, and the adults don't have answers. This isn't just a missing persons case – it's a cultural fracture with ramifications we can only barely understand. We owe it to the public to show them what's real."

A Finnish local reporter mutters something about this reporting being in bad taste, but Keith ignores it. Naturally, he'd say that, having a tourism industry in Lapland to help protect. People care more about the financial impact of Christmas here than they do about the holiday itself. All the twinkle lights and garland in the world can't cover up those motivations.

Keith reaffirms the start time tomorrow morning and moves on to another few reporters he hasn't spoken to, planting the same seed. That is just icing on the cake. By the time he's made his third lap around the plaza, the idea not only has momentum – it has large-scale agreement. The media will be there in force. Most of the reporters are already making equipment checklists and sharing concerns about signal bandwidth for their broadcasts. Some are wondering if props will be involved, like framing an empty sleigh in the shots. It's a clever idea, but overkill.

Keith stands by the Arctic Circle pedestals and watches a couple of families take pictures. His mind isn't on the scene. He's busy mentally watching the headlines write themselves. This isn't going to be just a story – it's going to be *history*.

Chapter Fifty-One

STOWE BESSETTE

They are becoming regulars at this café on the corner that is conveniently located between their hotels. The golden lamplight outside and the twinkle lights strung up around the room provide the perfect amount of Christmas ambiance. The faint sound of street musicians playing carols outside drifts through the large front windows.

Caught between lunch and dinner crowds, the café isn't full. A few tourists have wandered in, but the five weary faces huddled around a small round table are largely the only customers. Half-empty cappuccino cups, cocoa mugs, and dishes for the shared plate of croissants litter the table. They aren't here to eat. They are here to plan.

The red envelope was delivered that morning as instructed. The task was completed, but not without a sense of letdown. They all wanted to know what Santa had to say, and the woman who was the recipient wasn't sharing its contents. She barely had time to thank them before hightailing it out of the area. It left them with more questions than answers.

The contention is over what to do next. A divide over their next steps has emerged. The group is split fifty-fifty, and nobody is budging. The only person not weighing in is Julie, who looks content to listen to the arguments for each of their two options.

Johan leans back, folding his arms. "We dropped off the card like we were instructed, but running back to Rovaniemi doesn't solve the problem. Santa's still missing, and Switzerland is the only lead we've got. We should help Ellie and the FBI guy there. It's a lot for two people to do on their own."

"This Keith Meadows moron is *not* going to let this go," Hanna shoots back. "You've seen all the headlines. The world's media is turning this into a massive crisis. Parents must be on the brink of panic, and nobody is stepping up to reassure them that things are going to be okay."

"Why should that fall to us?" Johan asks.

"Who better than the people tasked with delivering Santa's cards?" Stowe counters.

Wyatt sips his cappuccino and sighs. "I understand the urgency, but media perception won't matter if we don't actually *find* Santa. Ellie and our reluctant FBI agent are already in Geneva, but they can't do this alone. Johan said there were nine places on the list, not counting his leases near Zurich. With more people there, we can divide and conquer."

"It's a good lead, but we can't assume it's going to work out," Stowe quietly says. "We have a responsibility to the people to explain that the legend of Santa Claus is not the same thing as celebrating Christmas. You think things are chaotic now? Wait another two days if we don't work to explain that to people."

"That's short-term thinking, Stowe," Johan counters. "Every moment we waste is another moment that Santa is missing. Don't let some tabloid hack distract us from finding Santa and putting an end to all of this."

Stowe crosses her arms, jaw tightening. "I wish Keith Meadows were just some tabloid hack. He's a senior White House correspondent with a lot of name recognition, along with the ability and know-how to shape the narrative. People are going to listen to him, and I promise, he's hell bent on ruining Christmas."

"Why?" Julie asks, speaking for the first time since they sat down.

"He's a reporter who likes ratings."

"I don't buy that, Stowe. There has to be something else."

"It doesn't matter what his motives are," Wyatt interjects. "We have to undermine his message. The easiest way to do that is to find Santa and return him to the village in time for Christmas Eve. That makes all this go away."

Stowe shakes her head. Johan hazards a glance at his wife, who does the same. Silence blankets the table, punctuated only by the café's hum and the occasional clink of cutlery filling the void. There is no consensus, and she isn't holding out hope of a compromise. It's a fork in the road, and they can only pick one path.

That is, of course, unless they split up. It's not the worst idea, but it somehow feels like the wrong choice. Santa brought Stowe and Wyatt in. He bought them to Julie. He brought Johan and Hanna to them at the Louvre. It feels like he wants the group together, so she isn't about to offer splitting up and going their separate ways as an option.

"We're going in circles," Stowe moans. "We're not going to move each other off our positions."

"Agreed," Wyatt says. "So, what do you want to do?"

Stowe thinks about it. She, again, thinks about the separate paths plan one last time before dismissing it. It's all or nothing. Fortunately, there are five of them at this table – a nice odd number that leads to a clear solution.

"We settle this democratically and put it up for a vote."

"All right," Wyatt concurs. "All in favor of going to Finland?" Stowe and Hanna signal yes. "And going to Switzerland?"

Wyatt and Johan's hands go up to shoulder level. They all turn to Julie. She didn't vote either way, and she's the tiebreaker.

Julie sits with her fingers laced around a mug of hot chocolate as her eyes move from face to face. She has listened to the whole debate without saying anything, and definitely doesn't look keen on weighing in with her thoughts. Now, she's the one who gets to make this decision. She shifts her weight in her chair.

"I'm new to this group. I shouldn't be the one who decides."

"The length of time we've known you doesn't matter, Julie. Santa sent us to find you, so your opinion has equal weight here."

Johan nods, as do Stowe and Hanna. The assurance doesn't appear to have assuaged her concerns. She exhales sharply.

"Okay…I don't think either of you is wrong," Julie begins, her voice low and tinged with nervousness. "But this isn't just about logic. This is about trust that Santa knows what he's doing."

Stowe and Wyatt nod as Julie pauses, tapping her mug with her fingernails, emitting soft clicks against the porcelain. "We need Santa back. That's not up for debate. But if he wanted us to search for him, I think what he wrote at the end of the card would have been different."

She turns to Stowe and Hanna next. "And fighting the narrative in Rovaniemi seems like a good idea, but getting people to believe us is a big ask. The fact is, Santa is missing, and the only thing that will restore the fragile belief people have in Christmas is his return."

"So, what's it going to be?" Stowe presses.

They all wait for the final vote to be cast and the verdict delivered. They will need the jet to fly to Paris to get them, regardless of whether it flies north or south when they take off. After another deep breath, she utters the words that set their course on the next leg of this journey. And just like that, the tie is broken.

Chapter Fifty-Two

SAINT NICHOLAS

There is peace in silence. For Saint Nick, it's one of life's truest pleasures. The world is noisy, and there is nothing quite as relaxing as stillness and the hush of night. The silence in the chalet is broken only by the soft creak of old wood and the steady hum of the heater rattling as it labors to beat back the cold.

Sure, Santa absolutely loves the sound of carolers and the melodies of the Christmas music they sing. He loves the sound of sleigh bells and the excitement in children's voices when they speak to him. But he still loves silence. There is a magic in it that recharges his batteries. It may be why he enjoys the comfort of his remote part of Finland so much.

Santa Claus stands near the foot of Fallon's bed, his warm eyes twinkling in the dark. She stirs almost immediately, as she has every night before. Her eyes open, still sleepy but somehow even brighter than they have been on previous visits.

"Santa?" she whispers, already sitting up under the covers.

He smiles. "Hello again, Fallon."

She beams, brushing her tousled hair out of her face. "Can I ask you a question?"

"Of course, my dear."

"Are you still working on my Christmas wish?"

"I am," he says gently as he sits on the end of her bed. "I've been working very hard on it. It's a very important wish."

"Will it be soon?"

"Very soon."

"I have more questions," Fallon says in a hushed but excited voice, pulling the covers off her and kneeling on the bed with her lower legs tucked under her. "Do you really live at the North Pole?"

"I actually live in Finland at the Arctic Circle."

"Why do they say it's at the North Pole?"

"Well, writers a long time ago put that in stories and poems. Authors like to embellish their works with flourishes like crazy plots, fantastical worlds, and remote or unfamiliar places. The North Pole is uninhabited and shrouded in mystery. It's also really snowy. People like that at Christmas."

"Do you have elves?"

Santa smiles. "I have a chief elf. Her name is Aurielle. She has rainbow-colored eyes and makes the best hot cocoa you will ever taste."

"Really?"

"She is very special…just like you."

"That's a really pretty name…Aurielle."

"Fallon is a pretty name, too."

"I like hers better."

Time is already growing short. Santa's expression shifts slightly. It's not darker, but it is more serious. He crouches so that he and the girl are at eye level.

"Fallon, can I ask you something important?"

"Of course, Santa."

"Do you know Kram?"

She scrunches up her nose. "Yeah. He and Skut are *really* big. Sometimes, they are mean."

Santa's eyes twinkle. "I know. They need some Christmas spirit. I think you can help with that if you want to."

Fallon nods vigorously.

"Well, there's a very special gift for Kram in the unused bedroom down the hall. There's a great big red bow on it."

Fallon's brow furrows. "Why is it in the other room and not under the tree?"

"Because it needs to be brought out and given to him at just the right time," he confides in her. "Tomorrow morning, when you wake up, could you bring it down to the living room for me?"

She straightens up proudly and nods vigorously. "I can do that."

"It's kind of heavy," he adds gently. "It will take all your strength."

Fallon lifts her chin. "I will do it for you, Santa."

His smile deepens, and his heart is warmed by her unwavering sincerity. "Thank you, Fallon. That means more than you know."

Just as the words leave his mouth, the door to the bedroom flies open. Light explodes into the room when the switch is flipped, ushering away the stillness of the night in an instant and the calm it carried with it.

Fallon shrinks back in surprise. Santa slowly stands, turning toward the doorway. He knew this moment was inevitable.

Trent stands in the threshold dressed in pajamas, his face twisted in fury, his shoulders squared like a man ready to strike. The light above casts sharp shadows across his features, and the wildness in his eyes makes Fallon's breath catch. He almost looks evil.

"Well…isn't this sweet?" Trent screeches through clenched teeth, his voice not much more than a low snarl.

Fallon gasps. "Daddy—"

"Go back to bed, Fallon," Trent snaps, not taking his eyes off the man in red. His voice is sharp, dangerous, and likely nothing like the father she knows.

Santa doesn't move. He stands his ground with quiet strength, shielding the girl with the simplest of gestures: presence. Trent steps into the room, the weight of years of control slipping off his shoulders.

"You just made the biggest mistake of your life," he says, his words tainted with a venomous tone. "You had one rule – do not interact with my daughter. You broke it."

Santa looks down at Fallon and then back at Trent. His voice, calm as still water, breaks the tension.

"I did. She has a kind heart."

Trent's fists clench at his sides, his breath sharp. "There will be consequences."

Skut and Kram arrive at the doorway. They wither under the acidic glare from their boss.

"How did he get in here? You two are supposed to be watching him."

"I was," Skut argues. "I was right outside his room the whole time."

"Then you fell asleep."

"I didn't! I swear! There weren't even any tracks in the snow leading to the main house. I have no idea how he could have gotten in here."

"We will deal with this in the morning. Fallon, go back to sleep. Kram, you will remain posted in this hallway outside the door until morning. If you need to use the bathroom, pee yourself. Skut, take Santa back to the guesthouse. You will remain physically with him at all times. Handcuff him to you if you need to."

"But Daddy, he won't be able to grant my Christmas wish!"

"He can't grant it. He's not Santa Claus, Fallon. There is no *Santa*."

"But there is!"

"Go to sleep. Now!" Trent turns his attention to St. Nick. "You are going to pay for this tomorrow. I swear it."

Chapter Fifty-Three

SPECIAL AGENT GAVIN KINNAIRD

The wind picks up across the frozen parking area outside of Geneva, stinging Gavin's cheeks as he marches toward the vehicle with his arms crossed. He can see Ellie's expression – a dark thundercloud of aggravation. He climbs in and slams the driver's door of the rental SUV a little harder than he meant to. Frustration will do that, and there is plenty of that at the moment.

"Six down, three to go," she mutters, putting on her seatbelt. "And we've got nothing but locked doors and zero signs of life."

"It gets worse. Local police are calling it quits."

"What? Why?"

"Oh, they have a laundry list of reasons, starting with their thinking that this is a waste of time and ending with it being late and they want to go home to their families."

"That's stupid."

"About which reason? They aren't necessarily wrong about the first, and the second is undeniably true," Gavin concludes, tensing his jaw to steel himself from the verbal onslaught sure to ensue from the passenger's seat.

"Oh, don't go 'Agent Scrooge McGrinchipuss' on me again."

Gavin glances at Ellie before leaning back in his seat, pinching the bridge of his nose. "Wouldn't dream of it. But nine places…nine long shots. I knew this list was a stretch, but I didn't think we'd come up completely empty."

"You'd think at least one of them would have had some hint of someone staying there. Who the hell rents nine places within driving distance in the same country and doesn't stay at any of them?" Ellie questions.

"Rich people. And, for the record, we've only checked six of them."

"Look at you turning into the optimist," she says, nudging him playfully in the ribs.

"Whatever."

"Where is the next target?"

"A couple of hours away," he says, checking the view out the windshield. "Assuming the weather holds. We should find a place to crash for the night and pick this up again in the morning."

Silence lingers between them for a few heartbeats as Gavin points the SUV east.

"All right. Let's stop somewhere first," Ellie says, appealing to Gavin. "I'm starving."

"Good idea. We've been running on adrenaline and coffee all day. There's a little village about five kilometers down the road. I'm sure there is an inn there we can spend the night in, and they'll have a café."

"Perfect."

Ten minutes later, the pair is seated at a small wooden table in a cozy Swiss café that smells like cinnamon and strong espresso. A fire crackles in the hearth, and their coats steam slightly from the warmth. Both of them settle on something hearty since they haven't had a decent meal since they left Lapland. The waitress takes their order with a tired smile and disappears behind the counter.

Gavin scans the menu again to make it less obvious that he's eyeing Ellie, whose attention has drifted to the couple seated at the next table, who are having a conversation with friends. The quartet couldn't look more different. Although all of them are dressed in sweaters, two look like they just came out of an oven that was set to bake at 450 degrees.

"You guys," the woman says, her voice full of awe, "this place…it's not just beautiful. It feels enchanted."

The man she is with nods, angling his phone so their friends can see images of the turquoise water stretching to meet the towering green peak of Mount Otemanu. They look mesmerized.

"You can't explain it until you're there. It's like the air is lighter. The water actually is about fifty shades of blue. That's how the workers at the resort characterize it. And at night, the stars don't just shine—they blaze. We sat on the deck of our overwater hut every night and just listened to the waves and watched the sky for hours."

"You're making us jealous," their friend laughs. "It sounds unreal."

"It *is* unreal," the woman confirms, tucking a strand of her blonde hair behind her ear. "But it's not just the scenery. There's something about being there that slows you down. Like… you start noticing things again."

"Island time," the friend concedes.

"Yeah. I mean, the way the hibiscus flowers smell in the morning. The rhythm of the ocean. Even each other." She glances at her new husband, and he smiles back at her, squeezing her hand.

"And the people there are just as magical," the husband chimes in. "Everyone greets you with a smile. There's this warm, genuine kindness at every resort. We had dinner on the beach the last night, and the chef came out just to ask if we liked the food. He was a native of the islands, and the recipe was passed down to him from his grandmother. It's like every meal comes with a story."

"Okay, okay," their friend says, holding his hands up in surrender. "We get it. Bora Bora is paradise, and you two are disgustingly in love. But seriously, it sounds amazing. You guys are glowing."

Ellie watches them intently while trying not to make it obvious that she is staring. As the conversation moves on from tropical paradises, Gavin notices the shift in her expression. It's not sadness…something more akin to reticence.

"You okay?" he asks gently.

She turns back to him, resting her chin on her hand, the flirtatious spark returning to her eyes. "Yeah. I'm just picturing you lying face-down in the water…wearing a snorkel mask."

Gavin smirks and wags a finger at her. "I see what you did there. I hate to disappoint you by shattering the image, but I'm more of a 'stay-on-the-boat-and-judge-others' type."

"Pity," she says, grinning. "You'd probably rock a wetsuit."

"You wear a wetsuit for diving, not snorkeling."

"Oh. I'm from Montana. I shouldn't be expected to know these things."

He chuckles. "Fair enough."

Ellie leans forward, the humor in her voice giving way to something quieter. "So… your fiancée. What's—"

"Ex-fiancée."

"Fair enough. What was she like?"

Gavin hesitates, eyes drifting to the window, where snowflakes lazily drift past. "She's shy. Reserved. Especially around people she doesn't know. Jules doesn't speak up much unless she really trusts someone. But…she's also warm and gentle. She loves kids, animals, and has a big heart. She even volunteers at a children's literacy center on the weekends."

Ellie nods slowly, her tone even softer now. "Not like me, then."

He looks back at her. "Not in some ways. You're…confident and bold."

"The byproduct of growing up on a ranch with two brothers."

"Maybe. But your sense of right and wrong is more than from your upbringing. You're quick to inject yourself in a situation that needs fixing."

"She doesn't do that?"

"Only if it's an argument between eight-year-olds. Jules is much better with kids than adults. She has no ego and can't understand people who put themselves before others. And she hates being the center of attention. She'll walk into a room, and nobody will notice. You walk into a room, and people *see* you."

"I thought you were going to say that they hear me."

Gavin bobs his head from side to side before winking at her. "That, too, for sure. Jules isn't like that."

"But you love her," Ellie says, her tone reflecting that it's not a question, but a test.

"I do," he replies without hesitation. "Regardless of what's happened, part of me always will. Jules is sweet and kind, and caring. That's the reason she put the ring in an envelope and wasn't around when I opened it. She didn't want to see the hurt on my face."

"Where I'm from, that's called being chicken."

"I thought that, too, at least, initially," Gavin admits, fighting to push stop on the vivid recording of that moment playing in his mind.

Ellie sits back in her chair, her fingers drumming softly against her glass of water. "She sounds like someone worth holding onto. Why won't you fight for her?"

"Because…because I can't make somebody want to be with me."

Before Ellie can reply, the waitress returns with steaming bowls of stew and fresh bread. They both eat in silence for a while, their earlier ease replaced by something heavier, more uncertain. They know each other's stories and the hurt…the heartbreak…the pain that comes with them. The question is, where do they go from here?

As the meal is being devoured, the conversation moves to less painful things than stories of love and betrayal. They talk about family, work, dreams…almost first-date kind of topics. When they finish eating and pay the check, they step back out into the cold and trudge over to the SUV.

"The inn is right around the corner," Ellie says, checking her phone's GPS. "The next address on the list is two hours away, and it's the closest one. We should start early tomorrow. Say, seven?"

"Sounds good," Gavin confirms.

"Think he's there?"

"Let's hope so. Tomorrow is the day before Christmas Eve. We're running out of time."

Ellie stares at the map on her phone. "It's a sleepy town, and the ski chalet would be a perfect place to hide."

"All three of the places left on the list are," Gavin moans. "So were the other ones we checked. Unfortunately, we won't know until we get there."

"Do you want to try one of the others instead? We can do the farthest one out and hit the closer ones on the return to Geneva."

Gavin fires up the vehicle. "Nah. At this point, the more we scratch off the list, the better. Of the three, that one is the easiest to drive to from Geneva if you have a fat old man in a red suit tied up in the back."

Ellie nods. Gavin notices that the silence between them no longer feels tense. It's somehow more…complicated. He likes this woman. She likes him. He wonders if, in a different place at a different time, something could come of that.

And somewhere between their disappointment over failed visits and the dwindling leads, an unspoken understanding between them is beginning to form. They are finding comfort in each other's company. He wouldn't have banked on that a few days ago. It's amazing how life works sometimes. Gavin only hopes that the inn has two rooms available. She is starting to erode his willpower.

Chapter Fifty-Four

KEITH MEADOWS

2 Days Until Christmas

Keith Meadows leans back in his chair. The small café in he heart of Santa's Village is completely empty this early. Tourism here is down, of course. Why would anyone want to visit this place when the main attraction isn't here? Visitors don't come to see any old Santa Claus. They can get that at any shopping mall in the States and any Christmas market in Europe. They are here to see *the* Santa Claus.

He takes a sip of his lukewarm coffee – the third cup he's had so far his morning. For a journalist, caffeine isn't a luxury so much as it's a necessity. The coffee is good, but it doesn't match the exhilaration of driving a narrative.

His latest article on Santa has been picked up internationally. Nearly every article questioning the whereabouts of Santa refers to his reporting. He has always been a big name in Washington. Now, he's becoming a household name globally.

Keith scrolls a series of new news alerts with a slow, satisfying swipe of his thumb. Every major news network is churning out breaking news headlines now, complete with grainy photos, wild speculation, and talking heads dissecting his latest exposé. They know what gets attention at Christmas, and the clicks and views that come with it.

"Santa missing? Global Christmas crisis unfolds" — CNN

"No sleigh, no sightings, no hope: The North Pole goes dark" — The Guardian

"Parents scramble to explain Santa's disappearance to kids" — NBC News

"End of an era? Father Christmas vanishes days before Christmas" — BBC

He grins. This is almost too easy. He has taken a fringe rumor, a mere whisper of concern from the frigid wastelands of Lapland, and helped it blossom into an international crisis with all the elegance of a controlled explosion. And Keith is the one who lit the match.

The key, he knows, isn't simply the reporting of facts. That happens every day, and any idiot can do it. In the modern age, it's about getting traction. That's what makes a Coldplay Kiss Cam video or people dumping ice water over their heads years ago go viral. Facts, on their own, don't earn clicks. They need a narrative to generate emotion because feelings trump evidence every single time. Outrage will always take center stage over nuance. The moment he framed the story not as a curiosity but as a *cover-up*, the internet did the rest.

A globetrotting Santa Claus pretending he's the real deal as he meets a sick child in St. Louis. Fine. That same Santa going missing less than a week before Christmas? Better. A conspiracy by everyone involved to hide the truth of his disappearance, or kidnapping, so as to not cause a panic? Bingo.

"You want widespread reach on an article or news clip?" he had once asked a junior producer when he first took over his role as a senior White House correspondent. "Don't ask what people believe. Ask what they're afraid of. Then hand it to them, dressed like fact."

And now? Now the world is afraid. Parents are whispering to each other at school pick-up lines as they get ready for Christmas break. Senators in the U.S. are posting to social media to demand answers. Religious leaders are issuing statements, with the Christian ones stumbling to explain that the holiday is about Jesus Christ, not a mythical man living with reindeer and elves at the North Pole. Even the White House has been boxed into silence. That must be driving MacKenzie Walsh crazy. Keith is willing to bet she'd much rather be talking about recess appointments right now.

Keith glances at his phone. The number of reads on his most recent article is insane – now in the tens of millions and climbing. The number of shares is topping even the most salacious celebrity scandals. Hashtags on social media are trending in multiple languages.

#WhereIsSanta
#SantaTruth
#ChristmasCoverup

His inbox is exploding with interview requests and network offers. Even the click-hungry and ever-skeptical Ben Haverson has gotten with the program. His email explained that two major cable news networks want to book him on a primetime show, and a popular podcast is begging for an interview. That raises his profile, and with it, the number of fans he has who will read every article he writes.

Keith closes his eyes so he can savor this moment. It's the sweet, intoxicating taste of vindication. Sure, some people will call him the Grinch, just as they did last year. The polite critics will call him a buzzkill, while the more aggressive ones label him a villain and surround that proclamation with a plethora of curse words.

But truth doesn't care about public opinion. And, while this is to a degree personal, Keith has been careful not to characterize this crisis as that. People needed to stop lying to their kids, plain and simple. The world needs to grow up.

A red-suited figure passes the window, and for a half-second, Keith tenses—only to realize it was one of the actor stand-ins milling around the village, looking more lost than festive. The traditional outfit is the biggest giveaway. The Santa that captivated the world last year looked like a Scandinavian toy maker. The only time he wore anything resembling the Santa outfit most Americans know was in Italy.

"Imposter," Keith mutters aloud to the empty café, reaching for the remainder of his coffee. "There is no Santa. This is what happens when fairy tales get too comfortable."

Children aren't lining up for pictures with him. They know he isn't the man they saw on television last year. He's a fraud. Now, Keith will expose as a fraud the St. Nick that everyone is beginning to believe in, as well. Twenty-four hours. That's all the time that separates him from the realization of a dream and a lifetime of fame.

Santa's disappearance isn't just news. It's the story of a generation, and it will forever be known that Keith Meadows wrote every word of it. The world is changing, and myth needs to change with it. He did what Congresswoman Camilla Guzman couldn't do when she tried to ban public depictions of Santa Claus. He is going to shatter the belief.

Stowe Bessette and Wyatt Huffman will certainly have something to say about that. Those two are true believers spinning tales about Christmas magic. Part of him hopes they find Santa Claus…or at least find out who took him. That will be yet another wrinkle to the story.

Keith tilts his head, letting a cold smirk tug at the corner of his mouth. This is the story that will change everything for him. And it will all be because Ben Haverson insisted on another big story because of what Stowe and Wyatt provided last year.

"Keith Meadows," a familiar voice says from behind him.

Speak of the devil….

Chapter Fifty-Five

WYATT HUFFMAN

Stowe and Wyatt find Keith Meadows exactly where they expected him to be –enjoying a coffee and stoking the fire as the world burns. Maybe that's a little extreme, but there are a lot of nervous people tuning into what's happening in tiny Rovaniemi, Finland. Wyatt gently grasps her arm.

"Stowe, what are you going to do?"

"Rip his head off."

"I like your energy…but that may not be the best approach to deal with this moron," Wyatt says, not having a better alternative to offer.

"Okay, you're right. I'll tone it down."

She rips the door open and doesn't hesitate to turn and angle toward the reporter's table. Wyatt knows that walk. It's her angry walk, and nothing good will happen when she reaches her target.

"Keith Meadows," she snaps, storming up to him. "You despicable piece of shit!"

"That was toning it down?" Wyatt mumbles as he comes up alongside her.

"Yup."

The reporter's trademark smirk is already forming as he studies her face. "Stowe Bessette. Good morning to you, too. I was wondering when you and your trusty sidekick Wyatt would show back up in Rovaniemi. Have you enjoyed your travels?"

"What the hell do you think you're doing?" she asks, ignoring his question.

Keith gestures around him theatrically. "Having breakfast. Oh, and reporting the news. On-location. I came by to visit Santa Claus, only it appears he isn't here. But you and Wyatt are. And the FBI, if you can believe that. You've got to admit, the irony is delicious."

"I've read your articles. You aren't reporting the news. You're trying to *kill* something that millions of people believe in."

Keith folds his arms. "Wrong, Miss Bessette. You have spent the past two years trying to convince the world that Santa Claus…your Santa Claus…is somehow real. I'm trying to *free* them from that comforting lie. There's a difference."

"You know it's not a lie," Stowe shoots back, her voice rising. "You were there last year. You *saw* what Santa did. You watched him bring happiness and joy to others every step of the way. You saw the magic."

"What I saw," Keith coolly states, "was a clever production that would make a reality television show franchise blush with envy. It was all smoke and mirrors, but you still managed to get the world believing he's a saint with sleigh bells. But he's just a symbol that people like *you* keep propping up because you're too scared of what happens when he's gone."

Her jaw clenches. "You want to talk fear? You're the one exploiting it. People are scared because they feel like they're losing a part of themselves…something that makes the holiday special and gives them hope."

"And that 'hope,'" Keith says, leaning closer, "is entirely built on fantasy that sets kids up to believe in a magical fix for every problem. It makes adults nostalgic for a past that never really existed, and children dependent on getting gifts that parents can't afford. You know what belief in Santa really does? It teaches disappointment. It teaches them that miracles come from strangers, not effort. That they're only good if they're rewarded with gifts."

Stowe's eyes blaze. "That's not what he professes! Not at all."

Keith smirks. He's gotten under her skin, and the worst part is, he knows it. Stowe always tried to keep an even keel when she was in Washington. She has seen how becoming overly emotional can be weaponized against someone. She wasn't always successful then…and she isn't now.

"If Santa Claus is so magical…" Keith leans toward her, lowering his voice. "Where is he, Stowe? You and Wyatt have been looking for him for almost…what? A week now? Tell me – did you find him?"

Stowe hesitates for only a couple of seconds, but it's more than long enough for the seasoned reporter used to sparring with the White House press secretary while cameras are rolling.

"That's what I thought. I'd say good luck with the rest of your search," Keith purrs, glancing at his watch. "But I think you're about out of time. Tomorrow is Christmas Eve, and when I'm standing in that plaza there with no Santa Claus to be found, the world will finally see he isn't the epitome of Christmas magic. It was all make-believe."

To this point, Wyatt has let Stowe march on this crusade by herself. She wanted this confrontation. His money is always on her to win any argument she engages in. She's smart and tough. Those are two of the traits near the top of the long list of reasons why he loves her.

That isn't the case this time. Keith just took her to the woodshed. Wyatt is about to respond when Stowe turns away, her fists clenched at her sides. She brushes past him, not looking back.

"Tell your girlfriend not to bring a candy cane to a knife fight the next time she wants to tangle with me, Wyatt."

He looks down at the jaded reporter. "Enjoy the moment, Keith. Like the Christmas holiday, it won't last forever."

Chapter Fifty-Six

SAINT NICHOLAS

The back door is yanked open, and Skut and Kram escort Santa through the gourmet kitchen to the living area of the main house. The two mountains of men are nearly expressionless. He can understand why. It was their job to watch him and ensure there was no interaction with Fallon. They failed, not that there was ever much chance of them succeeding in that mission.

The warmth of the chalet's grand living room stands in stark contrast to the cold suspicion in the air. Trent is seated on the leather sofa, a steaming mug of coffee cradled in one hand, his eyes fixed on the flickering fireplace. He doesn't turn his head when Santa is ushered in and stops ten feet behind him.

"I'm surprised you brought me in here," St. Nick says, his tone calm but cautious. "I figured you'd prefer to keep me tucked away in the guesthouse."

Trent still doesn't immediately look at him. "Against my instructions, you've taken it upon yourself to meet Fallon. There's no point in hiding you from her anymore."

Skut and Kram pull Santa by the arms to the front of the sofa so that Trent doesn't need to crane his neck or turn his body. The man nods, and the two beefy guards step back to the walls like shadows fading into the natural wood siding.

"You had one rule – no contact with my daughter," Trent continues, his gaze now snapping to St. Nick, ice behind his eyes. "I was crystal-clear about that rule. I was crystal-clear about the consequences. Yet, you still broke it."

"Yes," Santa said, nodding slightly and folding his hands in front of him. "I did."

"Why?"

"I needed to learn the truth. I have to admit, kidnapping me is a rash thing to do to prove a point."

A heavy silence falls between them, broken only by the pop and hiss of the burning logs. Trent glares at him…or through him.

"Do you have children, Santa?" Trent snaps. "No, of course you don't. You have *no idea* what it's like to be there every day, doing everything for her. Then one day, she looks you in the eye and—"

His voice cracks, and Santa's eyes soften. "You asked her who she loved more, you or me. And she said me."

Trent's jaw tightens. His eyes brim with a volatile mixture of fury and grief. "Did she tell you that?"

"No."

"Then how could you know?"

"Because I'm Santa Claus."

Trent shoots out of his seat, spilling his coffee in the process. He moves right in front of St. Nick and points a finger at his face. "You are not Santa Claus! Santa Claus is a myth. He doesn't exist."

"You're angry," Santa replies evenly, unfazed by the aggressive action. "And I can't say I blame you. With everything you've gone through, hearing that out of Fallon's mouth must have been unbearable."

Trent turns his back to him, moves to the fireplace, and picks up the poker from the black, wrought iron stand. He stabs the logs, causing them to pop and shoot off embers. The silence stretches again, and Santa notices the white-knuckled death grip Trent has on the tool. He is doing everything in his power to keep his anger under control.

"Fallon told you what happened?"

"She did."

"Did you tell her why you're here?"

"No," Santa replied. "What I do know is that she doesn't remember the comment she made to you."

Trent glances at St. Nick and narrows his eyes before replacing the firestoker. "Why not?"

"She's a child." Santa's voice is quieter now. "But this isn't really about who she loves more. It never was. You're trying to find a place where you don't feel rejected. Your wife rejected you after your son died. You believe God rejected you because he took your son away. And now you believe Fallon is rejecting you. Her comment wounded you, but that has more to do with your pain than her lack of love."

"She forgot the moment," Trent says, his voice barely audible. "But I didn't. How could she love a myth more than her own father?"

"After your wife left, you changed."

"You don't know that!" Trent snaps, turning back to face Santa.

"I do. You were the world to her…and you still are. But you've been miserable, and I'm a symbol of joy. She said that because she longs for a happier time when your family was…a family. She misses those times. She misses her brother."

"What happened was a tragic accident," Trent seethes, "one that cost me *everything*. Fallon is all I have left. I am not going to lose her to a man pretending to be magical!"

Santa doesn't respond with fear or anger. He doesn't answer with words. He simply bows his head.

"You broke the rules," Trent goes on, breathing hard. "You were warned. No contact. You crossed the line."

He turns toward the silent giants flanking the room. "Skut. Kram. I gave you your instructions before we arrived in Finland. That time has arrived. You know what to do."

The bodyguards move forward in sync, slow and deliberate. Trent turns to face Santa, a sinister smile creeping across his lips.

"I may not be able to kill the myth of Santa Claus," he says, his voice like iron, "but I can kill the man who wears the suit."

A loud dragging sound echoes from the hallway. Everyone turns to see Fallon waddling into the room, a determined look on her small face as she lugs a red sled nearly twice her size. A big red bow is taped to the front, flopping with each step.

She stops just inside the room, breathing heavily. "But he *is* Santa!"

Skut and Kram pause mid-step. Trent stares at his daughter, speechless. Fallon turns to her father with pleading eyes.

"He visited me to give me a Christmas wish."

She drops the sled with a thud and marches up to Santa, hugging his leg. Trent looks at his daughter – his fiery reason for breathing – and something in his anger begins to crack.

"Please don't hurt him."

The room falls deathly still. Trent's hands are balled into fists at his sides. His mouth opens, but no words come. Even the fire seems to go quiet. Skut looks over at Kram, who is riveted at the sight of the sleigh resting on the hardwood floor.

"It can't be…it's not possible. Is that…?"

"*Schneefeuer.*"

"What?" Fallon asks, turning her head up at Santa.

"It means *Snowfire,*" Kram says. "It was the sleigh I built when I wasn't much older than you are now, Fallon. I thought it was gone forever."

"Not gone," Santa assures him. "Just misplaced."

Kram blinks, confusion flashing across his face. Even Skut looks confused. "How? How did it get here?"

"I'm Santa Claus," he simply replies, as if it explains everything. And somehow, it does. "The cookies I baked my first night here are called 'Wish Cookies.' You snuck two of them when you thought I wasn't watching."

"I didn't make a wish," Kram argues.

"Not out loud, but you thought about *Schneefeuer* and how much you missed that sleigh. I simply granted your wish to see it again."

Trent's restraint is shattered. "I *am done* with this! You think this is a game? You manipulate my daughter, you twist her memories, and now you're corrupting my own people? You *are not* Santa Claus!"

"But he is!" his daughter shouts.

"Be quiet, Fallon!"

Fallon looks up at him, frightened, still clinging to Santa's leg. "Daddy! Please stop!"

But Trent doesn't stop. His face grows redder. He points at Santa with a shaking finger.

"Skut. Kram. Take him out of here. Now! Drag him back to the guesthouse or wherever else he *won't* be seen again."

Skut looks to Kram, who doesn't move. He hesitates, looking back at his boss for guidance.

"That was an order!"

Kram straightens his shoulders and thrusts out his chin. "I won't do it."

Trent's face contorts in disbelief. "You *work for me*."

"No," Kram says, his eyes never leaving Santa. "I protect people. I protect you. I won't hurt anybody who doesn't deserve it."

The silence that follows is deafening. Skut seems willing to wait to see how this plays out, unwilling to take on his almost equal-sized partner. Trent feels outnumbered, and that has only managed to enrage him further.

Kram turns to Fallon. "That sled is something I built in my childhood. I never even used it once, but I want to now. Would you like to go sledding with me?"

"Okay, Kram!" she chirps, beaming.

"Please, call me *Alaric*. That's my real name."

"Alaric," she repeats, testing it out. "I really like that name."

"Thank you. I haven't used it for a long time."

She runs over and throws her arms around him in a quick hug and then darts for the stairs. "What about you, Santa?"

"I'll be fine. You two go outside and have fun."

"Okay! I'll be right back! I'm gonna put on my snow pants and get my coat."

The sound of her footsteps fades up the stairs. Trent stands there, breathing heavily, glaring at his guard. Alaric meets Trent's stare. The power dynamic in this Swiss chalet has completely shifted.

All four heads turn when the sound of shuffling on the porch commands their attention. Without so much as a knock, the front door swings open, and a well-dressed woman storms in. She stops when she has them in full view before looking around. After a moment, her eyes settle on Santa Claus before shifting one final time.

"My God, Trent…what have you done?"

Chapter Fifty-Seven

STOWE BESSETTE

Stowe needs to walk. The air is sharp, and the cold pinches at her cheeks, much like it does on the mountain in Vermont. Home. She almost wishes she were back there, enjoying the holiday without the stress of having to defend Christmas again. The first two times, they had Santa to do that. This time, it looks like they are on their own.

She picks up her gait, needing the brisk movement to burn off the tension she feels in her shoulders. Stowe is not as outdoorsy as many of the residents in her state, but nature always seems to help her disconnect, relax, come to peace with her situation, and refocus. With the snow on the ground and the tall trees around her, this almost feels like winter in Vermont.

She needs the crunch of snow beneath her boots and the distraction of scenery to ride out the emotional storm raging inside her. Keith Meadows struck a nerve deeper than she expected. It wasn't just his smug deconstruction of Santa Claus or his arrogant assault on Christmas – it was that he got to her. She let him get under her skin. That's what stings the most.

Stowe hears the soft tread of boots behind her. Wyatt is trailing at a respectful distance, far enough not to intrude, but close enough to know he is there to support her. He always seems to naturally understand when to be near and when to hold back. That's one of the many reasons she loves him so much.

They've come a long way. When they first collided in that house office building corridor, she couldn't stand him. He was too much like Bobby Sinclair, the man who broke her heart. It was during the trip to this very village that she opened her heart to him. That, maybe more than anything she has ever done, changed her life for the better.

Stowe can't remember the last time she was this angry. Maybe once or twice in her life. She was devastated and angry when her parents died. She misses them dearly and lives each day with the knowledge that they are watching over her. Sometimes, she gets signs. Blue was their favorite color, and whenever she spots a blue jay or notices a blue object that otherwise looks out of place, she knows they are there with her.

Her anger at Bobby was far different. The pain ripped her heart in two when she found the man she thought she loved in bed with another woman. Betrayal is the worst feeling imaginable, so she knows what Ellie is going through. Meeting and falling in love with Wyatt helped heal Stowe's trauma. What will heal the trauma of failing Santa and allowing a charlatan to ruin Christmas for millions of people?

She passes Santa's Office without glancing up at it. Joulumaantie Road stretches gently before her, and she crosses it without a second thought. The sound of laughter and the whine of engines drift from the snowmobile park to her left. Families are lining up, bundled in winter coats, scarves, and hats, to take laps riding the machines. It's not like they can visit Santa. He isn't here, and she couldn't find him.

It isn't until she reaches the wooden fence that borders the reindeer enclosure that she stops, and Wyatt comes up alongside her. He doesn't say anything at first, content instead to let her speak when she's ready, without pushing or nagging or pleading, and definitely without telling her that she's overreacting. Wyatt won't offer weak platitudes that it will all be okay. At this point, she doesn't see how it will be. He probably doesn't either.

"Sorry."

Wyatt shakes his head. "Don't be."

"I lost it back there."

"You didn't lose it. Losing it would have been stabbing him in the eye with an icicle."

"He would have deserved it."

"No doubt, but that would only have added to our problems. Keith Meadows is a snake. He turned your passion for Christmas and desire to find Santa Claus against you. He played on your emotions because that's what he does."

"I still let him get under my skin."

They watch a group of children inside the enclosure feed a pair of reindeer, both bending their antlers gracefully to nibble treats from mittened hands. The parents are intent on standing back and enjoying the moment, with one capturing it on video to preserve the memory. It's a sweet, innocent moment that those families will cherish forever.

"He's a White House reporter. He gets paid to get under people's skin, Stowe. If I learned anything from watching him last year, it's that he pokes until people bleed. The fact that you're bleeding just means you care more than most."

Stowe looks at him, tears now streaming down her cheeks. "I feel like we let Santa down."

Wyatt nods, and she buries her face in his coat. "Yeah, me too."

"What are we going to do?"

He inhales sharply. "Not go down without a fight."

"How?"

She turns her head up to look at him, and he holds her face in his gloved hands. "We get with Johan, Hannah, and Julie and come up with something. Santa put us all together for a reason. We have to trust that he knows what he's doing and fight back the best way we know how."

She smiles weakly, wiping under her eyes with her sleeve. "With hope and cocoa?"

He grins. "Exactly. We should see if Aurielle can bring us some of hers."

They walk in silence again, this time back toward the Christmas House. The Village administrators let Stowe, Wyatt, Julie, Johan, and Hanna use the same space Ellie and

Gavin did. There is more than enough room for the five of them to hang out and brainstorm.

Warm light spills through the frosted windows of the secluded cabin. Inside, Johan and Hannah are on the couch, legs curled beneath them, mugs in hand. Julie sits cross-legged on the floor with a steaming cup and a notebook in her lap. Aurielle is standing over them with a tray, causing Wyatt and Stowe to smile at each other.

"It looks like she beat us here."

"Christmas is all about small miracles," Stowe muses.

When they enter the cozy sanctuary, the warmth wraps around them like a blanket. They each hug Aurielle, who already has their piping-hot cocoa ready. How she knew…well, Stowe is going to file that in the forever unanswered questions repository. If there is any room in it at this point.

Johan looks up and notices Stowe's face instantly. He sets his mug down. "Is everything okay?"

Wyatt answers before she can. "Not really. We had a run-in with Keith Meadows. It didn't go well."

"Who?" Hanna asks. "Oh, right, the moron reporter that hates Christmas."

Stowe turns to Wyatt and lets him handle the explanation of what happened during the run-in with Keith Meadows in the village coffee shop. Julie raises her eyebrows after hearing how angry Stowe was. She hasn't seen that side of her before. It's not something she is proud of.

"Stowe, you don't strike me as the type that lets jerks like this Keith Meadows guy get the better of you," Hanna concludes.

"I didn't handle that confrontation well," Stowe admits. "It's Christmas, and I have loved this holiday—"

"Forever," Wyatt interjects.

"I got emotional, and that gave him what he wanted." Stowe sits down beside Johan, rubbing her temples and closing her eyes. "Aurielle, if this is one of Santa's games, you need to come clean now. Keith Meadows is intent on doing real damage to Christmas."

The chief elf grimaces. "I assure you, it isn't."

"Then, who was giving us the red cards in Paris?" Wyatt asks. "Who sent them to Johan, Hanna, and Julie? Was it you?"

"It wasn't."

Stowe still isn't sure she believes the young woman. It has all the hallmarks of Santa, but if he was taken against his will…. There is no plausible explanation.

"Well, then maybe Santa wasn't kidnapped at all."

"We know that he was, though. We saw the evidence. Ellie and Agent Scrooge are convinced of it."

"Keith is going to hold a presser in the plaza tomorrow morning and show the world that Santa isn't here. He's going to cause a panic with parents and shatter the dreams of millions of children unless we stop him."

Julie reaches over and puts a hand gently on her arm. "Stowe, do you think the children give a damn what some grumpy cynic says in a press conference? Christmas isn't a thesis to be defended or a myth to be debunked. It's a feeling. A shared understanding that kindness, belief, and generosity still matter. And people *want* to believe in that."

"She's right," Johan confirms. "Meadows isn't the enemy. Neither is the media. Apathy is."

And just like that, the fire is back in Stowe's chest. It's not anger this time, but resolve. She doesn't know what form their fight will take yet. But she knows one thing: The spirit of Christmas can't be defended with logic.

Stowe nods at their newest friend. "So, how do we fight apathy?"

Wyatt leans forward, placing his steepled hands in front of his mouth. "I have an idea. We might not know the first thing about combating press insanity, but I know one person we can ask who does, for sure."

Chapter Fifty-Eight

WYATT HUFFMAN

Wyatt can be cryptic when he wants to be. Despite Stowe's pleading, he doesn't tell her who he's calling. She only realizes it when he turns on the speaker and sets his smartphone on his knee. Another pang of jealousy hits her. It's all over Stowe's face. Nothing ever happened with the woman and never will. She really should get over it.

The line crackles before MacKenzie Walsh's clipped, no-nonsense voice comes through. "Wyatt! Merry—well, I suppose we're past holiday pleasantries. How's the search? Are you calling with good news?"

He sighs heavily. "I wish we were. You're on speaker with Stowe."

"Hi, Stowe."

"Hi, Mac," she says, quickly sticking her tongue out at Wyatt to his amusement. "We're back in Santa's Village. The whole trip to Paris…well, other than meeting some old friends and making a new one, it felt like a wild goose chase."

Wyatt glances at Johan, Hanna, and Julie and offers a weak smile before lowering his eyes. He's grateful to have met them, but would be lying if he didn't expect the red cards to lead straight to Santa.

"At least you got something out of it. Outside of that, it was a complete bust?"

Stowe explains everything that happened in Paris, from the red cards appearing out of thin air to the chance encounters that they led to. She goes on to explain what they learned about the lead on Santa's kidnapper and how Wyatt's sister and the FBI agent are tracking that down in Switzerland.

Wyatt admits that it's a long shot that Santa is at any of those locations, and even if he is, the odds of getting him back to Finland in time for the press conference are remote. He explains that he thought the cards would lead to something, but never finishes the thought as his voice trails off.

"There is a chance that we missed something, but if we did, I don't know where," Stowe concedes.

"And there is no sign at all of Santa Claus?"

"No. Outside of getting the cards, not even a whisper."

"Did he deliver them…or, arrange it?"

"We have no idea. We asked Aurielle, but she insists it wasn't her. Of course, she could be lying."

There is a pause. "One of Santa's elves lying…that would be a first. Not that I have much interaction with elves. On the other hand, I know a lot of liars. Speaking of which, what about Keith Meadows? Have you run across the slime trail he leaves in his wake yet?"

"That's actually why we're calling," Stowe says, shifting her position on the sofa. "We did. It didn't go well. He's planning a Christmas Eve press conference that will go out live on all networks internationally."

"That sounds about right," MacKenzie moans.

"He's going to destroy what little belief people have left in Christmas, Mac," Wyatt interjects, sticking his tongue back out at Stowe. "It will ruin the experience for millions of kids. We need to find a way to stop him."

MacKenzie lets out a dry chuckle, tinged with fatigue. "You want to stop a journalist with a grudge and a god complex, in the middle of a media circus, on the most emotionally charged night of the year? Don't think for a second that I don't share that thought every day. Guys, you worked on Capitol Hill. You know better than most that you can't control the press."

"I'm not asking to control them. I want to... I don't know. Redirect them. Reframe the story. Something."

"Any ideas?" Stowe asks, picking up for Wyatt.

"Yeah. Find Santa."

"Other than that? You deal with the press every day. You must have some tools in your bag that we can use."

The White House communications director is a senior official responsible for developing and managing the overall messaging strategy of the president and the White House. The role involves coordinating with the press office, speechwriters, digital teams, and other executive branch departments to ensure consistent and effective communication with the public, the media, and other stakeholders.

Anybody who succeeds in the job has strong political judgment and strategic communication expertise, for starters. They also must be able to manage a crisis, display leadership, and, most importantly for this conversation, have a lot of experience in media relations.

"The best advice is to avoid getting yourself in their crosshairs to begin with," she admits. "That's why I didn't want the White House anywhere near this. But, since that ship has already sailed for you two, the best you can do is manipulate."

"Manipulate?" Stowe asks.

"Look, I'm not proud of using every trick I've learned in this job, but I can tell you this much: Keith Meadows is the kind of man who thrives on attention. The moment you try to silence him, he'll spin it into martyrdom."

"That didn't work for him last year," Stowe muses, thinking of the months of abuse he took in the aftermath of his actions at the St. Louis children's hospital.

"Which makes him even more dangerous now. This is redemptive for him, and he won't pull punches because of it."

"So I've learned," Stowe mutters.

"Trust me," MacKenzie continues, "that conference tomorrow will go from spectacle to crusade. He wants to be the guy who 'exposed' your Santa as a complete fraud. If you try to take that moment away from him, he'll light himself on fire just to get the headline."

Wyatt scowls. Stowe closes her eyes, likely fighting the same helplessness creeping in that he is. "So, what am I supposed to do? Just let him go on national television and torch Christmas in front of the whole world?"

"No," Mac says firmly. "You make his argument irrelevant. You give people something bigger, something real. Keith is betting everything on doubt. You need to go all in and show them hope instead."

It's a nice thought. Wyatt looks at Johan, Hanna, and Julie before setting his eyes on Stowe. She doesn't look overly enthusiastic about fighting that battle unless she knows she can win it.

"Will that be enough?" Wyatt asks.

"I don't know, but it's the only card you have left to play. Just know something going in – Keith Meadows isn't just a cynic. He's cruel. He's made a career of tearing down people and ideas and calling it journalism. He will *not* fight fair."

"I know," Stowe whispers.

"I have to head out of here. I will see—"

She stops.

"What?" Wyatt asks.

"I will be watching you tomorrow. Best of luck to you both."

They say their goodbyes, and Wyatt ends the call, tossing the phone on the cushion next to him. He pushes deeper into the back cushion and closes his eyes, feeling helpless to do anything.

"She works at the White House?" Julie asks.

"Yeah, MacKenzie Walsh is the president's White House communications director."

"That's impressive," Johan says.

"It sounds like an important job," Julie adds.

"It is, but you couldn't pay me enough to do it. Most of her job is crafting messages. MacKenzie is brilliant at it. I don't know where to start."

"Stowe...you've always known December 25th isn't just a date," Johan chimes in. "It's a belief, and because of that, you have more Christmas spirit in your little finger than most people have in their whole bodies. If you can remind people of that – really remind them – then Keith's stupid little press conference will be nothing more than static."

"I appreciate the kind words, Johan. I do. But you don't know who we are up against. Keith Meadows is conniving in a way I could never hope to be. Going up against him in his arena is hopeless."

"It's not hopeless," Hanna says. "But it *is* war, just the kind that doesn't use bullets or bombs. Don't fight him head-on. Use a different approach."

"She's right. If this Keith guy is just creating doubt and spectacle for headlines, we can win by giving the media a better story."

Stowe doesn't respond to Johan or Hanna. With a blank look on her face, she stares at the logs burning in the fireplace. The fire is an appropriate metaphor. If they don't find a way to derail this press conference, she fears that is what will happen to Christmas – it will go up in flames until the only thing left is ash.

"What story do we have that hasn't been told?" Wyatt asks, looking at Julie, who shrugs.

"Don't look at me. I'm a third-grade teacher, and I don't do public speaking."

"We have a story," Stowe says, slowly nodding as she stares at the dancing flames in the fireplace. "We have his story. His message. We need to tell that story louder than Keith tells his."

Wyatt nods. It's not the best plan, but a good one today is better than a perfect one that's too late. Tomorrow is Christmas Eve, and the world will be watching this small city in Finland. And regardless of whether Santa comes back in time, he and Stowe are going to make damn sure they remember what he stands for. Maybe it will have an impact, and maybe it won't. The world will determine that. But unless Ellie and Gavin work a miracle, it's all they have.

Chapter Fifty-Nine

SAINT NICHOLAS

Trent gawks, his mouth hanging open at the sight of the lovely woman standing in the middle of the chalet. The awkward stillness drags on for what feels like hours. Santa doesn't say anything. It isn't his place, at least right now. This is between them, and Trent will find his words once he gets over the shock of seeing her again.

"Geneviève?"

She remains silent. Trent blinks, still stunned into silence. Santa takes in the woman. She is tall and graceful, carrying herself like someone who has learned how to shoulder pain with dignity. Her eyes are sharp, but there is a weariness in them.

"Mommy!" Fallon screeches, coming down the stairs, racing over, and throwing her arms around her mother's legs. Geneviève bends down and cups her daughter's face in her hands.

"Hello, sweetie."

Trent's voice cracks as he speaks. "What…how did you know we were…what are you doing here?"

She rubs her daughter's back before looking up, flicking her eyes past Trent and toward the man standing just behind him.

She points. "*He* brought me."

Santa Claus stands near the fire, his expression patient and timeless. He's not surprised to see her, but isn't being smug about her arrival. St. Nick is just present in a way only he can be.

Trent looks between them, confused. "How? You brought her here?"

"I did."

"How?" Trent demands. "You haven't had access to a phone or computer…and how would you even know who she is or where to reach her?"

"I'm *Santa Claus*."

"See?" Fallon says. "He's Santa Claus!"

Geneviève reaches into her coat and pulls out a red envelope. She holds it up, allowing the light to catch the gold ink. "This was delivered to me in Paris. You *kidnapped* Santa?"

"No, silly! Santa came to deliver my Christmas wish!"

Geneviève looks down at her daughter and smiles. "Fallon, I need to talk to your father for a little bit. Adult stuff. Is that okay?"

Fallon nods enthusiastically, then turns to Kram. "We're gonna go sledding. Come on, Alaric!"

They disappear out the door together, Fallon skipping with the big, lumbering man struggling to keep up. Skut excuses himself to give them some privacy. He's fairly sure the enormous bodyguard isn't too far away.

Geneviève's face tenses, but her voice remains level. "What is this, Trent? Why would you do this? Is this a way to get back at me?"

"Why would I care about punishing you? You walked out on me, remember? It's not like you would even care!"

Santa steps forward, his hands clasped before him. "What Trent did had nothing to do with you. His actions, however misguided, were out of love for Fallon and his relationship with her."

Trent opens his mouth, then closes it again. He turns away, running a hand through his hair as he stares at the fire. "I don't even know what to say."

"Then don't talk," Santa says gently. "Just listen."

Santa looks at both of them now – two parents, their souls scarred by overwhelming grief, standing feet apart but miles away.

"You lost your son. It was a tragic accident that caused unspeakable pain," Santa gently says. "And instead of leaning on each other, you leaned away. You retreated into your own sorrow, built walls…wore masks. You tried to be strong *alone*, when the strength you both truly needed was standing right beside you the whole time.

"You didn't want to hurt each other with your pain," Santa continues after neither of them refutes his words. "So, you buried it. But in the silence, resentment grew. Misunderstanding grew. Anger grew. You—"

"Our son died because Trent wasn't watching him!"

"You know that isn't true. You know what I wrote you is the truth, and that's why you're here now. Your husband got distracted for a moment, and a moment was all it took. It could have just as easily happened to you. Passing the blame won't bring him back."

Geneviève swallows hard, her gaze locked on the floor.

"And the one who needed you both most – Fallon – got lost in the middle. She didn't blame you for what happened, Trent," Santa says, stopping him with a look. "Nor does she blame you for being upset and angry, Geneviève. But she *felt* the pain of the accident. She sensed the cold and distance that grew between you two. She felt her family falling apart like pages being torn from her favorite Christmas book."

She steps closer. Her voice, when it comes, is quiet. "Santa is right. Everything he wrote in that card is right. I blamed you. Or at least…I thought I did. I told myself I did. But the truth is, I was angry at everything. At the world. At God. At the sky for letting it happen. I needed someone to blame – and you were there."

Trent turns toward her, his jaw tight. "I blamed myself."

"I know," she whispers. "That's what makes what I did so wrong…and what hurts the most."

"You were both broken emotionally," Santa interjects. "Instead of reaching for each other, you turned away."

Tears begin pouring down Trent's face. "I lost our son—and then I lost *you*, too. I miss him every single day."

"So do I."

For a long moment, neither moves. Time seems to stand still. Finally, Trent takes a shaky breath. "We have…a lot to talk about."

Geneviève nods. "Yeah. We do. Santa? What was Fallon's Christmas wish?"

He smiles. "For her mommy to forgive her daddy. For her daddy to forgive himself. Most of all, to have her family back."

Tears begin flowing down both their faces. But Santa doesn't see anger or even pain in their eyes anymore. He sees understanding. He sees hope. And with both comes the promise of a brighter future.

"I don't know how we fix this," Trent admits. "So much has happened."

"We don't have to fix it all today," his wife says softly. "But we can start by *trying*. And maybe…maybe remembering how much we still love our daughter. And each other."

Santa tilts his head slightly. After all these years, he has come to understand people. He knows their hope and dreams, their pain and emotional baggage, and most of all, what the heart really wants. That's how he notices the spark in Trent's eyes when he looks at his wife…really looks at her, and for the first time in a long while, sees the woman he fell in love with. The one he built a life with. The one who stood beside him through the best and worst of everything until that tragic day.

"I don't even know how to begin to thank you. What you did…bringing her here, helping us talk again…it's more than I deserved. But I have to ask…" Trent hesitates. "After everything I did. Can you forgive me?"

Santa studies the man in front of him. Once hard and angry and bitter at the world, he has now cracked wide open, showing his vulnerability. It isn't a plea for mercy. It is heartfelt regret and yearning for forgiveness. Santa nods.

"I already have, Trent. But forgiveness is only the beginning of this journey. The real challenge is *what you do now*. You've taken the first step. The next ones…well, they matter even more. Reconnect with your wife. Continue loving your daughter. Be present. Be kind. And be patient."

The words land softly but powerfully, as if a weight has been lifted from Trent's shoulders that he didn't even realize he'd been carrying.

"I want to be a family again," Geneviève says, her voice low. "Like we were before. We were good. I loved that life. I miss it."

"Love doesn't vanish," Santa interjects one final time. "It gets buried. It breaks. But it *can* be put back together if you're willing to try. If you both are."

Trent nods slowly. "I am."

St. Nick takes a step back, his expression softening. "Family is the most important thing, Trent. *Family*. Don't ever forget that."

With a twinkle in his eye and a nod, he turns and heads for the back door that leads to the guesthouse. There is still so much to do and so little time to accomplish it in. When he reaches the kitchen, he can't resist stopping and looking back at the pair, who are now embracing in the center of the living area.

"Oh," he says, glancing over his shoulder. "Please tell Fallon I have made good on my promise to deliver her Christmas wish. Tell her that I'll be watching her."

"We'll let her know," Geneviève says, before looking up at her husband. "How will he do that?"

Trent stares into his wife's beautiful eyes. "Simple. He's Santa Claus."

Chapter Sixty

SPECIAL AGENT GAVIN KINNAIRD

The mountain road winds like a ribbon through towering pines and jagged rock, flanked by snowbanks. This is not like driving in Virginia. It isn't even close to a winter trip to the Appalachian Mountains. This is the Alps, and Gavin is grateful for the snow tires the vehicle is equipped with. They are required in France and Germany this time of year, and although there is no equivalent Swiss law, the government does require cars to be "roadworthy." To the car rental company, that means snow tires.

That doesn't mean the agent doesn't have a death grip on the steering wheel. His knuckles turned pale white as their SUV made the climb up here, much to Ellie's amusement. It's easy for her to think he's being dramatic – she isn't the one who's driving, and he's betting her neck of the Montana countryside is about as flat as Virginia.

Just ahead, nestled in a clearing, emerges a sprawling chalet constructed with weathered stone, wood beams, and a steep roof to shed the mountain snow. Smoke is curling from the chimney like a welcome flag. That's a good sign. They at least know that somebody is home.

"I think this is it," Ellie says, moving closer to the windshield.

Gavin pulls into the gravel driveway and catches movement in his peripheral vision. "Whoa—!"

He brakes hard, forcing the burly SUV to slide to a halt just as a red wooden sled comes rocketing down the steep hillside to their right. It shoots across the driveway and skids along the gravel until it crashes to a stop when it hits the snowbank on the other side. A large man, bundled in flannel with a wool cap, begins laughing hysterically with a girl, no older than five or six. He stands and helps her up.

"Well," Gavin says, his foot still stomped down on the brake pedal. "That was dramatic."

Ellie leans forward in her seat, studying the man. He's huge. "Does he look familiar to you?"

"Yeah," Gavin says slowly. "He was in the footage at the entrance. He was one of the three guys who came to the village."

She looks at him and smiles. "The seventh time is a charm. I think we found our hideout."

Gavin shifts the vehicle into park and kills the engine. They step out of the SUV, boots crunching on the snowy driveway. The big man looks up, but he isn't alarmed – at least, not like someone who assisted in kidnapping Santa Claus and is holding him against his will. Gavin would have expected aggressiveness, or even gunfire. If the big man is armed, he isn't telegraphing it.

The girl, cheeks flushed pink with excitement, waves at them. Gavin didn't know what to expect when they found the trio, but it certainly wasn't this. She looks genuinely happy.

"That sled is *fast!*" she chirps, bouncing on her toes as the man pulls the sled off the ground and stands it on its end.

"That's why I call it *Snowfire*," the man says, ruffling her hair. "I built it to be *really* fast."

Ellie smiles, but her eyes never leave the man's face. "Nice ride."

He gives a friendly nod. "Thanks. Sorry about cutting you off like that. We don't get many visitors here, and this thing isn't easy to stop. Can I help you two?"

Ellie opens her mouth but hesitates. She remembers having agreed to let Gavin do the talking. He's the federal agent, and he warned her before they began checking the addresses her brother supplied that this could be dangerous. Although it isn't shaking out that way. A man sledding down an alpine slope with a young girl may not be the last thing he expected, but it's near the bottom of the list.

"We're…well, I don't know how to say this…we're—"

"We're looking for Santa Claus," Ellie says, cutting him off.

The girl's eyes light up. "Oh! He's inside!"

Gavin and Ellie turn their heads and stare at each other with wide eyes. Could it really be this easy? After tracking the plane and rolling snake eyes on the first six places they visited, are they about to be walked inside to meet the Santa half the world has been looking for?

The man's easygoing expression falters for just a second. "This is going to require an explanation."

"You think?" Gavin says.

Ellie narrows her eyes. "Where is he?"

A sheepish smile tugs at the man's lips. "He's inside with the boss. A lot has happened this morning."

"I can take you to meet him!" the girl shrieks. "He's *really* nice. He made my Christmas wish come true! Come on!"

She grabs the big man by the hand and tries to drag him up the drive to the front door. Ellie and Gavin trail them. The agent is on high alert, but she is absorbing the moment like the four of them are at the end of the yellow brick road and about to meet the wizard.

"After everything, we are being walked into a chalet by a little girl to meet the Santa Claus who was kidnapped?" Ellie asks. "Do you think he's in there sipping cocoa?"

Gavin exhales slowly, shaking his head. "I was just thinking the same thing. Honestly? I don't think anything would surprise me at this point."

"My brother says you get used to that feeling when Santa is involved."

"Doubtful," Gavin mutters.

The man gestures toward the heavy wooden door. "You might want to wipe your boots. The boss hates snow on the floor and makes me clean it."

The agent reaches into his coat and retrieves his weapon. He doesn't want to take chances, despite the current placidity. Ellie puts her hand on it and shakes her head.

"You're not going to need that."

"Are you willing to bet your life on that?"

She nods at the little girl, who is pushing against the heavy wooden door as the big man slowly opens it. "I'd bet hers on it."

She's right. If Trent Quinlan is in there, he isn't going to endanger his daughter. Still, it's a risk. It's against procedure. But this is an assignment to find Santa Claus, not take down a Colombian drug cartel or a human trafficking ring. He tucks the weapon back into his coat.

The heavy door is finally pushed open, and the four of them step into the chalet. Warmth washes over them immediately. The air is thick with aromas of chocolate and pine. The room itself is spacious and open, with huge windows overlooking the Alps, thick cedar beams, glowing firelight from a rustic fireplace dominating one wall, and a vaulted ceiling that stretches toward a chandelier made of antlers and brass.

In the center of the room, a man and a woman stand locked in the most loving embrace Gavin has ever seen. Both of them have red eyes and wet cheeks. They heard everyone enter, but weren't bothered enough to let it interrupt this moment.

"Mommy! Daddy!"

The girl breaks free of the big man's hand and races across the room, flinging herself around their legs. The family sinks into a tight, tearful hug. This is the strangest assignment he has ever been handed, and watching Santa's kidnapper hugging his family is the cherry on top of that sundae.

Gavin gives the family a respectful moment before stepping forward. "I'm Special Agent Gavin Kinnaird with the American Federal Bureau of Investigation," he says, his voice firm but calm. "And this is..."

"Ellie."

She smirks. Gavin guesses that her days of playing an agent have come to an end.

Trent Quinlan grimaces and stands straighter. His wife appeals to him with her eyes. "I'm assuming you're here about—"

"Santa," Ellie says bluntly. "Where is he?"

"He was here," the woman answers, finally releasing the embrace of her husband and grabbing his hand instead. "That's why I am. I got a card from him in Paris. Well, not him…some people delivered it to me when I was taking pictures."

She holds up the red card. Ellie closes her eyes and shakes her head. Gavin's mind races as he tries to put all the pieces together. There are going to be a thousand questions hurled at them by Wyatt and Stowe when they get around to telling this story.

"Five of them, right?"

"Yeah," she says, furrowing her brow and cocking her head. " How did you know that?"

"It's a long story," Ellie concedes. "Where is Santa now?"

"He may have gone to the guesthouse," the big man in the corner says. "I can take you there."

Gavin's expression darkens slightly, and he keeps his eyes trained on Trent. "Did you take him against his will?"

"It's…complicated."

"It's really not. Let me help you out," Gavin says coolly. "Kidnapping is illegal, Mr. Quinlan."

"I know. I made a huge mistake. But I don't regret it. It led to this moment," Trent says, moving his eyes to his wife and then down to his daughter. "I may be getting my family back."

"There are a lot of people worried that you are ruin… jeopardizing Christmas for millions in the process," Gavin says, redirecting his language with the young girl in the room. "There are going to be consequences for that. I think you need to—"

"Let's get the full story first," Ellie says quickly, cutting him off. "We can sort the rest out later. They aren't going anywhere. Go find Santa."

Gavin exhales through his nose and nods. "Fine."

"This way," the big guard says gruffly. "I'll take you to the guesthouse."

Gavin turns to Ellie. "Keep an eye on them. He still kidnapped Santa. Don't let them lull you into a false sense of security. This situation is still dangerous."

He expects Ellie to make a snarky response about how he's overreacting. That's her usual M.O. Instead, she just smiles softly and nods.

"I've got them. Go get Santa."

"Fallon, come help me make hot chocolate for everyone," her sledding partner commands.

"Okay, Alaric!"

The two of them retreat to the kitchen. Ellie sits on the sofa with the Quinlans, eager to hear their tale. Gavin follows the second man through the chalet, listening to his boots thudding softly on the timber floor. This guard, if that's the role he plays, is even bigger than the broad-shouldered man hurtling down the mountain on the cherry-colored sled. This guy has an unmistakably military posture and dresses like someone more in his element on a firearms range. He is wearing a black thermal shirt under his sweater and cargo pants. The man is painfully trying to fit into the Swiss Alps motif.

They pass a row of plush and elegant rooms that are clearly designed for luxury retreats and exit through a mudroom. It's already beginning to grow darker outside. That ought to make for a fun drive off this mountain. To his right, Gavin can see the outline of the peaks in the distance. This is a beautiful place.

Not far from the main house is a smaller, cozy, and somewhat isolated cabin with a warm glow emanating from the windows. Gavin's breath clouds in front of him as the men approach the door. His instincts buzz with tension. Inside that guesthouse is either the man at the center of this surreal mess, or one more twist in a case that has already torn reality to shreds.

Gavin is ready for both as the big man steps onto the small porch and pushes open the heavy wooden door. The living area greets them with silence. Shadows flicker across the log walls as the fire in the hearth sputters its last embers. A single armchair sits before the fireplace, empty.

"Santa?" Gavin calls softly, almost laughing to himself at the absurdity of calling Father Christmas like he is a Labrador Retriever.

He looks at the man, who shrugs. The agent moves into the living area with measured steps, noticing the smouldering coals in the fireplace. It hasn't been tended in some time.

"He should be here," the guard says. I don't know where else he could have gone."

"Where did Santa sleep?"

He points at one of the small bedrooms. Gavin nods and crosses the floor and pokes his head in. No one. There are no belongings of any kind in the sterile bedroom. If he hadn't been told otherwise, he'd bet that nobody had slept here in months. The bed is made to perfection, and a single red card resting on the pillow catches his eye.

He walks over and eyes the elegant gold lettering that shimmers in the soft light.

Gavin

His name. He stares at it, almost waiting for the ink to disappear or transform into something else.

"How is this even possible?" the agent mumbles.

Gavin picks it up, his hands trembling despite the warmth of the room, and slides his finger under the flap of the envelope. The writing inside is penned in the same golden ink on a piece of green paper:

You and Ellie must return to
my home, where your destinies
await.

Gavin stands motionless, reading the words again and again. Santa was definitely here, and is now gone. But to where? And how? They were here to rescue him, but it's clear that St. Nick had other plans. How is he going to get back to Finland? Is he going back there? The instructions are for Gavin to, but why?

"Is everything okay?"

"I don't know. Can you take a look around the grounds to see if footprints are leading away from here? Santa must be on foot."

"Will do," the big man confirms before leaving the guesthouse.

Gavin pulls out his phone. How the hell is he going to explain this? He pulls up the contact and hits send. It's picked up on the second ring.

"Hey, Agent Kinnaird. Things are coming off the rails here. Please tell me you have news," Wyatt pleads.

"Good and bad. We found our kidnapper. He's holed up in a chalet just outside of Verbier. We're here now."

"Thank God!" he hears Wyatt say with a huge sigh of relief. He thinks he can hear Stowe squeal in delight in the background. "What's the bad news?"

"Santa has vanished without a trace."

Chapter Sixty-One

KEITH MEADOWS

Keith Meadows has never been on a bigger stage. Yes, that includes the White House Press Briefing Room. In there, he is only one among a sea of faces. Perhaps a prominent member of the press corps, but he still gets only a question or two. The press secretary at the podium on the dais calls the shots.

Not here. This is his baby…his doing. The assembled members of the media are here because of his reporting and his idea to hold a press conference that Santa is bound to not show up for. Standing in the center of the plaza and staring at a virtual sea of microphones and news cameras from every major network on the planet is exhilarating. He can understand why politicians and government officials love it so much.

All the carols, garland, and twinkle lights in the world can't mask the tense mood here. The frigid Arctic air is thick with equal parts anticipation and trepidation. International journalists jostle for position in the crowd to get the best angles. There is a hushed din of whispered predictions from tourists about what will happen. There are easily two or three hundred people here to witness this moment. His moment. His vindication.

After a year of ridicule from colleagues and his editor and being labeled "the Grinch" by the public, the social media mockery is about to come to an end. Keith is about to expose the foremost symbol in the world's favorite seasonal fantasy. His hard work is paying off. He may not have learned who kidnapped Santa, but he's about to blow the lid off the cover-up, and that is worth millions of clicks and views itself.

He steps into the middle of the circle formed around the center of the plaza. There is no platform or podium – the administrators of the village wouldn't let them set one up. They didn't want this to turn into an event. They failed. It has already become one.

"Ladies and gentlemen," Keith begins, his voice crisp with self-satisfaction as a hush falls over the crowd. "We are gathered here today in the very heart of this magical village to answer a simple question – where is Santa Claus?"

He looks around theatrically, spreading his arms. A number of people join him in the fruitless search. Most of the crowd looks hopeful that he will appear. The journalists are counting on him not arriving in time…or at all.

"Where is the jolly old man in the red suit? Where is the man who enchanted America with his testimony two years ago and the world with his travels last year? The one who made it look like he was delivering Christmas miracles? The one who had the world believing that he was real?"

There is absolute silence. Keith smirks, savoring the moment. "I hereby issue a simple, fair request: If Santa Claus isn't missing, let him come forward. If he is, I challenge any authority present to tell us the circumstances surrounding his disappearance."

He steps back dramatically. A murmur ripples through the crowd as everyone looks around. Eyes turn to the buildings surrounding the plaza, and especially Santa's Office. Nothing. Cameras that pan the area zoom back in on Keith, whose smirk broadens into a grin.

"Exactly," he says, pivoting back to the press. "Because Santa Claus is missing. Christmas might well be canceled, and nobody here will tell you the truth."

"Santa Claus is missing," Stowe Bessette says from behind the first rank of onlookers.

She is dressed in a simple winter coat with no hat, probably not wanting to mess up her hair. Stowe steps into the center of the crowd as Wyatt Huffman stands at her side. Another woman joins them, but Keith doesn't know who she is. Another pair who almost look like they are locals hang back slightly.

"That's what we're all here for, right? You are making it sound like the world has lost something. But I need to remind you that we haven't. Christmas doesn't vanish just because a man in a red suit is not here to usher it in. It's real spirit – the true meaning – is something deeper, older, and for Christians, the birth of Christ." Santa Claus is a symbol and an important one. He represents magic and wonder, generosity and belief. But he is not the *source* of those things. We are. You are.

"What Santa *is*," Keith says, his voice rising with glee, "is a carefully constructed illusion. A sentimental lie that you helped create over the past two years. And finally – *finally* – we're tearing it down. The world deserves to know that the magical Santa we've been waiting for is not only missing. He never existed. He's the manifestation of a story…myth…a brand…a symbol that doesn't mean anything. Not anymore."

Reporters hold up their recorders or take video on their phones. Some are shocked, and others are amused. Keith doesn't care. Let them spin his words however they want. He is right, they are wrong, and he has already won. He can see it on Stowe's and Wyatt's faces. Doubt is seeping in that they can salvage this. Here's breaking news for them – they can't. For the first time in two years, the myth that is Santa Claus has failed to show up on cue.

"Christmas isn't about Santa. It's not about gifts or commercialization. That's what he has been trying to teach us for the past two years. It's about hope," she says, her voice softening. "Not blind hope, but the kind you build in your heart. It's about choosing joy in a broken world. It's about family and community. About slowing down, just for a moment, to remember that we belong to each other."

"Who took Santa, Miss Bessette?"

"It doesn't matter. Regardless of whether Santa is here, the magic he embodies is alive," Wyatt interjects. "Look around you. It's in this village. It's in the people who are watching the broadcasts being beamed around the world. It's even in you, Keith…if you let it be."

He knows what they are trying to do. It won't work. Trying to reignite the spirit of Christmas but portraying it as a quiet, powerful, and unbreakable force is futile. These people are here for Santa. Their kids are here for Santa. Nothing else matters.

Chapter Sixty-Two

STOWE BESSETTE

Timing. For the majority of Wyatt and Stowe's journeys with Santa Claus, it has been on their side. He showed up when he needed to at the hearing. Everything about their trips to Vienna, Florence, Marrakech, and St. Louis last year ran like a clock, even when the slightest little thing could have sent the whole adventure spiraling. Timing is what they need now. Only, it isn't happening.

They found Santa and the man who had him. Thanks to Gavin and Ellie, they learned why he was taken. All St. Nick had to do was get on the plane with them and come back to Finland. Only, he disappeared without a trace. Stowe thought he would be here waiting for this press conference. The man seems to have the ability to come and go as he pleases. Just ask the United States Customs and Border Patrol. After two years, they still don't understand how he got into and left the U.S. There is no record of him leaving St. Louis either.

But Santa isn't here, and Keith Meadows is making the most of it. Stowe's monologue about the true meaning of Christmas was compelling, but it won't assuage the people here demanding to see Santa Claus. If there was a time for a grand entry, this is it. When she looks around the plaza and back at his office, he's nowhere to be found. Even Aurielle is looking forlorn as she watches this unfold.

The snow is falling more heavily now and beginning to blanket the plaza with a fresh dusting. The twinkling lights of Arctic Circle lampposts reflect off the icy cobblestones and the snowflakes drifting to the ground. Families who gathered in muffled joy at what they hoped would be the appearance of Father Christmas are beginning to look dejected and forlorn. The pain in the ass reporter from Washington is determined for them to stay that way.

Keith Meadows isn't finished. Not by a long shot. He steps forward after her plea to remember what Christmas is really about, his shoulders squared beneath his wool overcoat, his gloved hands outstretched from his sides.

"That's it?" he shouts, drawing the attention of the countless reporters and onlookers. "We held this presser with a challenge – produce Santa, or admit that he isn't here for Christmas. Instead, you give us some ridiculous spiel that Christmas can go on without him? To pretend that his absence doesn't at all matter to this holiday? Admit it, Miss Bessette, you came to Finland to find him, and you failed."

Stowe turns slowly, her eyes narrowing at the obnoxious reporter. Wyatt slides his hand up and grasps her arm, likely concerned that she might launch herself at Keith and pummel him to the ground. It's probably a sensible precaution. That's what she wants to do.

"You want to talk about failure, Keith?" Wyatt says, calm but stern. "Try looking in a mirror."

The crowd oohs, and the corner of Keith's mouth curls. "Oh, so clever, Mr. Huffman. Will you tell the world's children that Santa isn't coming, or just admit that he isn't real at all? Go ahead…all these cameras are trained on you. Say the words."

He motions to the cameras still rolling, as the reporters around them wait for a reply they can turn into headlines. Stowe doesn't know what to say. Apparently, Wyatt is equally at a loss for words. Everything they war-gamed leading up to this moment has been tossed out the window.

"You fed the lie," Keith says, his voice rising after not receiving an answer. "And now you're trying to bury the truth beneath warm holiday clichés. People deserve answers! The children deserve answers."

Stowe's expression darkens. "They deserve better than what you're giving them."

"Oh, please." Keith scoffs. "You and Mr. Huffman helped turn the most sacred holiday in the world into a Hallmark movie. If Santa Claus isn't important to Christmas, as you say, then why are you even here? Huh?"

"We were asked to be," Stowe confesses. "But you're missing the—"

"I'm not missing anything," Keith barks, jabbing a finger at them. "The truth is, Santa is missing. You didn't find him. You didn't save him. You didn't save Christmas."

Wyatt's jaw clenches, but it's Stowe who speaks. "And what have *you* done, Keith? Besides sowing fear, pointing fingers, and packaging it all into headlines?"

Keith's mouth opens, but Stowe is determined not to let him get in a defense to that.

"You say the world wants to know the truth. Fine. Here it is. Christmas is not a press release. It's not a ratings stunt or a scandal to be uncovered. It's the raw, radiant celebration of joy that exists not because of gifts or appearances, but in spite of what the world throws at us."

"Tell that to the millions of children who don't think there will be gifts under their trees this year or the millions of parents who think they don't need to go Christmas shopping for them."

"What do you know of children?" the woman behind Stowe asks, moving forward. "Do you have kids, Mr. Meadows?"

"No," Keith admits. "But—"

"But what? That your heart is so big that it's filled to the brim with concern for the world's children? No, I don't think so. You care about the story and the ratings that come with it. Since we're talking about truth here, why don't we start with that one?"

Keith bristles at being called out. "And who are you to think you know any better than I do? I don't see a wedding band on your ring finger. Do you even have kids?"

"No."

"See?"

Chapter Sixty-Three

WYATT HUFFMAN

Julie steps in front of Stowe with fire in her eyes. In the few days that they've known her, she has always seemed a little meek and unsure of herself. Not anymore.

She hadn't planned on speaking. At least, that was the plan. When they were plotting out what to tell the world, she didn't really want to be a part of it. Julie isn't a politician or a celebrity. She wasn't with them in either of the past two years. The mild-mannered woman from the Washington suburbs is involved in this year's Santa escapade for reasons none of them have figured out yet. Maybe they now have their reason.

Bundled in her winter coat and scarf in the center of this plaza with all eyes and cameras trained on her, she is the center of attention. It's the last thing she wanted until she did. Now, as the crowd of reporters jostles for space with microphones outstretched and cameras recording, it's her turn to take on the villain of the story they are writing. Or, at least, one of them.

"I'm a third-grade teacher. That's how I know children, Mr. Meadows."

Wyatt studies Keith's face. He didn't see that coming. It'd be better if the reporter were embarrassed enough to want to retreat, but that's not what happens when someone has an ego the size of his. He is looking for a way to spin this or otherwise disqualify Julie's opinions. That's what they do in the Beltway.

"Not what you were expecting to hear?" Julie presses.

"That doesn't mean you're a child psychologist."

She laughs. "No, not a trained one, but that's half of my job. Helping young minds develop emotionally is just as important as teaching A-B-Cs. I'm not here to speak for Santa Claus. But I spend every day with kids who are learning what this season is supposed to be about – and I think the world could stand to remember a few things.

"Christmas isn't just a day on the calendar. It's not about who has the biggest tree or the most expensive gifts. It's about kindness. It's about looking around your classroom – or your community – and asking, 'Who needs a hand? Who needs to be seen?'"

Her voice quivers for a moment, not from nerves, but from the weight of her words. This is a woman who clearly loves her job.

"In my third-grade class, we have a rule. When someone is sad, you don't ask why because they might not want to tell you. You sit next to them. You draw them a picture. You offer a cookie from your lunchbox. We call it showing up with your heart."

Julie's voice is growing stronger as she shifts between glaring at Keith and warmly staring into all the cameras at the people watching from home.

"Christmas teaches us that giving doesn't mean losing. It means growing together. Two of my kids, Sophia and Alex, just last week turned a classroom argument into a holiday card exchange. If we could only all settle our disputes that way.

"My students are seven or eight years old. Most of them still believe in Christmas magic. And you know what? I do, too. Not the kind with flying sleighs, but the magic that happens when people stop thinking about themselves and start thinking about each other."

Julie points gently to the crowd. "You ask if the spirit of Christmas is lost. I say it's not lost – it's drowned out by noise. We just have to listen again. To children. To each other. To the part of us that still hopes."

The reporters are all riveted. Julie's words are simple, true, and as comforting as warm cider in the cold morning air. The only person who isn't moved is Keith, who looks every bit the White House correspondent ready to push back on Julie's conclusions as if she were the press secretary spinning a story from the podium.

"You don't think that the notion of Santa not delivering presents to them on Christmas will be the least bit disheartening?"

"To some, maybe. But I have twenty-three students who wrote letters last week about what they'd give if they were Santa Claus. Not one of them said toys. They said: 'I'd give someone a friend.' 'I'd give someone food.' 'I'd give someone time with their mom.' They understand what Christmas is and what Santa represents.

"Seeing what someone needs and doing your best to give it to them – even if all you have is a smile, or five minutes, or your best crayon. Children have figured that out. Why haven't we? Why haven't you, Mr. Meadows?"

Julie steps back behind Stowe. No one claps, but some eyes in the crowd are glistening, and the silence that follows feels like reverence. Wyatt is about to say some final words when something unexpected happens.

"I couldn't have said it better myself," a booming voice bellows from behind them.

Chapter Sixty-Four

SPECIAL AGENT GAVIN KINNAIRD

The tires squeal as the jet's landing gear kisses the snow-dusted runway. Outside the window, Gavin can see that Rovaniemi looks half-swallowed by the gloomy winter. Snow is falling again. The dull, gray skies above the city reflect the mood as people contemplate a Christmas without Santa. He watches the distant line of fir trees whiz by like sentries guarding the edges of the world. Finally, the jet completes its roll-out and departs the runway for the taxiways leading to the private jet hangars.

Gavin unbuckles his seatbelt before the plane fully stops. Unlike on a commercial flight, he doesn't have to worry about the flight attendant barking at him. From what he's seen, the rules on private charter flights are far more relaxed.

"We're late," he mutters, checking his watch as if he could rewind time with his glare alone.

"I know. The press conference must've started already. We may be able to catch the end of it if we hurry."

Ellie grabs her coat and bag, already pulling up the app on her phone to secure a car for them. There is no time to get a rental. They could be at Santa's Village in the time it would take them to fill out the paperwork at the rental counter in the main terminal.

He is already at the door when the flight crew lowers the stairs. "Let's go."

They hurry down the steps and into the bitter cold. A breath-clouded scramble to the parking area is followed by a tense wait for the rideshare to pull up. Ellie stares at the digital map on her phone. It should be here....

"There it is," Gavin says.

A black SUV finally pulls into the private airfield lot with its engine running, and the driver barely masks his confusion over the urgency with which they climb in. He already knows the destination and seems to take their pleas to step on it for an additional tip to heart. Ellie leans back into the warm leather seat, catching her breath. Gavin sits beside her, unzipping his coat and looking out the window.

The driver pulls out and points the SUV at the airport exit. Gavin and Ellie made small talk on the flight up here from Geneva. The only thing they didn't talk about was the one thing he feels the need to address. It's unlikely there will be a better time to do this. Whatever path lies ahead, it will be harried and stressful. This is the last time he will get the chance to issue this final report.

"Your husband's not cheating on you," Gavin says without preamble.

Ellie blinks. "What?"

"You heard me."

"And you know this how?"

"I mentally finished my profiling," Gavin says, his tone clinical and his words matter-of-fact.

She stares at him, her eyes wide with surprise but still accusatory. "You haven't even *met* my husband."

"I don't need to. I've met *you*," Gavin says, finally turning to her. "And you've talked about Billy this whole trip with sadness, with frustration, but never with fear. You're upset, but not angry like someone who's been lied to or betrayed. You sound like someone who's been ignored. There's a big difference I see in those two things."

"You're wrong. Billy admitted where he was. He said he was with Missy."

"He did, but he never said *why* he was there."

"You're an FBI agent. You can't be that stupid! Why else would he be?" Ellie practically shouts, causing the driver to peek in his rearview mirror.

Gavin shrugs. "I have no idea, but I know when someone's projecting suspicion. And I've heard you talk about him every day for the past week. He doesn't fit the profile of a man who steps out on his wife."

"I didn't realize there was a profile for that."

"Oh, yeah," Gavin says. "There's a profile for everything. Human behavior isn't as mysterious as people think it is once you start paying attention."

Ellie waves a hand dismissively before looking away and watching the tall pine trees scream by outside the window. "You still can't be sure."

"No," Gavin says softly. "I can't. But I firmly believe that something else is going on and that there is an explanation for his behavior."

"Yeah, like cheating on me with Missy Petersen."

Gavin laughs. "See what I mean? Projection. Do you want the thought of your husband cheating on you to be true?"

"Of course not!" she snaps.

"Are you sure? You said that you thought your marriage was in trouble before this happened. You said that the two of you had fallen into a routine and become distant. Could this be you looking for a way out of it?"

"You don't know me, Agent Kinnaird."

"No, I don't…not well, at least. But that doesn't mean I'm wrong, and your lashing out just means that I'm hitting close to home."

"And they call *me* the armchair psychologist. If that were true, don't you think I'd know it?"

Gavin presses his lips together. He needs to tread lightly. It's bad enough that he blurted this out of the blue, and he's been pressing his opinion since they climbed into this car. He needs her to listen, not tune him out. He knows in his heart that he's right.

"You are remarkably self-aware, Ellie. You're smart, strong, and confident… You're also too close to this to see things the way I do."

"Is that why you resisted my flirting with you, or do I just suck at it that badly?"

The question catches Gavin off guard. It's not because he didn't recognize it, but because she had the balls to straight-up ask the question. Most women would tap dance around that. Not this one.

"Partly. The other part is that my own heart was ripped out, tied to the back of a pickup truck, and dragged ten miles down a gravel road. We are both emotionally damaged, and I think we would have regretted a fling. I don't do regrets well. And, before you ask, yes, that's the *only* reason."

The silence in the SUV shifts. It's less emotionally charged and more reflective. Ellie still has her arms crossed defensively with her eyes locked on the scene outside the window. Up ahead, the glow of Santa's Village emerges on the horizon.

"What comes next?" she asks in a near-whisper.

"I don't know. I can profile, not predict the future. But I think it starts with going home and talking to your husband. Find out the truth – the whole truth. You can decide for yourself then."

Ellie pulls out the Bora Bora keychain she has had since finding it in the airport's lost and found. She rubs it gently between her fingers. Gavin is about to say something and thinks twice. Her thoughts are her own and don't need to be shared.

"Thank you."

"For what?" Gavin asks, turning his head to meet her eyes after not expecting those words to come out of her mouth.

"Being honest."

He nods, not inclined to discuss this further. He said what he needed to say. Up ahead, the story about the missing Santa Claus is unfolding without them. But Gavin has just told Ellie a different story – one that she hadn't planned on hearing but needed to. One that might matter to her far more than the whereabouts of St. Nicholas.

Chapter Sixty-Five

SAINT NICHOLAS

Santa eased himself out of the door to his office without causing the sleigh bells to sing their song. The large crowd gathered in the square had its attention squarely on what was happening in the center. Since nobody has occupied this office in over a week, why would anyone be watching the door now? There isn't a reason, so they aren't.

The journalist running this circus made his appeal. It was having the desired impact. Despite the impassioned pleas from Stowe and Wyatt, and now Julie Cooke, the mood is dour. Parents have pulled their children close. Grumbling punctuated the arguments exchanged in the middle.

He wanted to announce his presence earlier, but something inside instructed him to wait. So, he did. But now the time has come to bring cheer back to his village. The spirited defense of Christmas was something people deserved to hear, but the reporter is right – the people gathered in this square are here to see him. Santa has had enough of seeing the devastated looks on parents' faces and the sadness in children's eyes. His one sentence has changed that.

The crowd turns as one to see the unmistakable image of Santa Claus. He is wearing his best red coat for this affair, complete with the white trim that makes him look more like the traditional Santa or Babbo Natale. His boots crunch softly against the snowy cobblestones as the crowd gasps at the sight before them.

"Is that—?"

"It's him! It's Santa!"

Click. Flash. Click. Journalists and camera crews begin a mad scramble to capture images of him. The crowd parts to make Santa's journey to the center of the plaza easier. Santa walks forward to face a frenzy of photos. The videographers train their cameras and zero in on him as he steps into the open area and raises a gloved hand to silence the now-deafening roar of the crowd.

"My friends, I've heard some rather *extraordinary* rumors these past few days," Santa says, his voice deep and rich as waves of nervous chuckles ripple through the crowd. "Some said I was kidnapped. Others said I had disappeared. Some feared I had given up altogether."

He pauses, his eyes scanning the sea of faces ranging from curious children to skeptical journalists to relieved village workers to gleeful parents. The best looks are from Wyatt and Stowe. They will likely need an explanation or two for all this, but that's for another time.

"Well," he says, spreading his arms, "as you can see, reports of my disappearance have been greatly exaggerated."

A cheer breaks out. Children clap with youthful enthusiasm and genuine excitement. Reporters lean in a little closer, expecting another of Santa's now legendary sermons about Christmas. The crowd – and the people around the world watching – must feel an immense sense of relief. His reappearance will quell much fear and uncertainty. In a world where chaos and doubt often reign, his line is calming. But that isn't the message the people need to hear.

"But I must say," Santa continues, his tone gentler now, "it warms my heart to know how many of you are here today…and how many of you are tuned in and watching from afar. That so many were worried not only about my whereabouts but what it meant for this holiday. Let me tell you something I've known since the very first Christmas: The spirit of this season cannot be stolen. It cannot be buried, hidden, or locked away – unless we allow it."

The plaza falls eerily silent. There is no coughing. No excited whispers. No shuffling of feet. It feels like even the snow blanketing the ground is holding its breath.

"You see," he says, "Stowe and Wyatt and Julie were correct about everything they said. Christmas is not about the trappings, the toys, the lights, or the feast. Those are the reflections, not the flame. The true meaning of Christmas is giving, not just presents, but of ourselves. Of our time. Our love. Our forgiveness."

Santa has never liked being the face of Christmas. He considers himself a reminder of its *true* meaning, aware that his likeness taps into deep nostalgia, evoking memories of simpler times, childhood magic, and family traditions. There's a bittersweet sentimentality in being asked to remember what the holiday is truly about.

He steps forward, his voice firm but warm. "It is about seeing one another not through a lens of what we can take, but what we can offer. It is about receiving, not only the wrapped gift beneath the tree, but the hand that reaches out when we are alone. The smile from a stranger. The quiet miracle of someone remembering your name. Isn't that right, Milana?"

A young girl near the front, clutching a worn teddy bear, expresses shock, turns to her mother, and whispers, "He's real."

Santa's eyes twinkle. A female reporter in the front asks the question on everyone's mind. "Where were you, Santa?"

"I was never gone. Christmas was never in danger. Not really. Because it lives here," he says, pointing to Milana's mother's heart, "and there," he adds, nodding to an elderly man in the front of the crowd, "and in all of your hearts."

Cameras record the moment. Phones stream it live over social media. But none of that matters to Santa. What matters is the light now glowing in the faces of the crowd.

"You don't need me," Santa admits. "Not really. You never did. What you need is your family…your friends…and each other."

Santa steps back, voice rising just once more.

"It is Christmas Eve, and there is much for me to do. So, this holiday season, I want you all to do something for me. I want you to hug your children tightly. Call your parents. Forgive your neighbors. Be kind, even when it's hard. Be generous when no one sees. And when you wake up tomorrow morning, remember that it's not the wrapping paper that makes the day magical. It's the people you unwrap it with. Merry Christmas to all!"

And with that, the children swarm him, and reporters angle in to shout their questions. The plaza, once cold with uncertainty, now glows with something warmer than fire: Hope, and the knowledge that Santa, the everlasting symbol of Christmas, was never truly gone.

Chapter Sixty-Six

KEITH MEADOWS

Carolers in the plaza begin belting out "Joy to the World" with maddening conviction. The village, having all the traits of a funeral home this past week, is suddenly alive again. Men and women in elf costumes begin handing out sugar cookies shaped like reindeer and cups of hot cocoa to children and parents alike. It reminds him of the block party that took over Capitol Hill after the committee hearing two years ago. Santa's sudden reappearance has energized everyone, and cameras are capturing it live for the world to see.

To Keith, the festive music is grating in the background like tinsel-wrapped nails on a chalkboard. He moves out of the plaza to stand alongside one of the buildings to watch this train wreck from a distance.

"Damn it," he mutters.

Santa Claus was *gone*. Gone for *days*. Every source confirmed he wasn't here. Stowe Bessette even admitted it, for crying out loud. St. Nick was taken from this very place only to arrive back here like a conquering hero just in time to step on his moment. Again.

Keith knows he broke the biggest holiday story in history. Never has anything he reported gotten so much traction so quickly. That's what happens when a global icon vanishes, and he had the scoop. He began the trend of people questioning belief, myth versus man, and the logistics of faith. His reports created the headlines people were talking about. After this, they will be laughing.

He can feel the heat rising in his face. His phone is blowing up with text messages. His inbox is already flooding with memes of him wearing a Grinch costume. Again. It's like last year, only worse.

Social media has already seized on this opportunity. People from all walks of life have jumped into action, slapping on the tag #MediaScrooge. One particularly cruel GIF has mashed up his on-air report with Santa waving jovially to the reporters today. The caption: Awkward.

"It was supposed to be *my* Christmas," Keith mutters again.

Most of the reporters he knows regard the man in red as symbolic fluff. They are content to write glowing human interest pieces about department store volunteers or how NORAD tracks Santa's sleigh on Christmas Eve. Even the ones who made the trek to Rovaniemi didn't know how big this story could be. Keith wanted more. He *needed* this story to be real to make up for what happened in St. Louis last year. Tangible. Verifiable. Emotional. It was going to be his redemption.

Santa Claus was missing, and the world deserved to know how and why. He was the driving force behind the story. Ratings shot up. He was called fearless by his contemporaries. He was the face behind "SantaGate."

Now, live on global television on Christmas Eve, Santa has reappeared. Healthy. Laughing. Glowing. He didn't even deny being gone, saying that he was always here in spirit, or some nonsense like that. He just winked at the cameras after other reporters tried asking follow-ups. He knew that young child's name in the front. All that after Santa's surrogates stood in front of the cameras and desperately tried to assure people what Christmas is really about. Damn it.

Keith knows he will be radioactive after this. His post in the White House press corps may even be in jeopardy. Who will take him seriously? How will the press secretary not mock every hard question he ever asks?

What started as a disappearance or even a kidnapping has become a reemergence of joy. Gone are the conspiracies about the disappearance. Absent will be parental concern expressed to children around the world. What is left are the perils of alarmism and exploitation. Against all odds, Keith is now the main villain in this story.

The reporter turns to leave the village, his head hung and his jaw tight. That's when he hears the last voice he wants to hear right now.

"Saint Nick strolled into Santa Village and ruined your Pulitzer dreams live on television, eh, Keith?"

"He could still earn one," her counterpart muses. I even have the title: "*When Santa Reappeared, My Career Disappeared.*"

"Catchy."

Stowe and Wyatt broke off from the crowd for this ambush. They want their pound of flesh. After the beating he gave them in the café yesterday, he almost can't blame them.

"Are the two of you here to gloat?"

"A little."

"Savor the moment all you want. I was onto something. Santa *was* gone."

"He was," Stowe confirms. "And now he's here – like Christmas magic. You got too close to a myth of your own, Keith. You stopped chasing the truth and started chasing a narrative. That's dangerous, whether you are covering politics inside the Beltway or Christmas magic at the Arctic Circle. It's your biggest problem. You don't just report the storm, you become it."

He starts to say something, but words fail to materialize. Stowe is right, not that Keith will ever admit that to her or anyone else. That's how journalists make their names in today's society. They need to be central to the story to be remembered. It may be right, it may be wrong, but that's how it works. Not that he expects these two do-gooders to understand.

"Take the 'L,' Keith. Write your post-mortem to spin the events here. Not that anyone will read it."

"'*The Claus Catastrophe*' would be a good title," Stowe offers.

"People deserve the truth in this world," the reporter fires back. "There is no Santa Claus. That man is not Santa. He may know things, but he's still not real. The only thing you two accomplished today is to continue the global deception. That's it."

Chapter Sixty-Seven

STOWE BESSETTE

He's lucky it's Christmas. He's also lucky that Ellie isn't here to hear this conversation. The holiday may keep Stowe from wanting to strangle the reporter, but she isn't sure Wyatt's sister would care. Why is it that people are so enamored with destroying everything beautiful and good in this world?

"You wanna talk about the truth, Keith?" Stowe asks. "The truth is, Santa isn't *just* a man in a red suit. He's a symbol of something bigger. Wonder. Humor. Forgiveness. Family. He represents the best parts of us – the parts we forget too easily when we're busy chasing outrage."

"Look around you," Wyatt says, taking up the argument as he sweeps his arm toward the plaza. "This place, these people – this isn't a pageant. It's a reminder that kindness still exists. That laughter still matters. That belief isn't a weakness. It's a strength."

"All of those things were put in jeopardy because one man…one icon…was missing in action. Tell me I'm wrong. Tell me that's not why you were searching for him."

"Yes, we searched for him for that reason. And yes, there were moments we didn't know if we'd find him. But instead of feeding the flames of panic, we chose hope. We chose to preserve the joy that gives this season its meaning."

Keith takes a breath. "Where was he?"

"It doesn't matter."

"But it does, Stowe. That's the *story*."

"No, it isn't," Wyatt argues. "Did you not hear what Santa said? The *real* story is that the spirit of Christmas can't be stolen unless we let it. It lives in the way we show up for each other. The way we forgive each other. The way we *listen* to each other. That's the truth. That's what you should be reporting."

Keith waves his hand dismissively.

"You still don't get it. After last year and this year, it's still a mystery to you. Haven't you learned *anything*?"

Keith doesn't answer her question. The fire in his eyes wavers just slightly.

Stowe steps closer, her voice low. "You used to chase stories that mattered. But now you're content stirring up controversy."

Keith's throat tightens. "I told you. I report the truth, not myths."

Stowe nods. "Then report *this*. This is the truth you were looking for. Tell the people that the world didn't fall apart. Tell them that even in uncertainty, families came together and that joy didn't vanish this Christmas Eve. Tell them that Christmas isn't something you expose – it's something you protect."

The hush holds for a beat longer. Laughter rings from across the plaza as the crowd breaks into a rendition of "Santa Claus is Coming to Town." Keith looks away, clearly growing tired of this conversation. Or, is it something else?

"I know what you must think about me. Do you want to know the truth? The real truth? I didn't set out to destroy Christmas. I set out to destroy the *lie*."

Stowe raises an eyebrow. Wyatt folds his arms.

"Every year, we wrap this season in nostalgia and sugar and pretend everything's okay…that the world isn't on fire. That families aren't falling apart or that people aren't alone, broke, or one bad night from giving up. And who's at the center of that illusion? *Him*. Santa Claus. The all-seeing, all-giving ghost of joy."

"Is that what you think?" Wyatt asks.

Keith shakes his head. "It's what I know. When I was seven, my dad got laid off in November. By December, we were behind on rent and eating mac and cheese every night for dinner. My mom still tried to make Christmas magic. She cried herself to sleep the night she wrapped my gift…some secondhand truck she bought at a thrift store. And you know what I did? I asked why Santa gave other kids better stuff."

His jaw clenches as if he is reliving the painful memory. "Mom said maybe Santa had to spread things out, that he loved everyone the same. I believed her. Then I went back to school and saw the game consoles, bikes, and iPads that the rich kids got. I realized Santa wasn't real. Not in the way they said. Not to everyone.

"That was the one thing your Santa failed to address at the committee hearing two years ago. Christmas may be about spreading joy, but it isn't spread equally. The myth of Santa Claus may be about generosity, but it causes a lot of damage, too. So, yeah, maybe I *did* want to take him down. Not the holiday, but the monopoly Santa has on it. I wanted people to see the cracks. I wanted them to stop pretending."

Stowe finally understands. This is what materialism has done to the holiday. Kids are told to be good, and Santa will come. When he doesn't deliver what they want, there is disappointment. The whole meaning of the holiday is missed.

"You thought ruining Christmas would accomplish that?" Stowe asks.

"I didn't want to ruin Christmas. I wanted to *redeem* it."

"You still can," Wyatt points out. "Look at those people, Keith. This is something everyone can share. What happened in St. Louis last year was something that everyone could share. Not just the privileged. Not just the believers."

"Tell that to seven-year-old Keith Meadows," the reporter says with a scoff.

"Even as an adult, after what you have seen, you are still missing the whole point," Stowe concludes after emerging from her thoughts. "It's not about fancy toys under the tree. It's not about who gets what and why. It's about your mom still wrapping a secondhand truck bought at a thrift store. She loved and cared about you enough to do that when your family had nothing. *That* is what the spirit of Christmas is about."

He laughs dryly. Wyatt places a gentle hand on his shoulder.

"Christmas isn't about gifts," Wyatt adds. "That's the greatest misconception of all. It's about *feeling* something positive. Look at those people. Look at the happiness and joy. It's not just because Santa came back in time for Christmas. It's because they get to share this moment with each other. You can still be part of this, Keith. Or you can stand outside it and watch from afar. It's your call."

Stowe offers a faint smile as she and Wyatt turn to leave. "But either way, Christmas will go on."

Chapter Sixty-Eight

WYATT HUFFMAN

The Christmas caroling hasn't let up. If anything, it has gotten louder and more joyous. Some of the kids are running around the plaza, while others join their parents in singing. What a difference ten minutes makes.

Wyatt isn't surprised that Keith Meadows opted to find the exit. His soul is as black as coal, and his heart has the warmth of an ice cube. He could have made this experience more redemptive and something to learn from. He chose not to. In Keith's world, joy isn't newsworthy – only misery is.

His colleagues don't feel that way. Cameras are rolling, catching all the merriment in ultra-high definition. Journalists are conducting interviews with some of the parents around the square. Some are getting in on the caroling. It isn't quite the Christmas block party that erupted after Santa's testimony on Capitol Hill two years ago, but the feeling is the same.

"Wyatt!" a woman calls, coming into the plaza from the main entrance. She is waving both gloved hands like she is hailing a rescue helicopter.

Wyatt has to blink several times to ensure he isn't seeing things. His mother is wearing her puffy crimson winter coat that makes her look like a festive balloon, with a scarf draped around her neck like a battle flag. Just behind her is a man who thinks traveling to the next town over requires a passport.

"Mom? Pops?"

She envelops him in a tight hug. Her coat smells like cinnamon and dryer sheets. His father stands next to her, taller, quieter, but with a look of pride in his eyes. They have never had a good relationship, but it has been better than ever in the past year. He shakes Wyatt's hand, but then claps him on the shoulder in lieu of a hug. It may look cold and impersonal to most observers, but it's the kind of gesture among men in the Huffman family that says everything.

"Nana! PopPop!"

Stowe comes barreling across the square like a snowball in motion, her cheeks red, her dark curls bouncing under her knit hat that she must have just put on. Her grandmother barely has time to open her arms before Stowe collides with her in a joyful embrace. Her grandfather waits his turn before hugging her with equal intensity.

"I didn't even know you were coming," Wyatt says, his breath visible in the cold air. "I mean…why…how did you—?"

"Merry Christmas, Wyatt!" another voice cuts through the merriment from behind them.

MacKenzie Walsh strolls toward them, hand in hand with Cliff. The White House communications director looks decidedly less formal than usual in a wool coat lined with faux fur and a knitted reindeer hat that flops over one side of her head. Cliff looks like the poster boy for an outdoor clothing store.

Even more surprising is who is with them. Malcolm Chapman, his wife Janelle, and their young son Braylen trudge through the snow behind them, their boots kicking up white flurries. The boy stops dead in his tracks at the sight of the impromptu Christmas party the plaza has turned into.

"Whoa," he whispers.

"Surprised?" MacKenzie asks after hugs and handshakes are shared.

"We just spoke to you yesterday. You were in Washington!" Stowe almost shrieks. "When you said you had to get to the airport…?"

"We were meeting everyone at Dulles to get ready to come here. "I almost let it slip during our conversation," MacKenzie confesses with a grin.

Stowe looks at Wyatt, puzzled. He remembers. "You were going to say, 'See you tomorrow."

She nods.

"Why was it such a secret? And how were you all able to meet up for the flight over here?"

"Because our instructions were rather precise," PopPop explains to his granddaughter, triggering a flurry of movement.

His mother and Nana reach into their purses. MacKenzie digs through her coat, as does Malcolm. They all produce red cards with the same gold lettering that Wyatt has been reading for days now. His jaw hangs open. Stowe is equally stunned.

"We got *these*," MacKenzie says.

"Wait! You all got cards?" Stowe manages to ask.

Wyatt looks at his father, who shrugs. "I *mean*, who ignores a personal invite from Santa Claus?"

"She didn't shut up about it the whole flight here," Cliff says, nodding at MacKenzie. "I'm pretty sure she's gloating over getting an invite from Santa when her boss didn't."

Wyatt isn't sure if he means the president or the White House chief of staff, but it doesn't matter. MacKenzie playfully slaps his chest. They look happy. It's a far cry from the stress, misery, and general unhappiness she felt last year. He couldn't be happier for her – for both of them.

The gold lettering on the red envelopes, still clutched in their hands, seems to glow just a little brighter in the winter light. Wyatt takes a step back and surveys the cheerful crowd in the plaza before turning back to his friends and family. This is Christmas.

Stowe introduces Johan and Hanna as Wyatt looks around for Julie. She's nowhere to be found. Hopefully, she isn't being shy. The family is going to want to meet her.

"This place is *awesome*!" Braylen screeches.

"You haven't seen anything yet!" Stowe advises.

Malcolm and Janelle excuse themselves to join the party, as do the Bessettes, Cliff and Mac, and Hanna and Johan. Wyatt turns to Stowe, who is still hanging on his arm. Her heart is as full as his, not just from the reunion, but from the quiet understanding that something bigger than them has been happening all along.

"So…do you ever think we'll get a straight answer to the question?"

"What question?" Stowe asks, peering up at him.

"Whether this was Santa's plan all along?"

Stowe shakes her head gently. "You know that I gave up trying to figure that out a long time ago."

"Well, we should join in on the fun," Wyatt's mother finally says. "It's not every day we get to spend Christmas Eve in Santa's Village instead of at home."

"Speaking of that…if you're here, who is minding the ranch?"

"Your brother and sister-in-law have it covered," Wyatt's father explains. "We'll celebrate when we get home, and you and Stowe come to visit."

Christmas isn't only a day on the Huffman ranch. It's a weeklong event that lasts right up until New Year's Eve. It's been that way for as long as he can remember, and it's convenient for him since he and Stowe can spend the holiday in Vermont with her grandparents and then head to the Big Sky state to celebrate with his family.

He looks at all the faces…his parents, the Bessettes, the Chapmans, and even MacKenzie and Cliff as they mill about the crowd, sipping cocoa and talking to the tourists and locals who have filled the plaza. Family and friends all gathered at the Arctic Circle on Christmas. That's what this holiday should be about. He's still stunned that they are here.

"Where's your sister?" Wyatt's mother asks.

"On her way back from Switzerland, last I heard."

His father's brow crinkles. Of the three Huffman children, Wyatt is the only one who has ever spent any appreciable time outside of Montana. While Ellie at least has a yearning to see Bora Bora, Colt harbors no such desire.

"Ohh…Switzerland. How nice!" his mother professes.

Another man emerges from behind them. He thought the last people he expected to see here were his parents. He was wrong. Seeing Billy Olson standing there is something akin to watching an alien depart a flying saucer that landed in the backyard.

There are a hundred different reasons for that, but he can't process any of them. His only thoughts are whether the man was cheating on his sister and whether Ellie got her revenge by bedding the FBI agent she has grown increasingly chummy with. She hasn't said much of anything about her situation since they left Vermont, but he knows she is hurting. Any wife would be.

"Billy…I'm a little surprised to see you," Wyatt says, looking him directly in the eyes before shifting his gaze to his parents.

"So am I," a frosty voice says from fifteen feet behind the gaggle.

Wyatt grew up on a Montana ranch. That means he was fed a steady diet of Western lore growing up. One of his favorite stories was the Gunfight at the O.K.

Corral, the most famous shootout in American history that took place in 1881 in the booming silver town of Tombstone in the Arizona Territory. Despite its name, the actual gunfight occurred in a narrow lot behind the corral, not in it.

The Earps and Doc Holliday squared off against the "Cowboys," led by Ike and Billy Clanton, in a thirty-second gunfight that must have felt like it lasted twenty minutes. Though the story has been heavily romanticized, the real event was a complex tangle of politics, power, and personal grudges. This feels a little like that. He can only hope it ends better for Billy than it did for the Clantons.

"Hello, Ellie."

"What *are* you doing here?" she asks, her voice betraying that it's more an accusation than a question.

"I needed to see you."

"Well, I don't want to see you!" Wyatt's sister shrieks.

Billy takes off his hat and holds it to his side. He looks at everyone sheepishly before turning his attention back to his wife. "I guess I should explain some things."

"I don't want to hear it!"

The family patriarch takes a step forward. "Ellie! You need to—"

"I got this, Pops," Wyatt interjects, turning his attention to his sister. "Sis, remember what you once told me about closure? Get yours, or I will tell every man in town you've been ridden harder than Secretariat."

"That won't work on me," Ellie argues, welding her arms across her chest.

"Wanna take that bet?"

"Please," Billy pleads. "Just let me explain."

She looks like she's about to say something when Gavin leans in to her ear. "Remember what I told you on the way here."

Ellie doesn't say anything, but she doesn't walk away either. Wyatt knows his sister is twice as stubborn as any mule. If she really wanted this conversation over, one way or another, it would be. Billy takes that as a sign to continue.

"Let me finish what I was trying to explain before you flew an ocean away. I was at Missy Petersen's house like I told you, but it's not what you thought it was. I wasn't cheating on you. I was doing odd jobs for her."

"'Odd jobs?' Is that what the kids are calling it these days?"

"Ellie, please, hear him out," her father pleads.

The words carry weight. Not only did they come from the mouth of one of the most hardened ranchers in Montana, but he used the word "please." It's not completely unheard of, but it is rare. He's also the man who would have pounded Billy into the ground like a fencepost upon hearing the news. The fact that he didn't and traveled across the world with Billy in an aluminum tube at 35,000 feet says something.

"Fine. What do you mean by 'odd jobs'?"

"I was painting her back fence, fixing the floorboards and railing on her porch, and doing some plumbing. That's why I was wet that day. I got soaked from the pipes and had to take a shower. I was just...just doing handyman stuff."

"You *really* expect me to believe that?" Ellie says with a raised eyebrow.

Billy exhales. "It's the truth. I've been squirreling away whatever extra money I could make picking up jobs after hours. She has given me the most work. I took those jobs because I wanted to surprise you by taking you somewhere special for our anniversary. Somewhere you've always dreamed of going."

She blinks. Even Wyatt knows where that is.

"Bora Bora?"

He nods. "I know I should've told you, but I wanted to see the look on your face when I handed you two plane tickets for Christmas and told you to pack your swimsuit. But I fell short. I only have just enough for the airfare and maybe a day or two in Tahiti...I thought I could make it work without you knowing. I thought it would be romantic."

Ellie's expression softens slightly, the corners of her mouth twitching between disbelief and emotion. She looks at her father, who nods.

"It's the truth. Billy told me what he was planning months ago," the family patriarch confirms.

"You idiot," she whispers, stepping toward her husband. "You thought making me think you were cheating on me was romantic?"

He gives a sheepish smile. "It didn't work out that way in my head. I know we've lost some of the magic in our marriage. We are muddling through life instead of living it. I didn't...I don't want you to stop loving me because of it."

Wyatt feels Stowe snake her hands between his torso and arm and rest her head on his shoulder. Ellie sighs, removes her gloves, and takes her husband's face in her hands. To Wyatt's mild surprise, she's wearing her wedding band.

"You don't need to fly me to a tropical island to make me love you, Billy. But... next time, maybe just surprise me with dinner instead of sneaking around at Missy Petersen's house."

He laughs, relieved. "Deal. But for the record, she tips like a champ."

Ellie shakes her head, half-smiling as she leans in and kisses him. "You're lucky you're cute."

Chapter Sixty-Nine

SPECIAL AGENT GAVIN KINNAIRD

His time with the FBI may be at an end, but at least he can go out knowing he's still got it. The profile was spot on. Billy Olson wasn't cheating on his wife, just as he thought. And the payoff for being on the money couldn't be sweeter.

Regrets are powerful. If anything had happened between Ellie and him during this adventure, this moment would have been destroyed. He wouldn't have been able to sleep well knowing that. This is the way it should be.

Of course, that means he is still alone. He doesn't know if a relationship with Ellie would have worked…probably not, for a list of reasons. The first and foremost is the one that commands his heart. He is still in love with another woman. The thought begins to send him spiraling into sadness despite the joy of this place. And then, a vision appears before him.

He hasn't seen her in over a week. The pain from reading the letter she left is still real, clawing at his soul and perforating his heart. He should be angry…even enraged. But he feels neither of those two emotions.

Time feels like it bends around them. Everything from the murmur of conversations, the shouting of questions, even the carols sung by the people around them, blurs into silence. Jules looks happier, somehow softer around the eyes, but still unmistakably vulnerable.

There is a tightness in his chest that no breath manages to loosen. Part of him has rehearsed this moment a thousand times: what he'd say, how he'd act, the calm detachment he thought he'd display upon running into his former fiancée. The woman who had once promised forever before vanishing from his life with nothing more than a letter professing, *"I can't do this."* Seeing her now, near the top of the world, an ocean away from the place they called home, sends a wave of confusion crashing through him.

Even if they manage to talk like old friends, every word will feel like walking a tightrope over a canyon of unresolved feelings. This could be a chance for closure. He could also walk away from this encounter more unsettled than before. But seeing her here…it's stirred up questions nagging him since the moment he read her letter. Was she sorry? Has she missed him, too? Did she make the right choice, or just the safe one? Maybe he will get answers. Maybe he won't. But none of that answers the question of what she is doing here…unless…

"Jules, what are you—?"

"Well said, Miss Cooke," Santa Claus interrupts, stepping forward from the edge of the crowd, his eyes twinkling beneath his fur-lined hat. "The world has heard a great deal of noise this season – debates, accusations, fears that the spirit of Christmas is gone. But what you just reminded us all is that Christmas never leaves us. It lives in the small, quiet choices we make every day. In your classroom, I see more true Christmas spirit than in all the glitter and garland strung across shopping malls."

"Thank you, Santa. I was just hoping to…hoping to be as inspiring as you are."

"You are far more so, my dear," St. Nick assures her, resting his hand gently on Julie's shoulder. "You are a teacher, and the thousands like you are the real magic-makers. You give our children the most important lesson of all – that love, kindness, and compassion don't need a sleigh or a chimney to be delivered. They only need a willing heart. And that is the most precious gift of all."

Santa turns to Gavin, who can only offer a weak smile. He remembers not wanting this assignment. After what Ellie has told him in their time together, it's a good bet that this jolly old elf knows that, too. He doesn't know how this Santa Claus could, but he somehow beat them both back from Switzerland. So, that's something.

"Agent Kinnaird. I sincerely apologize for the wild goose chase. I hope I can make it up to you while you're here."

"There's no need, Santa. My reward is the happy ending you provided for all these people."

There is a twinkle in Santa's eyes as reporters swarm him once again. The questions about his whereabouts are relentless. They want details. That's all they want. Too many of them are still missing the point, even if others are seeming to get with the program.

Santa moves back toward his office, leaving Julie and Gavin almost alone in this part of the plaza. They stare at each other, each waiting for the other to make the first move.

"Well, this is a little awkward."

"So, you're the arrogant FBI agent Wyatt's sister was working with."

Gavin wants to take offense, but her smile tells him that she didn't mean it that way. It's how he was described to her, probably by Wyatt via his sister. And, yeah, he understands why she would think that. He was arrogant, but it was more resentment over the assignment than an actual trait. Gavin's fellow agents can be far worse.

"And you were the mysterious woman the red card directed them to meet up with in Paris. How did that happen?"

"It's a very long story – one I don't want to talk about right now."

Another awkward silence injects itself into the conversation until he can no longer bear it. "I understand. Look, we should probably talk—"

She holds her hand up. "Gavin, this is my first time in Finland. I want to do something fun, like maybe take a reindeer ride or go dogsledding."

"Oh. Okay," Gavin says, dropping his eyes and kicking at a clump of snow.

"Would you like to join me?"

It isn't a pity offer. When Gavin raises his head, he stares into her pleading eyes. She actually wants him to go…at least, he thinks she does.

"Are you sure? I mean…"

She extends her hand, and he takes it. "Yeah. I've never been more sure about anything in my life, outside of the moment when you proposed and I said yes."

Chapter Seventy

STOWE BESSETTE

The guests are warmly welcomed to the enchanting café at Mrs. Santa Claus's Christmas Cottage, or so it is called. The architecture is stunning and the decorations plentiful. The tables are arranged in a U-shape with place settings that rival a state dinner at the White House. The aroma of the Christmas feast being prepared is wafting from the kitchen, which she assumes should be closed on December 25th. But that isn't what makes this so enchanting.

Tonight is a special night. It's not because they are spending Christmas dinner with Santa Claus, but because of all the others they are having it with. Everybody is here – a development that Stowe never could have expected. MacKenzie and Cliff, the Chapman family, the Huffmans and Bessettes, Julie and Gavin, Johan and Hanna…family and friends, old and new.

What makes this so magical is that they are all together. It may be the first and last time that ever happens, making this moment of love and laughter something to be cherished. And that is the heart of Christmas.

Stowe sets her eyes on the one woman she hasn't spoken to yet. Sometimes, mysteries are wonderful things. The fun in life can be marveling at the unexplainable. This isn't one of those times. She wants answers and is determined to get them from the one person who might actually be willing to share some insights.

"Hello, Aurielle."

"Hi, Stowe."

"I need to know. Did you plan this whole thing with Santa?"

She grins and closes her eyes as she shakes her head. "No."

"You can understand why I don't completely believe you. Cards mysteriously showing up when we least expected them to…Julie getting one, Hanna and Johan…even our families and friends…if Santa was a captive, who else could have sent them?"

The chief elf shrugs, her rainbow eyes glistening in the warm light of the restaurant's candles. "I understand why you think that way, especially after last year."

"Then how? And don't say *Christmas magic*."

"Stowe, you and Wyatt should know better than anyone that Santa is an opportunist. Two years ago, he seized the opportunity to speak to your committee and tell the world about the true meaning of Christmas. Last year, he wanted to demonstrate the power of hope and love by granting a Christmas wish that was only possible when everyone came together."

"And this year?" Stowe asks. "What's the message for this year?"

Aurielle looks around the restaurant and gently places her hand on Stowe's shoulder. "I think you already know."

"I'm sorry to interrupt," Ellie says as she moves next to them.

"It's okay. Dinner is nearly ready, so I need to ready the final preparations. If you'll excuse me."

Aurielle doesn't walk – she glides. Stowe watches her effortlessly navigate between guests before disappearing into the kitchen. She wonders if actual elves are making this dinner. She shakes the thought from her head before turning to Ellie. Some things are best left a mystery.

"You've been on quite the emotional rollercoaster ride this week," Stowe says, getting a nod from Wyatt's sister. "Are things with Billy okay?"

"I honestly don't know yet," she admits. "I mean, I believe his explanation…"

"But?"

"Why would I have ever thought that in the first place? I think we have some work to do on our marriage. What about you? This is your third Santa adventure."

"Yeah. I'm ready for a break," Stowe laughs. "I was really hoping…it doesn't matter."

Ellie gives her a knowing nod. "My brother loves you, Stowe. He has loved you every day since you were here two years ago. He's going to ask…eventually. Trust me."

"How did you know that was what I was going to say?"

She winks. "Ellie knows."

"Oh, don't you start with that, too!"

The two women share a laugh when Santa Claus steps toward them, looking resplendent in a red coat they have never seen him wear before. It must be formal attire in Santa's Village. He holds out a red envelope with gold lettering.

"I have gifts to hand out tonight after dinner, but I wanted you to have this one now," he says warmly to Ellie, placing it in her hand.

"I don't need anything from you, Santa."

"Maybe not, but you were instrumental in helping me return home. This small token of my appreciation is the least I can do. Please, open it."

Ellie blinks, confused but curious, and opens it. Inside isn't the usual card with gold writing. It's a voucher.

The Four Seasons Bora Bora
Seven nights
Deluxe Overwater Villa with Plunge Pool

Wyatt's sister is one of the strongest women Stowe knows. It takes a lot to surprise her, much less evoke a response like the one Santa just managed. Her jaw hangs open as streaks of tears race down her cheeks. She quickly wipes them away and tries to compose herself before turning into an emotional puddle.

"It's always a pleasure to make a Christmas wish come true, especially when two people share it," St. Nick says with a warm smile. "That kind of wish is more powerful than you know."

Ellie shakes her head gently. "But…it wasn't my wish."

Santa tilts his head, amused. "No? The poster you stopped to stare at in the airport? The keychain you picked up at the airport's lost and found? The couple you overheard at the café in Geneva laughing about their honeymoon there?"

Ellie's mouth opens slightly. She is caught between surprise and wonder. Stowe can't help but smirk. She's seen this happen too many times before. Each time is more magical than the one before it.

"You made the wish," he says, his voice soft. "Even if you didn't say it out loud. Even if it wasn't addressed to me."

She has barely recovered from the shock. "How do you know all that?"

He leans in, the faintest twinkle lighting his eyes like stars on snow. "I'm Santa Claus…and Santa knows."

He winks and turns his attention to his other guests as they begin making their way to the long Christmas table set up for them.

Ellie turns to Stowe, who shrugs. "I'd say you get used to it, but you never really do."

Chapter Seventy-One

SAINT NICHOLAS

The interior of the café glitters like a dream. In all his years, Santa has never seen it like this. Long wooden tables are decorated with pine boughs, glowing lanterns, and candlelight flickering gold across beams carved with ancient holly and pine. The garlands of spruce, dotted with silver bells, are hung from every rafter like always. A fire roars in the massive hearth, crackling and hissing as steaming plates of food fill the air with the comforting scents of roasted meat, cinnamon, and fresh bread.

That's not what is causing the feeling of warmth and joy. It's the laughter echoing beneath the vaulted, timber-beamed ceiling and the energy of the people in this room. These are his friends. Almost his family.

Santa Claus sits in the middle of the table, his crimson coat trimmed in velvet and gold. His face is glowing beneath a crown of white curls, his eyes twinkling as he watches Stowe and Wyatt, flanked by their families and surrounded by new friends who have become like kin during their unforgettable journey. Johan and Hanna trade stories with the Chapmans, with Janelle starting to show her belly in her sixth month of pregnancy. Little Braylen is about to get his wish for a sister like Alaya Tucker.

Ellie and Gavin swap tales with Billy and Julie. MacKenzie and Cliff are talking to Braylen, probably about the clocks he still so dearly loves. Christmas music plays low and sweet in the background as Aurielle is finishing distributing the dinner platters. The food is passed around as she takes a seat next to him.

He watches the scene before him with a calm smile, eyes resting on every guest like a silent blessing. He is not and will never be the jolly caricature of mall photos and wrapping paper. He doesn't pretend to be. Santa is older and quieter, with soft, creased eyes that have seen much and experienced it all. He slowly stands, causing his guests to quiet and lower their glasses, mugs, and utensils. The fire gives a loud pop, as if it, too, is listening.

"My friends," he begins, his voice warm and deep, "I'm sorry that this Christmas has been one completely devoid of the usual adventure. I will need to find a way to spice things up a little next year."

There is laughter around the room. Stowe and Wyatt shake their heads at the sarcasm.

"At Christmas, the spirit of selflessness shines brightest, reminding us that the season's true magic lies in giving without expecting anything in return. Whether it's offering time to a neighbor in need, sharing a warm meal with someone less fortunate, or simply being present for loved ones, these small acts of kindness ripple outward.

"But what of those who indulge an old man trying to bring joy to the world? What of those who set their lives aside to help that man when he is in need? I will truly be eternally grateful to Stowe and Wyatt, Gavin and Ellie, Julie, Johan, and Hanna for their efforts to bring me home."

There is polite applause and smiles all around the table. Santa means every word, but this dinner is not about them. At least, not entirely.

"They reflect a deeper understanding that the heart of Christmas is not found in what we receive, but in how we choose to lift up others, especially when no one is watching. Generosity isn't measured by the price tag on a gift, but by the thought behind it. It's in the handwritten note, the shared laughter, or the quiet act of forgiveness that restores a broken relationship."

Santa nods at Ellie and Billy, who lower their heads before looking at each other.

"But let us not forget that Christmas is not only for heroes or headlines," he says, bowing toward Wyatt and Stowe and then at Ellie and Gavin. "It is for *all* of us. It is for every parent who stays up to wrap gifts by candlelight. For every friend who sends a card to someone who needs hope. For every child who shares their toy with another who is less fortunate. And every stranger who offers a smile.

"Christmas is a reminder to us all. Not of gifts or toys or trees or songs, though I do love those things dearly. No, it is a reminder of something older, deeper, and increasingly forgotten as sands pass through the hourglass.

"It's the seat pulled up beside the fire for someone who had nowhere else to go. It's the letter written to someone you miss. The extra chair at the table, even if no one fills it, just in case they might. It's friends, found again after too long, and family forgiven after too much. Christmas is not perfect, but it's real."

He raises his glass. "My friends, another year has turned its page, and here we have gathered not for presents, but for presence. Christmas is not found beneath a tree but around a table. Its joy is not derived from the gifts exchanged but from the stories shared. Its magic is not conjured from empty ritual but the light we offer one another when the world grows dark.

"I toast tonight to not what we are given, but who we are and those we share our remarkable lives with. To family. To friendship. And to the spirit of Christmas that lives in all of us."

"To Christmas!" A wave of clinking glasses and cheers sweeps through the hall.

The room roars back to life as Santa sits. It's richer, somehow warmer now. The music comes back on as his guests dive into roasted meats, sugared fruits, buttered rolls, and bowls brimming with steaming potatoes and cinnamon-laced squash. There are mugs of spiced cider, glasses of wine, and flagons of dark beer downed. Plates clink as conversations continue and laughter echoes around the room. Santa's smile is even a little brighter, as he knows that this is something worth remembering. And the night still has plenty of magic left to it.

Chapter Seventy-Two

WYATT HUFFMAN

The snow has stopped, but the air still smells of flurries. Wyatt leans against the wooden pillar outside the restaurant's entrance. The golden light from inside spills out the windows and carries with it the laughter, warmth, and aromas of cinnamon and nutmeg from the cocoa and company inside.

Wyatt can't imagine a more perfect Christmas than this. He's surrounded by family, friends, and the quiet magic of Santa's Village, nestled against the imaginary line that is the Arctic Circle. The lights twinkle overhead like stars caught in the branches, casting a warm glow on everything they touch. This place feels timeless, as if Christmas itself had chosen it to live in spirit.

Everything feels like it led to this moment. From meeting Johan and Hanna to Malcolm and his wife to Julie and Gavin, the winding paths their lives have taken all converged in this place at this time. It's been a journey – one that could only be described as "magical." He has changed a lot because of it.

Stowe has changed, too. He remembers how much she despised him when they first met in the corridor outside the hearing room. It took a long time for her to open up about why. Her hardened edges were all because of Bobby Sinclair, the high school squeeze who later crushed her heart. But her armor melted away in the frigid Arctic air. Maybe it was Wyatt's warmth. He likes to tell himself that. Maybe it was Aurielle's hot cocoa. He may never know the real answer, only that it happened.

Even after the breakup and the drama of last year, their relationship has only become stronger. Gone is the uncertainty of where they stand with each other. Buried now forever is the past trauma of old loves. And now, he realizes something else – this isn't just a perfect Christmas. It's the start of something new. A life reshaped by wonder. A future guided by magic. Not Christmas magic or Santa magic, but one that a family makes with each other. He is a believer again, not just in the season or Santa Claus, but in the belief that things really do happen for a reason.

Santa slips out of the restaurant and finds Wyatt with his hands in his coat pockets, looking out at the pine trees standing guard around them. Wyatt heard the sleigh bells on the door. He heard the boots crunching the snow. He didn't need to turn to see who it was.

"Cold night," Santa says casually.

Wyatt doesn't look at him at first. "That's true, but it's also a little too warm for me in there."

Santa nods knowingly. "You have never really liked anything other than Montana winters and now the mountains of New England. You lived on a ranch and were the happiest when you were outdoors. You still like it that way. You carry the cold like a friend."

Wyatt chuckles before turning. "Some things you don't shake. Santa—"

"You're wondering if I planned all this." Santa looks at him with kind eyes that feel far older than time.

Wyatt doesn't bother denying it. "The thought has crossed my mind once or twice. You vanished without a trace. Kidnapped at gunpoint and spirited off to Switzerland. Yet, we received your red cards. We got puzzle pieces to find you. We solved the riddles you left for us."

"You did."

"We could have failed. It would have been easier if you had just told us where you were."

Santa presses his lips together. "Things had to work out the way they did. To answer your question, no, it wasn't planned. I never expected to be taken from this village with a gun pointed at me. I never expected to be loaded onto a jet and spirited off to a Swiss chalet. I never expected to grant a Christmas wish to Fallon or bring her mother and father together again. I made the best of a bad situation and decided to create some Christmas magic in the process."

Wyatt narrows his eyes. "I get that. But how did you *know* it would all work out? That Trent Quinlan wouldn't hurt you? That it would come together like this?"

Santa smiles, a twinkle catching the corner of one eye. "Santa *knows.*"

"Of course," Wyatt says, laughing.

"Besides, Christmas has a funny way of turning trouble into purpose. Perhaps that's what you need right now."

Santa reaches into the pocket of his red coat and produces a small box wrapped in forest-green paper, tied with a thin gold ribbon. It may be the best wrapping job he has ever seen. Either Santa did it himself, or Aurielle gave him a hand.

"I don't need a present from you, Santa," Wyatt says, holding his hands up.

"It's not *technically* for you," Santa replies, stepping closer and holding it out. "But you'll thank me later. Go on – open it."

Wyatt accepts the box slowly and graciously and brushes his fingers against the fine paper. He can't tell if it's the feel of the paper that causes his heart to flutter or the anticipation of what is inside the box. Suddenly, he feels like he did as a child on Christmas morning. His spine tingling, he unties the ribbon and lifts the lid.

His eyes grow wide. This can't possibly be happening. Nobody knew where…even with everything he has witnessed, Wyatt still can't believe St. Nick could pull this off. It's not possible. He looks up, startled.

"Is this…?"

Santa's expression softens. "It's the key to your future. I can't think of a better way to conclude Operation Polar Star."

"Polar…you know about that? How?"

"Wyatt, I love you, but please don't make me say it again."

"I know, I know…Santa *knows*," he says with a smile. For a brief moment, it feels like his own eye is twinkling.

Santa claps him on the shoulder. "Good. Now, you've stood outside by yourself long enough. Go find Stowe. She has her gift as well. I trust the two of them together will take you where you need to go."

And with that, he turns, sleigh bells chiming against the door as he steps back into the cabin's glow. Wyatt remains standing outside, his heart thudding against the wall of his chest. He stares up at the sky with a sudden sense that everything is about to change.

Chapter Seventy-Three

KEITH MEADOWS

The terminal buzzes with the quiet hum of the few tired travelers taking Christmas day flights and distant announcements in both Finnish and English. He thought he would be one of the few travelers here. Most people won't end their holiday celebration with friends and family until tomorrow. He was wrong. While the terminal is far from full, it isn't empty either.

Keith sits slumped in a molded plastic chair, his duffel bag at his feet and a lukewarm coffee in his hand. Most of the passengers on this flight don't look excited about the trip. He isn't one of them. He can't wait to get out of here. Of course, he isn't keen on returning home knowing what awaits, either.

His reporting from Rovaniemi made the waves he promised his editor. Of course, he didn't think Santa would make a grand entrance to ruin it all. Now, he's become notorious as a Christmas grinch. Many readers have accused him of "alarmism" and purposely trying to "ruin the holiday for millions." He isn't the cynical journalist out to kill the holiday magic as he's being portrayed. He was following a story and covering it with brutal honesty and investigative depth. At least, that's what he keeps telling himself, even if there was a darker intent.

Social media trolls are tearing him apart. He is the subject of countless memes, derogatory posts, and even threats. Imagine that at Christmas. But in the media, controversy is a double-edged sword. He's more visible than ever. Most of the well-known reporters in the world have gained their status because of being controversial.

That could mean his return to the White House press corps will result in his repositioning into hard-hitting political journalism, where his tenacity, sharp tone, and willingness to report unpopular stories are better assets. He's proven he can handle hostile topics and public scrutiny. That's valuable in D.C. In circles that prize truth over comfort, his reporting could earn respect.

That's the long-term outlook. In the short term, colleagues and friends will likely distance themselves. That's the path of the Christmas pariah. He won a couple of battles against Stowe and Wyatt and lost the wars. He's oh-for-two against Santa Claus. Now come the consequences.

Keith's phone vibrates, and he fishes it out of his pocket. He hesitates as he looks at the screen, sighs, and punches the "accept" icon. "Merry Christmas, Ben."

His editor doesn't miss a beat. "Is it really? Half the planet thinks you purposely tried to ruin Christmas. The other half knows you did."

Keith rubs his temples. He knows he will forever have to defend his reporting to the people. He didn't think he would have to for his editor. It was his idea for Keith to dig up a story that would rival last year's escapades. And he did. Unfortunately, just like last year, the ending wasn't the one he hoped for.

"Look, I was following the facts. Santa was missing. He was kidnapped."

Ben barks a laugh. "Oh, I know. And yet, he still managed to make it back to his village in time for your Christmas Eve spectacle. Damn convenient timing."

Keith bristles at the conclusion but remains silent.

"Too bad you didn't put a more hopeful spin on it. That would have made for some great television. If you had an optimistic outlook instead of playing the Doctor Doom angle, things would have worked out for you. It did for some of the other news outlets there. But nooooo, Keith Meadows had to torch the last shred of innocence left on the planet."

"I didn't *make* the story bleak. I *reported* it that way because it was."

That isn't entirely true, and Ben likely knows it. He chased the story, and facts are facts. But narrative matters, and Keith chose how that would look. To get attention, he had to make the situation dire. People respond to that. Sure, everyone likes the occasional feel-good story, as evidenced by the past two years. But they also crave drama. He only gave the people what he thought they really wanted.

There is a pause. "Yeah, well, bleak *sells,* apparently. Against all odds, our clicks and views approached last year's numbers. You were right – it was the story of the year."

Keith blinks. "Wait, what?"

"Of course," Ben continues, sounding more tired than angry, "you committed career suicide to deliver it."

The journalist chuckles in spite of himself. "So, what are you saying? Am I fired?"

Ben snorts. "God, no. But I'm not about to march you into the White House briefing room anytime soon. MacKenzie Walsh has instructed Dana to rake you over the coals the first time your hand goes up. I don't think you want any of that abuse."

"So, you're benching me."

"Until the smoke clears from the dumpster fire you lit under the Northern Lights, yes. Your brand is damaged. Time heals all wounds, and you are still a valuable asset, but you have some reputational damage to restore before you get back to work."

Keith leans back in the chair, watching a child press her nose against the window overlooking the tarmac. This might as well be a repeat of last year. It took him a month to get back in the game, but he still managed it back then. He can do it again.

"Take the rest of the week off," Ben adds. "Nothing is going to happen at the White House this week anyway. Everyone will be enjoying their post-Christmas hangovers and getting ready to blast the administration into the new year."

"And the recess appointments? I should be the one who gets in front of that."

"Like I told you before, who cares? The American people sure don't. They are too busy loading your stocking with coal. Take a break, Keith. Unplug. Get hammered on New Year's Eve. I'll see you when the year kicks off."

"Thanks, Ben."

His editor hangs up without another word. Keith sits still for a moment, feeling that the low buzz of the terminal is suddenly louder than before. The gate area is filling up. It's time to go home.

Keith's career isn't dead. At least, not as dead as he thought it was fifteen minutes ago. His wishful thinking about turning this disaster around has led him to a new truth. It's not a resuscitation that's needed – it's an *evolution*. He's a serious, hard-nosed reporter willing to chase the hard stories and has the scars to prove it. The Christmas story was his crucible. What comes next will define whether he becomes a respected truth-teller or just another loud voice people love to hate. America ultimately gets to decide that, but fortunately, he can help shape the narrative. He always does.

<h1 style="text-align:center">Chapter Seventy-Four</h1>

SAINT NICHOLAS

The warmth of the flames in the fireplace does not compare to the warmth from the people in this room. Some of them knew each other. Others barely know anyone. But they have all become fast friends, and none of his guests seems eager to leave and call it a night. After dinner was finished, they began milling around, talking and laughing as they had before the meal was served.

Santa may be the host, but he has tried to avoid being the center of attention. He wore his best clothing, which Aurielle was kind enough to leave out for him. His chief elf is going above and beyond after the scare she just had with his absence. Now, his coat is open slightly, and his eyes, as always, sparkle with something deeper than mischief – something ancient, knowing, and kind.

He turns his attention to the four adults gathered near the corner, their cheeks pink from the wine and their expressions caught between joy and amusement. He had almost forgotten that they had never met each other in person before today. You certainly wouldn't know that by watching them interact.

"Well," Santa says, coming over to the quartet, "I must say, Dorothy, that I'm grateful you didn't hang mistletoe *everywhere* in this village. I half-expected you to turn the reindeer barn into a kissing booth."

Dorothy blinks, her mouth falling open in surprise. "Santa! I mean…how on earth did you—?"

Walter chuckles and nudges her with his elbow. "Told you. You have a reputation now that extends all the way to the Arctic Circle."

She gasps, mock-offended. "I just like romance! Is that such a crime?"

Santa laughs, his shoulders bouncing with his amusement. "Not at all. It certainly worked for Wyatt and Stowe."

"You know that story? Did they tell you?"

Santa smiles at Nana with a twinkle in his eye. He absolutely knows the story, and not because his favorite couple told him.

Walter leans in. "You have no idea what it's like in December at our place. The woman decorates like she's trying to summon the spirit of Hallmark movies past."

"You hush," Dorothy says, giving his arm a light smack.

Santa turns to Wyatt's parents. "And Bridgit, Bill, thank you for coming."

The grizzled cowboy shifts his weight. His hands are buried in the pockets of his jeans. "Wasn't sure I would," he said plainly. "Flying and I don't exactly get along."

"He had a death grip on the armrest the whole flight," Bridgit teases gently.

Bill grunts. "I'm more comfortable in a saddle with hooves under me than a tin can with wings."

Santa smiles, stepping a little closer. "I know. Trust me when I say that it means a lot to Wyatt that you came. I know you haven't had the best relationship with your youngest son over the years."

"He told you that?"

"Wyatt is a very proud man…and private. Much like his father. He would never tell me."

"Then how?"

"Santa knows," St. Nick says with a smile.

Bill's eyes close, and he nods. He's heard all the stories by now and seems to accept that at face value.

"You and he have always clashed," Santa continues, "but not because you're opposites. It's because you're alike. Hard-headed. Strong values. Protective. Loyal to a fault. He got a lot of that from you. You and your wife raised him right. He is a wonderful young man."

Bill doesn't say anything, but his lips crease into a smile that Santa recognizes as paternal pride. He looks past Santa to where Wyatt is standing and laughing with Stowe as they talk to the Chapmans. For a moment, his mouth twitches like he wants to speak, but the words fail to materialize. They don't need to.

"And you did a great job with Stowe. The tragedy she experienced at such a tender age could have destroyed her. You lost your son, but you still had more than enough room in your hearts for your granddaughter. And she is a remarkably wonderful young woman."

Dorothy leans in, speaking low but earnest. "We were sort of hoping the two of them would figure things out. I knew Wyatt was her person the moment he walked into our home. He and Stowe are so good for each other. My heart was broken when they split last year."

"Even Bill was wearing black for a few days," Bridgit admits.

Walter nods. "The way they looked at each other…she hadn't smiled like that since she was a teenager. But you got them back together."

Santa shakes his head. "They did that themselves. I just provided an opportunity for them to rediscover the love they had for each other. It was always there, buried under fear and insecurity. Christmas is a time for taking off the armor. For risking something more."

"Speaking of risking something more…I'm not going to lie, we were all hoping that he was going to propose on this trip," Walter admits.

"They were in Paris. Stowe loves Paris," Dorothy chimes in.

"There is still time," Santa informs them.

"For what?" Bill asks. "Christmas is over."

"Ohh, there are still a couple more hours left. That's plenty of time for one last Christmas miracle," Santa says, both his eyes twinkling.

Chapter Seventy-Five

SPECIAL AGENT GAVIN KINNAIRD

The Christmas dinner was absolutely the most magical moment in Gavin's life. He was not in any rush to leave the warm glow of the hearth, and the new friends he had made gathered around it during a meal worthy of a Michelin-starred restaurant. But that's when Jules tugged his sleeve and asked him to get his coat.

The past day in Rovaniemi has felt like old times. While he and his former fiancée haven't been affectionate, they have talked and enjoyed Santa's Village just like the breakup never happened. It felt natural…and right.

But that doesn't mean what happened between them doesn't need to be addressed. Jules returned the ring he gave her without so much as a goodbye or a proper explanation. All he got was a letter…a heartfelt one, but still only a letter. Maybe the time for that conversation is coming.

They walk toward the entrance to Santa's Village, the fresh snow crunching softly beneath them. It always feels like it's snowing here. He guesses that makes sense.

Jules holds the red envelope Santa gave her only an hour earlier. Inside is a card, its gold script simple but clear:

Go to the entrance. Someone is waiting.

A black SUV is idling, and a man climbs out wearing a forest-green parka and fur-lined cap. "You must be Julie and Gavin. Hop in."

"Where are we going?" Gavin asks.

"Someplace special. It's not far."

The ride takes them north through pine forests and snow-draped hills until reaching a secluded cabin overlooking a frozen lake. Lights twinkle from the eaves, but there are no other lights on inside. The place is clearly closed for Christmas. Even as an FBI agent, this is a little creepy.

Gavin looks around. "What are we doing here?"

The driver takes a breath and exhales a white cloud in the cold air. "You'll see. Give it about ten minutes or so."

He walks away, leaving the two former lovers alone under the pine trees on the edge of a lake in a Lappish forest. Jules looks as uncomfortable as he feels. The time for the long-awaited and much-dreaded "talk" is finally here.

"I want you to know something, Gavin. When I gave back the ring, it wasn't because I stopped loving you," she says, her voice wavering.

He never questioned that, so he waits silently for further explanation.

She draws in a long breath. "When you proposed, I was sure I could handle it all… your job, the risks, the time apart. I told myself I was strong enough…that I knew what I was getting into. But over time, that confidence started to unravel."

Jules turns to face him, her eyes clouded with something between regret and fear.

"There were nights I'd lie awake wondering where you were, if you were safe, or if someone was pointing a gun at you in some alley while I was folding laundry or watching a movie alone. I'd get texts from you at midnight, and I'd stare at them, heart racing, wondering if they'd be the last ones."

She swallows hard.

"But it wasn't just the danger. It was the way the job owned you. When you were working a case, it felt like there was no room for me. Like I had to compete with something I could never touch. I started to feel like I was just a part of your downtime – something you could set aside when duty called."

Her voice cracks. "So, I gave the ring back. Not because I didn't love you. But because I was terrified that loving you wasn't going to be enough to survive a life built around fear and waiting."

Gavin steps closer. "Why didn't you tell me all that? Why didn't you talk to me first?"

"I didn't even know how to put it into words. And part of me hated myself for not being stronger – for not being the kind of woman who could just roll with it, like in the movies."

"So, you went to Europe?"

"I needed to get away…to forget. Then, I met Stowe and Wyatt. Seeing the love they have for each other…every day, it reminded me of what we had and what I still want…and how much I still loved you."

Gavin stands completely still as Jules speaks, letting each word hit him like a wave he hadn't seen coming. He had prepared himself for a polite, final goodbye. But this? This raw honesty? It rattles him.

"I thought it was too late…that I blew it. But when I saw you at Santa's Village, standing there looking just as unsure as I felt…my heart just jumped. Even after all the fear and second-guessing, all I wanted to do was run into your arms. At that moment, I realized it wasn't your job I couldn't live with. It was not being with you."

"I had no idea you felt that way," Gavin quietly says, his voice thick with guilt over missing all the signs. "Jules, I thought you were okay. You never said.…"

She offers a small, tired laugh. "That's the problem. I didn't know how to admit that I was feeling so vulnerable after promising you that I was strong. I didn't want to force a decision between the FBI and me. It wasn't fair to ask you to make that choice…and I didn't want to face the possibility that I would be the one who lost."

He steps closer, his eyes locked on hers now, vulnerable in a way he lets few people ever see him. "I should have asked. I should've noticed. You were always so supportive, always smiling when I'd get a call and rush out the door. I was stupid enough to think that meant you were fine."

Jules doesn't answer. She just looks at him as if searching his face/.

"I'm leaving the FBI, but not to win you back."

"I know, and I'm not coming back because you're leaving the FBI," she says, moisture welling in her eyes. "Losing you to your job would have been hard. Losing you forever because of that fear would be far worse."

A faint smile pulls at his lips. "Then maybe this time, we do it right," he says. "No more pretending we're fine when we're not. No more guessing. Just you and me, figuring it out. Together."

She tries to fight back her tears. "You know, I made a Christmas wish to Santa when I was a little girl. I was getting older, and it was probably the last one I wrote before I stopped believing in him. I wished to meet a wonderful boy, and that he would take me to a quiet place alongside a lake and pledge to be forever mine under the lights in the sky. My God, that place I imagined is so much like this.

Gavin grins and reaches into his coat. Julie stares at the ring he pulls out of his pocket, and then back at him. Her hands cover her mouth. "Oh, my God! You brought it with you?"

"Yeah," he says, a little embarrassed. "I guess I wasn't ready to let go."

Above their heads, the shimmering glow of the Northern Lights kicks into high gear. Ribbons of green hues dance across the night like a curtain of magic unfurling just for them. It's like the heavens themselves are smiling down on them…blessing this moment in time.

"Julie Elizabeth Cooke, will you—"

"Yes!"

She holds out her hand, and Gavin slides the ring back onto her finger – the one place in the world the gem affixed to the white gold band truly belongs. They kiss before turning their heads and lifting their eyes skyward. As Santa said, Christmas is about joy and family and a time for wishes to come true. This Christmas, they are getting all three.

Chapter Seventy-Six

STOWE BESSETTE

The horses' breaths puff like steam engines into the frosty night as the carriage creaks beneath a canopy of snow-laced evergreens. Lanterns swing gently from the corners, casting a warm amber glow over the powdery road. The snow that was falling softly has stopped, giving way to clearing skies punctuated by brilliant stars. The journey from Santa's Village through Rovaniemi has been nothing short of magical. All they need to complete it is a steaming cup of Aurielle's hot cocoa.

The driver wouldn't say where they were going. It wasn't until he made the turn and began climbing the hill that Stowe put the pieces together. The rhythmic sound of the hooves slows as the carriage pulls to a gentle stop at the ski lodge. Wyatt steps down first, offering a gloved hand to Stowe, who laughs at the familiarity.

"Wyatt," she breathes, scanning the slope before them. "It's the same hill."

"Welcome to Own-a…Ow-na-sh…Ounasvaara!"

"Seriously? It's been two years. You still can't pronounce our son's name?"

It's one of their oldest inside jokes. When they were outside at the end of Santa's congressional testimony, he commented about her family's affection for naming children after mountains. He said that if this worked out and they ended up married, they weren't naming their daughter Ounasvaara. Stowe simply said they would name their son that.

Last year, she thought the chances of that happening were zero. Their summer break-up squashed any chance of a future with Wyatt. Her heart ached, and his did, too. And it took Santa Claus to bring them back together.

They thank the driver and move around the front of the lodge. Ounasvaara is a year-round family ski resort south of Rovaniemi. It features ten downhill slopes with five lifts and several cross-country tracks during the winter. And, like last time, it's closed. That's to be expected on Christmas Day.

The corner of his mouth tugs upward as he leads her around the lodge to the top of the slope that fades into darkness farther down the hill. "Santa's got a sense of humor and, apparently, an excellent memory."

They stand at the top of the hill outside Rovaniemi, the same one where they first yielded to their feelings for each other. By accident or fate, or maybe by Christmas magic, they have become an enemies-to-lovers story that you find on the romantic fiction shelves in bookstores. This one has a decidedly holiday twist to it.

It is just as quiet here now as it was then and just as dark. The path to the top of the slope is untouched on this Christmas day. There are no footprints or sled tracks in the powdery snow. They walk hand in hand, gazing down the slope at the familiar silhouette of Rovaniemi. When they reach the top of the ski lift, a single wooden sled stands in the snow, waiting like a memory frozen in time.

"One more time?" Wyatt asks.

Stowe smiles and nods. "Let's try not to crash as hard at the bottom as we did last time."

She was scared that first sled ride down this dark slope – truly scared. The kind of fear that tightens in your chest and makes you question every decision that led you to that moment. The trail had looked impossibly steep, the night was almost pitch-black, and the sled too small and fragile for something so reckless. She remembers gripping Wyatt tightly, her heart pounding, wondering how she had let herself be talked into it.

But she climbed on anyway. It hadn't been bravery. Not really. It wasn't even the fear of being left at the top of a Finnish hill by herself. It was something else – something unspoken, magnetic, and inexplicable. Stowe had begun to trust him. Even then, with barely a reason to, she had felt drawn to Wyatt in a way she couldn't explain. And when they'd tumbled through the snow at the bottom, laughing, breathless, and tangled together in a heap of humanity, it had been more than just relief. It had felt like fate nudging her toward something she didn't yet understand.

Now, the hill stretches before them, quiet and cloaked in darkness, just as it did two years ago. They climb onto the sled with Wyatt in front and Stowe wrapping her arms tightly around him from behind. With a push, they are off. The sled takes the hill like a shot, speeding down the icy trail with wild speed and abandon. Now, years later, that same hill stretches before her. Still dark. Still steep. Still wild. But the fear is gone.

In its place is a certainty. Stowe couldn't imagine doing this with anyone else. It's not that she wouldn't hurtle down that slope beside another soul. It's that she wouldn't want to. The hill hasn't changed in two years, but she has. And now, with everything behind them and everything ahead, she knows exactly where she will land – not just at the bottom of a snowy Lappish hill but with him. Always.

The air roars in their ears, and the wind stings their cheeks as the sled rockets down the hill. Trees blur, and stars spin overhead. The night sings to them. As if on cue, the sled hits a bump at the bottom and flips, spilling them into the snow in a tangle of limbs and laughter. And, just like before, Stowe lands in a heap squarely on top of Wyatt, her face inches from his, breathless and laughing.

She brushes strands of hair from her face and kisses him hard and fast like she'd been waiting years for the moment. "I love you."

Wyatt grins up at her. "I love you, too."

"Well, it looks like we hit the same bump and shared another kiss. This is just like last time."

He reaches into his coat pocket. "Almost."

Chapter Seventy-Seven

WYATT HUFFMAN

Wyatt pushes his hand into his coat pocket and pulls out a small velvet box. Stowe's breath catches as he reaches over and opens it. The ring is simple and not ornate, yet still breathtaking. It's like it had been crafted out of a quiet moment that belongs only to them.

"Last time, I didn't ask this."

For a long moment, Stowe doesn't move. The wind whispers through the trees around them, and stars glisten in the clearing skies over their heads. The world moves in slow motion. Her eyes widen, then soften, and her mouth parts just slightly – not from surprise, but from the sudden rush of everything this moment means.

She stares incredulously at the elegant, slender band of brushed white gold and the single round diamond that rests in a low, delicate setting. The stone isn't massive. It doesn't need to be. It's the two tiny sapphires set flush into the band flanking it that make her eyes fill with tears. The deep blue gems are a subtle nod to a secret she has shared only with him. He remembered, of course.

"They're for your parents," Wyatt says softly, his voice catching as he notices her eyes wander to the sapphires. "You once told me blue reminded you of their strength. I wanted them to be with us…always. You've carried them with you through every part of your life. I want to carry you through the rest of mine. Every steep hill. Every dark night. Every wild ride."

He pulls the ring out of the box. It isn't flashy. It isn't loud. It's timeless, thoughtful, and completely, unmistakably hers.

"One more time. And every time after."

Her eyes glisten as she lets out a nervous laugh, staring down at Wyatt with a look that holds the weight of every memory they've ever shared – the good ones, the bad ones, and everything in between.

"Yes," she says.

"I haven't asked yet," Wyatt says with a grin.

Stowe brushes his face with her right hand. "You've said all you need to."

She pulls off her glove, and Wyatt slides the ring onto her finger with shaking hands. Stowe kisses him again, longer this time, and more sure. He never thought anything could ever beat the last two Christmases. Stowe was wrong. He was right. An engagement in Paris would have been romantic, but at the bottom of this hill in the same spot where they shared their first real kiss? Nothing could ever beat this.

They stand and brush the snow from their coats and pants and begin walking away from the base of the hill. The world feels hushed in that magical way it does only after something unforgettable happens. Stowe leans into Wyatt's arm, her hand clasped in his, her breath still visible in the crisp air. The adrenaline of the sled ride has faded into a warm afterglow. She doesn't bother putting her glove back on. She's too busy admiring the ring on her finger.

"You're an absolute lunatic," she whispers, eyes shining. "I can't believe you brought that on a sled ride down a mountain."

"It was worth the risk."

"Did you have the ring in Paris?"

Wyatt shakes his head. "No."

"Did you buy it here?" she asks, likely knowing that they never had enough time apart to make that magic happen.

"No. I've had it for a while now."

Stowe cocks her head. "Then how did you get it to Finland? Did my grandparents bring it when they came to Rovaniemi?"

"They didn't know where I hid it. As for how it got here…well, I'm sure there's Christmas magic involved in that."

Stowe grins. She knows what he's driving at. "Santa's a romantic."

"No doubt about it."

They walk, taking the same route to the road they did two years ago. Now, a new question creeps into Wyatt's head. This one isn't about his future with Stowe – it's how exactly they will get back to Santa's Village to celebrate. Will the carriage pick them up? He's about to ask Stowe when she gasps.

Just ahead, in a small clearing nestled between groves of fir trees dusted in white, sits a table adorned with small tea light candles. It's not a rustic bench or a snow-covered rock but an actual table. Small. Wooden. Very out of place. They share confused looks as they walk over to it.

A white tablecloth flutters slightly in the breeze, weighed down by a simple arrangement: a dozen soft ivory Christmas roses with dark green leaves and tinges of pink petals open wide despite the cold. At the center is an air pot with two ceramic mugs resting beside it. A folded piece of parchment lies on the table, labeled in delicate handwriting: *Aurielle's Secret Cocoa*. In elegant script is a recipe written as if passed down through generations – rich cream, a pinch of cinnamon, a whisper of vanilla, and something unnameable but "always stirred with love."

"We're going to get fat from drinking this every Christmas," Stowe whispers.

That's probably true. Heroin doesn't have the addictive properties that this cocoa does. And, although he has never tried that powerful drug, he doubts even it can make anyone feel as good as a mug of this does. It's as if joy itself were a warm beverage.

Next to the roses sits another red card, thick and velvety, with their names embossed in gold cursive lettering. Wyatt picks it up and pauses. It's likely the last one they will ever receive. These short Christmas missives have always marked the end of one journey and the beginning of another. She lets him have the honor, and it's with an almost heavy heart that he opens it, glancing inside before turning it so Stowe can read.

Congratulations!

Now you can live happily ever after.

Stowe's hand flies to her mouth, and tears of joy and wonder spring to her eyes once more. Santa knew. Maybe he has known all along. They always thought this journey was about others. Maybe it was also about them. They never personally asked anything from Father Christmas during their time with him. It turns out that Santa's true gift was the chance for them to find each other. They have long suspected that his magic is real. Now, they know it is.

They stand together in the snow and pour the cocoa, raising their mugs in a toast as the Northern Lights begin dancing across the Lappish sky. There are no sleigh bells, no crowds, no press, and even no Santa Claus. It is just them, cups of cocoa, the stillness of a Finnish forest, and a love that now belongs to forever.

The End

Aurielle's Secret Cocoa Recipe

A recipe whispered down from Lapland's northernmost kitchens, known only to those who believe in love, winter, and wonder.

Ingredients:
2 cups whole milk
1/2 cup heavy cream
3 oz dark chocolate (70% cacao), finely chopped
1 oz milk chocolate, for softness
1 tbsp Dutch-processed cocoa powder
1 tbsp brown sugar (packed)
1/2 tsp ground cinnamon
1/8 tsp ground cardamom
1/8 tsp sea salt
1 tsp vanilla bean paste (or extract)
A single drop of almond extract
A pinch of grated nutmeg (for garnish)
Whipped cream (optional)
Stirred with a cinnamon stick
Love (required)

Instructions:
1. In a small saucepan over low heat, gently warm the milk and cream until steaming—but not boiling.
2. Add the cocoa powder, chopped chocolate, brown sugar, cinnamon, cardamom, and salt. Stir slowly with a wooden spoon or cinnamon stick until the chocolate melts completely and the mixture is smooth and velvety.
3. Remove from heat. Add vanilla bean paste and the single drop of almond extract—never more, never less. Stir with joy.
4. Pour into warm mugs and top with whipped cream or a marshmallow snowflake.
5. Grate a whisper of fresh nutmeg over the top.
6. Serve immediately to someone you love.

A Note from the Author

Well, this is a little bittersweet. For an author, completing a series is an accomplishment – the realization of a dream that can span years or even decades. It's a to-do box checked. It's the satisfaction of telling the whole story.

It's also sad because I have gotten close to these characters and don't want to say goodbye. And, unless I someday find a compelling reason to revisit them, this is the final goodbye. I could see a future where there are more adventures with Santa, but I can't see how there is more of Wyatt and Stowe's story to tell. The happy ending missive at the end says it all.

I have to say that this probably ranks among the top three endings of any novel or series that I have written. Michael Bennit's final talk with his student staff in *The iAmerican* is on that list. I would also add Tierra Campos's chess match with Brian Cooper in *Decisive Endgame*. Perhaps a future book will replace one of those.

Some fun notes about this book. Ellie's desire to go to Bora Bora comes directly from my wife. We made that a reality in 2021, and the experience was unsurpassed. The description that Ellie overhears in the Swiss café is derived from my own travel notes. It is very pricey, but if you ever have the chance to visit, I highly recommend it.

Kram and Skut were not unique names. Kram is short for Krampus from Central European Alpine folklore, especially Austria, Germany, and surrounding regions. Traditionally, he's depicted as a half-goat, half-demon creature with horns, fangs, a long tongue, and cloven hooves. While Saint Nicholas rewards good children with gifts, Krampus punishes the naughty ones with a bundle of birch sticks or by carrying them off in a sack or basket. Not a good Christmas for that unfortunate child.

Skut is named after Scut Farkus, the red-haired, yellow-eyed neighborhood bully who torments Ralphie, Randy, Flick, and Schwartz in *A Christmas Story*. He's known for his raccoon-skin cap, intimidating demeanor, and memorable laughter. Despite his relatively limited screen time, he made a lasting impression as one of cinematic holiday's most memorable villains.

These two characters in *Finding Santa* are nothing like their namesakes, obviously. I wanted to include Christmas villains to see if anybody would pick up on it. I doubt many of you did. I know I wouldn't have. But it was a lot of fun to include.

I could have given Julie any occupation. Being a teacher made the ending work, but it was really my paying homage to Michael Bennit from *The iCandidate*. I began my writing career with a plot surrounding a high school teacher, and it was my way of paying tribute to that series.

There are also a lot of callbacks in this novel to the previous two books. There is also some fan service. I wanted to give a natural update on Malcolm and Janelle Chapman and bring MacKenzie and Cliff into the fold (the help with the FBI and the jet took care of that). I also wanted some time with the Huffmans, who, outside of Ellie, would not have been in the novel. I revisited some places and brought up some key moments in the series. Most of all, I wanted to bring them together as a big family right before the ending. I just thought it was an appropriate audience for Santa's message.

Speaking of Ellie, she wasn't initially going to be in *Finding Santa*. I had so much fun writing her sassy character in *Delivering Santa* that I couldn't resist including her in this one. Fortunately, I had only the bare-bones concept of the novel until late spring, so adding her in wasn't a problem and even provided the opportunity to add in some subplots.

I absolutely do love Christmas. Not the commercial aspect of it, but the spirit of the holiday. For many people, it is a stressful time, but it shouldn't be. That's not the point of the season at all. I'm an ardent believer in Santa's Christmas messages, and that's why I wrote these novels.

For those who didn't already pick up on it, there were three distinct themes in this series. That was determined early on, and why this was always destined to be a trilogy. The first novel delved into the true meaning of Christmas. The second explored generosity, togetherness, and the miracle of the season being within each one of us. This novel was all about family and friends, and the role they play in our lives.

I mentioned at the end of the last novel that The Santa Trilogy is meant to be a reminder of what should be important during the holiday season. I have done my part, and there are no more Christmas stories for me to tell. Now, I challenge you all to reflect on the lessons. Maybe it will make your Christmas holiday season a little more magical.

-Mikael

Acknowledgments

Thank you for spending some of your precious time reading *Finding Santa*. I hope this series warmed your heart and brought you some much-deserved Christmas spirit. Most of all, I hope you enjoyed reading the novels in The Santa Trilogy as much as I enjoyed writing them.

This is a story about friends and family. I am blessed to have both. Bill and Chris, Chris and Jess, Jenn, Steve, Amy, Billy (not the Billy in the story), Gabrielle, Stephan, Meg, and Aimee…thank you for all the Christmas memories you help make! To my mother, Nancy, sister and brother-in-law, Krissy and Ken, and my nephew Gibson – you make every holiday and family gathering special.

It has been a privilege spending more than a decade and a half of Christmases with my wife, Michele.

I have been working with my editor for a very long time now. It took a while to find one who could not only correct the mistakes in my novels (I love changing names and always seem to miss a couple in the manuscript), but also really help with their readability. Mike Waitz of Sticks and Stones Editing has been a Godsend, and I very much appreciate all the love and care he puts into reviewing my books.

The other challenge is cover design. There are a lot of fantastic graphic designers out there, but it takes a special one to understand what an author is looking for and find ways to incorporate that into a great cover. Dave at JD&J Design does that better than anyone. This may have been the easiest of the trilogy covers for him to design. I will have to present more of a challenge for him with future books.

And thank you, most of all, to my readers. Writing is a labor of love. I started this journey by writing novels that I wanted to read. It warms my heart that so many others have found them entertaining. I want to wish all of you a Merry Christmas, and may you and your families know nothing but peace and prosperity!

Mikael Carlson is the award-winning author of *The iCandidate* and the Michael Bennit Series of political dramas. He also wrote the Tierra Campos Series, Watchtower Thrillers, The Dancing Trilogy, and the dystopian America, Inc. Saga. *Delivering Santa* is his twenty-second novel.

A retired veteran of the Rhode Island Army National Guard and United States Army, he deployed twice to support military operations during the Global War on Terror. Mikael has served in the field artillery, infantry, and in support of special operations units during his active-duty career at Fort Bragg and in the Army National Guard.

A proud U.S. Army paratrooper, he conducted over fifty airborne operations following the completion of jump school at Fort Benning in 1998 and trained with the militaries of countless foreign nations. He never jumped out of Santa's sleigh, though. That aircraft would have been a great addition to his jump log.

Academically, Mikael earned a Master of Arts in American History and graduated with a B.S. in International Business from Marist College in 1996.

He was raised in New Milford, Connecticut, lives in nearby Danbury, and always tries to stay on the nice list.